JOIN SECTION X

AND NEVER MISS A MISSION!

Keep up to date with every Evan Boyd adventure at

www.benjaminshawbooks.com

Operation Hurricane

By Benjamin Shaw

MILL ROAD
media

For KJ & The Captain

PART ONE

"The laws of science do not distinguish between the past and the future." Professor Stephen Hawking.

It's Going To Get Ugly

The following takes place in our past – but firmly in our hero's future.

Square Maria Blanchard, Paris, France, 1986

Heads began to turn the moment the long, black vintage Mercedes had pulled to a stop outside Café Royale. Not only were cars like this a stark reminder of a time when Paris was in the grip of Adolf Hitler's terrifying 'SS', but parking wasn't permitted on the square, so having the brazenness to stop the old relic here was a clear signal that the driver didn't care much for local traffic laws, and anyone with a complaint should probably just keep walking.

There were a few rather interesting facts about the man sat inside the old car. Physically, he was nothing special. He was short, small and muscular, with sharp, weasel-like features. Had one of the many passers-by

6

felt like living dangerously and glanced into the car at that moment, they would have seen something that would have blown their mind. The man pulled back his sleeve to check his watch. The face of the timepiece was a small, black screen which came to life and flashed a set of large numbers, telling him it was 10.04 am - and it certainly didn't look like anything you would find attached to a wrist in 1986.

Hans Frisbeck sighed and looked around. The old square shimmered in the mid-morning sun. It reminded Frisbeck of a picture from a postcard or an old painting hanging on the wall of a grand house. Thick snow covered every surface, except for the black stones and rails making up the well-worn tram lines that guided the busy carriages around the city.

Despite the sun, the snow had been falling fast all morning, so the pavements were slippery and filled with people cautiously going about their business, without any inkling as to what was unfolding right under their noses. For Frisbeck, the morning crackled with a sense of danger, a feeling he was greatly accustomed to. He had visited many different countries and experienced all kinds of cultures; it was all part of his job. He had also learnt to be a patient man, good at watching people and doing as he was told. A further interesting fact about Frisbeck was his exclusive membership of an elite and savage team, tasked with one simple function: hunting. Frisbeck was sent to find things, to capture and return items that were important to people – and he never hunted alone.

Another large, black car approached, slowly crunching over the thick snow. It was followed by a powerful BMW motorbike and sidecar, carrying two men wearing goggles and helmets. The car hadn't even fully stopped before it spat out a mountain of a man. His name was Bakker; he had long arms that hung far from his sides, big legs that stretched out like a spider and huge features that seemed to be fighting for space on his face. Bakker took a long stride towards Frisbeck's car, across the path of an old woman carrying bags of shopping. The woman tried to step back out of his way, but Bakker was colossal; he took up the whole pavement, and he didn't even notice her as she slipped and tumbled onto the hard concrete. The woman dropped her belongings, gritted her teeth and cried out in pain. Frisbeck wound down his window enough to poke his ratty little nose through it, his small eyes pinched against the cold.

'Is he in there?' Bakker asked in his sharp, Dutch accent.

'Yes,' Frisbeck replied with a smile, revealing a set of broken, uneven teeth. 'For over 30 minutes.'

'Perfect, his stomach will be full – he will be slow. Let's go and get him.' Bakker walked out into the road and over to the man on the motorbike, who had been patiently waiting for his orders.

Frisbeck climbed out of the car and shut the door as Bakker talked to the other Hunters; he could feel the electricity start to fizz through his veins. The Hunter in the sidecar was a squat man called Nico. He hopped out and walked briskly down a side street and around the back of the café. Bakker stepped back onto the pavement and over the old woman. She straightened her patterned headscarf and with the help of a good Samaritan, began to scratch through the snow, picking up the shopping she had dropped. A crowd had started to form, a group of onlookers who sensed that something was about to erupt. Still, such was their air of menace that not a soul dared utter a word to the men dressed in black.

Bakker slapped a big, meaty hand on the door, stopped and turned his head, his long, dark hair swinging across his uneven face. He blinked slowly; his bulging eyes fixed on Frisbeck. 'No mistakes. We get him, then we get the hell out of this place. I hate snow.' Bakker didn't like the cold; they all knew he wanted to get home. And where exactly was home?

Well, the last and surely the most interesting thing about Frisbeck and Bakker and all the Hunters was, they weren't from Paris and they certainly weren't from 1986. Home was in a different time entirely – and a very long way away indeed.

Boyd was finishing his breakfast of fried potatoes and thinking about whether to order another. He was here to meet someone, a stranger, and they were late. Boyd didn't like hanging around anywhere longer than he needed to; although being a 15 year-old boy out alone wasn't rare in this time, the people in these small sections of town knew each other and Boyd clearly wasn't a local – far from it. Also, patience wasn't a skill he had ever managed to master.

The little café was decorated with family pictures on

the cream walls. It had a small bar on the right and a corridor at the back of the room leading down to the kitchen. Two older men sat on stools, drinking strong coffee from tiny cups; the café owner stood chatting on the other side of the thick, wooden bar. Boyd was the only other customer. He sat at the back of the room next to the corridor and didn't even look up as the door opened and the winter wind burst in like an intruder.

Then it died just as suddenly as it had arrived when Bakker filled the entire doorway. The huge man ducked his head through the entrance and, seeing Boyd immediately, he wound his way around two empty tables with the speed and grace of a ballet dancer. Frisbeck closed the door behind him. The men at the bar stopped talking and looked down at their little cups. The owner only dared to snatch a glance at the new arrivals, watching carefully from the corner of his eyes.

Boyd chased the last of his potato around his plate. He didn't need to look up to know that the sudden silence in the café meant trouble. It was something he had learnt to recognise over the last few days and, if he was honest, maybe even quite enjoy. He speared the potato and poked it into his mouth, savouring the flavour. As he did, he finally looked up at the huge man standing in front of him. Bakker was so massive that his head and shoulders blocked out the sunlight and even shaded Boyd from the light hanging on the ceiling. How does someone even get that big? It must be a family thing, maybe his parents were giants too – Boyd would remember to ask him, just before he knocked him on his backside.

Nico, the stocky man from the sidecar, was glad to be on his feet and walking. It had been absolutely freezing on the ride in; even his thick overcoat hadn't stopped him from shivering like a frightened dog. All this effort to find some stupid kid; he had no idea why they needed so many of them to grab a teenage runaway. Nico decided he was going to tell Bakker that he wasn't riding back in the sidecar, he would get in the car with Frisbeck.

Bakker had told him to go and wait around the back of the café, just in case the kid decided to make a run for it. If by some small miracle this boy did manage to get away from Bakker and Frisbeck, Nico actually hoped he did come this way. It was the kid's fault that he was here in this godforsaken place, in the worst winter he'd seen in his life.

'Yeah, come on, kid, come my way,' Nico said, laughing to himself. 'I can warm myself up by playing basketball with your head!'

Bakker stopped just one stride away from the table, watching as the kid hoovered up the last of his breakfast.

Frisbeck stepped alongside Bakker and leant around him, seeing Boyd for the first time.
'Seriously?' Frisbeck said, looking up at Bakker, an ugly smile cracking across his sharp face. 'This needs four of us?'

Bakker's bulging eyes seemed to darken, and he glared at his fellow Hunter. He understood Frisbeck's reaction; at first glance this was a 15 year-old kid, who looked like he was finishing a meal and about to ask his mum if he could go out with his friends. He wasn't much bigger than most other kids his age. He had thick, brown hair that hung over a pair of pale blue eyes. But if you looked closely enough, you would see it - the difference between him and other boys his age was burning behind those eyes.

Boyd quickly snapped a look at Frisbeck, his gaze narrowing as he smiled; he was ready, and he was going to enjoy this. Frisbeck felt a sudden uneasy murmur of discomfort in his stomach and wanted to look away.

Bakker broke the silence. 'Kid, finish up, we need to go. We don't want this to get ugly.' He picked up Boyd's hooded sweatshirt from the chair in front of him and held onto it.

Boyd put down his fork and picked up a large mug of hot tea. He ran his tongue around his teeth, looking carefully at the two men in front of him. 'It's a bit late for that, lads,' he said.

'What?' Bakker raised a big eyebrow.

'I said it's too late. It looks like it already got pretty ugly in here,' Boyd said, slightly louder, increasing the air of awkwardness in the small room. 'I was making a joke about how you two are not exactly pretty; but a joke tends to lose its impact when you have to explain it.' He sat forward and wrapped the fingers of his left hand around the edge of his big plate. 'I'm guessing you're not the brains of the operation, am I right?'

Bakker forced a smile. His thick, slug-like lips parted

to reveal a set of yellowed, tombstone teeth. 'The people I work for want to speak to you, so you're coming with us,' he said, leaning forward. 'Breakfast is over – let's go.'

Boyd looked around his table. 'A party? Well, why didn't you say so? Let's do this.' He leant in towards Bakker, as if to whisper. 'But my father raised me to clean up after myself, so any objections if I clear the table? You wash, I'll dry, okay?' Bakker screwed his face up in confusion.

Without warning, Boyd was on his feet. He swiped the heavy plate off the table with his left hand and brought it upwards, catching the big man flush on the jaw and stunning him with a loud 'SMASH'. Just as that piece of crockery connected, Boyd used his right hand to launch his mug at Frisbeck. Steaming hot liquid showered the Hunter, then the mug bounced off his nose and spun into the air above him. With both men stunned, Boyd flipped up the round wooden table and grabbed two of the legs. Holding it flat in front of him like a huge shield, he drove forward. The café owner's mouth dropped open as he watched a teenage boy use a table as a battering ram against two grown men.

Boyd forced them backwards, crashing through the two tables they had walked past to get to him. Both experienced fighters, Bakker and Frisbeck managed to stay on their feet as they shuffled in retreat, desperately trying to keep their balance. Then, as their legs hit the low windowsill, gravity took away all their choices. They crashed out through the front window of the café, taking the table with them. By the time their backs crunched through the snow and into the frost-hardened concrete, Boyd was already at the other end of the corridor at the back of the café.

The old woman in the patterned headscarf had collected her shopping from the pavement and was now sat on a tram, waiting to leave the square. She looked at the two men as they lay stricken on the cold floor and enjoyed a little smile to herself.

Nico was shadow-boxing to keep himself warm when he heard the crashing from inside the café. He quickly tried the door, thinking that joining a fight inside was a better option than waiting outside in the cold; the door was locked. He twisted and pulled on the handle to see if he could force it open, but it didn't budge. Then he felt the handle twist in his grasp. Someone on the other side was trying to get out but having no luck either. Almost as soon as the handle had started to move, it stopped again. Nico let go of it and waited. He heard a noise from inside, not crashing this time, something else. It was like moaning and it was getting louder. He leant into the door, put his ear against it and held his breath. Something was on the other side. Nico could hear footsteps pounding against the floor, getting closer, and the moaning built up into something more like a growl; was it some kind of animal?

Suddenly, the door and bits of its frame exploded outwards into the air and took Nico straight off his feet. On the other side of the door, like a human battering ram, was Boyd.

Nico hit the snow-covered cobblestones of the alley with a thud and the air shot out of him. The door was still sandwiched between him and Boyd, as the young man shook his head and took a breath. Nico let out a shallow cry before trying to free himself.

A hand appeared from the underside of the door and Boyd glanced at the ground in surprise. Under the door, dressed in the same black overcoat as those he'd just despatched from the café, was another man. Boyd didn't hesitate, he slammed his weight down onto the door, ramming into the thick wood with his shoulder once, twice, three times before the stocky man on the other side let out a tiny whimper. Boyd slid from the door, onto his knees and glanced back down at his adversary.

'I really hope you're one of the bad guys.' He gently tapped his hand on the man's cheek as he surveyed his surroundings and planned his next move.

Behind the alley he was on was a U-shaped apartment building. A set of steps ran up into a small playground at the back of the apartments. All he had to do was get across the playground, through an archway under the building and he would be on another street.

He was jogging towards the steps when he heard the *chug-chug* of an engine coming from the end of the alley. A beast of a motorbike with sidecar poked around the corner; the rider saw Boyd and pulled the accelerator back once, letting the motorbike roar out a warning. Boyd didn't hang around; he was already up the steps when he heard the engine snarl for a second time as the Hunter set off after his prey.

The playground was bustling with young children and parents building snowmen, whilst the older kids engaged in a serious snowball battle. Boyd darted straight across the slippery pathway, just about holding his balance when he heard the playground behind him erupt with a combination of screams, protests and the crackling thunder of a motorbike engine. Boyd cut through the archway and saw a small pile of bicycles leaning against the wall; he scanned them as he approached and quickly grabbed the only one that looked fit for purpose - a black and red BMX. He pushed it out onto the road and leapt up onto the saddle.

He risked a swift glance behind him. The motorbike was speeding across the playground, smoke coughing out of its big exhaust as the rider crouched down over the handlebars. If Boyd's heart hadn't been pounding before, it certainly was now. He began to rock the lightweight bike side-to-side under him, pumping the pedals with all his strength.

He headed away from the square as fast as he could, up into the narrow roads, lined with the houses, smaller shops and bars of the local neighbourhood. The bike was pretty fast, and Boyd was extremely fit but it wasn't long before the rider started to close the gap. He could feel the rhythmic chugging of the engine coming up through the road, but he didn't dare glance back again just now, he had to focus on getting away.

He quickly worked out he had two big problems: the first was, he was heading uphill, which wasn't ideal when you were being chased by a motorbike; the second problem was, however much he wanted to stay clear of the two men he'd just put through a window, he needed to be in that square to meet his contact. Boyd knew he must have been followed to the café and he couldn't leave his contact to deal with this kind of trouble on their own; he had to warn them and get them both to safety.

He was busy trying to come up with a plan when the man on the bike took a chance, drew in close and swiped his hand at Boyd, grasping the air right next to his arm. Boyd dropped his shoulder and just managed to slip out of reach, then he swerved between two parked cars and jumped up onto a kerb to buy himself some time. He was now heading straight for a group of worried-looking pedestrians.

Boyd glanced over his shoulder and darted back

through a gap onto the road, barely avoiding the shrieking gaggle on the pavement. Anger burned inside him. He pulled right and brought the bicycle towards the motorbike, keeping himself just out of reach. For a moment, Boyd was close enough to see the rider's eyes up close; they were grey and tired, but they creased with curiosity, wondering what on earth this kid was playing at, trying to decipher what his next move would be. Boyd didn't make him wait long.

He smiled at the rider before he swerved alongside the bike, lifted his right leg and kicked at the handlebars. The rider shouted in surprise as the machine turned sharply, setting him on a collision course with a stationary car. The man managed to brake enough so that the minor impact didn't damage the bike, but he was forced to stop and watch as Boyd powered off into the distance.

Boyd looked back to see the rider wrench the bike back into a straight line and rev the engine. Facing front again, he ducked and weaved between a gang of workmen who were unloading supplies from the back of a flatbed lorry. They shouted after him – the motorbike would have to slow to avoid them too, so Boyd pedalled for all he was worth to create more distance between them.

Up ahead, there was a narrow fork in the road, and in the middle sat a little restaurant, with doors on both the left- and right-hand roads. Boyd quickly hatched a plan; even as it came to him, he knew it was bordering on crazy, but what choice did he have right now? He would have to let the motorbike get close again. Boyd slowed and the rider cautiously began closing the gap, more wary this time. The big engine popped like a machine gun and Boyd felt a rush of adrenaline, a desperate need to pedal for his life; but he held his nerve and allowed the motorbike to get closer and closer.

He drifted over to the left-hand side of the road, the motorbike jerked left to follow. Boyd continued to slow as the rider brought the bike towards him. Boyd could taste the sooty, black exhaust fumes at the back of his throat now, but he had to wait just a little longer.

The motorbike rider was almost close enough to reach out and grab him when Boyd suddenly pinched the brakes on the BMX. By clamping them down for one, short burst he jolted to a halt, as the motorbike and rider darted up the left-hand side of the restaurant. Boyd quickly dipped the front wheel of the bike and went up the road to the right. He slipped his back wheel around in an arc as he stopped in a skid. He heard the motorbike screech to a stop on the other road and knew the rider would take three or four seconds to turn the big machine around and come after him.

Boyd waited until he heard the motorbike engine roar as the rider turned it back down the street. He lined himself up opposite the restaurant door, then he hit the pedals with everything he had. This was never going to work, surely?

Just then, a man with a huge moustache appeared, carrying a large box and filling the restaurant doorway. He was looking back inside, talking to someone, laughing and smiling. When he turned and looked up, the joy slid from his round face at the shock of seeing a teenager powering straight towards him on a bicycle. He shouted something in French, threw the box into the air and jumped out onto the pavement. A woman poked her head around the door before looking in total disbelief at Boyd. She ducked into the café just as Boyd pulled the front wheel up over the pavement. He then hopped the back wheel into the air a split-second before it hit the kerb, which lifted him and the bike clear off the ground. He tucked himself down against the handlebars, soared through the double-doorway and into the restaurant. He landed and quickly noticed the place was empty, except for some materials on the floor to his left. This must be where the workmen he had nearly collided with on the street had been unloading their tools and equipment – and they had left the double-doors on the other side of the restaurant wide open; perhaps luck was on his side after all.

Boyd saw the motorbike charge past the open doors and around the front of the café as he called out an apology to the owners. 'Sorry, don't mind me!' he shouted as he pumped the pedals twice, sailed through the café, narrowly missed the bar, hit the step in front of the doors, and glided through the air onto the street outside. He landed, wrenched the bike hard to the left and was darting back down the street before the motorbike rider even knew what was happening.

As Boyd swerved the workmen again, he leant out and grabbed a lump of timber that had been leaning against the van. They called after him again, cursing him with some impolite words he recognised in French - but it wasn't long before their voices were drowned out by the familiar sound of a motorbike engine, getting ever louder and ever closer. The rider was back, but it wouldn't be for long this time. Boyd sat up straight in the saddle and took a long breath. He stopped pedalling and began to free-wheel down the slight hill. The rider would be alongside him any second now.

Boyd weaved the bike from side to side and tossed the timber up into his right hand. He shifted his grip and spun the wood around a couple of times, getting used to the weight and feel of it. He knew, like the jump through the restaurant, that he was only going to get one shot at this, he had to make it count.

The rider eased off the throttle. Boyd was waiting until the motorbike got close, knowing his pursuer would be out of patience and wanting to end this for good. So, Boyd made it look like he was too tired to continue. He looked at the rider again – beneath the goggles, a thin smile was beginning to stretch out across the man's face. Then, all at once, the pleasure froze as he saw the ruthlessness in Boyd's pale blue eyes.

Boyd drew his right arm across his chest and slammed the length of wood down into the spokes of the motorbike's front wheel. He then quickly clamped down on the back brake of the BMX and skidded sideways; the bicycle slid out from under him and Boyd scraped along the icy concrete on his backside, before coming to a halt.

The rider wasn't so lucky. The block of wood spun around in the spokes until it hit the forks that held the front wheel, then jammed and stopped the motorbike dead. The engine screamed like a wounded animal as the back wheels flew off the ground. The rider gripped the handlebars in shock as he and the bike took off and flipped through the air, end over end before both came crashing to the street in a haze of snow and smoke.

Boyd stood up, grabbed the BMX, and casually pushed off, hoping the bike still had something left to give him. Like Boyd himself, it was battered but still up to the job. He skirted around the motorbike where the rider groaned, his limbs flapping about under the wreckage. Boyd powered away and didn't look back.

He rode into the square and slowly headed towards the café he had left only a few minutes earlier. The fight had drawn a large crowd; it's not every day two men leave a café through a window, wearing a table. They were up off the concrete now and arguing with two rather unimpressed policemen. Boyd allowed himself a little smile, before scanning the crowd. He'd never seen the person he was supposed to meet, but he had been given a description. His eyes danced across the sea of faces but he saw no sign of them.

Then, as if in slow motion, the weasel-faced man glanced over in Boyd's direction before quickly nudging his huge colleague. In the middle of a discussion with a policeman, the man-mountain turned sharply towards Boyd; his bulging, black eyes widened as his huge features contorted into a grimace.

'Oh, give me a break.' Boyd immediately pushed out into the road and headed away from the café. As he did, Bakker suddenly burst into a run with Frisbeck not far behind. There was a tram just setting off from the other side of the square; it was his best chance, and he had a head start. He would get away and then somehow come back to meet his contact.

As he carefully wove the BMX along the pathway and through the busy square, he risked a glance over his shoulder and saw Bakker literally throwing people aside as he quickly started to gain on him. Once Boyd was free of the crowds, he pedalled as fast as he could and got himself alongside the back of the speeding tram. He was edging close, getting ready to leap onto the platform at the back, when he heard a horn blare out and his eyes shot forwards; there, heading right for him, was an oncoming tram!

He had just seconds to get off this bike. Boyd grasped desperately for the rail on the back of the tram car. Just as he felt the cold metal bar in his grasp, his feet started to spin wildly and the bike weaved violently beneath him. The chain had come off but he was still sat in the saddle, being pulled through the square by the tram as the oncoming 40-tonne vehicle was now bearing down on him like a charging elephant.

There was nothing for it: Boyd launched himself and pulled with his arms for all he was worth. His body clattered down on the platform as his feet dragged along the road; he looked back in time to see the bike wobble on its wheels before being smashed into pieces by the oncoming tram.

Boyd hauled himself inside. The people on board looked at the dishevelled boy lying on the floor, puffing and panting. 'Good morning,' Boyd said as he pulled himself to his feet. 'Tickets please.'

They stared at him, mouths open. 'Tough crowd,' Boyd said, exhausted. He looked out of the back window and saw Bakker and Frisbeck closing in. 'Excuse me, pardon me, coming through.'

Boyd moved as quickly as he could through the packed carriage, accidentally kicking at shopping bags and treading on toes. How was he going to get out of this one? Just then, a scream erupted from behind him. Boyd's eyes shot down the carriage – Bakker had leapt onto the tram and was holding out an arm for Frisbeck. The stocky little weasel was running for all he was worth.

Boyd moved to the front doors, then jumped up and out. He grabbed hold of the metal railing running around the roof of the carriage and swung his legs up just as a growling Bakker arrived at the front door.

The big man snarled as Boyd's feet disappeared out of sight. Turning to the panicked driver, he grabbed him by his jacket and threw him straight out of the door after Boyd. The tram filled with gasps as the driver rolled twice between two cars before he quickly scrambled out of the road to safety.

Frisbeck arrived and Bakker shoved him behind the controls. The tram had levers and dials – none of them made any sense to Frisbeck.

'Sit here, keep an eye on these,' Bakker growled. 'Make sure nothing blows up when I do this.'

'When you do what?' Frisbeck replied.

Bakker pushed the heavy, gold lever that controlled the speed and the big tram suddenly lurched forward, accelerating into the back of the car in front. The passengers were thrown backwards and the tram filled with screams and shouts.

On the roof, Boyd had just got up on his feet as the tram's speed rocketed up. He fell flat onto his stomach and slid along the frosty, metal roof towards the edge. He shot over the side headfirst. If he fell off now, he would end up under the wheels. He threw his arms out and desperately grabbed for something, anything to stop him going over the side. Then his fingers caught hold of the railing on the roof, and he clamped them down. His legs flew over and he clattered against the side of the tram with a thump. Another car sped by, only just missing his feet, the driver holding down the blaring horn.

Boyd's face was tight against one of the tram windows. On the other side sat a man, chewing a large blob of gum and staring at him inquisitively. Boyd raised his eyebrows as the passenger lowered a set of curious-looking orange foam headphones. 'Any chance you could open the window?' Boyd asked. The man continued to chew his gum and slowly nodded, obviously not understanding a word he said, just smiling at Boyd like he was a madman. 'Thanks mate, you're a big help.'

Boyd felt his fingers starting to slip, he couldn't last much longer. He looked towards the front of the tram and saw Bakker's head poke out the front door, a smile twitching at the corner of his mouth. The big man suddenly ducked back inside. Another car whooshed by; it was travelling so fast that it knocked the breath out of Boyd. He tried to get a better grip but his hands were freezing cold against the metal railing; he held on, teeth gritted. The oncoming traffic was thick with cars and trucks, and the tram was going so fast now, he couldn't risk jumping off.

Through the window he saw Bakker pushing his

way between the panicked passengers, right up to where the smiling man sat, still staring out at Boyd. Bakker grabbed the passenger by the collar and threw him out of the way, before pointing a big, dirty finger at Boyd from behind the window. 'You're mine, boy!' the big man shouted.

'Boyd!' another voice called out; not Bakker and not from inside the tram. It sounded like it was coming from behind him.

Boyd flicked his head around and there, alongside the tram, was an old-fashioned army Jeep. Boyd was in no doubt, the woman behind the wheel was his contact, Rose. She was currently trying to edge the big, metal Jeep as close to the tram as possible whilst avoiding the oncoming traffic.

Suddenly the Jeep dropped out of sight as Rose slammed on the brakes and moved back behind the tram. Another line of cars and trucks sped by on the other side of the road and Boyd had to tuck himself in as a truck whizzed right by his back. His fingers wanted to give up on him – they ached so much they were practically numb – but he had to hold on just for a little while longer.

He carefully walked his feet up the side of the tram and put them on the window frame, his legs spread. Once these cars had gone by, the next time Rose got the Jeep close, he was going to try and jump for it. Boyd looked back inside the tram and saw an over-sized fist coming straight for him. Bakker's lumpy knuckles smashed into the window and it exploded, spraying shards of glass inside and out.

Boyd arched his back and sucked his stomach in as Bakker's hand, as big as a shovel, swiped at the air in front of him. The Dutchman then threw his right hand out towards the window frame and grabbed Boyd's ankle.

'You should have come quietly when you had the chance!'

Boyd saw that smile again; the big teeth were all different shapes, like the man had a mouth full of chipped stones.

'Boyd!' Rose called out again, as she weaved the Jeep back to the side of the tram. There was only a small break in traffic; Boyd needed to jump now.

'And you should have stayed under that table.' He lifted his right foot and slammed it into Bakker's big, ugly mouth. The man howled in pain as he fell backwards inside the tram.

'Anytime now would be good,' Rose shouted.

Boyd looked at the Jeep – it wasn't steady and there was a motorbike heading straight for it, with another truck close behind the bike. Rose moved the Jeep over to make a small gap for the motorbike but Boyd knew that there wouldn't be time for her to come back towards the tram and get out of the way of the truck. If he was going to do this, it had to be now.

The driver of the truck was already holding his hand on the horn; the bike rider had nowhere to go and started to wobble between the Jeep and the tram. Boyd closed his eyes. He let out a shout as he pushed off with his feet and flew backwards over the top of the motorbike. He spun in the air and landed hard on his stomach on the bonnet of the Jeep with a thud, quickly locking his arm around the big, spare wheel that sat on the top.

Without warning, Rose pumped the brakes and dropped back behind the tram, the oncoming truck flew by, clipping the Jeep's wing mirror and smashing it to pieces. Rose snapped a quick look behind, then pulled the handbrake and skidded the Jeep into a turn. Boyd hung on as she slammed her foot onto the accelerator and powered the vehicle back towards the square, away from the tram.

'You might have told me you were going to do that!' Boyd shouted.

'We didn't exactly have a lot of time to chat. Are you planning to ride the whole way on the bonnet or do you fancy joining me in here?'

Boyd pulled himself up and over the windscreen, he fell into the seat next to Rose. He was aching all over and breathing hard, while the 60 year-old woman next to him had barely broken a sweat.

'You must be Boyd,' she said, smiling. 'Welcome to 1986.'

A Class Act

Oakmead School, Bloomfield, Sussex, 2019

Boyd was bored. No, he was much more than *just* bored, he was starting to believe that boredom of this level could actually be lethal. He wasn't in the mood for school today. He had considered pretending to faint, asking to leave to go to the toilet and then not coming back, but he had tried both of those in the past few months and he knew he was on his last chance. His dad had been called to the school quite a lot already this year. He'd even jokingly suggested to Boyd that they paint his bedroom the same colour as Mr Providence's office and maybe install a filing cabinet seeing as Boyd liked spending so much time sitting across the desk from his headmaster. No, he couldn't do anything that might get him in trouble. He didn't want to put his dad through that and he couldn't bear that look he gave him whenever Boyd had let him down.

It's not that he didn't like school most of the time, it was being around the other people that bugged him. As Miss Oldroyd went over the key areas of the Treaty of Versailles, furiously scribbling on the board, Boyd looked around the class. Pixie Thorn and Courtney Marling were painting their nails whilst Jason Doswell and Colin Straker – nicknamed Doz and Strakes – were flinging pieces of screwed-up paper at the head of a boy called Fitzgerald Tork, whom everyone called Fitz. Lessons were all well and good, but he was expected to learn alongside these idiots, and he had no time for them. The only time he was genuinely happy at school was during cross-country running because it meant he didn't have to talk to anyone for an hour or so. The cross-country county championship was next week; Boyd was the best on the team and he'd been training like mad. He closed his eyes and blocked everything out, focusing on the fact that the last lesson today was P.E., and that meant cross-country.

Miss Oldroyd put down her marker pen and turned to face the room. Doz and Strakes quickly stopped bullying Fitz and tried their best to look intelligent while Pixie and Courtney lifted a textbook into place to hide their nail polish. Not that Miss Oldroyd would have said much: she was pretty timid and, much like Boyd, seemed like she just couldn't wait to get through each lesson and get away from everyone. Class 10B was known for the worst-behaved kids in the school and was also, unfortunately for Miss Oldroyd, her form group. So, every day, as they plodded in half asleep, she took the register and then at the end of the day, she had to try to control them as they buzzed and bounced, desperate to break out into the world. The headmaster, Mr Providence, told her that her form class was just testing her and if she passed, she would get a lovely pay rise. Never mind a pay rise, if she got through this year, they should give her a medal and name a wing of the school after her.

'Right, 10B, do I have your attention?'

'Yes, Miss Oldroyd,' came the bored, robotic response.

'Excellent. Seeing as it's Parents' Evening tonight, I won't see you for form group at the end of today, so I've got a couple of notices to give you now.' Miss Oldroyd picked up a slip of paper from her desk. 'Anyone involved in getting the Atrium ready for Parents'

Evening tonight should report to the Atrium at 3pm sharp and be ready to set up the displays. Next, you may recall that tomorrow is test day for anyone who missed the maths mock exam…'

She stopped as she noticed that Boyd was now fully asleep, his head slowly slipping down his arm. He let out a gentle, crackling snore. Miss Oldroyd was not much for shouting, but she could only be pushed so far. 'Boyd!' She used his surname, like everyone did, including his father. Miss Oldroyd's voice had risen to a tone and a volume that none of the class had heard her use before. Not quite a screech and not enough to shake the windows but certainly enough to make Boyd's head snap back into an upright position.

'Huh,' Boyd let out a noise that didn't resemble any word from the English language.

'Boyd, did you hear what I said?'

'Absolutely, Miss, every word,' he replied.

The class chuckled softly. He hadn't meant it as a joke, he was just trying to spare them both embarrassment. On reflection, it might be a bit late for that.

'Really? So, what was I talking about?'

'You, erm… You said something about Parents' Evening and then, to be honest, I might have nodded off – for which I can only apologise.'

Laughter burst out from his classmates. Boyd meant it, he wasn't playing for laughs, he was genuinely sorry. Miss Oldroyd was clearly fuming, Boyd hoped she was going to give him at least some credit for his honesty.

'I was talking about the maths test tomorrow, something that should interest you.' Miss Oldroyd placed both her hands on her desk and looked at Boyd with laser focus. 'As I understand it, you missed the last test and if you don't pass this one, Mr Providence isn't going to let you run in the county championships next week.'

Boyd sat upright, his cold, blue eyes narrowed.

'Ah good, I see that has got your attention,' Miss Oldroyd said.

Bully Boys

Boyd sat on the wall at the back of the school playing field, blinking against the scorching hot sun. It seemed like the whole school was outside this lunchtime; bags and jumpers had been thrown down, some used as goal posts, others as something to sit on. Everyone had something to do or something to talk about, all except Boyd, who kept himself to himself.

There was no one here he could talk to, no one who would understand. He kicked his heels against the wall and looked at the pathway that ran down the side of it. It led into the woods behind the school and this was the cross-country route they used for practice. He couldn't miss the race next week; he knew that if he ran he would win, and he had worked so hard for it.

But he was utterly hopeless at maths. Sometimes, he sat there with the paper in front of him and the numbers seemed to dance all over the page; none of it made sense to him. Numbers had no rhythm, no heartbeat – he felt no connection with them. When he ran, when he practised Taekwondo or boxing, he felt that connection. It was like he had a fire inside him to run the perfect race, or to pass a belt-grading, and that made everything feel right, just for that moment.

His father would always go on at him about how you have to do things you don't enjoy; that's part of life and if you don't learn that early on, you'll never be really happy. Maybe that's why he wasn't happy a lot of the time. He never felt like he fitted in but his dad said that this was all part of growing up. Boyd didn't want to hear that; he didn't want to know that this was normal, and everyone felt it. Looking out at this field, it didn't seem like anyone else felt like he did. He didn't even care if his dad felt the same when he was 15, he just wanted to do what made him happy because that was what life was about, surely?

Doz and Strakes wandered over. They had been talking to a group of girls. Boyd had half-heard the story Jason had told them about how his older brother had a motorbike that he allowed Jason to use and he liked to go to London on it at weekends. Boyd knew that wasn't true. Doz's older brother had a motorbike, but he didn't live at home; Boyd didn't think Doz saw much of his brother.

He'd invited Boyd to go out at the weekend on their mountain bikes, but Boyd told him no, which wasn't something many people said to Doz. He was big, tall and broad. He'd matured ahead of most of the other kids in their year and he used his size as power, forcing people to do whatever he wanted. But Boyd could see beyond the bully's bravado, and that Doz was also a little bit scared and a little bit lost. Even so, pretty much the last thing Boyd wanted was to hang around with him and his idiotic friends.

'Alright Boyd, you plonker,' Strakes said, followed by a snort at his own joke. The lanky, buck-toothed boy must have been as tall as Boyd's dad, who was about six foot three, but he was as thin as a rake. He tried to copy Doz's peacock walk but his feet flopped in front of him like a clown.

'Oh, don't start on him, Strakes,' Doz said, his big lips parting to show his perfect teeth.
He somehow managed to get away with being such a bully because all the teachers liked him. With his curly blond hair and his baby-faced good looks, along with his

easy manner, Mr Providence could never quite believe that Doz terrified every kid in the school.

Well, almost everyone. He wasn't even on Boyd's radar and this seemed to really bug the bully. No matter what he tried to do to scare or intimidate Boyd, it didn't work. It wasn't so rare for someone to disagree with him once but most fell in line after Doz had grabbed them by the collar of their shirt and pulled their face up to his. He'd tried that once with Boyd, just once. Boyd had put his arms up through Doz's and pulled them apart, pushing the bigger boy back a step, and breaking his grip. Boyd's strength had shocked Doz, so now he was wary of him and he didn't like to wind him up too much. But he did enjoy seeing how far he could go and trying to make him look like a fool in front of people.

'I take it you'll be failing the maths test tomorrow, then?' Doz said.

'Yeah, whatever,' Boyd replied, not interested. He wasn't failing the test; he knew that much for certain.

'I hear it's a new test, much harder than the last one. There were complaints from the government or something. Too many people passed it, so they upped the ante.'

'Are you joking? It's not the same test as a few weeks ago?' Boyd's head snapped around as he suddenly gave the big lad his full attention.

A football had rolled over towards them and a group of boys were walking over to get it back. Doz turned to see them and put his foot on the ball. Now was his chance to play to the crowd. 'So, you're never going to pass, you're thick at maths and you know it. Which means you won't be allowed to run next week.' Doz changed his voice, so he was sounding like a crying child. 'So, you won't get your special little medal and daddy won't be proud of his little soldier!' He turned to Strakes, who snorted.

A crowd had quickly gathered out of nowhere, everyone sensing the crackle of tension in the air. Unlike the bully, Boyd couldn't care less about what the crowd thought of him, or the fact that Doz was mocking him; he was just angry about them making a last-minute change to the test – this was a disaster.

Doz just thought that the look on Boyd's face was because he'd been defeated; and he wasn't going to let it pass without adding a wonderful full-stop. So, he flicked up the ball with his foot, bounced it once on his knee and hit a perfect volley, sending the ball straight at Boyd's face. The hard, leather sphere flew like a cannonball. Half a second later, a sudden '*CRACK*' sounded out as it stopped in mid-air. Boyd had caught it. There was a heavy silence as the whole school waited to see what would happen next.

Boyd jumped down from the wall. Strakes and Doz both jolted backwards and immediately wished they hadn't. It brought murmurs of laughter from the crowd, plus a couple of chicken squawks. Boyd stepped towards Doz and looked him in the eye. 'Why don't you and your overgrown clown here go for a run yourselves? Maybe in the middle of the motorway, at night.' Boyd shoved the football into Doz's chest with both hands, pushing him down onto his backside. The school bully was getting a dose of his own medicine, and the gathered throng erupted into collective laughter.

Boyd didn't notice. He was already halfway back across the field when Doz was up on his feet and drop-kicking the football with all his might, sending it deep into the woods for its owner to have to go and find. Boyd didn't care about Doz or Strakes or any of them; they could all get stuffed. He'd spent two weeks working out how to get a copy of the last maths test so he could make sure he passed. He needed a plan, fast.

Running Mates

Boyd slowed down as he ran over the hill, allowing a couple more people by him. Normally by now, he would be way out in front with perhaps one or two classmates trying to match him for pace, but today's cross-country training was always going to be different; the showdown at lunchtime had changed everything. If there was a new maths test, then it was in Mr Providence's office and the Prov, as he was known, always kept his office locked. Added to that, exams were kept in the Head's safe, which was in a cabinet behind his desk. This was the worst kind of problem for Boyd because it was a problem he couldn't solve alone, and he really didn't like relying on other people.

Boyd allowed three more classmates to go by and eventually, after what seemed like an age, Fitz Tork came alongside him, wheezing like a set of bagpipes. Fitz was small and skinny, with a mess of black hair that was never really styled and right now was stuck to his head with sweat. He panted like a dog in the sun as he glanced up at Boyd, then back at his feet, before suddenly looking up at the bigger boy in shock, clearly amazed at having caught up with the fastest boy in school. Then, before he could say a word, Boyd grabbed Fitz's arm and dragged him through a thick tangle of bracken, down a slope and off the path.

'What the hell are you playing at?' Fitz shouted as they burst down the bank and Boyd pulled him under a little bridge. Boyd held his hand over Fitz's mouth and put his finger up to his own lips.

Boyd didn't know an awful lot about Fitz, but the truth was, he really should have. Fitz idolised Boyd; he always tried sit next to him in class, always tried to find him at lunchtime and every school trip he made sure he was in the seat next to Boyd on the coach. He talked at Boyd for hours, week-in and week-out, and Boyd listened to none of it. He should have known everything there was to know about Fitz Tork but, in truth, there were just two things he knew for certain: one, he was known as 'Tork the Dork'; and two, Fitz once told Boyd that he could crack a safe.

49

Let's Get Cracking

Boyd and Fitz sat under the wooden bridge as their classmates trotted overhead. Fitz had just about got his breath back and calmed down before Boyd told him his plan. Now Fitz was inching back towards being hysterical.

'Sorry, you want me to do *what?*' Fitz yelped in amazement. Despite being so skinny, he had a babyface and right now it was screwed up like someone had put something disgusting under his nose.

'Not you, us,' Boyd said, crouching next to Fitz and gripping his shoulder encouragingly.

'Sorry, right; you want *us* to break into the Prov's office and pinch the new maths test from his safe?'

'Exactly.'

'Right, okay, let me think about this for a second.' Fitz rubbed his pale chin with his short fingers. 'That's going to be a "no" from me, I'm afraid. But this was lovely, honestly – great to catch up and everything. Oh, and by the way…' Fitz's voice then climbed to something very much like a shriek as he said, '…are you off your meds or what?'

Boyd clamped a hand over Fitz's mouth as another group of classmates clattered over the bridge. 'I get it,' he said sympathetically.

'Do you? Because I've got to be honest, from where I'm sitting it kinda seems like you don't.'

'Oh come on, I know it sounds insane, but where's your sense of adventure?'

Fitz's eyes widened, his voice suddenly becoming very high again. 'I left it at home with my P.E. kit,' he replied, pointing down towards the very small pink polo shirt and huge, baggy shorts he'd been given to wear from lost property. 'Heads-up, genius: when an idea sounds insane, it's usually because it is.'

'Okay, let's take this down a notch because your voice is so high, only dogs can hear you. You've got some questions, I understand, so how about we calm down and ask away.'

Fitz closed his eyes and took a deep breath; in through his nose, out through his mouth. 'Just one question,' he said, more relaxed this time.

'Go ahead,' Boyd replied.

Fitz picked up a stick and drew a box in the mud. He pointed to the box with the stick. 'The Prov's office is completely off-limits. Only prefects and the most trusted students are permitted entry.' Fitz drew two lines on one side of the box, to show Boyd where the door was. 'He keeps the door locked whenever he's not there.' Fitz picked up a stone and put it outside the box. 'It's Parents' Evening tonight, so he'll leave a student outside the room with a key and a walkie-talkie.' He tapped the stone with the stick, to show Boyd it represented the student. 'So, if the Prov needs anything, he calls and this chap comes running.' He lifted the stick and slapped it against his palm. 'This is before we even talk about the matter of the actual safe.'

'The safe is sorted,' Boyd said. 'I Googled it. Then went around the school and collected everything you'll need to break into it.'

'Oh, that's alright then,' Fitz said, sarcastically. 'How do you plan to actually get into the office and not get caught? Bradley Turvey got detention for stopping outside the door the other day, literally just for stopping. The Prov put "loitering" on the detention slip; Bradley had to ask me what the word meant. It's like 10 Downing Street – you won't get near the door.'

'Great question.'

'Thank you, I thought so.'

'The answer is pretty great too,' Boyd said, taking the stick from Fitz and tapping the stone. 'The guy at the door won't see us. We don't have to worry about walkie-talkies, keys, loitering or any of that.'

'Right! Because since lunchtime, you've developed the ability to walk through walls. I forgot! We're home and dry then.'

'No. That would be pretty cool, but no,' Boyd replied. He took the stick, flipped it around in his hand and speared it into the ground on the other side of the box. 'No one will ever know we were there because we're going into that office from below.'

Tunnel Of Trouble

Oakmead Secondary School was split into two main buildings: the old part and the new part, joined together by a long glass walkway. The music room was at the back of the old part of the school, which was made from crumbling bricks, was always cold and smelled liked wet dog. The Prov's office was also in the old part of the school but it was a big building, and it would take time to get there, especially with the route Boyd had in mind. Luckily, almost everyone else would be in the new school building for Parents' Evening, giving Fitz plenty of opportunity to work on cracking the safe.

'Follow me,' Boyd said, dropping a thin rucksack down onto the floor as he walked over to the piano in the corner of the music room. He started pushing it and the wheels squeaked as they turned, slowly at first – the big old instrument probably hadn't been moved in years – then they loosened up and gave in to the force as the piano rolled into the middle of the room. Mr Morgrave, the Head of Music, always liked to sit at his piano and be able to see the whole class, even when he wasn't playing on it. Just watching Boyd move the instrument made Fitz feel a little flash of excitement. They were doing something they shouldn't be doing, in one of the rooms of the school you weren't allowed in without a teacher. The excitement was bubbling inside him and he was already thrilled by whatever was coming next.

'Come on,' Boyd said, waking Fitz from his daydream. 'Make yourself useful; move the piano stool and roll up the rug.'

Fitz did as he asked, a big smile crawling across his face. He swayed and stumbled before plonking the heavy stool down in the middle of the room with a thump.

'Let's try to be a little more covert, shall we?' Boyd said.

'Sorry, yeah, of course,' Fitz replied. He rolled the rug back from the corner of the room and there, underneath, was a wooden hatch. 'Wow,' he said in a whisper. He got on his knees and carefully stroked the join where the hatch met the floor. 'Is this it?'

'This is it.' Boyd smirked. 'It's an old ventilation

tunnel that leads to the other rooms in the block. It's going to be a bit of a crawl to get to the Prov's office, but I figure if we make it in 20 minutes, we'll have at least 20 minutes to have a go at the safe and another 20 to get back here before they start shutting up for the night.' He smiled, then crouched down. 'But listen,' he added, 'god only knows what's down there, so be prepared, okay?' He stood up and went back for the rucksack.

'Whoa, hold the phone,' Fitz said louder, suddenly not so eager. 'What do you mean by that?'

Boyd picked up the bag and unzipped it. 'I've not been down there, and I doubt anyone has in years, so we just need to be ready in case we find… anything.'

Fitz held up his hands. 'Like what? Give me an example.'

'I don't know.'

'Are we talking body? Buried treasure? A missing Shakespeare sonnet?' His voice was building up to a shriek again. 'And how do you even know it leads to the Prov's office if you haven't been in there?'

'Relax, would you? I found a map, in the library – here.' Boyd took a piece of paper out of the bag and handed it to Fitz. It had been folded and unfolded so many times, it almost felt like it was made of cloth.

Boyd lifted the hatch and the damp smell that had always been part of the identity of the old school room suddenly got a lot worse. Now they knew where it came from.

'You found a map? What are we, the Goonies? I don't like this, Boyd, I don't like this at all. Let's find another way.'

Boyd pulled two head torches from the bag and handed one to Fitz. He took the map back and put it in his back pocket. 'Okay, like what?' he said, coldly.

'Oh, I don't know; you'll think of something, anything! But let's give this a miss, eh?'

Boyd put the thin bag on his back, dropped onto his chest and flicked his torch on; he was ready to go. 'If you're staying here, just tell me now and I'll go on my own.'

Fitz thought about how good it had felt to be somewhere he shouldn't be, how much he'd enjoyed seeing that stupid piano move from its corner. He thought about how school was always about doing the right thing, doing what you were told and never breaking the rules. Then he felt that buzz of excitement in his belly again. 'What the hell; I never really fancied going to college anyway.'

'That's the spirit.' Boyd lowered himself into the tunnel without another word and wriggled into place like a snake.

Fitz put his head torch on, flicked the switch and then followed him in. The tunnel was taller than he expected; they could both crawl on their hands and knees and once you blocked out the smell, it wasn't so bad. 'It's not like I could let you go alone, is it?' Fitz said. 'After all, what are friends for.'

Boyd stopped dead, his torchlight bounced up the side wall of the tunnel as he bent his head around, trying to turn to face Fitz. 'Let's get one thing straight, Fitz: I need you, okay? But we're not friends. I don't have friends, got it?'

Fitz didn't know what to say. 'Yeah, okay,' he replied softly, his voice now completely empty of any excitement.

'Now stop talking. I need to concentrate.'

While Boyd began to pull himself forwards again, Fitz remained still. He suddenly felt once more like this was all a huge mistake. He watched as Boyd's torchlight faded as he headed deeper into the tunnel. Fitz just stayed there in the dark, not sure what he wanted to do. It was too late to go back now, he decided, so he began to shuffle along the tunnel, trying as hard as he could to ignore how foolish Boyd had made him feel.

He soon realised that crawling on your hands and knees on concrete really hurts. The floor of the tunnel wasn't flat; it was knobbly and covered with loose bits of stone and goodness knew what else, and it wasn't long before his knees were burning in agony. 'Boyd, one second, hang on,' Fitz said, in a loud whisper. 'I think I've ripped through the knees in my trousers.'

Boyd stopped. 'Yeah, I think mine tore open after the first minute. Let's keep going and we can get you some plasters later.'

'How can you be so cool and calm about this? God knows what we're crawling through.'

'I'm not,' Boyd replied. 'This my worst nightmare.'

'Really?'

'Yep. I'm claustrophobic; I can't stand being in enclosed spaces.'

'Right. Whose plan was this, again?' Fitz asked.

'You're always sarcastic, aren't you, Fitz? Why is

that?'

'My mum says it's a defence mechanism, which basically means I use sarcasm to protect myself from idiots.'

'Interesting. I quite like it.'

'Really? Most people find it really irritating.'

'No, I think it's clever, it makes me laugh. Anyone who has a problem with it probably can't deal with you being smarter than them.'

'I'd never thought of it like that,' Fitz said, happy with the compliment. Boyd started moving again; Fitz followed.

He was just getting into a rhythm when something squished and crunched under his hand. He quickly pulled his hand away from the floor in panic. Fitz tried to shift his weight onto his right side as he shone his torchlight at his left palm. All he could see was black slime and what looked like fur. He recoiled in horror. 'Oh, god! Boyd, quick!'

Fitz panicked, tried to scramble backwards and lost his balance. Desperate not to put his left hand back down, he fell forwards. 'Boyd!' he shrieked, before his face slapped down onto the tunnel floor. Whatever it was his hand had found was now all over his cheek, neck and shoulder. 'Oh man! It's all over me. I'm going to hurl!'

Boyd shuffled back and turned around to face Fitz, the light from his head torch bobbing around, searching for the danger. 'Fitz!' he said in a whispered shout. 'What's the problem?'

Fitz had managed to lift himself up and was on his knees, his head bent over his chest. The smell was horrendous and now that *thing* was all over him. He felt like he wanted to burn his clothes and have someone hose him down. When he replied, he stuttered through quick, panicked breaths. 'Something proper gross, all over me, my hand.'

Boyd removed his head torch and pointed it at Fitz. He had slick, black goo on his cheek and over the shoulder of his school jumper. Boyd looked down at the floor of the tunnel. 'Fitz, I need you to promise me you're going to keep cool about this, okay? And promise me you won't throw up in here.'

Fitz opened his eyes and looked at Boyd in a state of panic. 'Just tell me,' he said through gritted teeth.

'You seem to have found a squirrel. The good news is, it's, like, really dead. The bad news is,' Boyd paused. 'Well, the bad news is, it's really dead. Which is why it's smells like that and it's not exactly solid.'

Fitz took a moment; his blinking became rapid. 'You're telling me I've squashed a squirrel? I'm covered in squirrel guts and stuff?' he asked, desperately trying to remain calm.

'Exactly. It's just squirrel guts and stuff. That's all.'

'Oh, "*that's all*", he says.' Fitz lifted his head to look at Boyd; it cracked on the roof of the tunnel, making a '*thunk*' sound. 'Of course, THAT'S going to happen, because my life is perfect.' Fitz cursed his luck.

Boyd stopped at the sound Fitz's head made on the top of the tunnel. He looked up and tapped above Fitz's head with his knuckle. Another '*thunk*'. He reached into his back pocket and pulled out the map. 'Oh, you little beauty,' he said, smiling.

'I have just covered myself in the festering insides of a decomposing rodent and you shake it off like I've got some broccoli in my teeth – marvellous. You really are a special kind of maniac, aren't you, Boyd?'

'Fitz, wait.'

'You're a magnet for this kind of thing, I can tell.'

'Fitz.'

'What have I opened myself up to? I should have seen the signs and stayed well away but no, not me. I'm my own worst enemy,' he said, getting himself really worked up now.

Boyd dropped his torch, and with his face illuminated by Fitz's beam he smiled and affectionately slapped his hands on both cheeks. 'Fitz, you little beauty!' He held up the map in front of his face. 'We're here!' Boyd said excitedly. 'We're directly under the Prov's office! Time to get your game-face on!'

Safe And Sound

Doz was feeling much better about himself now. The incident at lunchtime with Boyd had made him so angry but he would have his chance to get revenge; he always got his chance. Anyway, Boyd was a nobody. He had no friends, none of the girls seemed to like him and none of the teachers did either. He was always miserable and a total weirdo, so who cared what he did? And all the idiot had achieved at lunchtime was to make an enemy of Jason Doswell, which was never a smart move.

Doz had spent about five minutes being angry with himself after Boyd walked away. He'd told Strakes that Boyd had been really lucky to knock him over like that, that he was off-balance at the time and it had made it look like Boyd was strong, but he wasn't; not really. The only reason he hadn't followed Boyd and taught him a lesson was because he didn't want to get taken off prefect duty on Parents' Evening – he couldn't risk that. Boyd's punishment would have to wait and that meant that Doz could take his time and dream up something special for the weirdo, something that would really sting. But right now, he had a job to do and it was the most important job in the school. It showed everyone just how much power he had and it more than made up for Boyd's little lunchtime show. Doz settled down on the chair outside the Prov's office with the key in one hand and a walkie-talkie in the other.

Boyd knew that there would be complications getting into the Prov's office. There wasn't a rug or a carpet to worry about; nor did the headmaster have a lock on the hatch in the floor. In fact, as Boyd had sat in the office the week before, being punished for arriving for his French lesson through the window via the tree outside, he could barely notice the join in the beautifully varnished floor. But there was one problem. On top of the hatch, sitting in a wooden stand, was the Prov's pride and joy: his treasured acoustic guitar.

Boyd had made a mental note of the exact position of the instrument and decided that by gently opening the hatch just enough to slide his hand through, he could grab the guitar by the neck and lift it off the stand. He would then be able to push the hatch all the way open, the stand would slide off and he could climb out. In the worst case, the empty stand would maybe knock against the wall, but he was sure it wouldn't be loud enough for anyone outside to hear.

Boyd had handed Fitz a pack of lemon-fresh wet wipes from the rucksack and, although they hadn't got rid of the stains from his uniform, at least he smelt a lot better and he no longer had any dead squirrel on his face. He'd then used a piece of wood he'd found in the tunnel to scoop the carcass out of the way and flick it further down the crawl space before settling under the hatch into the Prov's office. 'Right, you ready?' he looked at Fitz.

'As I'll ever be.'

Fitz had taken off his head torch and positioned it at the ceiling. They could see where the concrete ended and the thick wood of the hatch began. Boyd pushed gently with the fingertips of his left hand at the top edge of the hatch and had his right hand ready to grab the guitar. Nothing happened. He relaxed, took a deep breath and tried again. Nothing, it wasn't budging.

'What is it?' Fitz asked.

'It's fine, it's just being stubborn, that's all.'

'Gently does it, though, eh?'

Boyd stopped and looked at Fitz.

'Trust me,' he said. 'I think it's been varnished shut; I've just got to give it a bit more welly.'

Doz was on his phone, flicking through the latest Instagram posts by Chelsea Football Club, thinking about how he could definitely play football as a job if he wanted to, when he heard the door at the end of the corridor open. He felt a rush of blood at the thought of some unsuspecting little Year Seven walking straight into his web of jurisdiction. Not a soul in the school was supposed to be here except him, and whoever this fool was, they were in the wrong place at the wrong time. But when he heard the thunderous nature of the footsteps and the long strides, his heart sank; this wasn't some young kid he could intimidate; it was the Prov, and that meant something was wrong.

'Doswell!' the headmaster's voice boomed, his Liverpudlian accent ringing as it bounced around the hallway.

Doz was out of his seat, on his feet and walking

towards the sound in less than a second. 'Yessir? What can I do for you, Mr Providence?'

The tall, wide teacher came into view. He was a physically imposing man of around 50 years old. He liked order; he commanded respect without ever demanding it and because of that, even people like Doz got a hollow feeling in the pit of their stomach when they felt they'd let him down.

He stopped when he reached his star prefect and put his hands on his hips. His usual white shirt and red tie were joined by a tweed jacket for Parents' Evening. 'What is the point in my providing you with a communication device, if you don't switch it on?' Doz looked confused for a second. 'It's called a walkie-talkie, Jason. The talkie part seems to be eluding you, sunshine.'

Doz immediately looked down at the radio he had clipped to his belt. 'Oh no. Oh sir, I'm so sorry!'

'That's alright,' the big headmaster said, cracking a smile. 'As it happens, it's good to get away from all those parents for five minutes.'

'Did you need something from the office, sir?'

'Yes, I wanted to show the head of governors some

plans I've been working on.'

'I can get them, sir.'

'It's fine. Relax. I'm here now.'

'But sir, it's my job,' Doz said, desperate to make up for his mistake with the walkie-talkie.

'Jason, just sit and chill out. I'm sure I can go into my office and find some paperwork without the need for your oversight.'

'Yes, sir, of course.' He chuckled and sat.

The Prov put his own key in the lock. 'If anything suddenly jumps out at me, you'll be right here though, yes?' He smiled and turned the key.

Boyd put the flat of his hand on the hatch and gave it a proper shove this time. It creaked as it gave way and popped upwards. Just as it did, he heard the door to the Prov's office open. Boyd stopped dead and held his breath. He couldn't let the hatch drop back down in case it made a noise, so he rested it on his head and looked out through the tiny gap he had created. It had to be a prefect coming in, probably looking for something the Prov had asked for.

'In the meantime, Jason, turn the walkie-talkie on,

for goodness sake.'

Boyd heard the voice and, beneath the desk, through the legs of a chair, he saw a pair of size-eleven, brown suede shoes step over the threshold and into the office. It wasn't a prefect, it was the headmaster. Boyd suddenly felt sick.

'Boyd! What's the hold up?' Fitz asked.

Boyd couldn't move his head; he was using it to stop the hatch from falling, so he reached down with his hand and put it over Fitz's mouth. Fitz moved to grab Boyd's hand but before he could, Boyd used his left hand to grab Fitz's head torch and twisted it, turning the light off. They were plunged into darkness for a moment, until the light from the tiny gap in the hatch started to seep through and their eyes adjusted. Boyd put his index finger over his lips, then pointed upwards to let Fitz know someone was in the office. The hatch was in the left corner of the room, directly in front of the back wall. The remainder of the back wall was taken up with cupboards and the Prov's desk sat in front of them.

Boyd slowly turned his head back around in time to see the Prov slip around the far corner of his desk and move towards the cupboards. He opened one of the doors and bent down to look inside. Now the Prov's chair was the only thing between Boyd and his headmaster as he was in the middle of breaking into his office.

The Prov was rifling through papers, clearly not able to find what he was looking for.

'Come on, what did I do with it?' he said to himself. He shuffled his feet closer to the cupboard and crouched down properly, onto his haunches. All the headmaster would have to do was gently nudge the chair out of the way and he would see that the hatch was no longer flush against the floor. There was nothing Boyd could do but stay as still as possible, make absolutely no noise – and pray.

'Ha! I see you!' the headmaster shouted.

Boyd tensed. *Oh god. Please. No.*

'You thought you could hide from me, did you?' The Prov's voice cut through Boyd's senses. His whole body suddenly went cold, as if he had been submerged in ice. He felt his legs began to twitch beneath him, every single part of him was screaming like mad to scamper back down the tunnel. But, just then, he saw the Prov slap a folder against his open palm.

'Gotcha!' he said, victoriously. Then the big shoes shuffled backwards, the cupboard door slammed shut and the Prov made his way back to the office door. He was still talking to himself as he went. 'The governors are going to love this,' he said cheerfully.

Boyd waited until the key turned in the lock, then he released a long breath as he moved swiftly and precisely. He pushed the hatch, reached through and grabbed the guitar by the neck. He lifted and twisted it so the hatch didn't make contact with the fat, wooden body of the instrument. He had already got away with too much today; he wasn't sure how much more luck he had left in the bank.

He pushed himself up and out of the hatch. The guitar stand slid back and gently clunked against the wooden skirting board. Boyd stopped for a moment and waited to see if there was any reaction to the sound from outside the room; nothing. He pulled the stand free and then let the hatch rest against the wall. Releasing the stand, he rested the guitar safely back in its rightful place. Next, he pulled the rucksack off his back and took out a bunch of what looked like plastic freezer bags; they were blue with elastic around the top. Grabbing one, he put the rest on the floor in front of him. One by one, he brought his feet out of the tunnel and stretched the elasticated blue bag over his shoes. Then he took off his jumper, turned it inside out and put it on the wooden floor next to the hatch.

Fitz watched every move carefully before Boyd gestured for him to follow his actions, but the smaller boy waved him away. 'Yep, I've got it,' he whispered, grabbing two elasticated bags and bringing himself up out of the darkness. 'Don't waste time talking to me; find the safe and prep the area.'

Boyd smiled and nodded. He walked over to the cupboard and carefully opened the nearest door. Bingo, right first time. 'Got it,' he said. He opened the bag and took out a tool belt from the school workshop.

Fitz was out of the tunnel now and was taking his jumper off. The wet, sticky patch where the squirrel guts and brains had seeped into the fabric wiping over his face as he pulled the jumper over his head. 'Ah man!' he said, a little too loudly.

Boyd gave him a look and they stopped moving for a moment. No sound from outside; they were safe. Boyd tilted his head and flared a look in Fitz's direction, letting him know that had to be their last mistake. Fitz nodded sheepishly, then put his jumper down and moved over to the cupboard. The boys sat close and whispered.

'What's this?' Fitz asked, pointing at the tool belt.

'Tools, for you to crack the safe.'

'What do you think I'm going to do with those? Build a shed? You don't literally "crack" a safe, you know. I'm not going to just shove a chisel in there, smash it with hammer and hey presto! We're in!' Fitz shook his head, his face screwed up in confusion.

'I don't know, Fitz - I'm not the expert. I didn't exactly have a lot of time.'

'Well, if this is all you have, we're in trouble.'

'Why? What do you need?'

Fitz looked at the safe. It was small and fairly new, but it had an old-fashioned numbered dial on the front. 'This is called a dial; I need to turn it and listen to what's happening inside. Which means I need a stethoscope.'

'A stethoscope? You mean, like a doctor uses?'

'Exactly like a doctor uses. Did you bring one?'

'Oh no, sorry,' Boyd replied, tapping his pockets. 'It's in my other trousers with my scalpel and my X-ray machine.'

'I see your sarcasm is starting to develop nicely.'

'Great, so we're stuffed then?'

Fitz thought for a moment and looked around. 'No, maybe not. Give me that drink bottle,' he pointed to a plastic bottle in the bin under the desk. Boyd passed it to him, and Fitz took off the lid. 'Give me your bag. Then see if you can find me some scissors, and some glue,' he said, his brain beginning to whirr.

He sat back on the floor, opened Boyd's bag, and rummaged around. He took out some headphones and put them down next to the bottle lid. Boyd added scissors to the pile of supplies. The bag was one of those hiking rucksacks that had a plastic tube running from a water container inside. You put the end of the plastic tube in your mouth and drank the water without ever taking the bag off.

Fitz took the scissors and held them over the material of the bag. 'Before I do this, do you mind if I rip this tube out of your bag and cut your headphones up?'

Boyd exhaled sharply and raised his eyebrows. 'Why not? Go ahead. I only saved for two months for that bag.'

'Excellent. Find me the glue.'

Boyd went back to the drawers and found some superglue. He quietly returned to Fitz and found that he'd already removed the drinks tube and cut the hearing buds from the headphones.

He was working fast. He cut a section of the tubing off the end and using the scissors he made a small hole a third of the way down the longer piece of tubing. He poked the smaller section of the tube into the hole and then glued it, making a 'Y' shape. Next, he drilled a hole in the bottle cap then attached it to the bottom of the 'Y' and poked the headphone buds into the two top sections and fixed them all with the glue.

Boyd watched it all come together and then realised he was looking at a homemade stethoscope. 'That's amazing. Will it work?'

'Probably not but it's all we've got,' Fitz replied, shuffling into position in front of the safe.

Boyd leant in, watching as Fitz popped the headphones in and placed the bottle cap on the door of the safe, next to the dial. 'You do know what you're doing, right?'

'No,' Fitz said, his face in pretend confusion. 'I

thought you brought me along for my charming personality.' He smiled. 'Yes, I know what I'm doing.' Fitz pointed to the dial. 'Behind here are wheels, which are known as "tumblers"; this type of safe has three wheels because it has a three-number combination. You with me so far?'

Boyd nodded unconvincingly. 'Yeah, of course.'

'Good,' Fitz said, genuinely pleased. 'I turn the dial and I listen carefully to a small rod that runs along these wheels. I'm listening for when this rod falls into a notch. I use a graph to map out the dial and…'

Boyd shook his head. 'No, you've lost me,' he said. 'I'll just get you a pad and pencil and keep quiet.'

'Perfect.'

Fitz began to slowly turn the dial, his homemade stethoscope pressed up against the front of the safe. Sometimes he turned the dial quickly, then slowed it down, and Boyd could hear the little clicks and clacks of the wheels turning inside the mechanism.

Boyd watched in awe as Fitz became completely lost in his work, muttering to himself and scribbling dots on a messy graph he had drawn on the pad. Boyd stood up and carefully stretched his legs. He didn't want to rush

Fitz, he needed him to stay calm and concentrate, but pretty soon they'd need to be back in that tunnel.

Fitz let out a long breath. 'Okay, I think I've got it,' he whispered. He removed the headphones and wiped his brow with his shirt sleeve.

'Nice one!' Boyd hissed excitedly, crouching down to the safe.

'Hang on, it's not a perfect science. Sometimes these numbers can be one or two out the first time.'

Boyd didn't speak; he let Fitz turn the dial. This time, he moved it quickly and deliberately, only slowing down when he clicked it onto three specific numbers. Nothing. Fitz paused and pursed his lips.

'What is it?' Boyd asked.

'Yep, I'm out by a number or two, I think. Hang on.' Fitz studied the graph and started spinning the dial again. He settled on two numbers and seemed happy. Then he took a deep breath. 'Cross your fingers,' he said as he turned the dial again, slowing suddenly, rolling it number by number until there was an audible 'CLUNK!' 'Crikey!' he whispered and stopped dead.

Both boys stifled a nervous laugh and had to look away from each other. Neither moved nor said a word, waiting to see if there was any sign of life from outside the office. After just over a minute, no key had hit the lock. Fitz looked back at the safe, slowly turned the handle on the front and pulled the door open.

'Right, let me get in there,' Boyd said.

Fitz stood up and straightened his legs for the first time in what felt like hours, grimacing as his joints creaked back to life. He picked up the homemade stethoscope, nodded and smiled at his handiwork before slipping it into the backpack. Meanwhile, Boyd leafed through the papers in the safe and quickly found the set of maths tests. He removed one of the tests, took out his phone and began snapping a picture of each page; within two minutes, he had everything he needed. He put the test back with the others, returned them to the safe, shut the door and closed the cupboard. Fitz put the glue, the pad and the scissors back, they put their jumpers back on and had one final look around.

Boyd turned to Fitz. 'Right, let's get out of here.' He moved the guitar to the right of the hatch, opened it up and climbed down into the darkness. He took off his shoe coverings and threw them into the tunnel.

'Wait,' Fitz replied. 'I found the dial set to zero.'

'What?'

'The dial, on the safe – when someone sets their dial to zero, it's not by accident, he probably does it every time.' Fitz went back around the front of the cupboard, leaving Boyd half in and half out of the tunnel. 'So, I just need to check that I put it back to zero, or he'll know someone's been in here.'

Fitz grabbed the handles on the cupboard and threw them open. Not considering the fact that the guitar was now right next to the cupboard, he stared in dread as the door collided with the bottom of the instrument and created a thundering, tuneless din. The boys froze in disbelief as the guitar continued to ring out like an alarm. Boyd snapped out of it first, reached out and clamped his hand around the strings, killing the noise, his eyes wide in panic. The handle on the office door started to turn.

Doz was almost at level 9 of a game called *Slayer Quest* but he kept getting killed at the same point. He managed to get to the waterfall and find the dragon eggs, but every time he searched under the nest for the Key of Kalbrack, he woke up Saydax, the Dragon Queen. She burst through from behind the waterfall and before he could get five direct hits with his fungus bombs to put her to sleep, she toasted him. He was just Googling a cheat so he could pass Level 8 when there was a massive '*CLANG*' from inside the Prov's office.

'What the hell?' Doz was on his feet and had the key in the lock within seconds. He turned the handle, opened the door, stopped and smiled at the scene in front of him. Then he realised he still had his phone in his hand. So, he lifted it up and snapped two pictures before turning on his heels and walking away. 'Man, you're finished, Tork!' Doz called out. 'You're so gonna get expelled for this one, mate!'

He casually trotted away from the office, heading down the corridor towards the covered walkway and the new part of the school to where all the parents, teachers and school officials were gathered to celebrate the wonderful centre of learning that was Oakmead Secondary School. Doswell would have to break up that little party and show them the picture of Fitzgerald Tork, his hands on the safe in the Prov's office; his face twisted in complete horror. Some days, he really loved being a prefect.

'Who was that?' Boyd shouted to Fitz, who was still in total shock, looking at the empty doorway.

'Fitz!' Boyd pulled himself out of the tunnel and walked around to the side of The Prov's desk.

'It was Doz. He um… I think…'

'Right, let's get that door shut and lock it from inside. Then we get back down the tunnel and by the time he's got the Prov back here, they'll be no sign of us.'

'No, he… um…'

'Fitz, listen! He didn't even see me and the Prov isn't going to believe Tork The Dork broke in here – and how could you have? Doz was outside the whole time. Let him tell everyone, he'll just look like a total nutjob! Earth to Fitz,' Boyd clicked his fingers in front of Fitz's face. 'We have to move, now!'

'He took a picture of me, on his phone.' Fitz's face was as pale as the white walls of the office.

Boyd reacted quickly, pulling himself out of the tunnel as he spoke at a machine-gun pace. 'Forget the tunnel; put the hatch down, put the guitar back and get to the music room. Put everything back as best you can.' He ran to the door.

'What are you going to do?'

Boyd stopped and turned. 'I'm going to get that phone and make sure he stays quiet.'

Boyd was away down the corridor in no more than three strides. He sprinted around the last bend before the covered walkway and saw Doz strolling down the long, glass walkway like he hadn't got a care in the world. Then he turned his head as he heard Boyd's footsteps. Doz's face dropped, instinct took over and he bolted. Like any bully, his natural reaction was to run from any kind of real trouble – especially when there was no one around to play brave for.

The new part of the school was built around something called an Atrium, which was a tall building with a huge floorspace in the middle that was open all the way up to a glass roof. This is where they held Parents' Evening, with stands displaying different school projects and even a stage for the school choir to perform a recital. If Boyd didn't catch Doz, he would run into the Atrium and show everyone the picture of Fitz at the safe and his chances of competing in the county championships would be all over. But for some reason that Boyd couldn't fathom, Doz didn't head towards the

Atrium. Once he made it through the walkway, he turned right and headed up the stairs. What the hell was he doing?

Boyd clattered through the double doors at the end of the walkway and immediately heard Doz's shoes smacking on the stairs above him. 'I want that phone, Jason!'

No reply.

Boyd took the stairs two at a time. As he threw himself up each level, he listened carefully just in case Doz left the stairwell to hide himself in one of the classrooms. Boyd reached the second floor but he could still hear Doz's feet pounding above him. The third floor was the last; above that there were no corridors to escape down, just the roof. Boyd's heart went up into his mouth as he recalled a small slice of a conversation he'd heard a while ago. Strakes had bragged about how he had been up on the roof during lunchtime and how he had the combination to the keypad for the door; Doz must be heading for the roof! Was he mad? No, Boyd understood now. If Doz got through the door at the top of the stairs, Boyd would never be able to get to him without the code. He couldn't let that happen.

Boyd quickly realised that he couldn't hear any footsteps anymore – was he too late? He dug deep and lunged up the final flight of stairs. As he came around the corner, the door was in sight but Doz was already through it, already moving across the flat roof towards the glass top of the Atrium. Boyd wondered why Doz hadn't just pulled the door closed behind him but as he ran he noticed it was one of those security doors that are made to close slowly to ensure no one got trapped outside; which meant Boyd still had a glimmer of hope. He hauled himself up onto the landing as the door was more than halfway shut, the afternoon sky slowly disappearing along with his last chance of catching Doz.

Boyd took one step and realised he wasn't going to make it, not like this. So, he used that step to launch himself. He hit the ground on his left-hand side and skidded on his hip across the smooth surface, his right leg extended out in front of him like a footballer in a sliding tackle. Just as the last shaft of light from outside was slowly being shut out, Boyd's right foot hit the door jamb and the heavy door stopped with a thud on his ankle. 'Aaaahh!' he let out a cry of pain. But he couldn't let it slow him down.

He grabbed the door handle, pulled himself up and went out onto the roof. The section he was on was flat and housed six big, white boxes that contained huge, whirring fans; the air conditioning for the new part of the school. There was a ledge running around the edge of this section of the roof and Doz was already at the far end, standing right at the edge. He looked at Boyd and smiled so wide, his eyes were almost lost in the creases of his face.

Doz put one foot on the ledge and jumped, disappearing from view. Boyd felt his breath catch. Had he just jumped off the roof? No, of course not – Boyd could see the glass top of the Atrium was just beyond the ledge. Doz had jumped down onto the surface that surrounded the Atrium roof.

Boyd followed and jumped without breaking his stride. As he landed, he tucked into a forward roll and then immediately came up into a run. Doz seemed to know the layout of the roof well, whereas Boyd was up here for the first time and was wary of getting too close to the edge or to the glass on the other side of him. Doz unexpectedly ducked left and moved towards the glass of the Atrium roof, which went up into pointed ridge, like the roof on Boyd's house. There was a walkway, like a ladder, that went over the top of the ridge and down the other side. Doz must know a way to escape from there, because he was crawling up the ladder, moving up the side of the huge, transparent roof.

Boyd didn't think about it. He was too angry to stop, he just stepped onto the first rung of the ladder and followed Doz out onto the glass. He tried to force away any thoughts of how stupid this was, but he kept hearing his dad's voice in his head.

'Situations get worse around you because you run on anger,' he would tell Boyd when they boxed together. 'You can't control anything if you let anger take over – be smart.'

He'd heard the same thing from his Taekwondo instructor when he'd lost the final of the sparring competition last year because he had let his opponent get into his head and wind him up. But even as he thought these things, even as he heard those voices telling him to be reasonable, to take a breath and calm down, he knew he couldn't do it. He *was* angry and there was no way he was going to let Doz get away with this.

Boyd looked down and saw the events of Parents'
Evening playing out beneath him. Large groups of
adults and students, all silently gathered. His dad was
down there somewhere, but he tried to put that out of
his mind for now. He reached the halfway point, in the
middle of one side of the glass roof and felt a knot in his
stomach; he was so far from the ground, suspended in
mid-air. Out of nowhere he heard a buzzing sound and
then the noise of the people below him broke up
through the air. Then, a scream.

'Oh no!' Doz shouted. 'Help me, please!'

Boyd looked up along the ridge of the roof: the top
window was opening right under Doz and he was losing
his footing. The Atrium windows were opened and
closed at a set time every day by a motor; the whirring
sound kept going as the windows slid open and Doz's
legs hung through the gap as he struggled to hold onto a
slippery panel of glass. Boyd stayed calm, looked down
at his hands and feet, and just concentrated on moving
fast, staying on the ladder and making it to Doz before
he lost his grip. He ignored the other boy's screams; he
ignored the people below them who suddenly began to
shout and panic as they looked up to see a student

dangling inside the big, glass roof.

'Quickly! I can't hold on!' Doz had managed to grab onto the steel bar that ran along the inside of the glass.

'Hang on!' Boyd shouted.

'I can't!'

Boyd reached him just as Doz let go. He grabbed the boy's left forearm and a handful of the sleeve of his school jumper. In Doz's other hand was the phone. Boyd was now the only thing stopping him from falling over 50 feet to the floor below.

Doz was now completely inside the glass roof, his legs swinging as he scrabbled around in a terrified panic. Boyd was lying down on the outside, with his head, shoulders and arms inside. The sound was almost deafening as the people on the ground reacted to the unbelievable scene playing out over their heads.

Doz looked up at Boyd, pleading with his eyes. 'Don't let me go, please.'

'I wasn't planning on it,' Boyd replied, seemingly cool and calm but inside, his heart was beating out of his chest.

Without warning, Doz's left hand lost its grip on Boyd's arm and he slid downwards. Boyd caught him at the wrist.

'Oh god!' Doz shouted. 'I can't do it. Please. I can't hold on!'

'I need to pull you up,' Boyd said, pleading. 'I need both your hands.'

Doz went to lift his right hand up towards Boyd, then stopped; he thought for a moment. 'You just want me to drop the phone,' he said. His face twisted with anger and disbelief.

'No, Jason,' Boyd shouted. 'I want to save your bloody life!'

Doz jutted out his chin. He wasn't going to do it. 'I'm not a complete idiot, you know!'

'Course not; just the bits you let everyone see. Doz, I need both hands or you'll fall.'

Doz shook his head and tried to work out how he had got to the point where Boyd was telling him what to do. He knew he didn't have a choice. He released the phone and it tumbled down through the air.

'Heads-up!' Boyd shouted and saw a set of concerned governors shuffle a group of parents aside. Everyone took in a sharp breath, then there was a momentary silence as they watched the phone descend and smash on the floor. Doz threw his right arm upwards and Boyd caught it, pulling him up.

'Climb over me,' Boyd said.

As Doz climbed over Boyd's head, Boyd grabbed his feet and boosted him out and over his back. Once Doz was out, he shuffled quickly back down the glass roof. Boyd just turned over and lay on his back, no longer scared of being so far from the ground.

'Don't think this means you're off the hook; you're done here, Boyd,' Doz said as he turned and jogged back the way they had come.

'Yeah, you're welcome,' Boyd said to himself. He sat up and looked out over the fields and trees of the Bloomfield Downs, still trying to get his breath back. Like always, he took the chance to enjoy the peace of being alone, because this time, he knew it wasn't going to last for long.

Suspended

'Suspended!' Fitz shouted. He and Boyd were alone in front of the school reception building. Fitz's mum and Boyd's dad were still inside with the Prov.

'It's not a big deal – next week is half-term anyway,' Boyd said, brushing Fitz off.

'So what? It still goes on my record! You could have told them I had nothing to do with it. They don't have the picture – it's just Doz's word against mine!'

'What's the point?' Boyd said. His last chance of running in the county championship had smashed to pieces with Doz's phone. Parents' Evening was called off, several of the attendees were talking about writing letters to the council about how on earth the school had made it so easy for two students to get up onto the roof, let alone almost fall through it.

Doz, of course, played the part of the victim to perfection. Boyd didn't care anymore. The championships were lost to him and nothing else mattered.

'What's the point?' Fitz shouted. 'The point is I'm suspended because of you. Thanks for that!'

'No one forced you, Fitz.'

Fitz didn't reply. He started to walk away, then stopped and walked back to Boyd. He'd never seen Fitz like this, literally shaking with anger. He fronted up to Boyd.

'Screw you,' Fitz said. Swallowing hard, he jabbed a finger into Boyd's chest. 'Y'know, I used to think this whole "iceman" thing was some kind of act, that people had you all wrong when they said you were just an idiot loner who didn't care. But I've watched you do nothing while losers like Doz and Strakes bully everyone; you just stood there, letting it happen. Even then I convinced myself you had a reason; you were still a good person underneath it all. *"Maybe it's because his mum died and his dad is a douchebag,"* I thought.'

'Watch it, Fitz!' Boyd gave Fitz a small shove, but the smaller boy came back at him, their chests bumping.

'Oops, sorry, have I touched a nerve, loner boy? Are you like this because daddy never bothers to spend any time with you?'

The reception doors opened, and Fitz's mum and Boyd's dad started down the steps towards the boys.

'Fitz, shut up, I'm warning you,' Boyd said quietly.

'Oh yeah and you'll do what, exactly? Hmm? What can you do to me now mate, eh? Oh yeah, sorry, my mistake.' Fitz laughed and stepped away. 'I remember now, we're not mates, are we?'

The laughter stopped, and Fitz's eyes started to well up with tears.

'That's the one thing you were right about today, you know that. You really don't have friends do you, Boyd? And now I know why.' Fitz walked away, towards his mum's car.

'Fitzgerald Tork, you come back here!' Marjorie Tork yelled as she stomped after him.

Boyd's dad didn't stop either. He walked straight past him, without a word or a glance.

The two men sat in a black Audi, parked at the side of the long driveway out of Oakmead Secondary School. The man in the passenger seat had tilted and turned the rear-view mirror so he could see the boys talking outside reception. Then two adults came out of the school building and the boys split, heading their separate ways. The man in the driver's seat was watching events closely in his wing mirror. His seat was pushed back as far as it could go; it was the only way he could fit his long legs in behind the steering wheel. He drummed his huge fingers as he watched the mother and son approach in their car. As they drove by, the big man turned his face towards the passenger because he had the kind of face that, if you saw it, you wouldn't forget it, so it was best to stay out of sight.

The man in the passenger seat didn't take his eyes from the other pupil. He watched as the boy and his father walked towards their car without exchanging a word. He could see from the boy's body language that he was boiling with anger, fists clenched, bursting for an argument; it was also clear that his father wasn't going to give it to him. They got in the car and drove past slowly. Again, the big man in the driver's seat looked away. He kept his huge, bulging eyes on the man in the passenger seat. The driver started the engine. His boss returned his gaze and turned his thin, snake-like lips up into a hideous smile that revealed a set of small, pointed teeth.

'I should follow?' the driver asked.

'Yes, please, follow them, Mr Bakker,' the man replied.

As the car pulled away, the passenger took out his phone and hit one button. 'Eagle, this is Van Cleef. We've found him.' He hung up the phone without hearing a word of reply. They accelerated after the other car. 'Don't be too eager, Bakker. We've done the hard part. When we strike, they won't know we are coming.'

Father And Son

Boyd woke the next morning to the sound of his dad moving around the house. He checked the time on his phone: it was after 9:30am, which meant Martin Boyd hadn't gone to work today. Martin had barely talked to Boyd last night and he was an expert at the silent treatment. Boyd had sat in the car on the way home and allowed his anger to boil and fizz, stubbornly refusing to start a conversation himself.

'Go to bed,' Martin had said as they walked through the front door, so that's exactly what Boyd had done.

Their home was a simple three-bedroom house in a small close in the town of Bloomfield. It was on an estate of about 100 houses, tucked away in the countryside, surrounded by hills and fields. Bloomfield was too big to know everyone but small enough that you couldn't help but bump into your teachers in the supermarket. It wasn't too far from London, just over an hour away by train, and Boyd's dad often made the trip to the capital, meeting a client in the city or heading to the airport and flying off somewhere for work. From the look of the leather bag at the front door, it seemed that his dad was going away somewhere today.

Boyd heard Martin in the kitchen. The kettle was boiling and the toaster popped. He decided to continue to avoid contact, to force his dad to make the first move. So he went into the lounge and found his tablet before making his way into the kitchen.

Martin Boyd was standing at the kitchen counter, reading something on his phone, drinking a coffee and eating toast. Boyd hated coffee, he couldn't stand the smell, so Martin always ate at the kitchen counter, never taking his coffee to the table. Martin's breakfast routine was always the same: the toast sat on the breadboard and he buttered a little bit of it at a time before taking a bite. Boyd took a seat at the breakfast bar, picked up the remote control and turned on the wall-mounted TV. He activated screenshare, so his tablet displayed on the television. Opening YouTube, he saw that one of his favourite YouTubers had dropped a new video.

FrakeNews was a site dedicated to exposing the truth behind unexplained events or revealing government cover-ups. Boyd loved it, Martin did not, which made it the perfect choice for this morning, Boyd thought. He had only started watching *FrakeNews* because his dad had told him that he wanted to discuss politics and world events over the dinner table. Boyd decided that if he had to talk about adult things that he didn't care about, he was going to get a different opinion to the one Martin got from *BBC News*.

It turned out he was surprised how much he enjoyed learning about world events. *FrakeNews* made this kind of stuff edgy and exciting, and most of the theories they came out with frustrated Martin, which was a bonus for Boyd. The reporter sat in shadow so you couldn't see their face and they spoke with a deliberately distorted voice. Mostly this was because the stories they reported on involved revealing the secrets of important and powerful people who had plenty of money, which made *FrakeNews* unpopular with politicians and businesses. Boyd clicked on the video and the familiar theme played through his headphones. The intro music was solemn, accompanied by the image of the clock on Big Ben in London, ticking faster and faster until it melted and exploded, leaving the title on the screen: '*FrakeNews* –

The Truth They Don't Want You To Know.'

The reporter came on the screen, just an outline of someone in a baseball cap. Next to the figure was an image of a passenger plane. 'Welcome to the truth. Last week, a plane took off from Heathrow Airport and by the time it landed in Paris, there was one less passenger on board.' The reporter's deep, robotic voice somehow still managed to be filled with intrigue and emotion.

Whoever was behind *FrakeNews* always started with that same line, 'Welcome to the truth.' Boyd had watched reports on the plastic contaminating the ocean, the refugees who had to leave their homes because of war and how governments weren't doing enough to stop global warming. They delivered their reports with so much passion and Boyd had learnt a lot from watching them. But it was the stories like this, which no one else even knew about, that really had him hooked.

'Yes, a woman has disappeared and almost no one is asking why. The story was picked up by a local French news outlet as they had a reporter on the flight but it was soon squashed by the British and French secret service – but here's the thing…' The reporter leant in, their face came closer to the camera, putting them even deeper into shadow. '*FrakeNews* has spoken to witnesses on the flight and the passenger went missing from the toilet of the plane. She went in, and she never came out. Her seat remained unoccupied for the rest of the flight. The plane was obviously sealed until landing, there were no recorded issues with the flight, with no unscheduled stops in between London and Paris. So, where on earth did this mystery woman go?'

Boyd sat forward, completely engrossed in the report.

'Well, firstly, thanks to *FrakeNews*, she's no longer a mystery. We managed to get a copy of the list of passengers who boarded the flight before the British government changed it and removed her name. And we can exclusively reveal that the disappearing woman is Miranda Capshaw: a British artist who lives in France.'

The image of a woman appeared on the screen and, for some reason, Boyd paused the video. Leaning forward, he studied the passport picture of the woman. She was around 40, with brown hair and a friendly, open face, and there was something familiar about her that he couldn't place. It continued to amaze him; the things adults did to each other. What had Miranda

101

Capshaw done to have someone make her vanish from the face of the earth? Where she was right now? And how on earth can you make someone just disappear from a plane in mid-air? He hit play again.

'So where is our mid-air toilet escape artist, you may wonder? And why on earth did the British government feel the need to erase her name from the flight manifest?'

The picture of the woman on the screen was replaced with an image of the Home Secretary, a tall man called Octavius Ogilvy. As the person in charge of keeping the country safe and secure, he was a frequent *FrakeNews* target, and was especially called out for not providing satisfactory answers to their questions.

'Mr Ogilvy, what has Miranda Capshaw done to receive such special attention from your secret service? We would love you to come on *FrakeNews* and shed some light on this. In fact, we won't stop talking about it until you do! Guys, until next time – demand the truth.'

The *FrakeNews* theme boomed out of the TV and then the screen went black. Then, the voice filled the room again, with the cryptic message that was played at the end of every video: 'If you have any information or a story that you think could be *FrakeNews*, go back to where it all started and find the time.'

Boyd had no idea what that meant but it all added to the drama of the videos – you didn't get this on the six o'clock news. He hit the screen of his tablet and paused the video. Martin had finished his toast and was washing up the bread board.

'Crazy, eh,' Boyd said. 'How can someone disappear like that, from a plane?'

'I've got to go away, not sure when I'll be back,' Martin replied, taking a sip of coffee.

Boyd pouted and said nothing.

'Okay, Boyd?'

'Yeah, fine, whatever.'

'Don't be dismissive. If you have something to say, be an adult and say it.'

'I'm not an adult and no, I don't.'

'Great.' Martin finished his coffee and began to rinse his mug. 'I'm disappointed in you, Boyd.'

'I got that, thanks.'

'You can't keep being that kid, you know that?'

'And what kid is that?' Boyd asked, his voice shaking with barely controlled anger.

'The kid who's able to convince himself that he has

every right to be unreasonable just so he can get what he wants, no matter who gets hurt. I know that other kids have a mother, and I can't help the fact that you don't but you can't let a situation like that define you. You have to define your situation.'

That was one of his favourite sayings and this time, he said it so calmly, with such a heavy heart, Boyd didn't know how to respond. He felt something inside him crack. It started in his throat; he swallowed, and it slid down into this stomach like a cricket ball. He didn't like what his dad was saying, he didn't want to admit that it was true and it didn't take long before Boyd let that feeling turn into anger, as he usually did.

'What would you even know? You're never here. You don't know anything about me!' Boyd stood up and shoved the stool back into place with a thump.

'Calm down, Boyd,' Martin said, his tone heavy with warning.

'Why should I? So you can give me another speech and then go and catch a plane somewhere? What's the point?' He walked to the kitchen door.

'Where are you going?' Martin asked.

'I take it I'm spending the night at Aunt Aurora's,

again, so I'm going to pack a bag. Don't worry about driving me, I'll get a taxi.' He left the room.

'Boyd! Hang on,' Martin walked to the kitchen door and watched Boyd run up the stairs.

'Boyd, please!'

Boyd's bedroom door slammed shut.

Aurora

Aunt Aurora lived in a small mobile-home park near the beach. Despite what he'd said to his dad, Boyd actually really enjoyed staying with Aurora. She hated it when he called her 'Aunt' – she was pretty cool and let him do whatever he wanted. He asked the taxi driver to drop him off at the end of the driveway to the park and paid the fare. He ducked under the gate and walked up the hill. The park was right over the road from the beach. You could smell the salt in the air and the afternoon sun glinted off the small, glassy fragments of sand in the pathway.

Being here immediately helped Boyd to relax. He knew exactly how he would spend the afternoon: he'd dump his stuff, grab his book and his headphones, and go over to the sand dunes where he could be alone. Then, on his way home tonight, he would stop and buy some chips from Alfonso, the old guy with a small, blue fish-and-chip van. Alfonso was always in the beach car park on Friday nights and he made the best chips in Bloomfield.

Boyd walked along the short track into the park. There were only seven homes in the whole place, six of which were parked on what was called a 'lot'. All the lots were similar; they had a mobile home, a space to park a car and not much else. Aurora's home was different. Firstly, she called it her 'van', whereas her neighbours called theirs 'static homes'; Aurora said this was because they were all snobs. Most of the others had cars outside; Aurora didn't have a car and didn't drive, she walked pretty much everywhere. All the other homes were on a flat piece of land, all on the same level, but Aurora's van looked like it had been added to the park as an afterthought. It was up in the top corner of the park, close to the road, on a raised patch of grass. So if you stood in the right place in the van, you could see over the hedge, across the small road and out to sea.

There was a tiny loft space on top of the van, and this is where Boyd slept. You had to climb a ladder from inside to get into it and there was only just enough room to lie down in there, but it was the best view in the park. Boyd always kept the little curtains open because he hated enclosed spaces and this way he could look out over the water as he fell asleep.

As he walked past the other vans, he could hear the familiar sound of Aurora's wood chimes. She had them hanging from strings on her washing line, on her awning, on every window and door, and they clacked and clinked constantly in the sea breeze. It had taken Boyd a while to get used to the noise when he first stayed there but now he actually found it soothing. It drove her neighbours mad but none of them ever complained to her face.

Boyd walked up the hill and saw Aurora's door was open. 'Aurora, it's me,' he called out.

His aunt appeared, stepping sideways through the narrow front door. Aurora was a big woman; not overweight by any means but she was very tall with square shoulders. She had big hands and big feet too, but once you noticed this – and there was no way you couldn't – you soon forgot it because Aurora had a kindness about her that was rare in anyone. Boyd felt like she really got him, but she managed to let him know that without the long speeches or the barrage of questions he got from other adults; she wasn't like anyone else he knew. Aurora showed him he was important to her without her ever having to say it, and it made him feel safer here than anywhere else in the world.

Today she was dressed in a long, floaty top and a pair of leggings that can only be described as 'colourful'; her hair was short, dyed dark red and messy. She was, as always, barefoot. She wore wooden beads around her neck and, as always, she had her big, silver ring that looked like an upside-down 'T' on the middle finger of her right hand. Boyd's dad had always called her a 'hippy', which a ten-year-old Boyd had to Google to see what it meant. As soon as he'd read the definition, it had made perfect sense. A hippy was someone who rejected the way most people did things and followed their own beliefs; it sounded like a great way to live. Maybe that's why Boyd liked her so much. Aurora didn't live by routines or appointments. She swam in the sea every morning at seven for an hour, whatever the weather. Other than that, she didn't seem to have any kind of commitments in her life at all.

'There's my Boyd!' she said loudly, her green eyes glowing. 'How's you, dude?'

If any other adult tried to speak to him like this, Boyd would probably want to throw up. But with Aurora, it just seemed natural. 'I'm good.'

'Yeah, so I heard,' she replied with a knowing smile and a wink. And that would be it. Aurora wouldn't judge him or ask for details, that wasn't her style.

'Dump your stuff, get to the beach,' she said, as if she had read his mind. 'There's a kite-surfing event down there this weekend and they're all out there practising today; it's unreal.' She tousled his long brown hair and gave him a playful shove.

Boyd smiled properly for what felt like the first time in a long time.

Boyd bought his chips and sat in the sand as the sun slowly slid out of sight. It had been a windy day, which was great for the kite surfers – he really had to have a go at that someday. As he wandered back, he saw a 4x4 truck parked on the grass bank outside the mobile-home park, tools and weeds in the back. Aurora had her friend Harry over for dinner. He was the gardener who looked after the park, mowing the grass and cutting back the hedges.

When Boyd got home, they were sat in the lounge.

'Boyd!' Aurora said with a smile. 'Harry's here.'

'Yep, hi,' Boyd said, eyeing the visitor suspiciously.

'Hello, son. Good day?' Harry asked, with an accent that was southern English, with a dash of Irish. He was sat on the sofa, his long legs crossed, his arms stretched out across the back of the furniture. Boyd guessed he was about 50 years old, tall with thick black and grey hair. He was a bit pink from being in the sun all day.

'Yep.' Instead of turning left and joining them in the lounge, Boyd went right and headed for the shower. Harry was one of those people who managed to be nosy without asking a lot of questions. Whenever Boyd turned around, he seemed to be there, watching and listening; Boyd didn't trust people like that.

Aurora and Harry weren't really together or anything, and Harry seemed too stuffy, too fussy, a bit like a soldier, not at all the type of person he imagined Aurora would enjoy spending time with. So, Boyd tried to make life as awkward as possible for his aunt's friend. He was rarely very polite, and always tried to let him know he didn't want him around. Thinking about it now, maybe Fitz was right, maybe this was why Boyd had no friends.

He had his shower and got dressed in some black jogging bottoms and a hoodie. He poked his head into the lounge and gave a quick, 'Goodnight'.

He reached up and pulled a small bolt to release the hatch that led into the shell. It made him think of yesterday and how close he had come to getting that test out of the Prov's office. Then he thought of the unbridled anger on Fitz's face the last time he'd seen him. Maybe the disappointment Boyd couldn't get over wasn't about missing the county championships; maybe it was something else that was eating away at him.

He pulled himself up into the shell and closed the hatch behind him. He lay there in the moonlight, the curtains open as always, and decided that when he woke up in the morning he could go back to the beach and spend the whole day there, watch the kite-surfing. He might even ask if one of the surfers would show him how it was done. He would forget all about Fitz, the county championship, his dad and everything. Maybe he would even ask Aurora if he could stay here the whole of half term; that would be exactly what he needed. As long Harry wasn't planning on being around.

Sand And Bullets

A light swept across Boyd's face, dragging him partially
out of his slumber. He had been dreaming he was in a
tunnel and couldn't find the way out. He could hear
voices calling his name: one of them was a woman's, and
although he didn't recognise it, he felt like he had to run
towards it. He'd had this kind of dream before, where a
mysterious woman was calling him and he couldn't find
his way to her. But when the light hit his eyes, the dream
slipped away. His heart was beating like a drum and he
was sweating through his clothes.

The light had disappeared now, and it took a
moment for Boyd's eyes to adjust to the dark once again.
When they did, he could see vehicles out on the road, lit
from behind by the moon. There were a group of people
on motorbikes, still moving but with their lights turned
off. Their engines rumbled softly over the sound of the
waves. Then they stopped and Boyd heard three soft
taps on the hatch beneath him. He pushed his duvet

aside and clicked it open. Aurora was staring up at him, her face was missing its usual warmth; something was wrong.

'We need to leave, right now, no time for questions.'

She didn't even sound like herself, but she didn't seem scared or panicked either. What on earth was going on? Rubbing his eyes, Boyd picked up his phone next to his pillow; it wasn't even three o'clock yet.

He lowered himself down onto the floor. In her bedroom, Aurora was throwing clothes into a bag. Harry walked back from the lounge, holding the TV remote.

'What's going on?' Boyd said, his eyes still only half open and stinging around the edges from lack of sleep.

Harry didn't reply. As he walked through the kitchen, he grabbed a big, heavy carving knife.

Boyd's eyes grew wide; suddenly he wasn't tired anymore. 'What are you doing with that?'

'Shhh,' Harry replied as he lifted the heavy knife up to shoulder height and walked towards Boyd. He stopped just short of him, outside the shower room. Harry held Boyd's gaze as he pointed a long arm back towards the lounge and clicked the remote control.

Suddenly the van was filled with the sound of the TV. He slapped the remote into Boyd chest. 'Hold this,' he said. Boyd was confused but did as he was told.

Harry dropped down onto the floor of the shower room, dug the knife into the floor and pulled up the plastic lino, revealing the bottom of the van. There was a thin line where the side of the van was joined to the bottom. Harry rested the knife on the joint and hit the top of it five times, moving the knife along the line as he did so. Then he stood up and gently pushed his foot on the joint; it went right through, cracking the floor of the van. Boyd could suddenly see bits of long grass through the gap. The floor had come away so easily, as if someone had prepared it for an emergency escape.

Harry returned, grabbed the control and turned the TV down. Why did he need to cover up the sound? And from whom?

'Listen, someone needs to tell me…' Boyd began to speak, but Harry stopped him, holding up a finger. Boyd fell silent except for a frustrated huff. What the hell was this? Why weren't they telling him anything? It was probably some kind of mistake, or someone that was no doubt here for Harry. Aurora came out of the bedroom with a small, flowery bag.

'I'll make this fast,' Harry said to them, really sounding like a soldier now. It made Boyd's hackles rise; he didn't like being issued orders.

'Some people are here; Aurora tells me that it's something to do with your dad.'

'What's that supposed to mean? What does this have to do with dad?'

'Just listen, will you?! All your aunt has told me is that these are not nice people and we cannot stay here. We go down through there,' he pointed to the fresh hole in the shower room floor, 'and my truck is just over the other side of that hedge.' He pointed through the wall of the van in the direction of his 4x4. 'You two get going and stick together. I'll follow and distract them if I have to. The truck isn't locked. The keys are under the mat.'

Harry turned to face Aurora. 'Get behind the wheel and watch for me. I'm parked on a hill, so when you see me in the mirror, release the handbrake and I'll start pushing the truck. If we're lucky, we'll roll quietly all the way down to the Ferryman pub. We can wake the landlord and call for help.' He turned to Boyd now. 'Once we're out of here, I promise, I will help you find answers.'

'What does that even mean?' Boyd replied, not quite ready to give in just yet. 'Answers to what?'

Then, the chimes tied to the awning began to tinkle and all three of them froze. It could be the wind, or it could be a cat, Boyd thought. But then the sound suddenly died with a loud '*CLACK!*' Someone had grabbed the chimes to stop the noise. Which meant someone was heading right for the front door.

'Go, now!' Harry whispered.

Boyd slipped on his Converse trainers and zipped up his hoodie as Aurora dropped her bag through the gap, then scrabbled after it headfirst. She turned her shoulders so she could get through and in seconds had wriggled out of sight. Boyd followed, down into the long grass.

The cold air suddenly hit him. The grass was wet, and the night had a different smell about it – it didn't feel natural to be out here, and it didn't feel right, running away. Aurora moved quickly, commando-crawling to the back of the van. Boyd glanced behind him under the van to see if Harry was following, but all he saw was tiny torchlights dancing across the grass on the other side of the static home and legs moving around in the shadows. He faced front again as they made it out from under the van.

Aurora saw a small gap in the hedge and barged her way through. Pulling his hood up, Boyd ducked his head and followed her. Once out onto the road, he looked back – still no sign of Harry. By the time he turned towards the truck, Aurora was already at the driver's door with one leg in the cab. She waved Boyd over and pointed for him to get in the other side.

'No, I'll help push,' he whispered. 'It'll be quicker with two of us; get in.' She smiled at his stubborn bravery. Then, all at once, the silence was broken. Men shouted and Boyd could hear what sounded like pops of air escaping.

'Get in the back,' Aurora shouted, not bothering to whisper anymore as she jumped in and started the truck. Boyd climbed up on the rear bumper as Aurora crunched the gears and hit the accelerator. As she did, Harry suddenly came into view. His head appeared over the hedge at the back of Aurora's van. He was running up the hill towards the top corner of the park. He was moving fast, almost as fast as the truck, but as they gathered speed, Boyd could see they were in danger of leaving him behind. Just then, Harry reached the top of the hill, jumped over the hedge like a hurdler and landed hard in the back of the truck, on top of the pile of weeds and grass. Pretty agile for a gardener, Boyd couldn't help noticing.

Boyd climbed over from the bumper and as he did, the popping sounds were joined by clanks against the bodywork of the truck. 'Oh my god! They're shooting at us!' he shouted at no one in particular. 'Do you hear me?'

'Yep,' Harry replied, dismissing Boyd and moving up towards the cab. He leant over to the open driver's window. 'Slide over,' he shouted to Aurora. She started to move, very slowly, keeping her hands on the steering wheel and her foot on the accelerator. Harry brought his right leg out of the flatbed of the truck and down onto the footplate below the driver's door. He opened the door and, grabbing hold of the truck roof, swung himself inside the cab and slammed the door shut in one swift motion. Boyd watched as Aurora slid over to the passenger side, the two of them timing it perfectly.

Aurora turned to Boyd and slid open the small rear

window of the cab so he could hear her over the engine and the sound of gunfire. She pointed to the passenger door. 'Get in this side, come on,' she said to Boyd.

Just then, the road behind them lit up and the night was alive with the thunder of motorbike engines. Boyd scanned the flatbed of the truck. He had a shovel, a fork and some barbed wire. Hanging on a hook at the base of the cab was an old leather bag, and inside it he found three heavy tent pegs. He looked back at Aurora and shook his head. 'No, I'm staying here.' He looked to the road in front of the truck. They were heading past fields and some houses, down towards the Ferryman pub, which was the last sign of life before you hit the sea. An idea kindled in his mind. 'Harry, take the left up ahead, into the beach car park.'

Harry started to protest. 'Boyd, we need to…'

Boyd cut him off. 'Just do it! Get inside the gate, then stop the engine and kill the lights.'

Harry swung the truck into the entrance as Boyd had said. There was an old wooden barrier and a rusted metal gate, but the barrier was always up, and the gate was never closed. Harry glided the truck straight through, pulled on the handbrake and turned off the engine. Boyd grabbed two sets of thick gardening gloves and passed a pair to Harry as he climbed out of the cab. Boyd nodded towards the barbed wire. 'Give me a hand here.'

Harry followed Boyd's lead. They put on the gloves and started unravelling the wire. Boyd was lashing one end around one of the old metal gateposts. Harry got hold of the other end and pulled it towards the opposite post. They had to be quick: Boyd could hear the motorbikes as they steadily popped and spluttered along the road. The riders were checking driveways and tracks for any sign of the truck. When Boyd and Harry had finished, the barbed wire was wrapped tightly around both posts and stretched across the entrance at knee height; that would do the job nicely.

'Let's go,' Harry said, removing the gloves and throwing them back in the flatbed.

'Hang on.' Boyd stepped back to the old barrier and started to push it down. Before he could finish, one of the motorbikes crept along the road into view. The rider was checking the entrance to the field opposite the beach. As he turned his handlebars, his headlight swept onto Boyd and the man quickly grabbed for the machine pistol strapped around his body.

Boyd let the barrier drop and ran for the truck. 'Go!' he shouted as Harry, already back in the cab, hit the button for the ignition. The big engine coughed into life and Harry stamped on the accelerator. In the side mirror, he saw Boyd jump onto the back of the truck.

As the motorbike came around the corner, the cab was flooded with light. The man skidded the bike to a halt and took aim. Suddenly, Harry's side mirror exploded as the man opened fire. 'Get down!' he shouted to Boyd and Aurora, the truck engine snarling as they tore off through the empty car park.

The man on the motorbike let his gun drop back to his side, pulled on the throttle and flew towards the entrance. Just as Boyd had hoped, he was distracted by the barrier and ducked under it at high speed without even looking for any other obstacles. As he cleared it, he brought his head up and the bike collided with the barbed wire, which bit into the machine just above the front wheel. The wire was supported by two metal posts that had been set in concrete for around 40 years – this wasn't a fight the motorbike was going to win. The machine spun wildly out of control, flying sideways and over the top of the wire before it flung the man through the air. Boyd watched as he hit the ground, rolled and skidded over and over on the rough gravel.

That was one down.

Another bike roared around the bend just in time for the rider to see his friend hit the dirt. He turned his bike to the left and powered up the hill next to the entrance, disappearing out of Boyd's sight.

Up ahead were a set of steps where the car park ended and the beach began. Harry dropped down a gear and put his foot to the floor. 'Hang onto something,' he shouted.

Boyd grabbed the wide silver roll bars that came down from the back of the cab to the side of the trailer and he bent his legs. Harry hit the concrete kerb going up to the steps, and the truck took off. As it did, the second motorbike suddenly appeared, bursting out of the sand dunes to their left and flying straight over the top of the truck in mid-air. Boyd ducked as the back wheel missed him by what could only be a few millimetres. He heard the scream of the engine and smelled the rubber as the wheel clipped the roof of the truck cab, just centimetres in front of his face. The truck smashed into the sand hard and Boyd bounced back up and out of the flatbed. He let out a cry of pain as he held onto the truck with everything he had before crashing back down in a storm of weeds, grass and sand.

Harry didn't take his foot off of the accelerator; there wasn't time. The motorbike landed to their right, back wheel first, in the shallows of the sea. The man skidded to a halt, squirting sand and water up from his back wheel as he did so. Then, with one rev of the engine, he was back in pursuit.

It wasn't long before he was right on their tail again. Boyd sat up in the back of the truck to see they were hurtling along a vast stretch of sand, with the sea to their right. The sand stretched back from the water and up into a hill. At the top of the hill was a steep ridge lined with bushes and trees, on the other side of that were the sand dunes Boyd loved to spend hours in. He could see the man was trying to get his motorbike alongside the truck, but Harry was weaving left and right, tapping the brakes. The man had to drop his gun back to his side so he could concentrate on not getting hit by the truck.

Then Boyd realised the guy was trying to get close so he could jump into the flatbed with him! He grabbed the old leather bag and tapped on the back window of the cab. 'Harry, let him come alongside us, on your left. Let's drive him up the hill towards the dunes. Maybe I can distract him, and you can knock him off.' Harry raised a thumb, looked in the passenger-side wing mirror and drifted to the left.

Boyd steadied himself. Reaching inside the bag, he pulled out one of the heavy tent pegs. It was made of thick metal that was folded into a 'V' shape. Boyd had seen this kind of peg before on the big white marquees people have at weddings.

He waited until the man got close and then launched one of the pegs; it missed completely but their pursuer had to pump the brakes to avoid it. The bike rider wasn't even sure what had been thrown, but it had certainly done the trick; the guy pointed at Boyd, clearly angry.

He dipped his head down as he weaved over towards the truck. Boyd threw another peg, at the bike itself this time. It dinged off the forks of the front wheel, hit the truck and spun into the air. The man slowed down and dropped back, further this time.

Then Boyd saw him pulling the strap around and

reaching for his gun. He flattened himself against the bottom of the flatbed of the truck just before bullets started to ping all over the place. But the ground was uneven, and the bike was bouncing around on the sand, so the man couldn't get a proper aim at his target. Still, he didn't need to be accurate. All he needed was one lucky shot and this would all be over.

Boyd felt around in the bag and pulled out the last tent peg; maybe one lucky shot was all he needed too. After a moment, the barrage of bullets stopped. He looked up; the assailant had dropped his gun to his side again and had begun to accelerate.

Boyd put his feet on the flap at the back of the truck and waited. He had to hold on; the truck was speeding along the side of the sandy hill and if he wasn't careful, he would slip to the other side of the flatbed and end up falling out onto the beach.

Using his left hand, Boyd threw the bag at the man, knowing it would have no impact, but he wanted to do everything he could to distract him. The man revved the bike engine and powered up the hill alongside the truck. Harry must have seen him make the move as he edged over just a little.

Boyd took his time before the threw the last peg; he held it in his hands, let the man see it and made out like he was trying to get his aim right. Then he let it go with everything he had, high over the man's head. Boyd had missed by a mile and he didn't care. He had done his job. He had distracted the man enough for Harry to pin the motorbike between the truck and the trees. 'Now!' Boyd shouted. 'Go Harry!'

Harry swerved left and the man wobbled and weaved. He took the motorbike all the way up to the top of the ridge to avoid the danger of the careening truck. He was so busy watching the truck, he didn't see the fat branches of an old alder tree coming at him at 60 miles an hour. The branch hit his chest and Boyd watched as his pursuer seemed to pause in mid-air then fall hard, back-first onto the sand. The bike roared up and over the ridge before plummeting to the ground and exploding out of sight in a ball of fire.

Two down.

'How cool was that?!' Boyd shouted from the back of the truck. Harry and Aurora looked behind through the rear window; their faces illuminated in the night by the orange glow of the explosion. In the distance, Boyd saw another bright light. 'We've got company,' he shouted.

'Hang on,' Harry called, 'I've got a plan for our last friend there.' He spun the wheel left and pulled the truck up and over the ridge towards the dunes. He reversed in and they bounced and bobbled across the surface towards the fire. Harry stopped the truck and jumped out.

'Are you nuts? We're sitting ducks; he'll see us!' Boyd shouted.

Harry grabbed the shovel from the back of the truck. 'Let's hope so. I want you to stand in the back. Don't move.'

'He'll shoot me!' Boyd protested.

'No, he won't. Trust me.' Harry started back towards the fire. He ran down into the bushes behind the truck and out of sight.

'What the hell is he doing?' Boyd asked.

'Let's listen to him. Just wait.' Aurora hadn't been herself since all this started. Boyd wasn't going to listen to her.

'Aurora, you're not thinking straight. We need to get the hell out of here. Now!'

'Boyd!' his aunt shouted, and her face had suddenly

changed. 'Stop being a brat and just do as you're bloody told!'

Boyd stopped cold, in total shock. 'Okay,' he replied and swallowed hard.

They didn't have long to wait. The lights from the other bike appeared, shining up into the night sky like the Bat Signal as the third man accelerated over the ridge and into the dunes. He was drawn towards the fire, looking for his friend. The chaser stopped the bike to take in the scene. The flames danced over his black leathers and jet-black motorcycle helmet. Standing there in the back of the truck, Boyd felt a knot in his stomach. Whatever Harry was going to do, he needed to do it now – and by god, it better be good!

The man looked at the truck, saw Boyd standing up in the flatbed and revved the motorbike engine. Sand flew up behind him as he tore away, heading down into the dunes, sitting high in the saddle as the big bike rocked and bounced under him.

'Aurora,' Boyd said insistently.

'Wait,' she replied.

The bike got closer.

'Aurora, where the hell is he?'

'Just wait.'

'Harry!' Boyd shouted into the night.

As the man brought the motorbike up towards the bushes in front of the truck, Harry stepped out and swung the shovel. His legs were bent, he swivelled from the hips and brought the sturdy old shovel all the way around from behind his head, just like a hitter in a baseball game. The shovel connected with the man's motorcycle helmet with a sickening '*CRACK!*' and Boyd watched as he flipped over backwards and landed flat on his chest, out cold.

The bike continued to roar onward and smashed into the back of the truck with a crunch, just as Boyd jumped clear. The last thought that went through his mind before he hit his head on a rock and lost consciousness was that he had never been more relieved to see Harry.

Trust No One

Boyd heard the woman's voice again; it called his name.

'Where are you?' he called back.

'Boyd,' she said again.

He was trying to move towards her, but it felt like someone was holding him back, like he was running through treacle. He felt a nudge and his body shook. His head felt numb, like his brain was made of marshmallow. Snatches of memory flashed in front of his eyes: a bright light, followed by an explosion, then he was face down in long grass. Was it all a dream? Surely it had to be, none of it could have been real. He couldn't hear the woman's voice anymore.

'I won't be long.' Harry's voice.

'Okay,' Aurora replied.

A car door opened and closed. Then the sound of a phone ringing through a speaker.

'Yes,' a man's voice answered the phone. Who was it? Boyd was sure he recognised him.

'It's me, any activity?' Aurora replied. Her voice was cold and impatient.

'None, and no trace of her. Something's up. What is it?'

Suddenly the pieces clicked into place. His eyes were closed, but he was awake and that was his dad's voice – Aurora had called his dad! Boyd opened his eyes to find he was on the tiny back seat of Harry's truck and everything flooded back to him. It wasn't a dream at all. He was just about to speak when something inside of him made him stop.

'We got hit last night, no idea who it was but they were clearly professional and very well informed,' Aurora said.

'Did the gardener lead them to you?'

'Unclear. He certainly knows how to handle himself, that much is clear. Where are you?'

'I'm trying to track down Miranda Capshaw, find out who she is and how she disappeared but…' The line suddenly exploded in static and noise. Martin cried out.

Aurora took the phone off 'speaker' but Boyd could still hear the commotion on the other end of the line. His dad was in trouble!

'Are you there?' Aurora said into the phone. 'Caretaker, are you there? Come in, Caretaker, please respond.'

Suddenly the driver door opened again, and Harry climbed in, holding a plastic bag. Aurora swiftly killed the phone call and smiled.

'They didn't have a cheese and onion, so I got you a ham and cheese,' Harry said, passing her the bag.

'Yeah, that's fine,' Aurora replied. She turned her head to look at Boyd.

He quickly closed his eyes. His heart was beating out of his chest, but he did his best to fake sleep.

'Is he still out for the count?' Harry asked.

'Yep, poor lad. Let's get him safe and tuck him up in a real bed.'

'Any word from Martin? Did you try him again?'

'Not a thing. It's not like him to not answer his phone.'

'What the heck has he got himself into, eh?'

Aurora turned away and started to cry. Or did she? Boyd wasn't sure if she was faking it.

'I have no idea, I really don't.'

Boyd didn't move a muscle; he didn't want to give

himself away. What had Aurora just called his dad, 'Caretaker'? What on earth was that about? Now she was lying to Harry about speaking to him. Boyd spent the next few minutes thinking. His dad was obviously in serious trouble and the two people he was with were lying to each other. And based on everything that had happened in the last few hours: Aurora's drastic change of personality, the call to his dad and the fact that Harry the Gardener had all of a sudden turned into James Bond, they'd both been lying to him too.

That's when Boyd made a decision; he had to get as far away from Aurora and Harry as he could and, if he wanted to help his dad, then he had to find this Miranda Capshaw and get some answers.

Harry stopped the truck outside a little pub in the middle of the countryside. Boyd sat up and pretended to yawn and wipe the sleep from his eyes.

'Here's my Boyd!' Aurora said, in an unconvincing attempt to switch back to being her usual self.

The blood rushed to his head and he felt a throb of pain as the fresh lump on his forehead started to pulsate. He gingerly lifted a hand to it.

'Ow,' he said.

'That's going to be a corker!' Aurora said.

'I'll see if they've got any rooms. Stretch your legs,' Harry said.

'I'll come in, I need the loo,' Aurora replied, taking her phone out. She looked back at Boyd. 'You'll be okay here?'

'Yeah, fine,' he said, yawning.

They got out and headed for the entrance to the pub. Boyd climbed over the passenger seat and out through the passenger door, keeping the truck between him and pub. He watched Harry and Aurora disappear inside, then scanned the area for any possible means of escape, but he really was in the middle of nowhere. The pub was on a long, winding road surrounded by hills and fields. All he had for company was a scarecrow and a man on the other side of the car park, loading bags into the back of a people carrier.

A young woman appeared from the door of the pub. Boyd did a double-take: it was Pixie Thorn from his class!

'Just once, it would be really nice to have a simple family break for a couple of days,' the man said, piling the bags in behind the seats. 'But that's impossible with you two, isn't it?'

Pixie just stood there, one leg bent, chewing gum, flicking through her phone.

'Oh, and I'll have that, thank you!' The man, presumably Pixie's dad, snatched the phone out of her hand and shoved it in his pocket.

'Hey!' Pixie whined.

'If you can't be nice to people, you can't have your phone. Tell your mother we're ready to go, please. I'll take your brother to the toilet.' He shut the boot and they both marched back inside.

Something caught Boyd's eye in the window at the front of the pub. It was Aurora, holding her phone to her ear and looking out towards him. He didn't acknowledge her; she wouldn't be able to see his face through the truck windows, but he could see hers. She was checking up on him. There was that feeling again, the alarm bell inside of him telling him he was better off on his own. He couldn't even trust his aunt anymore. Boyd didn't wait; he knew what he needed to do.

Aurora turned to head back to the front window and

check on Boyd. She nearly bumped into a young girl and her mum. The girl stopped dead and just tutted.

'Pixie!' the woman exclaimed. 'I am so sorry for that,' she said to Aurora.

'It's fine,' Aurora replied through gritted teeth, trying to get back to the window.

'You are very kind but no, *someone* is in a mood. What do you say, Pixie?'

'There's no need, really.'

'There most certainly is. Pixie?'

'Sorry.' Pixie flushed red as she managed a mumble from the corner of her mouth.

'That's fine,' Aurora replied, flashing a strained smile, and standing back to allow them through.

She made her way back to the window and saw Boyd was still stood, leaning against the other side of the truck. She tried Martin's phone again and it went straight to voicemail. When she turned, Harry had finished booking them in and was at the bar eyeing her suspiciously. She lowered the phone.

'All done,' he said. 'Martin still not picking up?'

'No. Let's get the bags, get settled and get some proper food.'

'That's a grand plan. And you can always try him again later, can't you?' Harry stepped away and headed for the door.

They came out of the pub just as a people carrier pulled away; its windows were down and Aurora could hear the woman from the pub, still talking to her daughter.

'I'm embarrassing? Really? I've never been so embarrassed in all my life, honestly, Pixie.'

'Well, you don't have to go through life being called Pixie,' Aurora thought, feeling sorry for the poor girl.

Harry went to the driver's door of the truck, opened it up and grabbed a small bag from under the seat. Aurora walked around to the passenger side.

'Right Sonny-Jim, let's get some food and…'

She stopped dead.

'Bugger,' she said quietly.

'What is it?' Harry asked.

Aurora didn't reply. She looked around the car park, her head on a swivel, then looked out towards the road as the family in their people carrier disappeared over the top of the hill.

'What's wrong?' Harry asked again as he moved

towards her.

Aurora pointed back at the truck, back to where Boyd was standing. Only it wasn't Boyd.

Leaning against the passenger door was the scarecrow.

Lord Of The Manor

The man drove the black Aston Martin around the twists and turns of the country roads of Bloomfield at speed, the huge tyres occasionally squeaking in protest as the supercar hugged the tarmac. He took a sharp left, down an almost hidden path, thundered over a hill and down into a valley; there in front of him was the beautiful stately home of Lockmead House. Made of yellow brick, the huge residence comprised a central building with four floors, and then attached on either side were two turreted wings housing five floors each.

The driver brought the Aston Martin up alongside Lockmead House, and from here you could see that the old home also had a two-storey wing in the shape of a horseshoe at the back, which created a courtyard at the rear of the house. There were many other buildings on the Lockmead estate spread out all over Bloomfield Downs, but this was where the driver did most of his work. He took the car around the back of the rear wing, through an archway, into the courtyard, and stopped sharply in front of a small door.

The driver was Antoli Bull, a man who looked like he had been constructed out of playdough. He was short and squat, like a sumo wrestler trapped in an expensive suit. His face was permanently pink and he had no visible neck, just a ring of fat around the base of his head. His muscles were not something he could hide, no matter what he wore.

His Italian black loafers kicked up dust from the courtyard as he marched towards the service door at the back of the house. As he walked, Bull pulled his pocket square handkerchief from his suit pocket and mopped a thin layer of sweat from his bald head. Just as he replaced the pocket square, the door in front of him opened. The man blocking his path looked at him without any emotion. He was Knowles, Private Secretary to Lord Ravensbrook.

'We were not expecting you, Mr Bull?'

Bull squeezed his frame through the door and headed directly for the stairs. Knowles moved after him. He didn't run, he never did, but he was very good at being extremely fast without looking hurried.

'No, this is unscheduled visit. I need to see His Lordship.' Bull's clipped English in his Russian accent echoed like a dog's bark in the large hallway.

'I'm sorry, sir, but he gave specific instructions not to be disturbed. He was home in the early hours and has only been in bed for a short time.'

Bull stopped as he reached the bottom of a huge, winding staircase. 'This is urgent, it cannot wait,' he said in a serious, low tone. 'You don't wake him? Fine, I tell His Lordship later that you refused.'

'His Lordship' was the formal way of addressing the man they both worked for: Henry Ravensbrook, lord of the manor. He owned Lockmead House and a huge amount of the Bloomfield Downs, inherited from his father and passed down through ten generations of his ancestors. He was a rich man who used his power for good and the people of Bloomfield loved him for it. He made contributions to scientific research, held an annual charity car event, threw huge garden parties for the public and was an infectious extrovert . Bull was one of his security consultants and one of the few who knew that there was much more to His Lordship than the generous adventurer the public knew him as.

Knowles passed Bull as they made their way up the stairs, looking almost as though he were hovering as he glided silently over the expensive carpet. As Bull reached the top of the stairs, Knowles was already at the door to Ravensbrook's private quarters. He knocked twice and entered.

'Your Lordship, I apologise for the intrusion; Mr Bull is here on urgent business.' Knowles waited for a response. However important Bull was in the grand scheme of Lockmead House, no one got to see His Lordship without Knowles opening the door for them.

'Very well,' came the groggy response.

Knowles stood back and held the door for Bull, who straightened the cuffs on his shirt and walked into the dark bedroom. The curtains were thick and lined, so despite it being daytime, there was no light in the room besides the dim glow coming through the open door. Ravensbrook was barely a silhouette to Bull, leaning up on his elbows, his thick, floppy hair tousled from sleep.

'I apologise, I wouldn't have insisted you were woken unless…'

'I'm awake now, so say what you have to say, there's a good chap.'

'Yes,' Bull swallowed nervously. 'Caretaker is missing, and…'

'Caretaker? Missing?' Ravensbrook interrupted him and sat bolt upright.

'…that's not all. Unfortunately, there seems to have been an attack on Hornet.'

'But Hornet had the boy.'

'Yes, she did.'

Ravensbrook swept his legs out of the bed and turned on the lamp. Suddenly the old-fashioned four-poster bed and the antique wooden cabinet beside it were illuminated. He reached out to it and picked up his red-framed, round spectacles and slid them into place. 'Then we really do have a problem.' He picked up the old black telephone by the bed and pressed a single button. 'We have a very big problem indeed, don't we, Mr Bull?'

PART TWO

Stowaway

Boyd was underneath bags and coats behind the backseat of Pixie's people carrier. He had run as fast as he could, grabbed the scarecrow from just inside the field next to the pub and propped it up against Harry's truck, then stowed himself away. Just as he had closed the boot, Pixie and her mum had come out of the pub, followed by her dad and brother, and they had set off.

Boyd had no idea how long they had been on the road but he did know that since they had departed, they had spent pretty much the whole journey arguing and blaming each other for their 'fun family weekend' coming to a premature end. He suddenly didn't feel so bad that he and his father didn't spend much time together outside of car journeys and boxing.

He felt a sharp stab of worry thinking about his dad – he had to do something; he had to find a way to help him. But how? He had absolutely no clue where he was or what kind of danger he was in. The only thing he did know for sure was that it had something to do with Miranda Capshaw, that woman who went missing from the plane. But who even was she? And if his dad was looking for her, why didn't he mention it when Boyd had put on the YouTube video about her on *FrakeNews*? Then there was the attack last night and Aurora acting so strangely… This was getting so far beyond nuts that he knew he couldn't just go to someone and ask for help; no one would believe him.

So, he was on his own then.

Unless, maybe not… Maybe there was someone who would believe his story, but would he even speak to Boyd if he asked him? There was only one way to find out.

An awkward silence had descended in the people carrier after the last round of arguments, so it was a relief when Pixie's mum put some music on. Boyd felt like he could breathe out. It also gave him a chance to carefully feel around in his pocket for his mobile without worrying too much about being heard. Strange, it wasn't in the pocket of his joggers or his hoodie. Then he suddenly remembered he'd thrown the phone back down next to his pillow in Aurora's van, and it was still there. That was it then, his only chance of reaching out for help was at Bloomfield beach and he couldn't risk going back there.

'Pixie! Put down the iPad now, please!' Pixie's dad bellowed, turning off the music.

'Hey, turn the music back on!' her brother squealed.

'You said I couldn't have my phone, you didn't say anything about the iPad, though,' Pixie argued back.

'Listen to your father,' Pixie's mum chimed in, wearily.

'God's sake, you always take his side, though,' Pixie protested.

'Put the iPad in the back or you won't have any electronics all weekend. I won't say it again!'

Wow. Her dad wasn't playing around now.

'Fine,' Pixie muttered.

'Music!' her brother squealed again. The stereo surged back into life and round five of the argument was done, all over in seconds.

Boyd watched as Pixie's perfectly manicured fingernails appeared over the back seat, clutching the iPad. She tucked it on top of the open rucksack, right in front of him. Boyd waited a moment before freeing his right arm and carefully easing the iPad back out of the bag. Pixie hadn't locked it and she was still signed into Facebook; perfect. Boyd opened her friends list, clicked on the search bar and typed 'Tork'.

Fitz and Pixie were not exactly best friends, but he knew that everyone in his class pretty much had everyone else on their friends' list. Fitz's profile appeared and gave Boyd the option to view his posts or write him a message; Boyd clicked the message icon.

He stopped.

Okay, how was he going to play this? Simple, he needed help and he had no one else – Fitz was his only hope. He tapped out the message.

The Hero With Two Faces

The Lockmead Learning Lab was a vast white building on the Lockmead estate. It wasn't far from Lockmead House and you could see it from all over Bloomfield Downs. But where Lockmead House was stately and old-fashioned, the Lab, as it was known, looked like a cross between an ice-cream and a spaceship. In the middle of the ground floor were several exhibits and information bases that introduced visitors to some basic but exciting elements of science throughout history. It traced the evolution of the planet, from the Big Bang Theory to the discovery of electricity and all the way up to Artificial Intelligence. A walkway around the inside of the building climbed up to the top, which housed an observatory with a huge telescope. Everything in the building was pristine white, just like the outside.

It was lunchtime and, like most days, the Lab was filled with visitors. Today it was a group of over 100 Scouts from all over the world. They were working their way around the facility, listening to talks and watching demonstrations from various scientists.

Just as they were about to have lunch, Lord Ravensbrook appeared. He had been all over the internet recently after leading an acclaimed archaeological dig in Brazil that had unearthed a new species of carnivorous dinosaur, and the bones were on display at the Lab. Alongside them were the pictures that had been beamed all over the world: Ravensbrook in his Indiana Jones-style hat, covered in dust, holding up the huge jawbone of the dinosaur – named the Megalovenator. It had not only made Ravensbrook famous, it had made him a global hero, with the media calling him a modern Indiana Jones.

Professor Reginald Yip, who had been on the dig with Ravensbrook, was talking to the group when the His Lordship came in through a door at the back of the main hall. He was dressed in a pair of cargo trousers and a long-sleeved black T-shirt. His hair was a thick, sandy-grey, swept back from his head. He was waving the hat he wore on the dig, smiling as his visitors began to clap and cheer. Everyone took out their phones and started shooting videos or snapping pictures of the real-life celebrity in front of them.

'Oh my, thank you!' Lord Ravensbrook said, bowing his head in appreciation. 'You are too kind. Thank you, gang, really.'

The noise started to quieten down.

'We love you Lord Ravensbrook!' someone shouted, then everyone laughed, including Ravensbrook himself.

'Bless you, I love you too. And welcome to the Lab, I hope you're enjoying your day.'

Everyone settled down in anticipation.

'This project is still a work-in-progress – it's not finished, and it probably never will be. Can anyone guess why?'

There was a moment of quiet before anyone put their hand up.

'Yes, young lady.' Lord Ravensbrook pointed to a tall, nervous-looking girl.

'Because there's more to do?'

'Yes, yes, I'd say you're right. There is always more to do, because we're still learning, all the time, so how can we ever be finished? Science is about learning from the past but also about building a future for mankind; the best kind of future, and I want to make sure we're right there, you and I, leading from the front.'

Everyone clapped. As they did so, Knowles entered through the door at the back of the hall and walked up behind Lord Ravensbrook. He smiled and leant in close. 'Hornet has been located; we will debrief her tonight. Your presence is required.'

'And the boy?' His Lordship asked urgently.

Knowles shook his head. Ravensbrook nodded. He then turned and smiled to the crowd.
'I'll leave you in the hands of the professor. Thank you so much for visiting us, your support means everything to our little lab. Goodbye – and remember; never stop learning!'

As Ravensbrook turned away from his audience, his smile evaporated. He whispered to Professor Yip, 'Give the insufferable brats whatever their little hearts desire and charge them full price. Oh, and make sure they're out the door by six. We're not a bloody charity.'

Knowles held open the door and they hurried out.

Crime And Punishment

Fitz's mum hadn't taken the news of his suspension very well. Marjorie Tork seemed constantly worried that her son was going to fail at school, ruin his life and be miserably unhappy. Up to this point, there was no reason for her to think that, but now he had been caught in the Head's office during Parents' Evening and been part of an escapade that involved a fellow student almost falling through the roof of the school, Fitz had to admit that she had sort of been proved right.

Fitz's dad, Roger, had told her that everything would be okay. Fitz had never been in trouble before and he would have a chat with Mr Providence to see if he could get the incident removed from Fitz's school record. Roger Tork was a short man, with brown hair slicked down onto his round head. He worked for the government doing something or other, Fitz didn't know exactly what. All he knew was, it meant his dad had to go to London every day and didn't get back until late.

His mum was of a nervous disposition. Even shorter than his dad, with tight, curly hair, her face twitched when she was anxious, and since Fitz's suspension, that was pretty much most of the time. Marjorie was a therapist who helped people talk through their problems and she saw her clients in a cabin in the back garden. She was trying to work now as Fitz was mowing the grass. Fitz hated mowing the grass at the best of times but pulling and pushing the huge mower all over the garden in a heatwave was really starting to get on his nerves.

'You need to have that done in the next 15 minutes, young man, I've got a client coming over,' his mum said, poking her head out of the cabin.

'15 minutes? You're joking?'

'I suggest you watch your tone and get it done.' Her disappointment was so great that she struggled to look at her son; every time she did, she whimpered and cried. He'd tried telling his mum that it was all Boyd's idea but that hadn't gone down well either. 'Then you're too easily led,' she had said.

His dad said that maybe it was a good thing Fitz had 'gone off the rails' now and no one had really got hurt.

155

Roger was sure that he'd learnt his lesson.

'*Oh, I have,*' Fitz thought as he blitzed the big old lawn mower around in the sweltering sun. 'I've learnt not to go anywhere near Boyd ever again.'

Fitz sat at the desk in his bedroom, draining a pint of water. He finished it, then started panting like a Labrador. He was absolutely shattered; he had never done so much manual labour in his life. So far, his mum had made him wash the car, clean his mountain bike and mow the lawn. He had been given tomorrow off, thank god, but on Monday morning he had to paint the front room. He usually got worn out painting Airfix models, so he was fairly sure that a week of this kind of punishment was going to kill him. He had even told his mum the songs he wanted played at his funeral, which she didn't find at all funny.

Fitz's room was pretty unique, and it was out of bounds for everyone else. It was always locked, even when he was in there. Inventing was his hobby, so he would take things apart, see how they worked, then adapt them and build something new. His room was littered with half-finished projects, various tools and notepads covered in ideas. A wetsuit hung on the open door of his built-in wardrobe; he'd told his parents he was going to take up canoeing, and they didn't even question the fact that he didn't own a canoe. The wetsuit had little bits of glass and mirror glued onto it and it was currently drying off under an old heat lamp.

At the end of the bed was a long desk. One half of it was taken up with piles of paper, a laptop and a desktop computer, along with three big monitors; while the other served as a work bench, with a soldering iron, a magnifying lamp and stacks of other tools. Four different-sized radio-control cars rested on the bench, all at various stages of rebuilding and each one with distinct modifications: one had a large mesh bucket attached to the top of it, and the wheels of the smallest car were under the large magnifying lamp. There were also two chests of drawers that had large technical drawings laid out on them. It wasn't like any other teenager's room Fitz had seen, but then, to be fair, he hadn't really seen that many except on TV.

He tapped the space bar on his keyboard and the computer screen came to life. Fitz hovered his thumb over a scanner that he had plugged into the desktop and the lock screen melted away. He immediately saw he had a Facebook notification, which was strange because he had social-media notifications set to only alert him if he got a direct message and he rarely got any of those. Fitz clicked on the little box in the right-hand corner of the screen and it opened up Messenger. There, at the top of the pile was a picture of Pixie Thorn – *that* Pixie, the girl from school. Her name was next to a carefully selected image and Fitz could see the first line of text from her message.

'Help me Obi-Wan, you're my only hope.'

His eyes grew wide. Okay, so what could he surmise from this? Firstly, Pixie Thorn liked *Star Wars*, which was a surprise in and of itself. Fitz never really thought of Pixie as a '*Galaxy Far, Far Away*' kind of girl, but it showed you never really knew someone. Secondly, she needed his help, on a Saturday, which meant she had been thinking of him at the weekend. In fact, now he thought about it, maybe that was the first and most important thing and the *Star Wars* reference came in a distant second. 'Keep it cool, Tork,' Fitz said out loud to himself.

Once he opened this message, Pixie would see that

he had read it, so he had to compose himself. Not replying to someone because you hadn't read their message was one thing but reading it and not replying because you were so hideously uncool you had no idea what to say was another thing entirely. Fitz now realised that he was sat there, looking at a message he hadn't opened and trying to work out what his reply should be without having read it. Time to man up – he opened the message.

'Help me Obi-Wan, you're my only hope. I'm in trouble, mate, and I need you. It's Boyd, in case you hadn't guessed, sorry about that. I don't have my phone. I know you hate me, but I've got nowhere else to go, please.'

Wonderful. Fitz desperately wanted to go back 30 seconds to when, in his head, this was still a message from Pixie Thorn. He found himself typing a reply straight away. 'Right. So how are you in Pixie's messenger?' He could see a response was being typed.

'I don't have my phone; long story and you can't tell anyone I'm in contact with you.'

'But you DO have Pixie's phone?????'

'I'll explain when we meet. Please.'

159

Fitz took a moment. He had spent the last two days being so angry at Boyd, he didn't think he ever wanted to set eyes on him again. He knew his mum only wanted the best for him and he had so badly let her down. It felt horrible seeing her hurt and he had convinced himself it was all down to Boyd. But now, sitting here, he knew the truth.

It had been his decision to follow Boyd into that tunnel; he could have said no. He got himself into that mess and he had to own it. He had always done as he was told, and he liked the excitement of going against the rules.

Plus, Boyd was in trouble, and if he had learnt one thing in the last few days, it was that the kind of trouble Boyd attracted was always the serious kind.

Parklife

Fitz walked into the Bloomfield Recreation Ground at 4:30pm. Boyd had said to be at the Rec for five that afternoon but in every spy movie Fitz had seen, you always got there early so you could stake out the meeting place and stay one step ahead. Boyd had told him to sit at an outside table at the community-centre café and wait for him, but seeing as Fitz was early and the only thing waiting for him at home was the job of dusting every single china nick-nack on his parents' dresser in the dining room, he decided to enjoy himself. He was wearing his dad's old Bloomfield Cricket Club tracksuit top over his usual shorts and trainers. On his head was Roger Tork's flat cap, along with a pair of large aviator sunglasses that stuck out from the side of his small, round face.

The only way Fitz could convince his mum to let him leave the house was an offer to walk their cockapoo, Tinker, who was currently pulling him through the car park much like a speedboat pulls a water-skier. If Fitz was trying to stay under the radar, he was failing miserably; Tinker Tork dragged him over to the football and cricket pitches, where he immediately decided he needed a comfort break. Luckily, his dad always had poo bags in his tracksuit top. He made his way over to the nearest suitable bin, which was under some trees next to the old Scout hut. This gave him the perfect view of the community centre café, plus both entrances to the park, so he would see Boyd approaching and be able to casually walk right over to him.

With the element of surprise and Fitz's brilliant disguise, Boyd would never see him coming. He thought about how he would do it, maybe he would cross the park in front of the café, then pretend he wanted a coffee. He would purchase his beverage, then walk over to Boyd at the table and say, 'Is this seat taken?' before pulling the sunglasses down and revealing his identity – magic!

Fitz had barely been under the cover of the trees for a minute before Tinker started to whine. The Tork family dog wasn't a fan of stopping when he was out on a walk and he didn't mind letting you know it. 'Tinker, stop moaning,' Fitz whispered as he carefully scanned the park. Tinker declined the request and increased the volume. 'Come on, sausage, give me a break for two minutes, eh?' Fitz looked down at his dog's little golden face.

But Tinker wasn't looking out at the wide-open space of the Rec, he was looking at the Scout hut behind them. Fitz turned as he realised someone was watching him but before he could get his head around to see who it was, he heard Boyd's voice.

'Is that meant to be a disguise?'

'No,' Fitz said defiantly.

'It is, isn't it?' Boyd said with a smile. 'That's you, incognito?'

'Listen, do you want my help or not?' Fitz said, finally turning to look at Boyd. When he did, he stopped dead and his mouth dropped open. Boyd was dressed in his hoodie and tracksuit bottoms; both were completely filthy, stained and dotted with rips and tears. 'Crikey! You look like you've been dragged through a hedge backwards!' Fitz exclaimed.

'Yeah, well, I ran through it forwards actually.' Boyd let out a small laugh from under his hood. Just visible, on his forehead, was a purple lump.

'What the hell happened to you?'

'It's a really long story and I'm still trying to piece it together myself. Did you see the news about an illegal party on Bloomfield Beach last night?'

Boyd had used Pixie's iPad to search the online news sites to see if there had been any reports about the gunfight on the beach. That's when he found that the police had made a statement about a rave that had turned into a fight; so whoever had chased them had somehow covered up the truth.

'Yeah, something about a fire and kids tearing around on motorbikes. What about it?'

'It wasn't kids. It wasn't a party.'

'How do you know that?'

'I was there, Fitz; I was the guest of honour. Someone tried to kill us – me and Aurora – and I have no idea why. I really need your help.'

'Tried to kill you? Holy crap! Um, yeah of course, come back to mine and we can sort this out.'

'I can't, Fitz. I have to stay out of sight until I know what the hell is going on.'

'It'll be fine. My parents barely know if I'm in the

house, so I can get you in and out without them noticing. But if you want my help, I need to know everything. Don't leave anything out, okay?'

'Okay. And Fitz, about the other day at school…'

'Forget it.'

Boyd nodded, relieved. 'What are friends for, eh?' he said, raising his fist.

Fitz lifted his and bumped it against Boyd's. 'Exactly.'

Full Of Surprises

It turned out that getting into Fitz's house without his parents' knowledge was the easiest thing Boyd had done in the last 48 hours. Despite it being a Saturday, his dad was at work and his mum was in her cabin office in the garden. Fitz pressed an intercom attached to the kitchen wall and linked up with his mum's office. There was a buzzing noise, then his mum answered.

'Yes?'

'I'm just going to have a shower, whack some washing on, then I'll make some noodles,' Fitz had said.

'Your dad and I are having spag bol later – you don't want any, then?' Marjorie had replied, clearly unhappy with her son's dinner plans.

'No, thanks,' Fitz replied and cut off the conversation.

Fitz's mum and dad had a shower room in their bedroom, which meant that Fitz had the main shower room in the house to himself. Boyd cleaned himself up and got back into Fitz's room as quickly as possible because he didn't want to risk getting caught. Fitz had laid out some clothes on his bed for him to try on. He was quite a bit taller and wider than Fitz, who had pinched some clothes from his dad's wardrobe. Boyd went for the plain items, swerving T-shirts emblazoned with Guns 'n' Roses tour dates or images of Elton John's face. When Fitz came in with the noodles, Boyd was sat on the bed in a plain grey T-shirt and a pair of old, faded black jeans that were ripped at the knee.

'Dad used to wear those to gigs,' Fitz said, as Boyd pulled on the jeans. 'But mum says he's too old for them now. He won't miss them.'

They would go well with his trainers, and Fitz had washed his hoodie, which was hanging to dry under a heat lamp. Fitz handed over a huge bowl of steaming noodles. He had thrown in some chicken and, by the smell of it, spiced everything up a bit with some chilli. Boyd looked at the bowl and then cast his eyes around Fitz's rather special bedroom. 'You really are full of surprises, Fitz.'

'You're not exactly a choirboy yourself, mate!' Fitz laughed.

Boyd had told him everything on the walk from the Rec to the house: his dad going away, the attack at Aurora's place and all the weird goings-on that followed.

'How did you even get out of Pixie's car without them seeing you?' Fitz had asked.

'They left the hotel so early, they didn't have breakfast,' Boyd explained. 'Pixie and her brother moaned every time they went past a service station on the motorway until her dad finally gave up and stopped. I got out when they went in for McDonald's.'

There was a moment of silence as they both concentrated on eating their food. Boyd's mind began to tick over, there was so much of what had happened that just didn't make sense to him, but what bothered him most was the nagging doubt about his aunt; he couldn't shake it off. When he was lying down in the back of Pixie's car, Boyd had wondered if he had been paranoid and perhaps a little harsh on Aurora. Maybe she was acting so out of character because she was just reacting to an exceptional situation. But when he had repeated everything to Fitz and ran it over in his head, he knew that something wasn't right. The phone call to his dad, lying to Harry, the way she totally changed in front of his eyes; he had done the right thing getting away from her, from both of them. He had no idea what his dad was caught up in, but he would find the truth the only way he knew how – by doing it himself.

'She called him what?' Fitz had asked when Boyd told him about Aurora's phone call with his dad.

'Caretaker.'

'What the hell is all that about?'

'I don't know, but I think I have a way of finding out – and that's where you come in.'

When dinner was finished, Fitz put the bowls on the cabinet next to his bed, alongside an existing stash that featured three mugs, two plates and several items of cutlery. Each sported the remains of a previous meal in varying degrees of mutation. Boyd looked at the pile and thought how his dad had reacted the one and only time he had collected a similar pile: he had placed it neatly under Boyd's duvet. Boyd had found it when he climbed into bed. Parents were all different, just like kids, he supposed.

Fitz had pulled over a small stool and Boyd was sat

next to him, in front of his array of monitors. 'So, this Miranda person who went missing from the plane – you have no idea who she is?' Fitz asked as he tapped his top lip with a pen.

'No.'

'And your dad gave no hint as to knowing her or anything about her situation?'

'We've been over this; none.' Boyd sounded antsy.

'Okay, chill out,' Fitz replied, in his high-pitched, anxious tone. 'It's worth asking again just in case some memory has been nudged loose now you've had some rest.' He tapped the pen on the desk. 'It's knowing where to start. Without any information or a sniff of a lead, it's going to be needle-in-a-haystack time. And he didn't even react when you watched the video on *FrakeNews*?'

Boyd thought for a moment, then sat bolt upright. 'That's it!'

'What? Come on, share with the group.'

'*FrakeNews*! They did the report on this Miranda Capshaw, they found her name before the government scrubbed it off the flight records – so, our starting point is whoever is behind *FrakeNews*!'

'Okay, I can see two problems with that straight away,' Fitz said in a serious tone. 'Firstly, why would they want to talk to us, we're just a couple of kids? And secondly, how do we find them? The whole point of *FrakeNews* is that no one ever finds them.'

Boyd considered the questions. 'Let's park problem number one for a second and jump straight to problem number two.'

'Be my guest.'

'There's that cryptic message at the end of every *FrakeNews* video about, "If you have something that might be *FrakeNews*… blah blah blah." So, bring up a video, let's listen to it.'

Fitz opened YouTube and selected a random *FrakeNews* video. It was the vlog from ten days ago about the unexplained power surges that had occurred all around the world.

'Skip to the end,' Boyd said.

'I'm on it.' Fitz clicked the arrow on the last minute of the video. He nudged it along to the last 20 seconds and found what they were looking for. The clip from the intro theme played in reverse, beginning with an explosion that drew inward and ended up as the clock on the Houses of Parliament. The mechanical voice spoke over the scene.

'If you have any information or a story that you think could be *FrakeNews*, go back to where it all started and find the time.'

Fitz hit pause and stopped for a moment.

'What do you think?' Boyd asked.

'Give me a sec,' he replied, waving his hand in the air as he was trying to think. He played the message again and scribbled on a pad next to his keyboard. Boyd looked down at it and saw that Fitz had written '*back to start*' and '*find the time.*' 'Okay, so they are probably not going to make this too difficult. Let's face it, they want people to send them information.'

'Right,' Boyd replied. 'And I think it's probably going to be an email or something secure, right? Because that way, they can pick and choose what stories they want to follow up.'

'Exactly. They can filter it.'

'Makes sense.' Boyd looked at the pad again. 'So let's go back to the start of the video and see what we can find, maybe?'

Fitz set the video back to the beginning. They

watched the opening theme but neither of them saw anything that stood out. He went back to the start and they watched it a second time.

'Okay,' Fitz said over a long exhale. 'So, this is the beginning and there's a clock.'

'Which fits in with, "find the time".'

'Right, but even when I pause it, there's nothing visible here. I don't know, maybe we're barking up the wrong tree.'

Something clicked in Boyd's eyes; they opened wide and he raised an index finger. 'Hang on, go to the *FrakeNews* channel page and open the first video they ever posted,' he said, excitedly.

'The what?'

'Their first video. It's not a report like all the others, it's about what they stand for and why we all have a duty to question facts we're told and stuff. It's got a different name. I can't remember now. Bring it up.'

Fitz closed the video and scrolled down through the long list of *FrakeNews* reports, over a year's worth, before getting to the first-ever post on the channel. There it was: the video was called '*FrakeNews* – everything they don't want you to know'. Fitz opened it and the usual titles began to roll.

'Stop it there!' Boyd said and Fitz hit the button on his mouse. 'Can you zoom in on the clock face?' Boyd asked.

'Yep, hang on.' Fitz took a screen grab of the image and then moved it over onto his MacBook and opened an app called *Clean Screen*. He carefully clicked all over the image as he expanded it, bringing sections of it into focus without worrying about the other areas.

'Can you see it?' Boyd asked.

'Yeah, I can see it's there, but I need to clean it up. Hang on.' After a minute of careful manipulation, there it was on the screen in front of them: on the second hand of the clock was an email address. Fitz already had one of his many Gmail accounts open and had copied the address into the addressee field. 'Now we get back to our first problem.' He turned to Boyd. 'What makes you think they are going to listen to a couple of teenagers with a wild story about hired gunmen on motorbikes tearing up Bloomfield?'

'It isn't a problem,' Boyd said, waving for Fitz to pass him the keyboard so he could type the email.

'Oh, it isn't? I'm glad to hear it.'

'Fitz. They're the only ones investigating these power surges; they're the only ones talking about a woman who has vanished into thin air. And now my dad gets snatched or something whilst he's looking for her? They're not just going to listen to us, they're going to help us.'

The Waiting Game

Fitz's dad got in late. Fitz went downstairs to say goodnight to him and his mum, and when he came back up, he arranged a sleeping bag and pillow on the floor for Boyd.

Much to Boyd's frustration, they still hadn't had a reply from anyone at *FrakeNews*. He had felt like they were making progress but now it was all in someone else's hands and he didn't deal well with that arrangement. He felt for sure that *FrakeNews* would leap at the chance to meet him and hear his story, then he would convince them that they should work together to find out where Miranda Capshaw had disappeared to. Fitz had set up an alert on his phone for the email account he had used to message them, but all was silent.

It was one o'clock on Sunday morning and Boyd was finding it impossible to sleep. He was sitting on the floor in the dim light given off from the various electronics in Fitz's room. Fitz was fast asleep, letting out the occasional snort as he rolled over. Boyd was doing the only thing he could think of to keep moving this forward: he tried to piece together everything that had happened since Friday night.

It felt like he was in the centre of a drama, and the only one without a script – like he was surrounded by secrets, all kept by the only people he had ever really trusted and now he was alone, without a clue as to why. He'd always had a sense of being detached from the people around him. What had Fitz called it? The 'iceman' act. But it wasn't an act and Boyd didn't seem to know how to fix it without feeling like a fraud. He was who he was because of the way he'd been brought up. He had never had a close bond with his dad, not in the same way other kids did. Whenever they were on holiday or out somewhere and they saw other families and the way they interacted with each other, Boyd and Martin always instinctively looked away. Boyd used to convince himself that the thing they were missing was his mother, but deep down, he knew it was more than that.

His mother had died giving birth to him, so he had never known her. His father didn't like talking about her and she didn't have any family, so for a long time it had felt like there was a huge piece of his life missing. His dad hadn't been able to look after him at first, so he had lived in some kind of children's home until he was five. He didn't really have any clear memories of that time, just tiny fragments, like blurred photographs, nothing he could really grab hold of and call his own.

Boyd had found that the best way to deal with being different was to just accept it, get on with things and not care about anyone else. He had never felt hard done-by; he had never felt jealous of other kids or like he had missed out. In fact, he had always felt lucky for the life he had, until now. Now he was angry and, without Fitz, he would have felt utterly lost and alone. But he knew that his dad had always done his best for him and now it was Boyd's turn to step up and do something for his dad. He had to believe that whatever he was involved in, he wouldn't keep anything from Boyd unless he absolutely had to.

Fitz stirred and rolled over. 'What's up?' he asked Boyd.

'Can't sleep.'

'Is it the rubbish pillows?'

Boyd chuckled. 'No, it's not the pillows. I've just got too much stuff going on in my head, that's all.' He stood up and went to Fitz's workbench.

Fitz climbed out of bed and rubbed the sleep out of his eyes. 'I do all my best work when I can't sleep,' he said, picking up one of the radio-controlled cars.

Boyd inspected one of the loose wheels from the bench. 'Oh, weird,' he said shuffling it in his hand to hold it by the hub. 'What's that on the tyres?'

'Just a little something I've been working on.' Fitz picked up a pencil, leant forward and brushed it along the surface of the tyre. Boyd could see 100s of fine hairs moving and fluctuating under the pressure of the pencil.

'You know how a spider…'

The phone vibrated on the bed where Fitz had left it. Boyd snapped his head around, his eyes flared open. Fitz threw down the pencil and dropped into the chair in front of the computer. He tapped the keys, his hawk-like eyes focused on the screen as he accessed the email account. Then the side of his mouth raised in a smile. He looked at Boyd.

'Monday morning, Waterloo Station. We're on, mate.'

A Hornet's Sting

You only ever had a meeting in Lord Ravensbrook's private office in Lockmead House if there was something very right or something very wrong. Unfortunately for those currently gathered, waiting patiently for His Lordship to arrive, something was very wrong indeed. This was his inner sanctum; this was where Ravensbrook could truly be himself, drop the act he put on for the public and indulge his true passions and desires without any concern for judgement. In this room, the decisions that shaped everything His Lordship had worked towards for almost 20 years had been made and witnessed by only his most trusted team of lieutenants.

It wasn't a grand room, not compared to the rest of Lockmead House, but it was a room that radiated power and purpose. Even if you hadn't ever been in there before, it felt somehow different to the rest of the house. The office was on the top floor, at the front of Lockmead

House, and you didn't even get through the door without Knowles opening it for you. Knowles was a tall man in his fifties, wiry, with long limbs and short, curly blond hair. His thumb was also rather important, because without it, the door to the private office remained locked for anyone but Ravensbrook himself.

The room was rectangular, with a large, round window opposite the door and bookshelves all around the walls stretching from the floor right up to the ceiling. There was a large table at one end of the office, plus an old leather sofa and a long coffee table. At the other end was a wide window that overlooked the driveway; in front of the window sat an old wooden desk. Knowles liked to tell the story that the desk was made from pieces of wood taken from the last-ever wooden battleship built in England, *HMS Victoria*. Lord Ravensbrook was certainly rich enough to make it possible.

As Aurora sat in one of the small, antique chairs at the desk, she noticed the piles upon piles of paper and folders stacked on the desk and all over the floor at this end of the room. It wasn't untidy but there were so many. How did someone operate every single day with so much to consider, so much to worry about? Aurora, which wasn't her real name and never had been, was someone who liked order. She liked to focus on a task and wouldn't stop until it was done to her satisfaction. Under normal circumstances, she wasn't the kind of person who would ever be anxious about a meeting such as this, but since she had failed at the task she was responsible for, she was determined to make things right.

The woman Boyd had known as his aunt for the last ten years was not the same person who sat opposite Lord Ravensbrook's incredibly luxurious, empty, leather captain's desk chair. Aurora Boyd was a lie, a fabrication that had been created as a female influence in the life of a young boy who no longer had a mother. That whole plan had been woven together here, in this room by some of the people who sat in it now.

Aurora stood as the door opened and Lord Ravensbrook entered with Knowles whispering in his ear. Knowles closed the door once His Lordship's two muscular Dobermann dogs had stalked through it. Named Hannibal and Khan, they were a fearsome-looking pair who responded to Ravensbrook's every command. His Lordship sat and the dogs perched either side of him like statues.

Ravensbrook put a leather folder on the desk in the middle of the piles of paper, pulled away an elastic fastening and opened it before sitting in his chair. Now he was seated, everyone did the same. Ravensbrook raised a hand to his face and pushed his glasses up nearly to his forehead. He strummed his lips with his forefinger as he looked through the papers. It was two in the morning; everyone was tired, but no one would dare question the timing of the meeting; there was work to be done.

Ravensbrook looked to Aurora. 'A scarecrow?'

'Correct.'

Upon hearing her voice, Khan, the dog to the left of Ravensbrook, let out a rumbling snarl. For some reason, he had never liked Aurora and he always let her know it. His Lordship paused and looked back at the notes. He gently twisted and turned the gold signet ring on his little finger. 'Interesting. He's a resourceful boy.'

'He is.'

The low hum of Khan's growl grew louder. Next to Aurora, almost directly in front of Khan, was Antoli Bull, the stocky Russian who had rushed to break the news of Boyd's escape to His Lordship. A nervous twitch made his leg bounce up and down every time he stole a glance at the hound. Khan bared his teeth.

'Boyd's temper is a problem for him, and it can cloud his judgment,' Aurora continued, not even glancing at Khan.

'But he is able to use his wits when he's in a bit of a spot and the pressure is on?' His Lordship asked.

'No, it's more than that,' she said gravely. 'He was in his element the other night; he relished the fight and he was completely relentless. If we let him fall into the wrong hands, Boyd could well develop into an unstoppable force that will derail everything we have worked for, and that's a risk we cannot take.'

Ravensbrook looked back to Aurora. Where her short hair was once messy and dyed red, it was now bleached blond and slicked back close to her head. Her relaxed, colourful clothing that had done so much to define her in Boyd's eyes was gone, consigned to the bin. She was now dressed in a pair of black leather trousers and a black leather motorcycle jacket; her huge frame looking strong and fearsome.

'You will fix this, Hornet,' Ravensbrook said, using

her codename.

'You doubt it?' she replied, disappointed rather than angry.

But the slight change in her voice was enough for Khan to leap up from the floor and let out a bark. Although it was aimed squarely at Hornet, Bull instinctively grabbed the arms on his chair and straightened up in fear. Hornet turned her head to face the powerful, snarling beast, twisted her features and bared her teeth like a wild animal. She unleashed a low growl, her green eyes piercing into Khan's own. She showed him that she wasn't scared; in fact, she was just in the right kind of mood to take him on and had no doubt that she would win.

Seeing the demonic look in her eyes, Khan shrunk back down onto his belly and whimpered. He looked up at his master apologetically. Just as quickly as Hornet had snapped, she returned her focus to Lord Ravensbrook and her face settled back to normal. Bull snuck a sideways glance at her; maybe it wasn't the dog he should be afraid of.

'If I didn't trust you, you wouldn't be here,' Ravensbrook responded.

'I'm pleased to hear that,' Hornet said. Her voice had reverted to its quiet, chilling tone. 'And Caretaker?' she asked.

'No word.'

'So, someone is putting all the pieces together,' Knowles said.

'So it would seem,' Hornet agreed. 'But who?'

'The Gardener?' Bull asked.

'Harry? No.' Hornet thought for a moment. 'He certainly isn't all he seems but he's not the sharpest tool in the box, which means he's probably MI5.'

Lord Ravensbrook closed the file and pulled his glasses back into place. 'Well, never mind that for now, your focus is the boy. I'm going to ask Bull here to give you full access to the Greenhouse. With the skills we have in there and your expertise on the little bugger, I'm confident that, whoever is sniffing around our prize, we'll get to him first.' The Greenhouse was a building on the estate that housed Lord Ravensbrook's cyber-espionage division; a team of experts who could trace anyone, anywhere.

His Lordship stood and walked to the door with Knowles and the two dogs on his heels. Bull raised his bulk from the chair and watched as Hornet stood up, the leather of her clothes creaking softly. He was supposed to be the muscle, the protector, but he doubted there was anything or anyone that Hornet would need protecting from.

Knowles opened the door, an invitation for them to leave. Hornet stood in front of Bull, with the ring on the middle finger of her right hand, the only fragment left of her former life as Aurora; except now she had turned it around the other way, so the sharp point of the 'T' faced towards the end of her finger like a spike.

'I hate those dogs,' Bull said with a dismissive sniff.

Hornet suddenly stepped in close to him. Even though she was a head taller than him, he could smell her musty breath. 'You know the thing about dogs, Mr Bull?'

The Russian shook his fat head so his neck fat wobbled like jelly.

'Canines didn't evolve on their own; we changed them. We like to think they are man's best friend until they bite, or they rip another living being into pieces, then we blame them for being unsophisticated. We are surprised to remember that they remain animals, still

187

wild underneath. They are unpredictable and fighting to survive in a world they don't control. Something you and I can sympathise with, can we not?'

Bull blinked quickly, unsure of how to respond.

'After you,' she gestured to Bull, allowing him to leave first. He was a proud Russian who had fought in wars and killed men with his bare hands, but he gladly followed Hornet's instruction. She left the room, eager to get started. Aurora was dead and gone, and it was time for Boyd to meet Hornet.

Rendezvous

'"*Waterloo Station, 8 am Monday morning.*"' Fitz read the message out loud. '"*Come alone. Buy a pasty and a copy of Total Film. Put the pasty in the bin outside Costa Coffee, then take a seat and read the magazine.*"'

Boyd and Fitz were sat at the desk in Fitz's room, reading the reply from *FrakeNews*.

'What am I getting into here?' Boyd said, shaking his head. 'This is crazy!'

'I know! What kind of lunatic throws away an entire pasty?'

'Not quite what I meant.'

'Oh, you mean the cloak-and-dagger stuff? Yeah, well I get it. They need to be careful. They're constantly uncovering government lies and exposing corruption in huge corporations. They have to watch their backs I guess.'

'Yeah, I suppose so.'

'So, you're going alone then? I've got to paint the

lounge tomorrow anyway.' Fitz attempted a smile, but Boyd could see he was disappointed.

'Priorities,' Boyd joked.

'Exactly!' He had enjoyed helping Boyd and, if he was honest, he had enjoyed the other day at school right up until Boyd had been so dismissive of their friendship. He had a bit of a hollow feeling in his stomach that his friend would be leaving in the morning and carrying this adventure on without him.

'You know, you're a bit rubbish on your own, so if you need me for anything, just ask. Or hit me up on Pixie's Messenger.'

Boyd laughed. 'I will. You're the first person I'd call. I mean it. Thanks for being a proper mate.'

'Alright, chill out,' Fitz mocked. 'I think I preferred you when you were being a douchebag!'

Going It Alone

Boyd sat looking out of the train window. As they got closer to London, the gorgeous green hills of Bloomfield were steadily replaced by railway depots and office blocks. Fitz had woken him at 5:30, given him a breakfast of porridge and a mug of tea, and a handful of cash he had stashed in a shoe in his wardrobe. He had also given him an old iPhone 4 with a direct line to Fitz's computer. It used a satellite to communicate directly with Fitz's email, so Boyd could send texts or leave voicemails for him and it couldn't be traced. Boyd didn't really understand exactly how it worked but he thanked Fitz; he wasn't keen on getting a new phone in case it could be used to track down his location.

Roger Tork's morning routine meant he always got up just after six, so Boyd had snuck out of the house by then and walked to the station in the morning air. It was going to be a scorching-hot day, and the first Monday of half-term meant London would be busy, so Boyd was actually pretty happy to be heading into the big city early. Part of him was glad to be alone. He was at his most comfortable without anyone relying on him to say or do the right thing, but he couldn't deny the fact that he had felt a rush of excitement working with Fitz again. It had made it all seem like a bit of fun, just a game. But the next step, he had to take alone. This was real, people were getting hurt – probably even his dad – and he had to find out why and who was behind it.

'*The next station is Waterloo,*' the public address system began to announce their arrival. '*This train terminates here. Please remember to take your belongings with you when you depart from the tra*in.'

Boyd saw the huge canopy over the platforms of Waterloo Station just before it swallowed the front carriages of his train as they slowed to a halt. People stood to gather their belongings and form queues by the doors while Boyd stayed in his seat and watched. Fitz had enjoyed pointing out that another clear advantage of having to leave so early was arriving at the meeting point ahead of schedule, allowing Boyd to scope it out, like Fitz had done in the Rec on Saturday. Boyd mentioned that this hadn't really worked out that well for Fitz but he appreciated the advice. However, it did cross his mind that it would give him the chance to see if he was being followed, which was the main reason why he was delaying his departure from the train.

Finally, he stood and walked back to the very last carriage. It was a twelve-car train, which meant when he leant out, he wasn't under the canopy, he was at the far end of the platform in the sun. Boyd covered his eyes and looked down towards the station but couldn't see anyone out of place. At this hour of the morning, not many people were getting on this train to head out of the city, so there would be little cover for anyone who was waiting for him to appear. Maybe he was being paranoid but considering his Friday night had consisted of being hunted by a bunch of armed commandos on motorbikes, he decided that paranoia wasn't the worst habit he could develop.

Boyd stepped out onto the platform, keeping his head straight but his eyes moving constantly, watching for anything out of place. The adrenaline was coursing through him and he was ready to run at any moment. He reached the gate at the end of the platform, took out his ticket and pulled his hood up over his head.

Ruthless And Skilled

Elliot Jagger was late. He parked his small electric car in the gardens of the Lockmead estate and quickly trotted towards a thick, wooden door in a high brick wall. Elliot was around 35 years old, extremely tall with large, broad shoulders. He never did any exercise; he found the idea of going to the gym absolutely revolting and was always flabbergasted when people were fascinated by his huge build. He didn't see it as any kind of accomplishment; not when his brain was clearly the strongest and most impressive muscle he possessed. He was the smartest person he knew, the smartest person he had ever known, and he wasn't expecting to meet anyone smarter than himself in the near future. *That* was something to brag about, and he never missed an opportunity to do so.

He was dressed in his usual tweed suit – an interesting choice on what was already becoming an uncomfortably hot day. He still lived with his mum, and she had used his car last night. He discovered this when he stepped out of the house and into the driveway this morning to find it completely empty.

'Oh, sorry love,' his mum has said without a shred of sincerity when he'd woken her up. 'I think I left it in the car park at the bingo,' she managed before she nodded back off to sleep.

So, Elliot had cycled to the bingo hall in town, locked his bike to a lamp post, folded himself into his little car and driven to work. His lateness meant that he was already flustered, but as he struggled with his briefcase, he lost his grip on his travel mug of homemade spiced ginger tea. A drop of the sacred liquid coughed out of the open lid and splashed down his shirt.

'Perfect,' Elliot muttered to himself. So, that was it then; today was ruined before it had even started. The universe clearly had it in for Elliot Jagger.

He swept a curly lock of loose blond hair from his eyes, gently placed the cup on the ground and pushed two fingers against the front of one of the dusty, red bricks next to the wooden door. The surface of the brick pinged outwards before sliding to the left. Behind the front of the fake brick was a keypad. Elliot put in his own personal, five-digit code and opened the creaking wooden door. He picked up his tea and headed towards the Greenhouse. It was a mammoth glass structure the size of a football pitch, with whitewashed side windows and a transparent curved roof that displayed the leaves of the various plants and trees within. A high brick wall surrounded the Greenhouse on all sides and Elliot had come through the only entrance. It didn't take a brain the size of Elliot Jagger's to work out that Lord Ravensbrook didn't use the Greenhouse merely to grow his prize tomatoes.

Elliot hurried to a glass door at the south end of the building and walked straight in. He entered a small, airless room that looked much like the little greenhouse at his grandad's allotment. To his right was a line of muddy boots and a row of coat hooks, all taken up by rain macs and wax jackets. On his left, leaning up against the white glass wall was a collection of garden tools; the different-sized spades and forks were surrounded by discarded gardening gloves and spray bottles of weed killer.

Opposite the entrance was another door, this one frosted white, just like the glass all around him. Elliot raised his right hand and pressed it against the glass just above the handle. What looked like a regular pane of glass turned black, and a red outline dotted around Elliot's hand. After a three-second wait, the red outline turned green and the glass returned to its original frosted white before the door's lock gave way with an audible click. Elliot himself had designed and overseen the creation of the security for all His Lordship's most private rooms and offices, and he knew that even MI5 had nothing as good as this. He pulled the door open and entered.

The Greenhouse was where some of the best hackers in the world worked together to ensure His Lordship's more secretive business interests ran smoothly. Well, to be honest, Elliot considered himself one of the very best hackers and counter-intelligence operatives in the world, but the rest of the team were nowhere near his level. Who did His Lordship call when he wanted to spy on a competitor? Elliot. Who was the man Ravensbrook requested when he wanted to hack one of the most secure spy satellites in the world? Elliot. And because of the systems he had designed, they could do it all from right here, in sleepy Bloomfield. Yes, Elliot Jagger was

The Man and he made sure to remind himself of that every single day.

Elliot had been hand-picked to work there. Mr Knowles had approached him one evening, suddenly appearing in Elliot's car as he was leaving his office car park. Back then, his work had been data entry for MI5, the home of the British security service. He was told that one of the most powerful men in the country was putting together a team to help him spy on business rivals, to infiltrate government computer networks and operate against everything MI5 stood for; Elliot accepted in two seconds flat. It was MI5's own stupid fault: they hadn't seen his potential and they didn't respect him at all, so it was a matter of principle. That and the fact that Lord Ravensbrook would pay him more money in a month than the British government were paying him in a year, so it really was a no-brainer. The only downside was, most of the team had been assembled before he came on board and he wouldn't trust half of the morons he worked with here to chip his PlayStation, let alone hack a London CCTV network. So, Elliot had to handle most of the big stuff himself, which was just the way he liked it.

Once you got inside the Greenhouse, you noticed that the plants you could see from the outside were actually on a mezzanine; a suspended floor that was way up in the roof. On the ground, there were no trees or bags of compost as you would expect; the whole building was one big computer room, full of screens, desktops and servers. The hum and the heat from the electronics was the second thing you noticed, but Elliot was used to that. His desk was in the middle of an enormous communications station that was situated on a raised platform, known as the Hive.

As he weaved his way towards it, Elliot could see that the people he was due to meet were waiting. Bull, that horrible Russian idiot was there, playing with Elliot's favourite stress ball. It was in the shape of a small sausage dog that was cocking its leg to take a wee and Bull was squeezing it between his fat, pink fingers. Elliot would have that out of his mitts as soon as he got up there. He could also see the back of a woman's head; she was sitting in his seat, watching one of the immense TV screens on the wall. Her blonde hair looked wet against her large head as she sat perfectly still, like a crocodile patiently lying on the surface of a swamp. A bead of sweat slowly made its way down the middle of his back as he quickened his pace.

He walked up onto the Hive and she spun around in the chair. She didn't speak, she simply fixed a set of penetrating green eyes on him and waited. Elliot couldn't help it, he stared at the woman and gulped like a little boy who'd been caught with his hand in the cookie jar. He felt his eyes grow wider, so he snapped his gaze away and concentrated on Bull. 'That's my favourite stress ball.'

'You are late,' Bull almost spat the words at him.

'I had an errand to run.'

Elliot decided it was probably best he didn't tell them it was his mum's fault – that might undermine his authority a little bit. He took the stress ball from Bull's hand and put it back in its place on his desk. He tried to keep his eyes on Bull, but he could feel the woman's stare burrowing into him. He risked a quick glance at her and noticed she had turned the corner of her mouth up into the smallest of smiles.

'You were supposed to run errand for *me*, 20 minutes ago,' Bull insisted, his accent thick and his tone angry.

'Yes, well, I'm here now, so let's get on with it.'

'Apologise.' It was the woman. She hadn't moved a muscle and Elliot hadn't seen her speak, but she had fired the word out in his direction.

'Excuse me?' Elliot replied, defensively.

'Close,' she said as she stood up. 'And you are excused.' She slowly extended her frame upwards. Elliot was surprised to find she was as tall as him and almost as wide but carried herself with a confidence that crackled out from her like an electric current. She picked up the stress ball from its place and squeezed it in her huge hand.

Elliot was not used to looking straight ahead and being able to make eye contact with many people, so this was all very new to him, as was the feeling of someone making his skin crawl. In her eyes, he saw a frightening unpredictability. Elliot didn't know if she was going to laugh, order them a pizza or rip his head off. He quickly decided he would do whatever she wanted, as long as she left him alone as soon as possible.

'Right. Yes. Sorry about being late,' he spluttered.

'Better.' She continued to look him in the eye.

'This is Hornet,' Bull said, standing to the side of them both, his bullet-shaped head barely reaching their chest height.

Hornet. Elliot had heard that name before. He froze in stunned silence. The woman noticed.

'You've heard of me.'

'Yes.'

'Good. You were asked to trace someone for us last night and we're here for the results.'

'I was? Oh, right. Yes, I was!' Elliot did his best impression of an enthusiastic, team-player. He turned and tapped out an unlock code on his keyboard, then scanned at the screen. 'Nothing yet, Hornet. But don't worry, when he does resurface, we will find him. I've got facial-recognition software running through the backdoor of MI5, so the minute he pops up on any major CCTV, we'll be on his tail.'

'Good.' Hornet glanced at the desk, picked up Elliot's travel mug and sat back down in chair. 'Then we'll wait.'

Hornet. Yes, he remembered now. Elliot recalled it had been his first-ever project for Lord Ravensbrook. It was ridiculously top-secret; only a few other people inside Lockmead had even heard of it. Hornet had been trusted with guarding Ravensbrook's most prized asset and Elliot had to help create a fake identity for her. At the time, he had been tempted to investigate Hornet's real past and see why she had been given such a massive responsibility. What he'd found had terrified him to the extent that he hadn't slept that night thinking about the things this woman had done. Hornet wasn't just one of Ravensbrook's trusted aides, she was a ruthless and skilled assassin, and now she was sitting here, in his office, casually sipping his tea.

'Spiced ginger, homemade. Very tasty,' she said.

Battle Station

Boyd had arrived 30 minutes before he was due to meet his contact from *FrakeNews*. He had decided on the train ride up to Waterloo that he was going to position himself somewhere and watch, just like Fitz had suggested. Whoever had chased them on the beach the other night was still out there and whatever they wanted, they wouldn't just give up. Maybe they didn't have his dad – maybe Martin had got himself free and that meant there was a good chance they would be watching Boyd, following him in case he met up with his father. He also knew he couldn't trust Aurora or Harry, so he had to try to stay one step ahead. He could barely believe it; last week he was at school, worrying about a maths exam, and now here he was, heading to a meeting with conspiracy theorists who tried to bring down governments and worrying about people trying to kill him.

Waterloo station was massive and, at this time of

day, absolutely heaving with people.

Most of them came and went in a few minutes, making their way to a platform or heading underground; and they pretty much all kept their heads down and ignored each other. The platform entrances were all on one side, with shops, cafés and a ticket office on the other.

Boyd was new to this. He stood alone for a moment, feeling miniscule against the large crowd, all his confidence starting to slip from him as he realised that this wasn't a situation he could control. Normally, if something was beyond his abilities, he would learn to master it; he would work at it and develop his skills. When he moved from boxing to Taekwondo, he had almost quit after his first week. His instructor, Mr Beeson, had asked him why he wanted to take up martial arts.

'Because I want to be the best,' Boyd had said, through gritted teeth.

Mr Beeson had laughed. 'Why don't you start by just being the best you can be?' he had replied.

Mr Beeson had taught him to set goals, to be his own harshest critic and his own toughest competitor. Boyd had learnt to evaluate situations and to try to be better at the things he could control and not worry so much about the things he could not, which wasn't something he was always good at. If he couldn't do something, if his skills took too long to sharpen, then sometimes he would cave in and walk away. Often, he just needed some time to cool off and then he would come back again the next week with renewed determination. The problem he faced now was that he didn't have a single clue what he was doing, he didn't know how to act or how to control the mess he was in, but he couldn't storm off like a stroppy kid – not this time. If he threw in the towel, he might never find his dad or know the truth behind all this, so he had to suck it up and learn fast.

He stood with his back to the coffee shop where he was supposed to be sitting and reading the magazine in 20 minutes. He looked up at the departures board as if he were just another passenger waiting for a platform to be announced. He kept his hood up and occasionally he would swing himself around and get a sense of his surroundings. He didn't waste a single second; his eyes darted to every face. He decided he would look at people's faces, then their shoes, bags and coats to make sure he had as many ways as possible to identify anyone who spent too long hanging around him. The coffee shop was right next to an exit leading out to a street that was heaving with commuters, buses and taxis.

Boyd ran it through in his head: what would he do if he were the *FrakeNews* contact? Or what if the people who took his dad were here waiting for him? He doubted that any of them would come alone, so he was probably dealing with multiple watchers. So, if he were in their shoes, which spot would he pick to watch from? He closed his eyes for a second and pictured the station layout behind him. There was a food concourse upstairs – he would certainly make use of that; you could look out over the whole station from up there. Then, he would put another watcher in the coffee shop, sat with their back to the wall, looking out at the station concourse so they could see the face of everyone who approached. Yes, that's how he would do it. Maybe this spy stuff wasn't so tough after all.

He checked the time on the phone Fitz had given him and saw he still had ten minutes before he was due at the meeting. Buying the pasty and the magazine was obviously a way for him to make himself known, a way for them to force him to show himself. So he had bought both items as soon as he had arrived and had them in a carrier bag. Boyd looked up at the departures board again and pretended that he was waiting for someone. He took out the dummy iPhone again and made out like he was getting a phone call. He turned, glanced upwards at the food concourse, and scanned all around it. There didn't seem to be anyone suspicious standing at the railings looking out over the station.

He looked inside the coffee shop and instantly locked eyes with someone. A man, sitting at the back, next to the door marked: '*Staff Only*'. He was dressed in a suit and hunched over a laptop but his eyes weren't on the screen, they were looking out at the concourse. The man had been looking directly at him and then quickly broken his gaze when he'd turned around.

Boyd, still pretending to talk into the phone, walked over towards the stairs that led up to the concourse but instead of going up, he stopped at the bottom and helped a woman with a pushchair down the last few steps. She thanked him and Boyd went around the back of the staircase. He pocketed the phone, stopped at the bench underneath the stairs and sat down next to a homeless man who was trying to keep a low profile, just like Boyd. Now he was out of sight from anyone at the coffee shop and anyone who was upstairs on the concourse. If someone was watching him, they would have to follow to see where he had gone, they would have to show themselves. He was flushing them out.

Two minutes went by and then he saw the man from the coffee shop walk along in front of the departures and arrivals board, a phone clasped to his ear. His head was spinning around, moving side to side – he was looking for someone. Boyd turned his face to the left, away from the man, but he could still see his reflection in a shop window. The woman with the pushchair that Boyd had helped down the stairs was trying to exit WH Smith but a small gang of teenagers were in her way. Boyd could see in her face that she was ready to snap but held it in.

He glanced back over towards the man in the suit, who wasn't even hiding it now, desperately searching the big crowd for someone. Boyd felt a churning in his stomach; was this the *FrakeNews* contact or someone more dangerous? How long could he stay here before they made a move on him? His heart was thumping. What if this guy worked with Harry? What if he was trying to get to Martin through Boyd? Boyd fought every urge he felt to run at the man and confront him; best to sit and wait, make him show his hand.

Then, he heard a shout from his left. He snapped his head around as the gang of teenagers burst outwards, running and pushing their way through the crowd. The woman with the baby shouted and Boyd saw why. One of the gang had her handbag. Dammit!

Boyd checked his watch, he only had five minutes until he was due at the meeting. Then he felt a twitch in his legs and before he could convince himself that this wasn't his problem, he was on his feet and giving chase.

The thief was fast, probably around the same age as Boyd but he had a head start and had probably done this before and clearly knew where he was going. The thief ran along the outside of the shops, where the crowds were not as thick, but they had the risk of colliding with anyone stepping blindly out of a shop and onto the concourse.

Almost immediately, two men stepped out from Burger King and into Boyd's path. 'Move!' Boyd shouted, bellowing over the noise of the crowd. One man turned his head but didn't shift his body quickly enough. Boyd dropped his shoulder and smashed between the men, sending cups of coffee and a bag of breakfast baps up into the air.

Shouts followed both boys as they charged at speed across the busy station. The thief ducked right at the coffee shop and headed out towards the street. He glanced back and Boyd caught a look at his face. Boyd saw that the 'he' was a she and probably around two years younger than him. Her face had been calm and relaxed until she saw Boyd was quickly gaining on her.

As he rounded the corner and went past the coffee shop, he saw the thief turn right, out of the station. He continued to shout warnings and people parted as he gave chase. When he reached the covered section of street outside the station, he dropped his shoulder, turned right and just about managed to stop dead before he hit a crowd of frustrated commuters. Directly in Boyd's path was a huge man carrying a briefcase, his suit jacket slung over his arm. The crowd was so thick, Boyd struggled to look through it and it didn't help that he was the only one trying to walk against the flow. Boyd stood his ground against the big man and tried to push to get through the crowd.

'Whoa! What's your problem, mate?' the man said.

Boyd ignored him. It was no use, he wasn't getting through here, the road was blocked with two stationary buses, coughing thick black smoke out into the hot, London atmosphere.

'I'm talking to you, son,' the man said again.

Boyd glanced at the taxi rank to his left; a long line of black London cabs idled behind a roped-off area and stretched all the way down the access road next to the station. The big man grabbed Boyd's collar and went to move him. Boyd looked up at the man for the first time. He was sweaty, red-faced, angry and spoiling for a fight.

'I'm chasing a thief, I just need to…'

'Right, 'course you are,' the man interrupted.

Boyd didn't have time for this. He swept the man's hands away in a single, upward motion. The big man was momentarily stunned and that gave Boyd the split-second he needed. He turned his body left and cleared the rope barrier in a standing jump; he was now in the taxi rank. The long queue of waiting customers started to complain as Boyd placed a foot on the bumper of the first taxi, before launching himself up onto the bonnet, then the roof. As he scanned the road ahead, the crowd on the ground erupted in response; some hollered in protest, others were unsure what was unfolding and decided it was best to get as far away as possible.

Boyd heard someone shout for the police when he saw the thief, already on the other side of the crowd, confidently strolling behind one of the stationary buses. The driver of the taxi climbed out, shouted for Boyd to get down and swept his arm towards Boyd's foot, missing it by a country mile.

A policeman appeared from the station and stopped. He had an irate crowd, people dangerously scattering all over the place and a teenager on the roof of a black cab. 'Alright, down you get, sunshine!' he called out and reached for his radio.

Boyd looked ahead and saw that the line of taxis formed a perfect escape route: a black, metallic pathway that led away from the baying crowd all the way back down the road towards the thief. His meeting with *FrakeNews* was going to have to wait. He took two steps on the taxi's roof and leapt off over the bonnet of the next taxi in the queue and landed on its roof. He didn't stop there. Letting the momentum sweep him forward, he did the same again, two steps before pushing hard, launching himself into the air and onto the next taxi. In just a few seconds he was on the roof of taxi number nine, the last in the line, and he couldn't stop himself – he came off the back of the cab and hit the floor with both feet, tumbled and rolled across the sticky, hot tarmac.

He sprung up on his feet in an instant, looking to where the thief had ducked behind the bus. She had grabbed a city bike and was disappearing around the corner. Boyd sprinted over to the bike rack just as a man was putting on his bicycle clips and taking his helmet from his bag. He couldn't believe he was going to do this, but it was his only chance. He grabbed the bike from the man, pushed away down the road and leapt into the saddle. So now he was a thief chasing a thief!

'I owe you one,' Boyd shouted to the stricken man and powered after the other bike.

The thief was quite a way ahead of Boyd, but her route was straight enough that when he sat up in the saddle, he could keep her in sight. What was he even doing? He had no idea. But something Fitz had said to him popped into his head, about how Boyd had always stood by whilst other people were bullied, and maybe this was his way of rallying against that. Whatever was driving him, it felt good to be doing something right for a change, and anyway, there was no way he could go back to the station now. It had felt all wrong from the moment he'd arrived, like the meeting was a set-up and maybe the people from *FrakeNews* were in on it. Whatever was going on, he would decide where the next meeting would be and it would be on his terms.

Boyd pedalled slowly; he kept his distance without losing sight of the thief. The roads were busy, but they were heading south, away from the station, and the cycle lanes were moving freely. Then, without warning, the thief turned left and darted through the entrance to a park. Boyd moved to quickly follow. By the time he had come out the other side of the small park, she was gone; she must have seen him following her. Boyd cursed himself for not being more careful; he cycled around the surrounding streets but there wasn't any sign of her, she had disappeared without a trace.

He turned a corner by some old viaducts when a pushchair suddenly rolled out from behind a wall and straight in front of his bike. Boyd had been looking the other way and was going way too fast to avoid it. He turned the

215

bike, desperately trying to stop but went through the side of the pushchair, falling on top of it and crashing down onto the ground. Boyd did everything he could not to put his weight down onto to the pushchair, but it was no use, they smashed into the hard concrete together. He rolled over twice and lay on his back for a second, winded and trying to figure out what on earth had just happened. How did a pushchair just appear like that? He suddenly realised he may have hurt someone – oh please let it have been empty.

Boyd scrabbled up onto all fours and saw it, lying on the road, spilling out of a tatty blanket was an old doll with one eye missing and a twisted smile on its face. He heard a robotic laugh coming from the doll and recoiled in dismay.

A pair of shoes came to a stop in front of him. Boyd glanced at them. Shiny, black Doc Marten's with white laces; He had seen a pair of those shoes already today. His brain quickly flicked through its memory banks and settled on a result: the stairs at the station. Boyd tilted his head up and there in front of him was the woman with the pushchair from Waterloo station; the one who had her handbag stolen. Next to her was the thief.

'You owe me a pasty,' the woman said.

Passing The Test

'So, who are you?' These had been the first words any of them had said to each other since Boyd had hauled himself up out of the road. At first, they had all stood in silence, weighing each other up. The teenage girl, whom he had assumed was a thief but had clearly been there to lure him away from the station, eyed him suspiciously. Boyd had waited for the other woman, the woman he had assumed was the victim of a bag-snatcher, to say something. This could all still be a trap, he had no idea who he was dealing with, but then, neither did they. He picked small chunks of grit out of his hands and gently sucked at the dots of blood they left behind.

'You're just a kid, so who are you?' the woman asked again.

Boyd guessed she was around 19 or 20 years old. She was a few inches taller than him, with her hair in short curls. She was lean, athletic and wore black leggings and a black vest top. The younger teenager didn't even look at Boyd; both young women seemed completely unfazed by how bizarre this situation had become.

'You got my email?' Boyd asked; it was time to test the water.

'Maybe,' the older woman replied, defensively.

Boyd paused, then shook his head and smiled. 'You're wasting my time.' He started towards the bike he had abandoned on the floor.

'If that's how you want to play it, why even bother coming?'

He picked up the bike and turned back to the woman. 'Y'know, people told me you guys were shady and fake, but I wanted to see for myself.'

'And you think you've seen us, do you, bro?'

'I think I've seen enough. You can't help me.' Boyd turned the bike around and climbed onto the saddle.

'I know what happened to her,' the woman said.

Boyd stopped. 'You know what happened to who?'

'You know and I'm not saying her name out here. If you really want to see us, follow me.'

Boyd looked over his shoulder. The teenager had gone, vanished into thin air, and the woman was walking towards a small café which was set into one of

218

the archways in the viaduct. Boyd thought for a second, but it was just for show – he knew he would follow her, he had no other choice, no other leads to follow. It was time to see what *FrakeNews* could offer him.

As he entered the café, the woman was talking quietly with a bald Italian man who was standing behind the counter, wearing an apron. Boyd couldn't hear what was said but the man fired him a wary look. She turned to Boyd.

'This way.'

They went into a storage room filled with large, industrial cans of olive oil and boxes of provisions. There was a small desk covered in paper and folders; the woman pushed a chair towards Boyd, he sat down. She perched on the edge of the desk, just like the Prov always did when he was giving out detentions. It meant she positioned herself above him, it gave her an edge, a sense of authority.

'So, your mother is wrapped up in this, how?' the woman asked him.

Boyd frowned. 'It's my dad, and he's missing.'

'Right. And you said your aunt is helping you?'

219

Boyd took a deep breath. 'Look, you know I didn't say that and if you'd have wanted me to prove I am the person who wrote to you, you should have given me a codeword or something. As it is, your pasty and magazine are sitting on the floor by a bench in Waterloo station because I thought someone was being robbed and I tried to help. But seeing as there was a homeless guy next to me, I wouldn't have my heart set on getting the pasty back in one piece.'

The woman was quiet for a moment. She looked Boyd up and down, taking everything in. Despite having spent a couple of nights at Fitz's house, he was totally exhausted, and utterly desperate; it must have shown.

'Okay,' she said with a straight face. 'We tagged you the moment you arrived and wanted to see what kind of person you are, so we staged the theft. We call it the "White Knight" test, and you passed. Congratulations.'

'Thank you.'

'I'm Skye.' She held out her hand.

'Boyd.' He took it and they shook.

'Let's get you a brew, and we can talk.'

'We've got a hit!'

Elliot Jagger put down his forkful of pancakes and responded to the urgent bleep coming from one of the computers in the Hive. He had set it up the night before, using what he considered his two most innovative creations. First, he had used a programme to drift through the cracks in MI5's computer network and pinch CCTV footage; he called it Pick Pocket. If Elliot wanted to take a little look at something a government or corporation had on their system, as long as it had been saved to the victim's network or shared with someone, Pick Pocket allowed him to digitally enter unnoticed and take a copy without leaving a footprint. As it downloaded the recent CCTV footage from all major cities and transport hubs in the UK, his facial-recognition software, Face Trace, began to search through it for Boyd's likeness; and now, huddled in front of the monitor, they were looking straight at him.

'When and where,' Hornet demanded. She was bent over the desk like a vampire about to sink her teeth into her prey.

Elliot hit some keys. 'Waterloo Station, the platform

10 camera at 7.58 am this morning.' They all checked the time; it was almost nine; they were an hour behind him.

'Now it knows his face, it will find him again, don't worry.'

'I'm not the one who should be worried. How long to find him?'

'It should be almost instantaneous,' Elliot said, adding a little dash of caution to his statement because, right now, Face Trace had not found any other hits.

'And yet, here we are,' Hornet hissed.

'Maybe your computer is stupid,' Bull said, as if it was a valid point that needed to be made.

Elliot turned his chair slightly to face the no-neck Russian. 'Ah, of course, you're right!' he responded sarcastically. 'I shouldn't have run it on the computer I modelled on your brain.'

'How about I smash it over your head, and we see if it works then, huh?'

Hornet had heard enough. 'Children,' she said sharply. 'I've done enough babysitting over the last few years.' She looked at the frozen image of Boyd's face on the screen. He was walking down the platform, towards the station. 'The software clearly isn't the issue. It's only found his face once, which can only mean one thing: he's hiding. Run this on from the point he exits the platform and you'll find that he puts his hood up. So, all we need to do is follow the movement of the hooded boy via the cameras. It's not the perfect solution, Mr Jagger, but it's hardly rocket science. Sometimes, even the most effective predators must adapt. Get on with it.'

Elliot hit play and they watched Boyd approach the ticket barrier and pull his hood up over his face. He flashed a look at Hornet, her mouth turned up in one corner as she licked her thin lips like a hungry lizard about to snatch an unsuspecting fly.

She looked at the screen as the hunched figure of a teenage boy was swallowed up by the huge rush-hour crowd at Waterloo Station. He might be an hour ahead of them, but he was alone, he was rattled and he would be desperate. 'Good,' she thought.

Elliot brought up a new feed from a camera inside the station and scanned the sea of people, looking for their target. Hornet tapped the screen with the sharp point of the 'T' on her ring, highlighting a hooded figure moving slowly through the crowd.

'And we're back in the game.'

Frake HQ

Skye got up and walked to the side wall. She stood in front of a shelf containing jars of pickles and tubs of flour, put her hands on either side of the shelves and pushed; the shelf and the wall popped outwards on a hinge to reveal a dark corridor. She turned, squared up to Boyd and held up a finger.

'Know this,' she jutted her chin towards him in defiance. 'I'm about to show you a level of trust that most don't get anywhere near because I can see that you're alone, scared and I think we can help each other. But just as I trust you, you trust me when I tell you to tread carefully, and if you betray me, even for your own noble reasons, I will end you. Do you get me?'

Boyd was transfixed. Skye's brown eyes were filled with conviction and left him in no doubt where he stood. He nodded. 'Sure.'

She stood aside and ushered him through the doorway. He stepped into a short, narrow corridor that was lit by one light fixed to a socket on the red brick wall. Thick dust clogged in his throat when he breathed in; he pulled his hoodie up and around his mouth. Skye closed the secret door behind them and walked to a small door at the end of the corridor. She tapped in a code on a keypad and Boyd heard a loud '*THUNK*' as the bolts retracted. Boyd followed her into a new space, eager to get out of the confinement of the hallway.

It was a vast open space made entirely of brick, down to the curved, arched ceilings; they were inside the railway viaducts. The place was massive, with sections divided up by wooden walls. Two old Land Rovers and a selection of mopeds and bicycles sat to their left, and metal racks on the wall displayed helmets, motorbike leathers, jackets, skateboards – basically every transport option you could want to get across London in a hurry.

Beyond the vehicles stood nine long metal dining tables with benches attached, and to the left of these a wooden partition built against the back wall housed a large kitchen. Inside, a few people were busying themselves with kettles and pans, getting breakfast started. They moved through the dining tables and towards a wooden partition that stretched the whole width of the building. Skye stood aside and motioned with her hand for Boyd to go through. 'Welcome to *FrakeNews*.'

Boyd stepped through the doorway into pretty much the coolest place he had ever seen. He suddenly thought how it was probably a good thing that Fitz wasn't here because they'd never be able to get him to leave. In front of him were metal racks filled with servers that formed a walkway. Once beyond it, he saw around 20 metal desks that looked like they had been put together with whatever someone could find dumped by the side of a railway line. The chairs were all different: some were office chairs with chunks of foam missing from the back or the seat, others were old dining room chairs that someone had clearly thrown away because they had seen better days. No one here had made any effort to give them a new coat of paint, or repair them, they just used them.

There was a set of stairs in the middle of the room and another set in the far corner; the upper levels looked like those portacabins you get on building sites. Skye headed towards the stairs in the far corner and Boyd followed. His eyes were searching the desks and the monitor screens as he walked through, desperate to see something that might give him a clue as to what Skye and her boss knew about Miranda, but he saw nothing. It was still early and there wasn't a huge amount of activity in the office right now, if you could even really call it an office.

Skye led them upstairs and into a small room with an old, tatty sofa, a dining chair and a coffee table. She sat in the dining chair and pointed him over to the sofa. There was a door to his left and the young 'thief' from the train station came through it, carrying a tray. She put it down on the coffee table.

'Thanks, Teela,' Skye said. The tray carried two cups of tea and a packet of Penguin biscuits on it.

'*Thank god*', Boyd thought; he was starving. 'May I?' he said, pointing to the Penguins.

'Go for it.'

He tore open the packet, took one, opened the wrapper and hoovered up the bar in an instant. He washed it down with a sip of the hot tea. 'So, how does your boss get away with having a kid like that working for *FrakeNews*?'

Skye raised her eyebrows. 'Well, strictly speaking, Teela doesn't work for *FrakeNews,* and as for my boss,' she paused, 'I think you need to forget anything you think you might know about us.'

'But you are going to help me, right? You wanted to know about what happened to me, about my dad.' Boyd suddenly had an awful feeling that he was wasting precious time.

'Boyd, relax. Let me explain.'

Relaxing was the last thing on his mind. He fought the urge to tip the table over and scream that he needed her to stop stalling and give him some answers. He took a breath and grabbed another Penguin. If he wanted to make any kind of progress, he had to trust Skye. 'Okay, I'm listening.'

'This is all me, everything you see around you and everything you watch on YouTube.' Boyd looked at her quizzically. 'The underground news organisation that the government and big business wants to silence – you're looking at it.' Skye held her hands out. She wasn't being arrogant; she was almost apologetic, as if Boyd would be disappointed in the news. 'I started putting it all together two years ago. I took in kids from the streets, people who had nothing and no one they could rely on and I put a roof over their head. If you go up those other stairs, there are rooms and beds; we all live here.'

'All?'

'There's about 20 of us; all young women with nowhere else to go. We all have skills that drive our cause forward. Teela can climb up a drainpipe, get through an open window and be gone before you even know it.'

'Well, I nearly caught her,' Boyd smirked.

'Yeah, because she let you. Kelsey is our mechanic, Delilah is our bodyguard. But our secret weapon is, every one of them is at home on the London streets, and we all know how to be someone that everyone else ignores. Who remembers the person sat in the doorway asking for spare change, huh?'

'Nobody.'

'Right, and we use that to fight against those people who stepped over us on pavements and had us thrown out of shop doorways night after night.'

'But how do you have…' He waved his hands around, gesturing at the building they were sat in. '… all of this. How can you?'

'Daddy was rich. I never knew him, he didn't accept me when I was born and my mother died, so I ended up in care, then on the streets. When my father died, turns out, he left me a few quid. They found me when I was admitted to hospital with an appendicitis.' Skye stopped and for a moment, it looked like she was fighting back tears. 'I never wanted his money, I wanted a dad - but I can certainly take what he gave me and use it for something good.'

She paused again. Then, she slapped her hands down on her knees, ending the topic of conversation. 'So, that's my history. Now it's your turn. It's about time you told me how you're linked to Miranda Capshaw.'

Boyd told Skye everything, from the attack on Aurora's van, the phone call between Aurora and his dad, right up to arranging their meeting at Waterloo. When he was finished, she asked him some questions about his dad.

Boyd told her that Martin worked for a logistics company called Hurricane. He didn't know what it was exactly that his dad did or even where the office was; he said Martin went away quite a bit for business.

'I think you need to get your head around the fact

that your dad's wrapped up in this somehow,' Skye said, trying to tread gently. She had already picked up on Boyd's tendency to react to a tricky situation by letting his emotions get away from him. He had done a reasonable job of gritting his teeth and holding it in so far, but Skye knew that talking about his dad's involvement might just provoke him. 'And if you're right, and Miranda Capshaw is at the centre of this, then I reckon we can help each other.'

'You'll help me find her?'

Skye tilted her head to one side. 'Well, it's not like on TV, where the good guys just follow a trail and it leads somewhere. There's a load of threads we could pull at here, some will get us nowhere and some of them will mean trouble. It's about knowing which one is going to get us closer to the truth. In our vlog about Miranda, we mentioned the power surges that had been happening, right? The thing is, we didn't put everything we know in those videos. I've got a team member who is in contact with three scientists inside three different governments and the reality behind these surges will blow your mind. Honestly, we could release this stuff and people would go ballistic; it would cause someone somewhere a proper headache.'

'So why don't you? Force them to answer you, make them tell the truth!'

'Because it's not ready, not yet. We don't know who that person is. It could be a group, a government, anyone. I'm a journalist, not an activist. I don't just want to spoil the party – I want to find the truth and make them take responsibility.'

'Okay, so what have you actually got so far?'

Skye paused a moment, looked at him and tilted her head. Then nodded to herself, picked up her cup of tea and headed back down the stairs.

'Come with me and I'll show you,' she called back to him.

Skye sat on one of the desks, and Boyd had taken the most comfortable chair he could find but was still pretty uncomfortable. She had asked a young woman to join them. She was around the same age as Skye, small to the point of being tiny, and had black hair with pink tips tied up into buns. She wore a huge white jumper with black animal print that looked like a duvet on her slight frame.

'I'm Azima.' She shook Boyd's hand and eyed him suspiciously.

'Boyd.'

The office area was busier now and it was pretty clear they all knew who Boyd was. The whole place smelled like engine oil and cooked food but Boyd could also sense an air of excitement that had been generated by his arrival. Before he had met Skye or her team, he had put all the responsibility on them to make sense of this craziness. Now, he was beginning to see how much it meant to them too, and he was feeling the pressure to deliver something that would help them get closer to the truth.

It was clear that Skye was going to take a backseat for this; it was going to be Azima's show. From the moment she began talking, it was clear why Skye had her as part of the *FrakeNews* operation. Azima's initial wariness melted away and her eyes shone with an energy and enthusiasm that pulled Boyd into her world. He was utterly captivated.

'Two weeks ago, there occurred a concentration of power in London that was beyond anything we've ever seen,' she said. 'It registered like an earthquake, causing

233

blackouts, and scoring an impressive six on the Richter scale. Power like that should have been devastating, but there wasn't a solitary sign of any outward pressure.'

'The mechanism they use to measure earthquakes?'

'Exactly, and this one came in at level-six, which is big.'

'How big?'

'So, imagine 60 million kilograms of dynamite.'

'Okay, that's pretty big! But you're saying some people just lost their Wi-Fi for a bit? I mean, no buildings fell down or anything?'

'This is my point, no outward pressure; it doesn't make any sense. Something that massive, and buildings should have been reduced to rubble. But nothing - not even a fallen roof tile.'

'Well the readings, the Richter scale, it must be wrong then, surely?'

'No, they're correct.'

'You can't know that.'

'We can,' Skye said as she leant forward with a knowing smile. 'Because we've spoken off the record to three government scientists who all have the same readings for both events.'

'Hang on; are you telling me that this had happened more than once?'

'Yep,' Skye said. 'Two events, occurring at different times. The media reported that there was a network failure around the same time as the London power surge. They used that story to cover up the blackouts and whatever; but it doesn't explain the surge itself.'

'You said this was two weeks ago at an industrial estate,' Boyd said. 'Let me guess, the second one happened a week ago, around the same time as Miranda Capshaw disappeared from that plane?'

'Within minutes of Miranda Capshaw's plane landing, it lost all power on the runway and a similar energy signature to the one in London was recorded in France.'

'That's not even the weirdest part,' Azima said. 'A few hours after the event in London two weeks ago, a man called Bishop disappeared without a trace from Hyde Park. Two power surges, two people go missing. Even if you believe in coincidences, that's going to keep you up at night.'

'So, you've got two events in two different countries. Both with massive readings on this Richter scale thing that would usually mean a whole lot of damage; but there wasn't a single brick out of place. Do you or your scientist mates know what caused them?'

'No,' Skye said flatly.

Boyd nodded. 'Good, glad we cleared that up, moving on then. How about you tell me what you *think* caused them?'

Azima and Skye looked at each other. Skye shook her head at her friend.

'Guys, you said this would blow my mind, and I've kind of been through hell to find you, so...'

Azima sat forward. Boyd could see she was dying to let him in on her theory. 'I think someone has created the means to partially contain a black hole, and they're opening it.' She smiled and nodded, waiting for Boyd to be impressed.

Boyd's eyes widened. He rubbed both hands over his face. 'Back up – a black hole? You mean, like the things you get in space that eat up everything and spin you into another dimension?'

'Well, I'm not sure you're grasping the exact science, but in theory, yes.'

'I should say, we don't know anything for sure right

236

now,' Skye said, making an effort to bring the conversation back down a notch.

'Well, that's a relief,' Boyd said. 'Because, for a moment, I thought you were betting everything you had, including my father's life, on something that sounds like a side-plot from an *Avengers* movie.'

'It doesn't make sense because you're not asking yourself why,' Azima said, looking up and smiling. She was building up to something here, they all knew it, and whatever it was, it clearly made Skye uneasy.

'I'm not sure Boyd's ready for this. Why don't we leave that for another time?' Skye said. 'We should focus on this other person who disappeared. This guy Bishop is our best lead to Miranda and maybe we can find a clue to whatever your dad is mixed up in.'

'No, hang on,' Boyd said. 'Azima's right, I want to know why someone would be opening black holes in the middle of London.'

'You really don't,' Skye said, shaking her head.

'He does,' Azima was convinced.

'He really, really doesn't,' Skye persisted.

'Oh, just tell me, for crying out loud!' Boyd exploded.

Azima jumped to her feet; she was still shorter than

Boyd and he was sat in the chair. She took a moment to compose herself, then raised her hands and held them in front of her, as if she was holding a sphere. 'The containment of the power source, the lack of outward pressure, this has the hallmarks of someone very seriously experimenting with dark energy,' Azima said with conviction.

'Dark energy? You mean the stuff that's out there expanding the universe?'

'Yes!' Azima clapped her hands together.

'So how does someone even contain that and why? Are they making it into a weapon or something?'

'No. I don't think this is about destroying anything,' Azima replied, a spark in her eyes as she built up to her big reveal. 'I think it's way cooler than a weapon. I think that someone has found a way to travel through time.'

Playing The Hero

Elliot Jagger was sitting at his desk in the Hive. He felt like a fly struggling to free himself from a tangled web, with Hornet arched over him like a spider. He was flicking from camera to camera as they traced Boyd's movements through Waterloo Station earlier this morning. Hornet's left arm was clamped to the top of Elliot's chair – which most people struggled to even reach – meanwhile her right hand was on his desk, just close enough to his mouse to really annoy him. She alternated between drumming her fingers on the desk or clenching her fist and lightly scratching the glass surface of the desk with the tip of her ugly, silver ring. It made a noise Elliot found unbearable; it set him on edge, like fingernails down a blackboard. Bull was sat in another high-back leather chair at another desk, his feet up, gently snoring. Elliot Jagger's worst nightmare had a name and it was 'Monday'.

'There,' Hornet said, as they watched a wide-angle

shot of the station from the main entrance. 'That was him. He's gone behind the stairs. Get us something from down the other end of the building at around ten seconds from this view.'

Elliot pulled up some files and opened one. He tapped in a time and, sure enough, an image appeared. They searched for a sign of the hooded teenager but found nothing at first.

'No cameras covering that location.'

'Roll it on.'

Elliot did so, letting the footage play and waiting for her next helpful suggestion.

'Wait, we have some action. What's that?' Hornet pointed to the right of the screen at what looked like a commotion of some kind.

'It's nothing,' Elliot said dismissively. 'Looks like a bag snatcher or something. If we watch this all day, we'll see half a dozen of those at least.'

'Wind it back and zoom in on it.'

Elliot turned his head, intending to give Hornet a look that questioned her order. But she was already facing him, her green eyes squinted and piercing into him like a spear. Elliot felt a sudden cold rush run through him, so he quickly nodded. 'Good plan, will do.'

'Stop!' Hornet snapped. Elliot stopped the video.

'There,' she said and pointed to the left of the commotion. A figure in a black hoodie appeared and gave chase.

'Might be unrelated, probably working with the thief,' Elliot pointed out. 'They could be a spotter or something – that's why they're running.'

Hornet tilted her head and looked at the image of the figure paused on the screen. 'No. Start downloading CCTV from around Waterloo, five miles in all directions should do it. Looks like someone decided to play the hero. That's my Boyd.'

Not My Problem

'Time travel?' Boyd asked. His eyes flitted between Azima and Skye.

'Yes,' Azima answered enthusiastically.

'We're getting ahead of ourselves,' Skye said. 'We don't know anything for sure yet.'

'But we know what the science tells us,' Azima insisted.

'And the science,' Boyd said, 'tells you that Doc Brown is out there somewhere, playing with a Flux Capacitor?'

'Okay.' Skye had heard enough.

'Doc who?' Azima looked confused.

'He's taking the mickey.'

'Taking the what?' Azima asked, confused.

'He's mocking us,' Skye said, wearily.

'No, I'm not exactly mocking.' Boyd held his hands up.

'No? So, what then?'

'This is it? *This* is what you have? I mean, guys, can you even hear yourselves? Time travel, for god's sake!'

Azima was deflated; her shoulders slumped. She turned off the monitor and folded up her notes. Skye looked at her friend and felt a flash of shame that she hadn't defended her.

'Y'know, I can see why you think this sounds crazy, I really can.' Skye said flatly.

'That's a relief.'

'Don't be such a prat, Boyd. This is Azima's work and she's bloody good at it. She isn't pulling this out of thin air.' Boyd shifted in his seat as Skye stood up. 'Just because something sounds crazy, doesn't mean it's not the truth. Stop thinking about what you think you know. The fact is that time travel has never been impossible; we travel through time every minute of every day. Is manipulating time improbable? Absolutely. But there are governments and corporations who pour tons of money into researching ideas that you and I would think are totally cuckoo. And that's the great thing about science: everything is crazy until it works, then it becomes genius.'

'Just for the record,' Azima broke her silence, clearly

243

still a bit bruised by Boyd's reaction. 'My contacts are scientific advisors to governments, and they're telling me that they have never seen anything like this. They have nothing to explain it, so we're already in the realms of improbable, you get that? Which means, whatever this is and whoever is doing it, they are breaking new ground and going to great lengths to keep it hidden – and it's linked to this Bishop guy and Miranda.'

'Which means,' Skye said, 'it's also linked to your dad.'

'And what if it's not?' Boyd said defiantly. 'What if I wait for you to investigate all this and it's got nothing to do with my dad? Why should I care?'

They all sat in uncomfortable silence. Boyd was frustrated, not because he didn't believe it but because this was massive, on another level completely. It wasn't something he could control, nor resolve quickly.

He was desperate for help and had imagined a professional team of journalists were the right people to turn to. But, in truth, the *FrakeNews* team were a bunch of kids not much older than him, with a cool place to hang out and a few computers. Skye and Azima looked at him like they were ready to throw him out.

'Please tell me why I shouldn't just go home, call the police and wait for someone to sort this out. Why should I give a damn? Come to think of it, why should you? This isn't our world, we're all kids. It's not my job to save you,' he pointed at Skye. 'Or you, Azima. Or anyone. That's why we have adults.'

'And if they can't do it?' Skye said with quiet anger.

Boyd stood up and looked her in the eye. 'Like I said: Not. My. Problem.'

'Code red!' a shout came across the office. 'Someone's out front.'

Azima turned around and tapped some keys on her machine. Skye held Boyd's gaze for a moment longer, then huffed at him with contempt.

'What's happening?' Boyd asked.

'Code red – someone's in the shop, asking questions,' Skye told him as she flicked the stand-by switch and the big monitor came back to life.

'Anyone know who that is?' Azima asked, pointing at the image on the screen.

There was obviously a concealed camera on the shelf behind the counter as Boyd was looking at a shot over the head of the bald Italian man. He could see a tall woman with slicked back blonde hair and a remarkably familiar face. His heart began to sink.

'Yeah, I do,' Boyd said sheepishly. 'It's the aunt I told you about, the one that went weird on me. That's Aurora.'

Skye looked from the screen to Boyd. 'Still want to go home and leave this to the adults?'

Boyd stayed silent, staring at the image on the monitor and gritting his teeth.

'Well then,' Skye said with a sarcastic tone. 'It looks like this just became your problem, doesn't it?'

A Bigger Prize

Hornet had gone into the café alone. Bull protested, of course; he hadn't beaten anyone up in a few days now and Hornet could see it was starting to get to him. She would have to let him give someone a little slap soon or he would be totally unbearable. But this wasn't the right time; this operation needed a light touch. She also knew that Boyd was probably long gone from here and that the small Italian man behind the counter really didn't know who the boy was; but he wasn't telling her the whole truth.

She was good at many things but spotting a lie was something she excelled at. You ask a simple question and let the person speak. If they have something to hide, the body language will tell you everything you need to know. Plus, a liar always tells you too much of the wrong thing.

Hornet climbed back into the passenger seat of the black Range Rover.

'We're leaving?' Bull asked from the driving seat.

'No. Keep the engine off. We wait.' Hornet took out her phone and hit a number. The phone rang, the call connected and the car filled with the voice of Lord Ravensbrook.

'News?'

'We had him going into a park on a city bike, not far from Waterloo. Then the CCTV goes black, no working cameras the other side of the park, and no sign beyond that, which means he's stopped somewhere in the immediate vicinity. I had Jagger trace the bikes and found two in the area; one of them outside a café. I've just been in there now.'

'And?' Ravensbrook was getting impatient.

'And the owner remembers him. Boyd was with a young woman and the owner was even kind enough to tell me what they ordered.' Hornet paused, she looked through the window into the little café. 'I'm going to put someone on watch at the café,' she said. 'I want to come back here another time, kick over some rocks and see what crawls out.'

'But you said the owner told you everything?'

'He told me too much, in fact. Oh, I believe he

doesn't know who Boyd is, but he told me Boyd had ordered two coffees. Boyd doesn't drink coffee, he can't stand being near the stuff. Which means the guy in the café is lying.'

'Okay. You're certain this the best way forward? You have been out of this kind of operation for a long time.'

Hornet glanced over at Bull, who wisely looked the other way, not wanting her to see his pleasure at Ravensbrook questioning her methods. 'My instincts are as sharp as ever. We don't need to rush in like a bull at a gate.' Hornet leant over to the big Russian and quietly said, 'No pun intended.'

'Meaning?' Ravensbrook asked.

'I'm going to stay in the area and get Jagger to throw a net around him and the girl. They'll pop up on CCTV again and when they do, they might lead us somewhere, or even to someone.'

'That's a risk, Hornet. You said yourself we don't want him falling into the wrong hands.'

'It is a risk. But you always said the boy was bait for a bigger prize. We know someone out there is using Hurricane technology. I think it's time we flush them out. Perhaps we can kill two birds with one stone.'

Hidden From View

When the Range Rover had first arrived outside the café, the young woman had been tucked around a corner, watching from a distance, waiting for an opportunity. It had come when the tall, leather-clad woman exited the vehicle and headed for the café.

The young woman, whose name was Blair, walked past the Range Rover. She moved quickly enough to look like someone in a hurry, but not so hurried as to draw attention from the big ape in the driver's seat. He didn't even notice as she unwrapped a piece of gum and then discarded what looked like a wrapper. In fact, she had passed the wrapper into her other hand and thrown a small listening device through the open back window of the Range Rover. When the tall woman had returned to the car, Blair sat out of sight and listened to every word.

A short time later, she stood from her seat on the

Northern Line train; not a single passenger looked up at her, no one paid her any attention. She blended in perfectly with the students and interns who weaved in and out of shops and stations all over London. Her jet-black bob was scooped up into a small ponytail and her clothes were industrial and functional: a pair of black combat boots, black jeans and a grey T-shirt. She completed the look with a tatty old rucksack; she could be on her way home from an art lecture or just as easily be a cleaner on her way to work, but Blair was neither. She was nothing of the kind.

Even though she was only 18 years old, she had travelled all over the world and lived a life most people four times her age would never be able to imagine. Most teenagers fortunate enough to travel are in search of something, they fill an Instagram account with waterfalls and sunsets, but Blair's search was entirely different. Since she was born, her life had been centred on the work of her father, Karl. The quest had taken them to countries most people her age wouldn't be able to find on a map. Blair hadn't just lived in these countries; she had fought to survive in them. She had spied, deceived and stolen her way through each and every place they had settled in. Then, when they had what they wanted, she and her father had moved on, leaving as little trace of their existence as possible; onto the next place to find the next person or the next item that could take them another step closer to completing their puzzle.

Blair's father believed they were finally getting closer, but they both knew they weren't alone in their hunt and every move now was crucial. She got off the train at Hendon Central and walked the short distance to the old, disused building they were currently calling home. The derelict headquarters for the German Trade Union Federation seemed like a good fit, seeing as her father was half-German. The building would probably be knocked down soon and replaced with expensive apartments, but no matter; Blair and her father never stayed anywhere too long. The windows were all either smashed in or boarded up, the outside was covered in graffiti and the land around the building was littered with broken office furniture, boxes of papers, discarded mattresses and anything else people didn't want or need anymore. It was perfect for them.

A disused building like this didn't attract visitors

and they would always find one that was too hard for homeless people to get into. Blair looked just like any casual teenager on her phone, except she wasn't checking a social-media feed, she was scanning every angle and direction for any kind of threat. She had taken a different route back to their base every time, just one of the many measures to ensure she wasn't being watched or followed. When they had arrived here a month ago, Blair has spent the night creating a hidden entrance that she could access speedily. The huge pile of rubbish sitting across the entrance looked completely impenetrable; it was around 20 feet high and sat between dense overgrown weeds and brambles.

Blair quickly ducked under a sheet of blue plastic and crawled through the back of an old desk. She turned and pulled the plastic back down, putting a brick on it to secure it to the floor. Then she carefully moved aside a sharp mesh of chicken wire and crawled under a row of wooden school chairs, which led her safely to the other side of the mountain of weeds. If someone was determined to get through her makeshift tunnel, they probably could do so, but the idea was to slow an intruder down.

Blair stayed in a crouch for a moment, closed her eyes and listened intently. When she was sure there were no sounds to concern herself with, she stood and walked to the nearest window. She climbed up onto the fat, concrete window ledge, reached over to her right and grabbed hold of a thick, iron downpipe. She pulled herself upwards; her feet left the window ledge and clamped around the pipe as she snaked up the side of the building, then in through the broken first floor window. Blair carefully lowered herself into a small room. Between now and the moment she had left the street, less than a minute had passed.

The floor was covered in broken glass from smashed light bulbs and shattered mirrors. Jagged pieces of splintered wood were piled up high and stuck out at all angles, making the room into a deadly obstacle course. When she had negotiated her way around each barrier without any harm, Blair stepped into a long corridor. She turned right and walked around the edge of the building, her hands out by her side, her face tilted up. Her father would be watching her on the camera she had set up, so she was showing him her face, letting him see that the visitor he was about to receive was a

254

friendly one. The last door was locked on the inside, so she waited. Her father would be working, and he could not be rushed. After almost five minutes, the silence was broken by the sound of locks being released and, at last, Blair pushed the door and stepped into the dank room in the cold, abandoned building that she now called home.

Whenever they had to choose somewhere new to operate, Blair's first job was to secure the building and make entry for any intruder as difficult as possible. But the room she stood in now, this was her father's domain, and he'd set it up exactly as he needed it. Blair attached a padlock to the inside of the door and slid various bolts into place. Karl was back in the far section of the large room, looking at a laptop and scribbling notes, completely lost in his work. He was surrounded by a set of desks set up in a 'U' shape. Spread out around him were various pieces of machinery, tools and technical drawings. In the far corner a generator gently hummed and coughed. Next to this, a large, wide object sat silent and ominous under a dirty, brown sheet.

Blair walked to the right, where their camp beds and a small stove were set up and placed her bag down.

'I need you,' Karl said, without looking up from the screen.

'Coming.'

Karl was around 55 years old, with thinning grey hair and a gaunt, haunted face. His nose and chin were both pointed and hooked; so much so, they seemed to be stretching out from his face and trying to meet up in front of his mouth. He had cold, grey eyes that matched the pale colour of his skin. He very rarely went outside, and Blair had to force him to eat and drink. The only thing he did consume with any regularity were foul-smelling brown cigarettes that made the damp, musty building smell ten-times worse.

'Anything to report?' Karl asked, still focused on his work.

'The woman who works for Ravensbrook is scratching around in the dark. They don't know anything about Miranda, they're getting desperate.' She paused. 'Like us.'

'Anything on the boy?'

'No, they lost him,' Blair said wearily.

Karl stopped. One of the cigarettes stuck out from between his yellowed teeth. He clamped down on it and drew in a breath; the end of the cigarette glowed like lava in the half-light of the room and a boulder of ash dropped onto the desk. He removed the cigarette from his mouth and slung it into an empty baked bean tin next to his computer.

'Have you lost faith in me, my dear?' Karl asked, clearly irritated.

'No, father,' Blair replied, unconvincingly.

Karl tilted his head as he regarded her. 'This journey has been our life for many years, but recently I've watched you change from an adventurous, wide-eyed child into a sceptical young woman - weary and full of doubt for what we're trying to achieve. Unless I'm mistaken?'

'You are mistaken.'

'That's good, my angel, because we are so close.'

'Are we? Are we really?'

'Have I ever lied to you?'

'No. But I think you've wanted this so badly, for so long, that you've let it consume you. You would believe it even if it weren't true.'

He paused, took out another cigarette and struck a match. His grey eyes seemed to shine in the flash of the flame before he discarded it into the bean can. He took a deep drag on the cigarette. 'You're worried about me, I can see that, but don't be. I have made the adjustments and the Chamber is finally ready.'

'It is?'

Her father's smile confirmed it. She had once again become the excited child he had missed so dearly. 'Absolutely.'

Karl moved away from the desks and over to the object while Blair followed. She watched as her father pulled away the sheet, revealing a tube that looked like a one-man submarine; it was copper in colour and was plugged into the generator. There was a clear glass window on the top of it and two white tubes that were attached to the old pipework in the corner of the room.

'When do I leave?'

'You have to go now. But listen to me, please. It will hurt, Blair. I can't begin to tell you how much it will hurt.'

'I'm ready for it. I understand.'

Karl placed the cigarette on the edge of the desk and held his hands up like he was praying. 'No, you don't. It will be more painful that anything you've ever known.'

She walked to her father and placed her hands around his. 'But it will be worth it. We've talked about this and it's the only way.'

'I'm rather afraid it is. On top of that, you'll also be walking directly into harm's way. We know for certain others will be there too.'

'You taught me to stay out of sight, remember?'

'I did, and you're so very good at it, but we need to know who else was there – we need to know why. That's the whole operation. Now, let's not waste time.' Karl broke free from his daughter, picked up the cigarette and put it between his teeth.

'I'll do whatever you need,' Blair said keenly.

'You need to make sure you hear whatever it was he told them, but do not, under any circumstances, disrupt their exchange. Bishop went missing that night and you jumping back cannot alter that.'

Karl walked over to the covered object and ran his hands over the sheet. 'Now, let's get to work.'

Blair eased herself down inside the Chamber and slid into what her dad called 'the sleeve'; it was more like a see-through plastic sleeping bag. Once she was in, she rested a small canister of air on her chest and put a breathing mask over her face. The smell of the old rubber in the mask always made her feel sick to her stomach, so she closed her eyes and fought against the reaction. Karl zipped up the sleeve and Blair was now in an air-tight bag, with only the sound of her breathing and her thumping heart for company.

Karl brought down the heavy lid with a thud that made Blair jolt with shock, then he fastened it in place with the bulky clamps. He picked up his laptop, took a deep breath and hit the 'enter' key. The generator began to rumble, knocking on the concrete floor as the white tubes attached to the buildings pipework suddenly stiffened and tensed. Karl looked in through the window at the distorted view of Blair's face through the thick plastic sleeve and the breathing mask; her eyes were wide and unblinking.

Suddenly, the water from the tubes began to fill the Chamber and Blair began to spin around inside it, rotating like a chicken on a spit. Karl put on a metal welder's mask as the lights around the window came on one by one and the speed of the spinning inside the Chamber increased until his daughter was no more than a blur of light and water; but he could still see her eyes, like a frightened animal with nowhere to run. Then, there was a sound like a muffled explosion, like a blue whale hitting the ocean after leaping into the air: 'WHUMP!'

The spinning slowed, the generator reduced back to a low hum, and now all the lights were glowing around the window on the Chamber, Karl could see that the sleeve was empty, his daughter was gone. Blair had jumped back in time.

Now their future was in her hands.

You'll Never Catch Her

The Dorchester Hotel, London – Two Weeks Ago

Arnold Bishop was desperately trying to keep a low profile. It had been a stressful few days to say the least and he had decided to leave his very nice flat and move into a hotel for a while. The Dorchester was expensive and full of rich people, which meant no one would pay much attention to a chubby, 50 year-old bald chap eating dinner alone. It still felt like an extravagance staying somewhere like this, and it bothered him that he had to. But since some uninvited guests had turned up at his flat last week and extracted information from him in several unpleasant ways, Bishop thought a short break somewhere he could remain anonymous was very much in order.

Even though he was doing his best to stay under the radar, he would be complaining to the manager the next time he went downstairs. The lift was out of order and seeing as his room was up on the eighth floor, Bishop had a lot of stairs to climb in the summer heat. He was fit enough, despite his expanded girth, but if he hated one thing, it was being hot, and right now he was dripping with sweat. He reached the top of the stairs and turned left towards his room.

His door was at the very end of the corridor and he was already dreaming about standing directly under the air conditioning unit as he opened it. As he entered his room, he was surprised to hear a *'PING!'* from the other end of the corridor. Sure enough, the lift arrived at his floor. Well, that *was* strange. Bishop was a suspicious man, and it had been a trait that had kept him alive in a profession that came with a short life expectancy. So he stood behind his door and watched through a crack as the lift opened to reveal two men, both in black suits.

He instinctively closed the door to his room and felt a surge of unwanted adrenaline. He was overreacting, getting himself worked up over nothing at all. The lifts had simply been fixed in the time it took him to lumber up the stairs; that was totally plausible. Of course, the alternative was that these two men had been sent by the same people who took him last week. They had tracked

263

him down and were about to extract him from the hotel.

He froze in place, his mind working in overdrive. He put his eye up to the peephole and saw both men walking quietly down the hallway, looking at the door numbers. He didn't recognise them, but he had been a spy for long enough to know when people didn't belong, and these guys were not here to change the towels. He had chosen this room because it had the service stairs right next to his door.

The men in black were still some way down the corridor, so Bishop had to move now to make the most of his head start. He gently pushed down on the door handle, stepped out, took two steps and then it happened – the one with the big nose snapped his head to the right and saw him. Bishop looked back at the man long enough to see that he didn't just have a big nose, he had a massive face on a huge head that sat atop a body the width of a small house. Bishop didn't wait for him or his shorter, rat-faced friend to exchange any words, he just bolted.

He burst into the stairwell and there, on the last step heading up towards his floor was an elderly lady. She glanced over her shoulder at a bellboy carrying two heavy suitcases and gave the man a piece of her mind.

'I don't expect to have to climb stairs at my age, you need to sort your lifts out.'

They both looked up at the sweaty man blocking their path. Bishop quickly reached out to the bellboy and grabbed one of the cases.

'Let me help you with that.' Bishop stepped towards the door, pulled it open and stood behind it, ushering the woman through.

Suddenly the smaller of the two men, the one with the rat face, scampered around the corner into the stairwell. Somehow, he stopped himself in the doorway, directly in front of the old lady. He had to grab her by the shoulders to avoid barrelling through her and knocking her to the floor.

'Good Lord! You want to slow down. You'll hurt someone.'

Rat Face screwed his face up in bewilderment.

'And you get your hands off me, young man!' The lady carried on as Rat Face regained his composure, released his grip and stood back out of the doorway.

'Yes, you're right. My apologies.' He forced a smile and nodded as she spoke. She wobbled through the doorway and out into the corridor.

Rat Face wasn't going to wait any longer. As soon as she was out of his path, he stepped through onto the landing of the stairwell. He looked at the bellboy in front of him and was about to shove him out of the way when he heard a little whistle from behind him. He turned and Bishop hammered him in the chest with the heavy suitcase. The force of it knocked Rat Face backwards into the bellboy. Bishop stood on his toes, watching as one of the men he was sure had come here to kill him fell backwards down 12 stairs, taking two suitcases and a 16 stone bellboy with him. He heard all kinds of snaps, unnatural crunches and yelps before he set off after the men. By the time they had settled in an untidy pile across the bottom of the steps, Bishop had launched himself over the handrail and down to the next flight of stairs. If Rat Face had come this way, then the smart money said that his house-sized friend with the big face was already on his way down to the lobby in the newly restored lift, which meant Bishop was now in a race to reach the front door first.

He got to the bottom of the service stairs, took a breath and walked out into the lobby. He was near the reception desk, which was on the right-hand side of the vast hotel foyer. The lifts were on the other side, over to the left of the entrance. In the middle was an enormous round sofa, with a large plant in the middle of it. Bishop could see the outside world, he could almost touch freedom, but between him and his escape was a bustling crowd of hotel guests.

The area around the reception desk was thick with suitcases, pushchairs, whining toddlers, flustered parents and bored teenagers. Bishop started to weave a pathway through, feeling out the shortest route to the exit. He risked a glance over towards the lifts but couldn't see any sign of the man-mountain. With a guy that size, Bishop could keep his head low and he'd still be able to see him coming.

He was about halfway through the queue of people at the desk when he saw the Mountain appear in the corner of his eye. The big man took a long stride into the foyer and immediately began to scan the crowd. Bishop swallowed down his fear, tried to keep his nerve and not let his fizzing adrenaline take over. He was an experienced spy who had spent a lot of his life very close to danger and still managed to dodge it; but he knew what these people were like and he couldn't help but be scared out of his wits. So what he should do and what he actually did were two very different things.

Bishop immediately stopped weaving and started pushing and shoving his way through the crowd. This led to the people around him starting to protest, which just made him even more anxious, so he pushed harder. Within seconds, any notion he had of getting out of the hotel without rousing suspicion had evaporated. He was causing a commotion that started to spread out around him like ripples in a pond – and now he had to run for his life.

He bulldozed his way free of the pack of protesters and, as he did, he saw that the mountain was now moving towards him, ready to cut off his chances of getting to the front door. Bishop looked ahead and saw he had one chance. It was a crazy idea, but if he didn't try it, then the big man would be on him in a matter of seconds.

He took a run up and leapt onto the round sofa, planting his foot between a boy, completely lost in his Nintendo Switch, and a man reading a newspaper. Bishop leapt, crashed through the leaves of the big plant and stumbled off the other side of the sofa, just as the Mountain was coming in from the right. As Bishop landed on the floor, another man stepped forward to berate him: a small, officious American, with short, spiked hair that gave his pale head a perfectly flat top. The man waved an arm weighed down with a big, gold watch. Bishop looked through him to the Mountain, who was allowing himself a confident smile as he closed in.

Bishop took two steps and powered upwards through Flat Top, hitting him in the chest like an American football player, lifting the tourist off his feet and forcing him backwards. Mountain was ridiculously huge, more like a character from a graphic novel than a real human; but the force of being hit by Flat Top was still enough to send him into a spin. The American and the Mountain tumbled backwards onto the floor and Bishop didn't hesitate – he burst past the tangle of limbs and made straight for the front door.

Blair was still very weak. Her mind was sharp, but she had so little strength that just walking here had left her completely exhausted. Her father had been right about the strains of making the jump, so she had found a place to hide and stayed out of sight for a few hours.

She checked the large bracelet around her wrist. Her father had clamped it on her before she'd climbed into the Chamber and she was pleased to see that all of the lights around the bracelet were still gleaming, which meant she had plenty of time. Her father had explained to her that the lights let her know how much power there was left in the Chamber back in her own time. If the lights went out, she would be lost here and could give up hope of ever getting home.

Blair knew where Bishop was going to be, she knew when he was going to disappear, she just didn't know how or why; but she was about to find out. She walked slowly along the edge of Hyde Park. It was a huge space and was probably quite beautiful, especially on a summer evening such as this, but Blair didn't have the luxury of looking at the world through the eyes of a tourist. Like every other place she had been in her life, she had a specific purpose. She looked out over the park, which was mostly empty now, and thought about the best place to position herself. Then she heard it – a scream from somewhere behind her.

Blair turned to see a man explode out of the door of the Dorchester Hotel. He stopped for a moment, his head spun left and then right, before he burst into a run, straight towards her. Instinctively, she knew this had to be Bishop. Her father's warning sounded in her head like an alarm; she couldn't come into contact with him, she couldn't influence what was about to happen, even though she had no idea what exactly *was* about to happen.

Blair looked behind her – the nearest entrance to the park was five metres away. She walked calmly, not too fast and not too slow, her legs still felt like jelly. She heard a car horn blast a warning and turned to see Bishop scrape himself from the bonnet of a taxi as he crossed the road towards the park. Blair made it to the entrance before Bishop was up on the pavement and as she turned into the park, out of sight from the road, she started to run.

Her legs immediately felt like they wouldn't hold her, the blood rushed to her feet and every muscle was screaming at her to stop. She ignored it, gritted her teeth and pushed harder. Somehow she was sprinting but she didn't know where she was heading to. She looked left and saw a bench sat in front of thick bushes. She reached it, skidded to the ground, and lay down behind it in the cover of the foliage. She immediately looked right towards the entrance, but there was no sign of Bishop. She closed her eyes for a second; the blood was throbbing through her legs and her heart was racing. She was in total agony, but she controlled it and swallowed the pain back down. She would have time to lick her wounds later but for now, she had to focus. Where the hell was Bishop?

Then her question was answered. First, a single arm and leg swung over the wall into the park, further down from the entrance. As he threw his other leg over and fell to the ground, two men appeared at the entrance around 20 metres away from him. Bishop was a big man, but he moved quickly. Blair could see he was fading, though, and even from this distance she saw the signs in his body language that he was resigned to his fate. He turned his head and saw the two men; they were jogging now. That was it, Bishop was done and he wasn't going to fight the inevitable – he knew it was all over.

Then the strangest thing happened, and Blair had to

almost hold her breath. Bishop reached the bench Blair had hidden behind, stopped and collapsed on it. He was panting like a dog in the sun, gasping from his exertion. The two men arrived; they seemed unhappy at having to run after him, like it was an inconvenience. Even before anyone spoke, Blair could tell that she was watching three people who knew each other. Not like friends or brothers know each other; more like two bullies tormenting their favourite victim.

There was a streetlamp next to the bench, and through the thick cover of the shrubbery, Blair could see the back of Bishop's bald head, gleaming with droplets of sweat under the light. She could also see the two men now. One of them was the biggest man Blair had ever laid eyes on, absolutely colossal, like a refrigerator in a suit. His face was powerfully ugly, everything just looked too big, it was like a child had drawn the image of a devil they saw in their nightmares.

'Why did you run?' the big man spoke, and his entire hideous face seemed to play a part in forming each word.

'I didn't exactly have a lot of fun the last time we got together, Bakker,' Bishop replied. He didn't sound scared at all, more frustrated.

'Oh, Bishop. That hurts my feelings.'

'Yeah, well, disappointment is one of life's harsh realities – deal with it.'

The big man, Bakker, laughed. The sound was deep and rasping, like a motorbike misfiring; it made the hair on Blair's neck stand on end.

'Why are you even here? I gave your boss everything he wanted. I gave you the kid and you paid me back with some rather poor hospitality. So whatever Mr Van Cleef wants this time, consider me unavailable.'

'You lied to us.'

'No, I did not.'

'You told us you didn't know where the Capshaw woman was. That wasn't true.'

'It was. I don't.'

'You telephoned her, Bishop! We know you did!'

Bishop was quiet. His breathing had finally begun to settle back to normal. 'I contacted her, yes. But I didn't know where she was, so, technically, I didn't lie to you.' He held his hands up, like a magician who had just made a dove disappear. 'You didn't ask me if I knew how to contact her, you just asked if I knew where she was. Wherever you came from, they didn't teach interrogation very well, I'm afraid, old chap.'

'You think you're so clever, you English, but you're just boring.'

'Oh, say it isn't so. I honestly thought we were onto something, you and me. Does this mean no third date?'

'Keep going with your jokes.'

'I mean, it's not like I was going to invite you over to mum's for Christmas dinner or anything, but I was planning to follow you on Instagram.'

Bakker took something out of his pocket. Blair couldn't see what it was, but she noticed a flash of silver as it caught the lamp light. Was it a knife? Were they going to kill him here, in front of her? Her breath snatched in her throat as Bakker stretched out a long leg and put it on the bench next to Bishop. The big man leant forward and rested an elbow on his knee. Then, almost in a whisper, so quiet that Blair had to strain to hear it, he spoke.

'You know something, Bishop? We'll find Miranda Capshaw and when we do, she will know that you gave up the kid. I will tell her that myself. We will have him very soon.'

'It'll be too late,' Bishop said, his bravado faltering under his quivering voice. 'You really don't get it, do you? It's all about her, you total cretin! And the fact is, you'll never catch her – she's already gone back.'

'Back? Back to where? What are you talking about?' Bakker looked at him, unsure if Bishop was just stringing him along.

Bishop leant forward and put his head in his hands.

'I asked you a question, Bishop. Where has Miranda gone back to?'

Bishop's shoulders began to move up and down, sobbing noises growing louder as he rubbed his eyes with the heels of his palms. Bakker turned his face towards his little friend and shook his head at the pathetic sight. But when Bishop pulled his hands away, it became clear that he wasn't crying at all; he was laughing at them.

'You're never going to tell me, are you?'

'Of course I'm not!' Bishop said. His laughter died out and he took a long breath. 'Whatever you're going to do, just get on with it.'

Without warning, Bakker raised his hand and there was a burst of light. Blair tried to blink it away. The light disappeared almost as soon as it arrived but as her vision cleared, what it left was something Blair would never forget. She quickly clamped her hand over her mouth to stifle a scream and watched as Bakker and his accomplice turned and walked out of the park, back towards the road. She allowed herself small breaths behind her hand and felt the tears pour down over her fingers. Because now she knew how Bishop had vanished without a trace.

What was left of the old spy oozed and dripped down through the wooden slats in the bench and onto the ground, Blair knew she had to get back to her father without delay. She had to tell him that the people hunting down everyone involved in Operation Hurricane had come back here from the future; and they had brought some toys with them.

I've Got This Friend

FrakeNews **Headquarters – Present Day**

'We need to go,' Boyd said, panicking. 'We need to go now!'

He had watched his aunt talking to the Italian man behind the counter in the café and now she was sitting outside in a 4x4, seemingly going nowhere. His heart was beating out of his chest. He felt like he was being chased, even though she was out there and he was in here. Surely there was no way she could really know where he was.

She looked so different. On the black and white camera, Boyd could see her hair was light, like she had dyed it blonde and her clothes were so completely different to anything he had ever seen her wearing. This, along with everything else he had discovered in the last hour, just made him feel like his life was turning into some kind of nightmare. Maybe that was it, maybe he was still asleep in the van on Bloomfield beach and he would wake up to find that none of this was real.

'Boyd, listen to me,' Skye grabbed him by the shoulders, shaking him out of his daydream. 'It'd take an army to get through the doors of this place and that's even assuming anyone would know where to look.'

'Think about everything I've told you. Now put that together with everything you've told me. Do you want to bet on these people not having an army?' Boyd shrugged her off and started looking for his rucksack.

Skye tilted her head, then nodded. 'That's a fair point but you need to calm down and think this through.'

Boyd stopped and took a deep breath; he realised his fists were clenched so tight by his sides, his fingers were digging into his palms and his knuckles were pale white.

Skye pointed at the image of the Range Rover on the screen. 'We've got a camera as flat as a two-pence piece set into the logo on the café sign. So, if they make a move, we'll see it coming.' She turned to look at Boyd. 'They tracked you here, which means they've either been following you all along, they accessed CCTV or they hacked the email you sent. But, they aren't sure where you are now - which means, she is sitting there, banking on you letting your emotions take over and deciding your best option is to run for it.' Skye sat down at the screen and pulled up the other chair. 'She knows you pretty well, I reckon.'

Boyd knew instantly that Skye was right; they were safer in here. He just had to come to terms with that feeling of not being able to control the situation;. he was going to have to wait it out. 'So, presuming we get out of here, someday soon, what's our next move?' he asked.

'A closer look at this guy, Bishop.'

'The one who no one's seen in two weeks?'

'Right. We got into his bank accounts.'

Boyd's eyes widened. 'Illegally?'

'No, Boyd, we asked his mum really nicely.' She rolled her eyes. 'Yes, of course we did it illegally! Anyway, he rents a flat not far from here.'

'How far, exactly? Can we get a bus?'

'Typical teenage boy! It's a half-hour walk, sweet pea, if you reckon you can manage it!'

'Just to remind you, I've been shot at, thrown around in a car chase and pedalled halfway across London to get your handbag back, only to find it wasn't stolen in the first place. So, I apologise if a brisk walk across town doesn't exactly sound like my ideal way to spend an afternoon,' Boyd said with a smile.

Skye laughed and held her hands up. 'Fair point.'

'Surely the police would have been through this Bishop's flat already, though, right?'

'They don't know he's missing; no one's reported it.'

'So how do we know he is actually missing?'

'Because MI5 have been talking about him.'

'Did his mum tell you *that*?' He smirked.

'No – someone there talked to someone here.'

'Okay, so we should get ready to leave. We need to be over there as soon as this lot have left.' Boyd pointed at Aurora's Range Rover on the screen.

'We can go tomorrow, when Hae is back,' Skye said.

'Who's Hae?'

'She works for me. She has the ability to make doors open, if you get me. So, we wait. Unless you know someone else who can pick a lock and disable an alarm system?'

Boyd smiled. 'Funny you should ask,' he said.

Escaped Prisoner

Fitz had spent most of the morning doing everything in his power to avoid starting the painting in the front room. He had loaded the dishwasher, put some washing on, unloaded the dishwasher, hung the washing out and was now gluing his mum's favourite vase back together. Fitz was inspecting seventeen pieces of broken china under the magnifying glass on his worktop when the computer pinged; Boyd was calling.

Fitz opened the channel so they could speak and put on his headphones. 'Boyd, you okay?'

'We need you up here, as soon as possible.'

'I'm grounded, remember? I'm an actual prisoner in my own home.'

'Listen. I'm going to send you an address. It's a flat we need to break into. Get your backside on a train and meet me there. I've got to go.' He hung up.

'Boyd!' Fitz yelled into his computer. 'Boyd!' No response. He sat back in his chair. 'Oh, for crying out loud,' he said quietly.

'Fitzgerald, are you going to get on with this painting or what?' Marjorie Tork called up the stairs.

'It's next on my list.'

'Glad to hear it. You know I can't abide the smell of paint; I'll be outside in my office.'

'Of course, mummy dearest.'

'Sarcasm, young man – is the lowest form of wit.'

'But the highest form of intelligence.' Fitz muttered.

'Excuse me?' His mum called out.

'Nothing.'

Fitz got out of the chair, grabbed his rucksack and started packing some supplies for a trip to London. Breaking into a flat – that was a step up from getting suspended. It would be easy enough, depending on the alarm system.

When he had everything he thought he might need, Fitz put the bag aside and thought about the painting.

He made a clicking sound as he looked around the room, his brain whirring, shuffling through one idea after another. Then it came to him – he knew exactly how he was going to paint the front room without actually being in the house.

A Fly On The Wall

Roger Tork had been told he could leave work early and take the afternoon off. Normally this would be a welcome surprise, especially in half-term and with Fitz at home. But today wasn't normal at all for more than one reason. Firstly, his son was painting the front room at home today and the boy was prepared to do virtually anything to get out of doing the job. He also knew that the smell of paint set off his wife's migraine headaches, so the opportunity of a half-day at home was not quite as sweet a prospect as it had first sounded.

Another reason today was far from normal: his boss had told the whole team to go home – the entire floor, every single one of them. Roger had watched as they packed up and were shuffled out the door. Working for the Home Secretary meant you often stayed at the office long into the night, came in at weekends and gave up a large slice of your life to help keep the country safe. The modest glass office was always buzzing with government workers and visitors;. There was a constant hum of people on phones and days were packed with meetings and conferences – it was part of the reason why Roger enjoyed his job so much.

So when the Home Secretary, Octavius Ogilvy, sent everyone home on a Monday afternoon, Roger knew something was very wrong indeed. Whatever was going on, it had something to do with that odious little toad, Percy Hoggsby, who apparently didn't have the afternoon off and would remain glued to the Home Secretary's side. This was not good news for Roger, not good at all. Roger and Percy were constantly competing for Ogilvy's attention and recently, Percy had been winning. Roger couldn't let that continue. So, whatever little scheme Percy was cooking up, Roger was determined to uncover it. He reminded himself that he wasn't doing this to be a snoop. He wasn't a bad person, it was just that Percy was a treacherous little slimeball and sometimes, the Home Secretary needed protecting from himself.

The day had been drifting along a familiar course; Roger was sitting at his desk, working on a speech for Octavius, when Percy scurried from the lift, leading two unannounced strangers towards the Home Secretary's office. Roger immediately stopped typing and watched with great interest. The two men made it as far as the waiting room outside Octavius's office. Only a moment later, the Home Secretary came out, walked anxiously by the two men and told everyone to head off home, as if it was the most natural thing in the world. Of course, most people packed up and headed out as quickly as possible. But with just one look at these two characters, Roger knew he couldn't go anywhere until he had found out what was going on.

One of the men was so tall, he had to duck to get through doorways. Roger had tried not to stare at him, but he looked like a reflection in a hall of mirrors; every feature, every limb looked like it was magnified to horrific proportions. He resembled the result of some kind of experiment. Roger had quickly looked away when the man's shark-black eyes menacingly flicked towards him. The other man was smaller but also broad, like a rugby player, and he sported thin, slicked back black hair that shone almost wet against his pale skin, as if he'd swum here. Both were dressed head-to-toe in black and were far removed from the usual type of suited visitor they received here at the heart of the British government.

Roger had packed his things, grabbed his jacket and headed towards the lift, but he only went down one floor. There was clearly no chance that Roger could get into Octavius Ogilvy's office, but luckily, he didn't need to.

Roger had noticed a few months ago that good old Percy seemed to have a lot of information from meetings he hadn't even been in. He also noticed that Percy liked to go on his 'little walks' around the building to 'work on his daily steps' – so one day, Roger followed him. Percy had headed down one floor to the stationary cupboard and disappeared inside. Roger had waited until the little reptile had left and then searched the room. On the bottom shelf, right at the back, behind a box of Post-it-notes, was a small box. Roger had opened it and found a small receiver with a set of headphones. The little rat had bugged the boss' office and had been listening to every word the Home Secretary said! Roger hadn't taken the evidence to Octavius because he knew it would come in handy some day; it seemed that day had arrived.

Roger stood in the cubicle of the men's toilet and popped the headphones into his ears just as Percy ushered the two strange visitors into the Home Secretary's office.

All Friends Here

'Thank you, Percy. You can toddle off home now,'
Octavius Ogilvy said as he removed his reading glasses
and put down the note his assistant had given him. He
didn't look at Percy Hoggsby; he was too busy staring at
his visitors. Ogilvy's chubby, sweaty face wobbled with
indignation as he tried to act like a man in control. The
Home Secretary was a large man who wore his pinstripe
suit trousers high above his ample waist and held them
in place with thick, red braces. His hair was almost gone
but what was left was dyed black and manipulated into
a hideous comb-over in a vain attempt to disguise his
obvious baldness. He took out a handkerchief and
dabbed carefully at his brow, ensuring he didn't disturb
the carefully crafted bird's nest on his head.

'I'll stay, thank you, Octavius.'

The reply from Hoggsby caught Ogilvy off guard
but before he had a chance to question it, the man with
the wet black hair stepped forward.

'I see from your reaction to my note that we understand each other,' he smiled, revealing a set of almost triangular, pointed teeth.

Ogilvy flinched at the sight. The man had a chilling smile, like a piranha fish. 'I understand nothing. Absolutely nothing,' Ogilvy said, shaking his head. As he did, his plump chin swayed back and forth over the knot of his tie.

'Come now, Octavius, neither of us has time for games,' the man said again. His voice was low and scratchy, like he needed to clear his throat. 'A one-word note, and you send the entire office home? You know what it means, you just don't know why I am here.'

'Well, perhaps you can help a chap out on that score – who are you?'

'My name is Van Cleef and this is my colleague, Mr Bakker.'

Ogilvy glanced quickly at the colossus of a man who was standing next to Percy Hoggsby. Percy was a tall, slim man with pale skin and a frizz of ginger hair. But next to Bakker, Percy looked like an infant of a different species entirely.

'And what do you know about...' he lifted the note

290

from his desk… 'this?'

'Hurricane?'

Ogilvy visibly shuddered.

'Well, my information is vast and extremely accurate. I got it first-hand, in fact.'

Ogilvy snorted in anger and turned to his assistant. 'Percy, listen, I must insist, off you pop home now, please.'

Hoggsby didn't move.

'Percy! I don't want to get into disciplinary action, but I will!' Ogilvy banged his hand on the desk.

'Please, Home Secretary,' Percy stepped forward, 'don't embarrass yourself.' Hoggsby lifted the lapel of his suit jacket and underneath it was a solid-gold badge pin.

Ogilvy stared at it in wonder; it was a large capital 'T', the bottom of which was sharp like a spike. He hadn't seen that emblem in a very long time. As he turned back to Van Cleef, he saw that his visitor had pulled a necklace out from under his black shirt; on the chain was the same emblem.

'You see,' Hoggsby said. 'There's nothing to fear. We are all friends here.'

Ogilvy's shoulder slumped as he sank into his large, leather office chair and desperately tried to make sense of what was happening in front of him. The chair squeaked and creaked with every deep breath he took. 'What is your interest in Hurricane? It was all a very long time ago. I was barely involved, truth be told.'

'Tut-tut, Octavius. I know that's not the case,' Van Cleef said, a lizard-like smile stretched out across his face.

'You can't possibly know anything!'

'But I do. A very dear friend of mine was there when it all unfolded, and he happily provided me with all the juicy little details.'

'Oh, is that so?' Ogilvy threw his hands in the air like a child throwing a tantrum. 'And pray, what else did your dear friend tell you, hmm?'

'He told me that if I came back here and spoke to you,' Van Cleef said as he leant forward and put both hands on Ogilvy's desk, 'we could work together to build a power the likes of which most men can only dream about and the world will be ours for the taking.'

Ogilvy looked into Van Cleef's wide, maniacal eyes. 'Who on earth told you that?'

'You did Octavius, my friend. You did.'

Except for his rapidly blinking eyes, Ogilvy sat perfectly still.

'You see, you're the man who gave me the account of what happened on Hurricane Island.'

'Impossible! I never speak of it. And anyway, if I had met you before, I am fairly certain I would remember.'

Van Cleef stood up straight. 'You're correct, we haven't met before. Our conversation about Operation Hurricane doesn't happen for another 20 years.'

Ogilvy's lips slowly parted as his chins dropped, covering the knot on his tie. 'Do you mean to tell me that you're here from… you've come back here…'

'You will come to me many years from now and you will tell me everything. Then you will send me here with a simple message; we need to find the boy, today, right now.' Van Cleef pointed to the phone on Ogilvy's desk.

'I suggest you make the call – we need to bring the Guild back together before we run out of time.'

This Is My Fight

'So, who's your mate?' Skye asked him. They were still sat watching Aurora's 4x4 on the monitor. Boyd had his chin on the desk.

'Fitz? He's not really my mate.'

'You're not exactly a warm and fuzzy type, are you, Boyd?'

'I might have heard that somewhere before.'

Skye laughed. 'Well, whoever he is, you'd better be able to vouch for him. I've broken so many of my own rules in the last couple of hours, letting you into our world, and now I'm trusting this Fitz kid too. If either of you screw me over…'

'You'll end us, I know. I remember the speech. We won't, you can trust me, and Fitz is as loyal as they come.' Boyd let the words hang in the air for a moment. 'I guess he is my friend; probably the only one I've got.'

'Then do yourself a favour and don't let him down.' Skye finished a bottle of water she had on the desk.

Boyd sat up and looked at Skye. She turned to face him. 'Can I ask you a question?' he said.

'Depends what it is.'

'Why do you take all these things on? You're not much older than me but while I'm getting suspended for cheating on a maths test, you're posting videos online about the government and being threatened by the Home Secretary.'

'Ha! Yeah, old Octavius. Dude's a charmer, isn't he?'

'Azima said he's doing everything he can to try to find out who's behind *FrakeNews*?'

'Yeah, but our people are good, and we're used to staying out of sight. He's a slippery fish, and he's very careful to make sure he doesn't do any of his own dirty work.'

'So just put something out there to show everyone what he's like.'

'Easier said than done. Like I said, he's careful, but he's a solid-gold douchebag, I'm sure of it. It wouldn't surprise me one bit if he was up to his neck in all of this.'

'I still don't get why you bother. You've got tons of money, right? So, buy an island and get away from him; get away from everyone.'

'Stick my head in the sand? That's your answer for everything? Nah, not my style. See, I feel the exact opposite of everything you said earlier. This *is* my problem, because this is my world and it should damn well be a fair one.'

'You think I don't agree with that?'

'It didn't sound like it.'

'No, I do. I just don't think it's our fight right now.'

Skye tilted her head. 'So, whose fight is it? The "adults"? What if they're part of the problem? Like Ogilvy and his crew – how are they helping me or you? Can you trust your aunt? – or your dad? Maybe we leave it to them to sort the world out? No, the world is full of fakes who pretend to care and cowards who stand back and leave it to someone else to wade in and do something. Well, not me. I got given a voice, so this is my fight. It's everyone's responsibility to ask "why" and to shout "stop" if they see injustice. And if Azima is right about what someone is doing out there, then we need to stop it.'

'But if Azima is right, then surely it's a good thing? We could fix so much stuff if we had the chance to go back and do it all over again. Imagine a world without

Hitler or Bin Laden – what would be so bad about that?'

They had both turned away from the screens now, totally engrossed in their debate.

'See, you're immediately thinking that this would be like *Back To The Future*, or Indiana Jones taking on the Nazis, when it just won't be like that, Boyd.'

'You don't know what it could be like.'

'I do, trust me on that.'

'How can you say that?'

'Imagine the most hateful, corrupted person you can think of and now imagine they have the ability to travel through time. Do you really think they're going to go back and stop bad things from happening? No. You can't dream up what they'll do because you're a million miles away from being as twisted as they are. Something this heavy never ends up in the hands of good people. Trust me, if they succeed then the world is about to get a whole new set of problems. So, if I can stop it, damn right I'm going to.'

They both turned back to the screen and sat in silence for a few minutes. Then Skye took her feet off the desk and clicked on the other screen, bringing up the images captured a few minutes ago by the café camera.

There she was, Aurora, but not as Boyd knew her.

'She looks like she could do some damage.' Skye followed this with a whistle.

'She looks so different,' Boyd replied, confused.

'You said she was a hippy, all baggy tops and beads.'

'She is – or was – that doesn't even look like her.' Boyd leant forward, hit the space bar and the screen paused. He saw the sneering look Aurora was giving the café owner, like a predator toying with her prey. 'That's how she looked at me the other night.' Boyd stared at the screen and narrowed his eyes. 'I'd never seen her be like that before. Now the hair, the clothes; it's like I don't know who she is.'

'I think we need to start working on the premise that maybe you actually don't; maybe she's never been who you think she is.'

Both of them were suddenly drawn to the other screen as Aurora's Range Rover slowly pulled away.

'Sweet,' Skye said. 'Let's go and do some breaking and entering.'

Another Fine Mess

Roger Tork had bought himself a white-chocolate
Magnum in the newsagents on the way home from the
train station because he figured he deserved it. He had
made good his escape from the office toilet as soon as
the man who called himself Van Cleef had told the
Home Secretary that he had to make a phone call. Since
then, Roger had spent his entire train journey trying to
work out what on earth was going on.

What was Hurricane? How would Octavius Ogilvy
send these two characters to meet himself if he didn't
even know them; and how the hell had Percy Hoggsby
managed to speak to their boss like that and not get
himself fired? Whatever it was, it sounded like a heap of
trouble that Roger didn't need. He had never heard
Octavius Ogilvy so scared – petrified, in fact. So he
would keep an eye on it from a distance and leave it to
Percy to get covered in whatever mess was coming.

Roger sat in his car, ate his Magnum and tried to put

it all out of his mind. Once he finished the ice cream, he headed for the house. As he opened the front door, the smell of paint hit him immediately. He set his briefcase down in the hallway and decided he might as well see how the poor lad was getting on – he might be ready for a tea break.

He opened the door to the front room and slowly scanned the scene in front of him; his jaw dropped in sheer disbelief. All the furniture had been moved into the middle of the room and covered in plastic sheeting. There, on the floor, was a modified radio-controlled car. Fixed to its back was a wire basket containing an industrial-sized paint pot. There was a piece of hose trailing out of the pot and into a nozzle attached to the car roof. This nozzle was twisting and turning, spraying paint over the walls. Sitting behind the paint pot in a cradle was an iPad, the screen of which had a set of dimensions and calculations on it. Roger looked closer and saw that they were plans and measurements for the front room.

He had to hand it to his son, it was an ingenious way of completing a truly hideous chore without actually having to be there to do it and, for the most part, the plan was working pretty well. The only problem, which Roger felt compelled to step in and sort out before his wife inspected the work, was that Fitz hadn't factored in the windows. So, much like the walls, they were also now a very nice shade of yellow desert sunbeam.

Break And Enter

Bishop's flat was in a smart, modern-looking building called the Oxo Tower, which overlooked the River Thames. Boyd hadn't stopped looking over his shoulder the whole way. Seeing Aurora turn up at the café like that had knocked him sideways and even though Skye had done her best to keep him talking, he felt like he wanted to be sick; his insides were twisting and turning. He couldn't shake the image of his aunt from his mind. Skye was right, he was starting to believe he didn't know her at all.

They were standing by the railings, looking out at the river, when Fitz approached them. 'I told you you'd need me,' he said with a smile. He held out his fist and Boyd gave it a bump.

'So, what did you tell your parents?'

'I didn't tell my parents anything. I'm grounded, remember?'

'But they'll freak when they find out you've done a

runner!'

'Nah, it'll be fine. I'll help you guys out and get back before they even know I've gone. Piece of cake.' Fitz looked at Skye and gave her a suspicious smile. 'And you are?'

'A nobody. Shall we do this?' She marched through the middle of them and headed towards the flats.

They both followed. Fitz looked at Boyd and raised his eyebrows. 'You seem to have a knack for associating yourself with such friendly people.'

'She's fine, give her a break.' Boyd shook his head.

'Oh, I see!'

'What? What do you see?'

'Hey, mate. Relax, I get it.'

'What? Oh, you think that I… no, absolutely not.'

'Hey, so she's a bit old for you. Look, I didn't say a word.' Fitz smiled.

'You didn't need to, and, for the record, I don't fancy her.'

'Okay, that's good.'

'Yeah, exactly, because we need to stay focused on what's important here.'

'You're right. And, because that means the path is

clear for me to utilise the Tork charm…' Fitz pretended to lick two of his fingers and stroke them across his eyebrows. Then he smoothed his hair and sniffed at his armpits.

'Wow.' Boyd raised his eyebrows. 'She doesn't stand a chance, does she?'

They both laughed as they walked around the corner and caught up with Skye. She was leaning against the wall and they couldn't be sure how much of their conversation she had overheard. They both stopped dead. Fitz stifled a laugh and Boyd opened his eyes wide.

'Who is this clown again?' Skye asked.

'Whoa!' Fitz said, clutching his chest as if her words had hurt him.

'This is Fitz,' Boyd said.

Fitz stuck out a hand. 'Charmed, I'm sure.'

'And right now, he's our best hope.'

Skye rolled her eyes. 'Wonderful. This way gentlemen.' She led them down a set of stairs to a single door. 'Lucky for us, it's a basement flat, so we won't be bothered while you work.'

Fitz looked at them both. 'So, let me get this

straight… getting me suspended for breaking into the headmaster's safe isn't quite enough for you; now you want me to break into someone's flat? Who even lives here?'

'A guy called Bishop,' Boyd said, shaking his head. 'And don't worry, he won't be bothering us. He's gone missing; he's very probably dead.'

'Oh well, that's fine.' Fitz exclaimed, his voice climbing up an octave. 'Has it even crossed your mind he might be in there, decomposing in his recliner in front of *Bargain Hunt*?'

Skye took a deep breath and spun around from the door. 'Look, are you going to pick the lock or am I going to get Bruce Banner here to turn green and smash the door down?'

'Hang on a minute,' Boyd protested. 'Was that aimed at me?'

Fitz laughed. 'She's got your number, mate!'

A hint of a smile flashed across Skye's face.

Fitz got on his knees in front of the door, eyed the lock and removed his backpack. 'Okay, back up and give me a minute. We won't be outside for long; it's nothing complicated. Just keep an eye out up there for anyone walking by.'

He slipped on a pair of surgical gloves and unrolled a leather pouch, which was full of what looked like small screwdrivers.

'What are those?' Boyd asked.

'It's my set of lock picks,' Fitz replied. 'Luckily, I rarely leave home without them.' He snuggled up to the door of Bishop's flat and regarded the lock.

'You're not going to be stubborn, are you? Not today, not for me?' he said, peering down his nose into the mechanism.

'Is this part of the Tork charm you mentioned?' Boyd asked sarcastically. 'Are you using it on the door right now? Because honestly, I think the picks would be a lot quicker.'

Fitz selected two picks, looked at them individually and then gently placed them both in the lock. 'You know, Boyd,' he said as he started to gently turn the picks, 'someone at some point made a grave mistake in telling you that you were funny.' He continued to lightly tweak the lock. 'And, as your friend, I see it as my responsibility to right that wrong.'

The door clicked. Fitz turned the handle and it

swung open. 'Boom,' he said as he rocked back and rested his back against the wall. He then raised his hand to gesture them inside. 'And that's how it's done.'

Boyd went in first, then Skye; Fitz followed and shut the door. He reached into his rucksack and took out two more pairs of gloves. 'May I suggest you both take these.'

Boyd and Skye each took a pair of gloves and snapped them over their hands.

'The alarm wasn't set.' Boyd lightly stroked the keypad in the hallway.

'Of course not,' Fitz whispered. 'That's because he's in the lounge, stuck to his armchair, turning into fungus.'

'No,' Skye said seriously. 'If he was, we'd have been able to smell him from outside.'

'Comforting.' Fitz screwed his face up. 'And I don't want to know how you know that.'

'So, what exactly are we looking for?' Boyd asked as they stood in the hallway.

'I'm not sure,' Skye said.

'I thought you had a lead or a tip-off or something we could use as a starting point? You said you had his bank records.'

'We do. If there's something in here, we'll find it. Be patient.'

'Not his strongest suit, unfortunately,' Fitz said.

Skye walked deeper into the flat. There were just four doors off the hallway and she pushed each one open. The first was the lounge. Fitz peered around the door to confirm that Bishop wasn't sat in the armchair. In fact, after a quick look in the kitchen, the bathroom and the bedroom, the one thing they noticed was just how clean and tidy the whole place was.

'Doesn't look like anyone has been here at all, except a very thorough cleaner.' Skye wiped her finger over the small table in the hallway and inspected it. Not even a speck of dust.

'Maybe that's the point,' Boyd suggested. 'You said MI5 knew he'd gone missing? From what I've seen in films, they'd turn the place upside down, then put everything back and scrub any trace that they'd ever been here.'

'Well, let's presume that whatever they were looking for, they didn't find it.' Skye pointed at Boyd. 'You take the bedroom.' Then at Fitz. 'You take the lounge. I'll do the kitchen and toilet. Holler if you find anything.'

They split up and started work. 30 minutes later, Fitz and Boyd headed for the kitchen where Skye was finishing up going through the fridge freezer.

'Nothing,' Fitz said and let out a frustrated huff. 'No passport, no computer, it's just weird, like a show-home.'

'Yeah,' Boyd agreed. 'Everything looks new. If he's gone anywhere, he left most of his very dull clothes here.'

'You want to see weird, you should see his fridge,' Skye said. 'It's basically empty. The cupboards too, not a scrap of fresh food in the place, but his microwave has certainly seen some use.'

'Yeah, that's not so hard to imagine for a bloke living on his own.' Boyd said.

He and Fitz sat down at the small dining table, both looking around the room, racking their brains for inspiration.

'Let's go back to basics – what was it MI5 told you about Bishop?'

'Hang on,' Fitz blinked rapidly as he turned to Skye. 'You actually spoke to MI5?'

'Not me personally, one of my team. But our contact there didn't give us any specifics, just that he suddenly went off-grid around the time of the surge and we should take a proper look at him.'

'What could he have known that meant he had to disappear?' Boyd asked, more to himself than anyone else.

'If I had to put money on it, I'd say Bishop was a spy.' They both looked at her quizzically. 'Who doesn't have a passport or a computer? Also, he has a new toothbrush and a new tube of toothpaste in the bathroom too; so, at a glance, it looks like he's still living here, but why are they brand new? He wanted people to think he was still here but he's on the run from something. You said yourself his clothes are dull, right? So he is someone who makes a point of trying to blend in; he doesn't want to stand out. Put that together with MI5 talking about him like he's a person of interest and I think we've got ourselves a spook.'

'It's strange,' Fitz said. 'But I'm suddenly reminded of how dangerous it feels to be sitting in his flat uninvited and we don't seem to be making any progress. So, unless anyone has any bright ideas as to where he might hide his little spy bits and pieces, I am going to pinch one of the microwave pizzas he has in the freezer and suggest we make tracks out of here, pronto.'

'Hang on.' Boyd clicked his fingers – an idea had come to him. He opened the dishwasher; it was empty except for knives and forks. He walked over to the bin and pressed his foot down on the pedal, and the lid popped open. He stuck his hand down inside and pulled out take away cartons and boxes for frozen ready meals.

'What are you thinking?' Skye asked.

Boyd moved over to the hob and looked at it carefully. Then he opened the oven door and pointed to the back of it.

'Clean as a whistle,' he said, again, almost to himself.

'Right, we've covered this, someone has cleaned the place,' Skye said.

'But they didn't empty the bins, or clean the microwave; so why take the time to clean the oven?'

He got down onto his haunches and stuck his hand in the oven.

'What are you doing, Boyd?' Fitz asked.

'The oven,' he replied, still feeling around inside it.

'It's not been cleaned. It's never been used.' Then he stopped moving, his eyes widened.

'What? You've found something? Tell us you've found something!' Skye said excitedly.

Boyd pulled and they heard a small ripping sound. He brought his hand out of the oven. 'I've found something.'

Lock And Key

Boyd was holding a small piece of metal with a strip of brown packing tape hanging off it.

'How did you know to look there?' Skye asked him.

'The guy doesn't ever use plates. There are no pots or pans or oven trays anywhere and all he eats is takeaways or microwave ready meals. Plus, my dad always hides stuff in the oven when we go away. He says no thief ever thinks of looking there, so it's like a safe you never have to lock.'

'Maybe your dad's a spy too,' Skye said, not entirely joking. Boyd ignored it. 'What is that?'

'It's an Allen key,' Boyd held it up.

'Like the things you use to put furniture together?' Fitz said, confused. 'Why the heck is he hiding that?'

'Because whatever it opens is really important to him,' Boyd said, looking at the key. 'Okay, we go back to our respective rooms and we look for anything that has a hex-shaped screw on it.'

'A what?' Skye shook her head.

'Any piece of furniture that is held together by a screw with a hexagonal head.' He held up the Allen key. 'This opens something in this flat and we need to find it.'

They split up again and within two minutes, Boyd was calling them into the bedroom. He had taken the key with him and started to remove the legs from the bed. By the time he called them in, the mattress was against the wall and the bed frame was on its side with three legs missing.

'What have you got?' Skye asked.

Boyd held two of the legs in his hands and tapped them together; the sound was exactly as you would expect from two pieces of solid wood being hit together. He put one down, picked up the third leg and repeated the exercise – the sound was different. He waved the third leg in the air. 'The bottom of this one is hollow.'

Boyd ran his gloved fingers over the leg, looking for a way to open it. Fitz and Skye got in close.

'There's a seam there,' Skye said, pointing to a faint line in the wood.

'Yep, he's sealed it with glue or something,' Boyd said.

'He's done a great job, really professional,' Fitz pointed out.

'Maybe he missed his true calling; maybe he should have been a carpenter. You should leave him a note, y'know, in case he comes back,' Boyd said sarcastically.

'Pass me that pen, I'll write it now.'

'Boys!' Skye brought them back down to earth. 'The sooner we figure out how to open this, the sooner you two can get back to your playdate.'

Boyd looked at Fitz and shook his head. Fitz raised his shoulders.

'What? She's right. Come on Hulk, just smash it open.'

Boyd gave a sarcastic smile and gently tapped the leg against the metal frame of the bed. Nothing happened. He gave it another tap, harder this time, and the piece of glued wood came away, revealing a screw with a hexagonal head.

'Sometimes, a little force is just what's required.'

Boyd set to work and soon the screw fell to the floor and the bottom half of the leg came away from the top. He reached inside and took out a roll of papers, which he held out for Skye to take. She flattened them out on

315

the chest of drawers and started reading. Boyd then pushed his fingers deeper down into the leg and took out another roll of papers, but this one was a thick wad of money with an elastic band wrapped around it.

'Jackpot,' Boyd said. 'I think we can be pretty sure that our assumptions about Mr Bishop weren't too far off the mark. Who keeps a wad of cash hidden like that?'

Fitz raised his eyebrows at the cash, then turned to Skye.

'What have you got?' Fitz leant over.

'A diary maybe? Lots of notes in code against certain dates,' Skye replied.

She handed the sheets over to Fitz. Boyd stood next to him and tried to make something of the scribbles.

'Okay then,' Fitz said, tapping the page in front of him. 'Looks like he was having meetings with some fella called Vic right up until he disappeared.' He pointed to certain days on the pages. 'That's the only pattern I can make out. So, who the heck is Vic?'

'If this guy is a spy, that could be a codename, which means it could literally be anyone in London,' Boyd said.

'Doesn't even have to be in London,' Fitz said

wearily. 'He could have been calling them, they could be anywhere.'

'No, wait a second.' Skye held a hand up. 'That name, Vic – that's ringing a bell. I know I've seen it somewhere.'

'Okay, so think,' Boyd insisted.

'Yes, great advice. Thank you, Boyd. I am trying.'

'Then try harder. This is important.'

'And it would be loads easier without you on my case,' Skye snapped at him.

Boyd looked at her coldly. Fitz pulled a face.

'You two sound like my parents,' Fitz said and laughed to try to break the tension. 'Last month, my dad bought a hot tub on the credit card and my mum went ballistic; they spent two weeks arguing about it…'

'That's it!' Skye's eyes grew wider. 'Credit card!'

She took a thin file out of her bag and opened it up. She pulled out a bunch of papers that she had hastily thrown into the file and frantically started leafing through them. She picked up the Allen key and used it to go down through each entry, line by line, until she found what she was looking for.

'Vic!' Skye flicked the paper with her finger. 'Gotcha!

Fitz, you're a genius!'

'Finally, the recognition I deserve,' Fitz replied.

'Bishop's credit-card statement shows that he bought drinks at The Old Vic theatre on the same exact dates in the diary. So Vic isn't a person...'

'...it's a place,' Boyd finished Skye's sentence and exhaled deeply. 'Looks expensive, maybe he bought two drinks - maybe he was meeting someone there.'

'Well, if he did,' Fitz said, holding the diary pages, 'then he was due to meet them again today.' He showed them the page, then checked his watch. 'Matinee performance starts in an hour. Anyone fancy a trip to the theatre?'

The Scalpel

'SOLD OUT.'

Boyd, Skye and Fitz stood staring at the sign on the pavement outside the theatre.

'So, what now? We're going in, right?' Fitz asked.

It had only taken them ten minutes to jog from the Oxo Tower on the Thames but now the clear blue sky of the morning was starting to fill with clouds as the first drops of a summer downpour fell. Fitz pulled the collar up on his rugby top, desperate to get off the street.

'One of us needs to go in, obviously,' Skye replied.

'What, with a sign around our necks saying, "Are you here to meet Bishop?"' Boyd said testily.

'No, listen! He must have had a ticket to get in there and sit at the bar, right? No trace of him buying any on the credit card and no ticket stashed away in his flat. I bet you anything there's a ticket sitting in that theatre waiting for him to collect it. He probably paid for it in cash.'

'Well,' Boyd said, 'there's only one way to find out.' He started to walk towards the front steps.

'Where do you think you're going?' Skye asked him, grabbing his arm.

Boyd looked down at her hand. 'I'm going in there to collect the tickets.'

'I don't think that's such a good idea, do you?'

'She's right,' Fitz said. 'This person Bishop was meeting could be anyone, could be one of the assassins who tried to hit you the other night.'

'Relax, Fitz,' Skye smirked. 'It's a London theatre on a weekday afternoon. Let's keep the drama on the stage, yeah?'

'So why is it not a good idea for me to go in, exactly?' Boyd asked, agitated.

'How can I put this without bruising your fragile ego?' Skye tapped her finger against her lips. 'Sometimes you need a sledgehammer…' Skye gestured towards Boyd… 'and sometimes you need a scalpel,' she said, holding her hands to her chest. 'Now is the time for the latter. This may require some diplomacy, and if things don't go to plan, I am good at talking my way around a situation.'

'And I'm not?' Boyd's eyes narrowed.

'You said it, not me. Not only that but Fitz actually makes a good point: what if the person Bishop was meeting knows who you are? Then we get nothing. You need to wait here.'

'No chance.' Boyd shook his head.

Skye turned to face him. 'Listen, we are running out of time and I'm not going to argue with you; stay put and watch the entrance. I can handle this. I've got my phone if anything goes wrong, okay?'

'She's right,' Fitz said, ruefully.

'Fine,' Boyd conceded. 'Go on then. But be careful.'

Skye smiled, then turned and casually joined the crowd heading for the front doors.

'We should wait over there,' Boyd pointed to some trees across the road. He put his hood up as the rain started to beat down onto the hot pavement. They crossed the street, and both tucked in under the trees.

'This is better,' Fitz said. 'Whoever he or she is, we might even get a look at them from here.'

'He,' Boyd said through gritted teeth.

'Well, that's a bit sexist. Spies can be women, Boyd.'

'Not this time.'

A tall man with black and grey hair in his forties walked around the corner on the other side of the road. He had pulled the collar of a leather jacket up to guard from the rain. Boyd pushed Fitz further back under the trees as the man glanced across the street in their direction. Boyd peered around a tree trunk.

'I should have known,' he said.

'Who?' Fitz insisted. 'Who is he?'

'That, is Aunt Aurora's friend: meet Harry the gardener.'

Two-Minute Warning

Skye had taken her seat in the theatre. The ticket was in Bishop's name and he had paid for it in person. Skye had turned on the tears, telling the box office manager that her uncle had bought it for her as a birthday present before he died. They let her in and gave her a free programme. Now she just had to wait.

'Ladies and gentlemen, the performance will begin in ten minutes. Thank you,' the voice over the public address system said cheerfully.

The orchestra began warming up and Skye was thinking that maybe she should stand at the back and get a good view of everyone as they took their seats, but before she could move, a well-groomed man in his forties, dressed in a smart shirt and an expensive jacket, dropped into the seat next to her. Skye composed herself, stared straight ahead, and kept silent for a moment. When she felt she had a little more control over her thumping heart, she turned towards him. He was looking at his programme.

'You were expecting someone else, I think,' Skye said, trying to sound confident.

The man started to rise from his seat. 'Be at the bar in two minutes, or I'm leaving.' And he was gone.

'Are you absolutely sure it was him?'

Boyd tilted his head at Fitz.

'I've known the guy for a year, Fitz. We also enjoyed a rather eventful evening together last Friday. So yes, I'm sure it was him. We need to get in there now.'

Fitz stepped in front of him and grabbed his arms.

'Wait one second. This wasn't in the plan.'

'You're talking like there even is a plan! We're making all of this up as we go along. Now move out of my way.'

'No, Boyd. Hear me out.' He raised his hands but stood his ground. 'Like Skye said, we wait here and watch. The scalpel approach, remember? Let her do what she needs to do. Plus, they're in a building full of people and we are watching the exit. Where can they go?'

Boyd's teeth were gritted, he was breathing like a

rhino ready to charge. But he couldn't argue with the logic in what Fitz was saying.

'Okay,' he said begrudgingly. 'We wait.'

The theatre hallways were emptying as customers made their way to their seats, ready for the performance. Skye was moving against the crowd as she nudged her way through the tight corridors, then around a corner and into the small bar. There were a few stragglers still drinking at a table and Bishop's contact was seated at the bar, two glasses in front of him. She walked over and perched on the stool next to him. He stared straight ahead, still not looking at her.

'I took the liberty of ordering you a gin and tonic, just like Uncle Bishop used to like.'

'Thank you.' Skye took a sip, not because she wanted to have a drink but because she needed a moment to compose herself and think this through.

Since Boyd had turned up at *FrakeNews*, everything had moved at a million miles an hour and Skye hadn't had a chance to sit back and hit pause. What had started off as a missing woman had soon been linked to these unexplained events; then the Bishop angle had come into it. Now Boyd had shed more light on things, but he had brought with him a whole new set of problems and potentially a group of people that were a real threat to her and everyone she cared about. All of this seemed to flash through her mind in a second as she sipped the orange juice and felt its sharp taste bite into her tongue. So she had to play this like one of them, like she knew what she was doing. So many people relied on her, she couldn't give this man any idea who she really was.

'So, I am guessing you know what happened to Bishop,' she said, with an air of authority that surprised even her.

'Do tell,' he replied, dryly.

'Things got a little hot; he's gone to ground.'

'Right.'

'He sent me.'

'Did he really.' The man didn't phrase this like it was a question.

Skye gave him a tiresome look. She was getting into character now, thinking like a spy.

'Listen, if you don't want what I've got, that's fine,' she said and turned to face him. 'But Bishop told me that when the chips are down, you're a person I can trust.'

He laughed in mid-drink, snorting into his glass.

'Well, that is very odd,' he said, turning to face her. 'Because Arnold Bishop wouldn't trust me as far as I could throw him.'

She quickly looked away from his cold eyes. Dammit, she had overplayed her hand. Well, one way or another, Skye was about to find out what kind of man Bishop had been meeting with.

'Well then,' she said as coolly as she could. 'It seems like you have a bit of a problem.'

'I do?'

'Yep. Because he *did* trust me, which means if you want to know what he knew, then you need me.' She turned to face him now, playing it cool, her body language exuding confidence. 'And let's be honest, there's not a lot you can do to me in a packed theatre, is there?' She took another sip of her drink, not sure if she was being courageous or utterly reckless.

'Look around you, lass,' the man said, holding his hands up. 'There's no one left but you and me.'

Skye did, and saw he was right; the whole bar had emptied. Other than the two of them, the only person in sight was the man collecting the glasses.

'Oh, Mick and I go way back. He won't help you,' the man said. 'This wasn't Bishop's place to meet, it was mine.'

Skye put her glass down and smiled. 'This changes nothing, mate. You need me and we both know it. So, what now?' she asked him.

He spun around on his stool and narrowed his eyes. 'Now you and I are going to go and have a little chat with someone.'

'I'm not here alone,' Skye said, coldly.

'Good, I'm counting on it,' the man replied with a knowing glint in his eye. 'Because we want a word with your friend, too.'

The Sledgehammer

'I don't like this at all.' Boyd leant against a tree as he chewed on the skin around his thumb. He hadn't taken his eyes off of the front of the theatre in the last five minutes.

'We wait, you heard her,' Fitz insisted. 'If we charge in there and she's fine, we blow the op.'

Boyd finally turned to Fitz.

'The "op"? What do you think this is? *Mission: Impossible*? We're kids, for crying out loud, and we're standing out here while someone in there is in trouble.'

'That's never bothered you before.'

Boyd took that on the chin. 'Yeah well, maybe what you said about that actually got through to me.'

They stood in silence for a moment. Fitz could see he was going to have his work cut out to stop Boyd bolting over the road.

'Screw this.'

Boyd ran to make the other side of the road before a

bus and a courier bike collided with him. Fitz waited for a break in traffic and followed as quickly has he could. As he went into the foyer, he heard the man behind the counter at the box office calling to Boyd, who was already halfway up the stairs to Fitz's left. Fitz realised that they weren't going to get anywhere if this guy called the police. He approached the box office and used the fact that he was flustered to his advantage.

'I'm so sorry, we just got a text from our mum – our nan has been taken ill. Have you got a first aider?'

The man turned away, probably looking for his radio, and Fitz followed Boyd up the steps two at a time with all the speed he could muster. But with the head start Boyd had, there was no way Fitz was going to catch up. He stopped on the first floor, put his hands on his knees and took some deep breaths. Then he heard a glass smash and what sounded like raised voices.

Fitz cautiously trotted along the corridor. He heard music begin to drift out from the auditorium; the performance had started. Then something caught his eye to his right. The barman was face down across the bar, pinned in place with by a corkscrew through his tie. Boyd was hunched over him, twisting one of his arms

330

around his back. Next to him on the bar were two half-empty glasses and an Allen key.

'Boyd!' Fitz yelled in shock, probably louder than he should have.

Boyd had his mouth to the ear of the large barman, who clearly didn't have a clue how he had ended up being quite so seriously threatened by a 15 year-old boy.

'Listen, son, you just need to calm down,' the man said, his voice shaking.

'I'm not your son, *mate*,' Boyd almost spat the reply. Then he reached for a jar that was sitting on the other side of the bar and slammed it down next to the barman's head.

'Now, I know you know exactly who I'm talking about, so either you tell me where they went, or I'm going to take these…' Boyd looked at the jar '… these pickled eggs and one by one, I'm going to shove them…'

'They left by the side door about three minutes ago,' the barman spluttered.

Boyd didn't say a word. He released the barman, who stayed where he was for a moment, almost unable to believe what had just happened. By the time he managed to release himself and straighten up, the man from the box office appeared in a panic.

'Mick, have you seen two teenage boys running around up here anywhere?'

The barman pulled his tie back into place and rubbed his neck, his face still flushed.

'No, mate. No one's been here since the show started.'

Nowhere To Run

'There they are, just up ahead.'

The rain had passed over and the hot sun had dried out any sign of it ever having arrived. Fitz's blood was clearly still pumping from seeing Boyd's activities with the barman.

Boyd grabbed his arm. 'Just slow down, hang back a bit,' he said.

'Are you joking?' Fitz turned his face to Boyd, who looked like he was ready to explode. 'Hang back? We can see them, they're right there. Let's get her.'

'Look at the way she's walking with him. Skye does not need rescuing, Fitz. She's taking care of this.'

'You've changed your tune – a minute ago you were throttling a barman!'

'Yeah and now I can see she's okay. We're going to follow and let her handle it.'

Fitz nodded. They walked up past Waterloo station and Boyd instinctively pulled his hood up as they did so. A moment later and they were heading back towards the Thames but this time, Boyd knew exactly where they were going.

The queue wasn't that long; Boyd suspected that was because of the rain shower earlier. They managed to tuck into the queue a couple of groups behind Harry and Skye. Boyd kept a close eye on Harry, trying to work out if he knew he was being followed, but it didn't seem like it.

What in god's name was Harry even doing here? What did he have to do with Bishop? Boyd would see what he had to say for himself as soon as he had a chance to ask him a few questions. Any minute now, Harry's options were about to drastically diminish.

Boyd glanced up at the massive, white Ferris wheel stretched out above him as he and Fitz followed Harry and Skye into a passenger capsule of the London Eye. The door shut behind them and they began to rise into the skies above London. Harry had nowhere to run, and nowhere to hide.

Section X

The capsule was far from full; Boyd and Fitz had been the last of a small group of people to enter their car and by the time they were on board, Skye and Harry were already looking out over the river side. Boyd positioned himself at the opposite end and kept them in his eyeline.

There was a hum of conversation as families chatted and tourists held up their phones, capturing selfies with the London skyline across the Thames in the background. There were a few elderly tourists sat on the large wooden bench in the middle of the capsule amongst a collection of bags, rain macs and umbrellas that people had left there as they all lined up by the windows for the best view.

'I think my dad works down there,' Fitz said, staring down at Big Ben and the Houses of Parliament. 'Not sure where exactly.' Then a thought hit him. 'Oh crap, I really need to think about getting home soon!'

'Seriously?' Boyd asked, still not taking his eyes off

the same spot, closely monitoring Harry's every move.

'You have no idea how scary my mum is – I need to think about damage control here.'

'Uh-huh.'

Boyd wasn't listening. He had noticed Skye say something to Harry and when he responded, her face dropped. Skye's eyes suddenly flicked around the capsule until they found Boyd; his left eye was probably just visible from under his hood. Skye held his gaze before mouthing a word.

'Sorry,' she said, her face creased with emotion.

Boyd moved, heading around the right-hand side of the bench so he could approach Harry from behind. He stepped over bags and outstretched feet as quickly as he could and was almost close enough to grab Harry when an umbrella handle caught him around the left elbow in a python-like grip. It spun Boyd around just as a woman stood from the bench and moved in front of him, blocking his path. She was small, barely even five feet tall, with short, choppy, silver hair. A pair of large, thick-rimmed spectacles seemed too big for a face that was somewhere in the region of 70 years old. She wore a faded old wax jacket over a crisp, white blouse and plain, black trousers.

'Steady on there, young man. Let's not make a scene,' the woman said, looking at Boyd with a wide, serious smile.

Boyd noticed that her accent had a slight tinge of the Midlands about it, like a kid named Josh he knew at school but nowhere near as broad. Boyd took hold of the umbrella and went to move it, but it didn't shift with the ease he imagined it would.

'What the hell is that thing?' he asked the woman.

'Just one of our little toys,' she said, her frosted blue eyes twinkling. 'Now, I think we could all benefit from a little chat and we don't have much time, do we, Harry?'

Fitz had come around the other side of the bench to stand next to Skye.

'Are you okay?' he asked her.

'I'm fine. You both need to hear this,' she said.

As the rest of the tourists in the capsule moved around, elbows out and nudging for space, eager to get the best pictures for their Instagram, none noticed the meeting that was taking place in their midst. Without any discussion, Boyd, Fitz and Skye, along with Harry and his friend, all moved as a group over to the other side of the car. It wasn't the best position for sightseeing, so they didn't have to fight for room with all the tourists.

'Hello, Boyd,' Harry said. 'You seem to have an uncanny knack for survival.'

'Yeah, something I've had to learn pretty quickly over the last few days. Who the hell are you, Harry? Is that even your name?'

'It is,' the mystery woman said. Harry turned to her and rolled his eyes. 'Oh, give over,' she said. 'It's time we give the boy someone to trust, wouldn't you say?'

'Ha!' Fitz let out a laugh, followed by a snort. 'Him, trust? Good luck with that!'

'And who are you?' Boyd eyed her warily.

The woman cast her eyes around the capsule, then started to speak softly: 'What I am about to tell you does not go any further than this group. I hope that everything you have all witnessed in the last few days will help you to realise that you are mixed up in rather a deadly game; lives are very much on the line. So, I'm going to be blunt and I'm just going to have to hope you are ready to hear it. To be frank, we need you, Boyd, and you need us, so we have a limited amount of time to judge whether we take a leap of faith and work together.'

Boyd looked the tenacious woman directly in the eyes. 'You can trust us.'

'Thank you. My name is Ophelia Bletchley.' She removed her glasses and polished them on a handkerchief she pulled from her sleeve. 'I'm head of a branch of the secret service called Section X; we handle scientific operations.'

'I've never heard of it,' Skye said confidently.

'Well, when you're in the spy business, Miss Rake, that's rather the point.' Skye responded with an icy look. 'We aren't very well-funded, and there aren't many of us – in fact, within the intelligence community we're a bit of a joke nowadays. We chase down conspiracies and keep a watch on the crackpots. We are often affectionately referred to as "the Toy Department" because it's our job to monitor the nasty little buggers who try to bring the rather incredible and impossible stuff into reality.'

'Something like, I don't know, time travel?' Boyd said, fixing his eyes on Ophelia for any sign that she knew exactly what he was talking about.

'Ah, you've been doing your homework,' Ophelia

said with a smile; then she nodded towards Skye. 'Although I presume that little nugget of information is down to you, Miss Rake.'

'Call me Skye. So, Azima was right? Someone is actually travelling through time; that's what's causing the power surges?' Skye said, eagerly.

'Section X can neither confirm nor deny such a statement at this time.'

'That's a "yes",' Skye said, flaring her eyes at Boyd. 'I really hate to say I told you so.'

'Back up a sec – time travel?' Fitz said with a disbelieving tone. 'Are you having me on?'

'As I said…' Ophelia started before Boyd interrupted her.

'Yes, we know, you can neither confirm nor deny it. So, you wanted me to follow Harry and Skye, but why? What the hell have I got to do with all this?'

They stood in silence for a second or two. Ophelia was no longer looking at Boyd, but over his shoulder. 'Yes, I needed you to follow Harry. It's just unfortunate for us that it seems someone was also following you.'

Boyd's eyes darted around the car; he couldn't see anyone suspicious at all.

'In the next car. Do you know who that is?' Ophelia asked, pointing past Boyd.

As he turned and looked over his shoulder, the capsule suddenly jolted to a halt. Passengers stumbled; some fell against the glass surround of the capsule as a chorus of panic began to rise. Boyd looked to the car behind and through a cluster of faces he saw Aurora, staring intently at him with those fierce green eyes.

'She certainly seems keen on you,' Ophelia said.

Hornet lifted the radio to her mouth as she steadied herself.

'I said to stop the cars, not to slam the brakes on for god's sake.' She released the button and the radio let out a squelch.

'Sorry,' came the reply over the airwaves. 'Do you want support now?'

Hornet rolled her eyes before pressing the button and speaking into the radio again. 'You mean they haven't left yet?'

'Not yet, no.'

'Then yes, get them in the air for God's sake! He's seen me, he knows we're on to him and if I know Boyd, he's about to do something very stupid.'

'Allow me to enlighten you: her name is Hornet,' Ophelia said. 'She's a highly skilled assassin, working for an exceptionally nasty man who runs a covert operation we've been keeping a very close eye on.'

Boyd shook his head, as if someone had just hit him with something heavy. 'Hornet?' he repeated.

'Yes, Hornet. I know, as code names go, it's a tad dramatic, isn't it? She's been off the grid for quite a few years.'

'Yeah, well, she's been my Aunt Aurora for the last ten of them.'

'Yes, we were aware of that, obviously.' Ophelia gestured towards Harry.

Boyd looked towards Harry. 'And how do you figure into this, Romeo?'

'X-One sent me to keep an eye on you.'

'X-One? Who is X-One?' Skye couldn't keep quiet any longer.

'That would be me,' Ophelia jumped in. 'Head of Section X. Big cheese, top dog. I am "X-One".'

'So, mate.' Fitz looked at Harry, chuckling. 'Does

that make you, Number Two?'

'No,' Ophelia shut him down. 'Sorry to disappoint you, Fitz. There is no Number Two.'

'I'd see a doctor about that, if I were you.' Fitz laughed, then realised that his audience was not amused.

'We have what looks like a group of trained mercenaries and a stone-cold psychopath in the next car over,' Harry said. 'Let's try to stay on track if we can. What we need to do is get you three somewhere safe.'

'There's not a lot they can do to us up here, surely?' Fitz offered.

The London Eye had stopped just at the point where their capsule was at the very top, with Hornet's car alongside theirs.

'Well, they've managed to bring us to a halt. I suggest we don't wait to find out their next move,' Harry said in reply, looking towards Ophelia. 'If we can somehow force their hand.'

Boyd had been quiet. He was looking at the other capsule and watching all the goings-on with careful consideration. Hornet, or whatever she was supposed to be called, seemed to be organising her troops. Any unfortunate members of the public who happened to be in the capsule along with her were all now cowering on the floor on the opposite side of the car.

'He's right,' Boyd said and nodded towards Harry. 'Looks to me like Hornet has at least four other people in that car with her and I don't think they're going to stay put and wait for Christmas.'

He headed for the door to the capsule and ran his hand along the rubber seal. When he turned back, Skye was looking at him with confusion, but Fitz knew his friend had gone over the situation in his head and reached a conclusion, and he knew it probably wasn't going to be anything sensible. Harry was still saying something when Fitz interrupted.

'Shut up.' Fitz held up a hand and Harry stopped, more than a little surprised. 'I think Boyd is about to do something crazy.'

Ophelia and Harry turned to see Boyd, his hands raised, pushing on the door to the capsule.

'How do you reckon we get these open?'

Before anyone had a chance to respond, there was a hiss and the door slid aside. Boyd stepped back as a howling wind whipped into the car, taking his breath away and the air was suddenly filled with shouts and screams. He looked at the door, then out at the other capsules.

'It wasn't me,' he said. He was right, every capsule door was open. He turned to Skye and Fitz, his face set like stone, deadly serious. 'Look, we all know they're coming for me. So, I have a plan.'

'Boyd, don't be stupid!' Skye shouted.

Boyd looked at Ophelia and pointed towards Skye. 'Tell her,' he said. 'Tell her I'm right!' he shouted over the noise.

Ophelia breathed deeply. 'I'm afraid so – all of this – it leads back to him.'

Despite figuring out as much, the news still hit Boyd like a truck. He swallowed deeply, before nodding.

'So, what's your big plan, hero boy?' Skye said nervously.

'For you guys to get somewhere safe, I need to get out of here and lead them away.'

'Hang on a tick,' Fitz jumped in. 'We are 135 metres off the ground. You know how high that is?'

'No,' Boyd shook his head.

'Well, it's 135 metres, which is really flamin' high!'

'Then I'd better not fall off.'

Boyd looked out the door. Fitz was right; they were ridiculously high up, and Boyd had no chance of making it to a surrounding building. The London Eye was just a bigger version of the ferris wheel at Bloomfield funfair, and there was no way down unless he somehow used the structure itself.

Boyd got down on his haunches and looked out of the door at the structure beneath him. Much like the wheel on his bike; the Eye had spokes in the middle that led to a narrow rim. Coming out of this rim was a support framework, and outside of this, in cradles, were the capsules that the passengers travelled in. From where he was now, it was at least a three-metre jump to get down to the support framework. He knew he could make it.

He looked over to Hornet's capsule and saw two men at the door, nervously starting to climb down the cradle onto the framework. They were coming for him, so he had to do this now.

Boyd grabbed Ophelia's umbrella and slapped it against his palm. 'This is pretty strong, right?'

'It should be, it's made from tungsten steel,' she said.

Boyd then desperately searched the car with his eyes for something, anything that he could make use of. An elderly woman was sat on the bench with her shopping bag at her feet, completely calm among all the madness erupting around her.

Boyd put on his best smile. 'Afternoon, madam.' He pointed at the bag sitting open on the floor. 'May I borrow those?'

'Makes no difference to me, sonny. We're not going anywhere, are we?' the woman shrugged.

'Much obliged.'

Boyd took what he needed from the shopping bag and grabbed Harry and Fitz. 'You two, listen. I've got a plan.' He outlined it quickly before turning to head for the exit.

Skye and Ophelia were watching the two men from the next capsule who were now crawling along the support framework of the London Eye, slithering like snakes towards their car.

'They're coming,' Skye said with utter disbelief. 'This is seriously messed up. I can't believe they are actually doing this!'

'Boyd, hang on,' Ophelia said. 'Before you run off,

you need to know something.'

'I've got a few questions myself but they're going to have to wait.'

'That's fine, but this can't wait,' she said gravely.

Boyd straightened up and faced her.

'Hurricane isn't where your father works; it isn't a company at all. It was a top-secret project from many years ago. It was something that went very badly wrong.'

'Why are you telling me this now?'

'Because if you don't make it, if these people get hold of you, they are going to lie to you and I need to know that you won't let them get into your head. Like I said, we need you, Boyd. Which is why I have to tell you something that I wish you never had to hear.'

Boyd nodded gravely.

'You're a smart lad, I'm sure you've figured this out already, but Martin Boyd is not your father, any more than that odious woman over there is your aunt.'

Boyd's breath caught in his throat. Ophelia was right; of course he'd come to the realisation that Martin wasn't his real father. But now, hearing it said out loud, it felt like someone had dropped a huge weight on his chest. He just stared straight ahead. Whoever Martin was, whatever his involvement in all of this, Boyd needed to face him; he needed answers. Everything that divided the two of them were the same things that made them so similar, it's why they'd always struggled to get along; he was a chip off the old block. Boyd swallowed hard.

The small, stern woman in front of him melted a little at the sight of the broken boy in front of her. Ophelia tilted her head and put both hands around his face.

'Now, you listen to me, my boy. We will deal with this, all of it. We will make sense of it for you, I promise you that. But right now, all I can tell you is this; I'm so very sorry, love. I really am.' She gently tapped his face, a signal to shake it off and find his focus; they had work to do.

Boyd pulled away and nodded. He turned, the umbrella in his hand, and made for the door.

Skye stepped in front of him and blocked his path. 'What the hell do you think you're playing at, hero boy? It's not your problem, remember?' she said, her eyes full of tears, doing everything she could to stop him stepping outside.

'It's time I stopped dragging everyone else into my problems and dealt with this myself.' Boyd gently moved her aside. 'If they want me, they've got to catch me first.'

The Eye Of The Storm

Boyd stood at the door, the wind beating his face. He hooked the handle of the umbrella through his belt loop at the back of his jeans and jumped.

He landed hard on the frame and coughed out a burst of air as his chest hit the metal. He frantically wrapped his arms around the structure. The wind was ferocious at this height, battering him like a boxing opponent, unleashing punch after punch as he clung on for dear life. He looked down, wide-eyed, as his legs kicked at thin air and all of a sudden, he felt nauseous and dizzy. His arms were numb and he was losing his grip. He willed himself to hold on, closed his eyes tight and focused on steadying himself. Beneath him was a criss-cross of smaller bars and if by some miracle they managed to stop him falling, hitting them was going to hurt a lot.

He swung one of his legs over the bar in front of him, pulled himself up and straddled the structure. He looked back to the car he had just jumped from; it seemed so far away from down here. The two men in black were already coming around either side of the capsule he had just leapt from, and they looked pretty unhappy that he was going to make them chase him. Boyd could see no sign of Fitz or Harry.

'Come on lads, get a move on,' he said to himself. Boyd sat there on the bar, stranded high above London as his two pursuers carefully crawled around the capsule, using the cradle Boyd's car sat in to steady themselves. One of the men, a bald, bullet-headed man who didn't seem to have a neck, looked directly at Boyd.

'This would all be much easier if you just came to me.' He spoke in English with a thick Russian accent.

'Yeah, but that would take all the fun out of it, don't you think?' Boyd played it cool as he sat and swung his legs like a kid on a swing.

Inside the car, Fitz and Harry, with the help of the elderly lady – who introduced herself as Enid – had been carrying out Boyd's instructions. They had taken the two bags of Enid's baking flour, a novelty Union Jack bowler hat borrowed from one of the other passengers and Skye's water bottle. They cleared a space on the bench and set to work.

'Not too much water,' Enid had told them with a glint in her eye. 'Otherwise they won't hurt.'

Ophelia moved backed from the door. She had a phone at her ear as she waved Skye over. 'My dear,' Ophelia wrapped her hand around Skye's forearm. 'You need to call your people and tell them to get out. They must leave now.'

'Why? They won't be able to break into our place.'

'We can't take the risk. Tell your team to leave and scrub all your files. It would be handy if you have anyone who can speak to the science of all of this. Someone we can borrow…'

Skye took out her phone and held down a key. Someone answered the phone at the other end. 'It's me. We've been compromised. Wipe everything, take the back-ups and get out. Oh… and put Azima on the phone, now.'

Boyd was doing his best to keep his two chief

pursuers as angry and distracted as possible. 'Isn't it great to feel the wind in your hair?' Boyd said to the angry, bald Russian. 'Oops! Sorry. Did you know that they can take the hair from your butt now and sew it into your head? You should give it some serious thought.'

The Russian gritted his teeth and glared back. 'When I catch you, little boy, I am going to rip your arms off and beat you with them. How does that sound?'

'Painful, to be honest.'

Boyd looked up at the opening to the car and there was Harry holding a Union Jack bowler hat, his arm cocked and ready like a cricketer ready to launch the ball at the stumps.

'Heads up,' Boyd said and nodded towards the door to the capsule.

Harry and Fitz had rolled the wet flour into several small, hard balls and they began to let fly: Harry at the bald Russian and Fitz at the taller man on his side of the car.

The shock of being pelted with an unknown projectile immediately knocked the gangly goon off-balance. Fitz's first missile hit him in the chest and he instinctively brought a hand up to the point of impact. Before he had a chance to get both hands back on the frame, a second flour bomb whizzed by his ear and then a third slapped him hard on the cheekbone, right under this eye. That was enough to disorientate the man completely; both hands came away as his brain demanded him to take evasive action.

Boyd held his breath as the tall man lost his grip and came away from the wheel. He tumbled through the air for less than a second before crashing into the support frame with a crack, and somehow he latched his long fingers around the steel, just managing to cling on.

The Russian had taken a more sensible option and had simply tucked himself down, huddling for cover. Harry's direct hits had him pinned down, but he wasn't going anywhere. That was fine, Boyd didn't need him to. He just needed both men distracted, and now he could make his move.

Boyd quickly swung himself around, dropped his legs down and kicked at thin air.

'Boyd!' Skye called out to him. 'What the hell are you doing?'

He turned and saw that the bullet-headed Russian

had started to move. The taller man, who had fallen through to the support frame, was now below Boyd, walking along the narrow rim of the wheel. In a few more careful steps, he would he within touching distance of Boyd's legs. Harry and Fitz were still throwing the projectiles but both pursuers were expecting them and now they knew they were no more than weaponised dough balls, they weren't having much of an impact.

'Don't watch this part!' Boyd shouted to Skye with a smile as he let go of the bar and dropped through the support frame, landing on the rim.

He quickly spun around to face the tall man, who bent and twisted his long arms and legs as he moved along the rim, like a spider crawling across its web to feast on a fly. The man's skin was covered in pockmarks; his thin lips were wet with spit. Boyd let him get close, waited until the man could see the ice blue of his eyes, then dropped out of sight. The Spider's hand swiped through thin air where Boyd's head had been less than a second before. Spider looked down, expecting to see Boyd tumbling through the white metal frame towards the ground, but instead he saw him hanging from the rim by his fingertips and moving swiftly around the wheel, hand-over-hand like a kid on a climbing frame.

'What are you waiting for? Go after him!' the Russian shouted at his friend. 'Get down there!'

Just then, the Russian's radio buzzed. Hornet's voice was just audible over the howling wind. 'Bull, change of plan. Listen up.'

Spider did as he was told and continued his walk along the rim as before. He couldn't work out why the boy was hanging from it by his hands – this was going to make it so easy to catch him.

Boyd knew exactly what he was doing. When he looked out at the London Eye from the capsule, he saw that the frame was attached to the rim every few metres. So he figured that he could wrap the curved handle of the umbrella around the rim of the wheel and slide for a few metres before hitting the next frame. Then all he had to do was move the umbrella over the frame connection and slide down again. It seemed simple enough in his head but now he was actually about to slide down from the top of the London Eye using an umbrella, he had to admit it wasn't the best idea he'd had all week.

He grabbed the umbrella from his belt loop and put the handle over the rim of the wheel. He couldn't quite make out the shouts of protest from Skye and Fitz; his friends were so far above him that the wind was whipping their words away. What he could hear was Spider, clunking through the steel frame above him, his big boots getting ever closer to stamping on his left hand. He tried not to think about how far up he was, how he was being chased by a group of assassins who wanted him dead, or how he was about to entrust his life to an umbrella. He just wrapped both hands around it, closed his eyes and pushed off.

Boyd came to a stop against the next section of frame with a gentle bump. He opened his eyes. 'Well, that was a piece of cake,' he said to himself.

He had been right at the top of the wheel so it hadn't been a steep slide, but sliding along the next section was going to be a different story. Boyd grabbed the rim and moved the umbrella along. Wasting no time overthinking it, he took his left hand off the rim, grabbed the umbrella and slid down the rim once more.

This time, when the brolly stopped, Boyd's legs carried on and crashed into the spokes. He let out a cry and felt a burning pain through his shoulders, but somehow, he didn't let go. Looking down at his legs, he noticed all the people on the ground, many of them with their phones out, filming the thrilling scenes playing out high above of them. Boyd quickly repeated the action and, this time, saw the faces of the tourists in the car nearest him as he flew by them. He was starting to enjoy himself.

Just as he was steeling himself to make the next slide, Boyd heard a far-off sound, like a beating drum. He swung his head around in the direction of the sound and saw that Spider was no longer giving chase. In fact, he and bullet-head were now way up above him, crawling back up towards the capsules. What the hell where they up to? Boyd stayed put as the strange noise got louder, sounding less like a drum now and more like air being sliced apart by a heavy set of rotor blades. Then, it came into view: an imposing black helicopter tipped forward, chopping through the sky like a shark cutting through water. Somehow Boyd didn't think this belonged to *FrakeNews*, or Section X; this was Hornet's reinforcements and they were moving in for the kill.

He brought his feet up on the rim and, holding onto the umbrella, quickly began to pull himself back up towards the cars. Boyd did his best to concentrate on where he was putting his feet whilst he snatched a look back towards the skyline, searching for signs of the helicopter. It was getting closer now, surely only moments away, and Boyd saw that the Russian was nearly back to Skye's capsule – he was running out of time.

Then he saw her coming around the side of the car he had departed only moments ago – Hornet and two more men. How could he have been so stupid? He hadn't saved anyone. He had tried to play the hero, just like he had done at Waterloo Station; just as Hornet knew he would, and he had left his friends completely unguarded.

Boyd put the umbrella back into his belt loop and moved as fast as he could back through the frame. He had to make it to that capsule before she did. What had Ophelia called her? A "highly-skilled assassin"? And Boyd had left his friends within her reach.

He let his anger drive him on. When he reached the section directly under his capsule, he looked up and saw the soles of the Russian's boots, plus three pairs of the same black boots belonging to the other men, but no sign of Hornet. Boyd was about to shimmy up the frame when his breath was taken away by the force of the helicopter. It rose alongside the London Eye, just metres away from him. The '*THWAP!*' of the rotor blades and the power of the air hitting him knocked him back against the steel bars. He struggled to open his eyes as the wind held him down. When he managed to part them into a squint, he saw the long, black machine rise and hover over the big wheel before a rope ladder dropped down from its belly.

'Oh no!' Boyd shouted to himself, as the Russian lunged out and grabbed for the ladder.

Boyd didn't have time to think about what was going on in the capsule before he heard a scream. Hornet appeared at the door, pushing Skye close to the edge. Her face was twisted with pure terror. The Russian caught the ladder and put his foot on it. Just as it looked like Skye was beginning to fight back, Hornet shoved her out of the capsule and Boyd stopped breathing. He watched helplessly as she fell, limbs flailing, until she was caught by a waiting henchman.

Hornet jumped after her, then pushed a petrified Skye towards the ladder. A moment later, Harry jumped from the capsule and landed on top of Spider. They tumbled through the steel frame, right next to Boyd. Spider grabbed at his ankle, his face screwed up and his teeth gritted.

Before Boyd had a chance to respond, Harry kicked at the man's arm. 'Go, get her back!' he shouted before lunging at the other man.

Boyd hauled himself up and onto the top of the frame just as Skye was pulled into the cab of the helicopter, and Hornet and her team scrambled in behind her. Boyd reached the top of the frame, the London skyline silhouetted behind him as he pulled himself to his feet. The bullet-headed Russian smiled from the helicopter as he started to pull up the ladder and gave the order for the pilot to swing away into the sky.

Boyd took two steps across the frame and jumped with everything he had left. His heart seemed to stop beating as, for a second or two, he was soaring forward and upwards, almost like he was flying. Then gravity kicked in and he started to drop downward. As he did, he desperately reached out towards the ladder with everything he had, stretched until it physically hurt, but it wouldn't be enough.

For just a split-second, Boyd's mind drifted to what it would be like to fall from here. Would he end up in the Thames? Would he survive? As soon as it had come, the thought was overtaken with another; he reached around to the back of his jeans, grabbed the umbrella, and chopped through the air with it, like an axe. It caught on the last rung of the ladder at the same moment that the helicopter started to roar away.

Boyd was pulled with it at savage speed; he had given up hanging from one thing and traded it for hanging from another, only this one was moving at around 50 miles an hour. He quickly got his other hand on the ladder and started to climb.

'Come and join the party!' was the shout from above as Hornet held out her hand.

He had no choice; he reached up and took the treacherous woman's hand. She pulled him into the helicopter and as he was sprawled on his belly, he felt a hot sting at the back of his neck. His vision immediately started to blur as the strength in his body drained away.

The helicopter started to bank left and Boyd was helpless to stop himself rolling over. The last thing he saw was Skye's face, her familiar hard-as-nails expression now firmly back in place.

'Keep your head, Boyd,' she said earnestly. 'These fools won't beat us.'

Hornet laughed. 'Kids these days – they think they know everything.'

Everything Changes

It only took a moment to bring someone back from a jump, but the minutes that followed could be crucial, because you never knew what effects they might be suffering from. Karl had known subjects to be unconscious, or in excruciating pain, and he silently hoped that Blair would be spared both.

As the noise subsided and the light dimmed, Karl released the catches on the lid of the Chamber and opened it. There, inside the sleeve, floating in the water, was Blair, conscious but breathing hard and fast. Karl released the valve to empty the water, unzipped the sleeve and pulled his daughter into his arms. 'Alright, I've got you. I've got you.' Water spilled over the concrete floor as Karl removed the breathing mask and tilted Blair's head towards him. 'Take a long breath, stay calm and take your time.'

Blair was gasping at the air around her, desperate to catch her breath as she tried to speak. 'Father,' she managed, heaving and choking.

'It's okay, take a moment, we have time,' he reassured her.

She shook her head. 'No, listen, we don't...' Blair steadied herself. 'Bishop was killed,' she said, then gasped again. 'Bishop was killed by travellers from the future.' Her eyes flickered before she passed out in her father's arms.

Karl lifted her carefully from the Chamber and carried her across the old warehouse to her bed. He gently rested her weary body down and covered her with a blanket. Then he stood and thought for a moment in the darkness, stroking his face with his long fingers.

This changed everything. He had to make sure Blair got her strength back. He knew what he had to do.

PART THREE

Solid Ground

Fitz had watched the helicopter disappear out of view with a sense of total helplessness. The men had stormed into their capsule, taken Skye and there had been nothing he could do about it; there were too many of them and they were too strong. Now they had flown out of sight with Skye and Boyd in their clutches and his stomach churned with an anger and frustration unlike anything he had ever experienced.

The authorities had got the London Eye moving again and by the time their car reached the ground, the police were taking statements and trying to figure out what had gone on. Harry had used one of Spider's own shoelaces to secure him to the railing inside the capsule.

Ophelia had quietly made another phone call before giving Fitz and Harry a clear order: 'When we get to ground level, absolute quiet and follow my lead.'

Fitz did as he was told. He didn't know what else he could do; he was in a complete state of shock. He had come up to London to help Boyd and Skye and they were gone, missing, facing God knows what; and he hadn't done a thing to stop it. He felt an instinct to run away from these people and go home, but he would be no help to Boyd at all if he did that. Only a few days ago, this had all seemed like a game, an adventure, and now he could see it for what it was: it was about life and death.

Their capsule settled to a stop at ground level and Ophelia reached her hands out, taking hold of both Harry and Fitz. She held their arms tight and mumbled some thanks and prayers as they made their way across the concourse and away from the London Eye. Ophelia could put on a convincing act when she wanted to, looking for all the world like an old lady who had been through a terrifying ordeal. A couple who had been in the same capsule were talking to the police and pointing in Harry's direction.

'Okay, nice and quick now, please, team,' Ophelia said. 'Around the corner you'll find a green van; that's our man.'

One of the policemen approached and raised a hand to Harry. 'Can I have a word, please, sir?'

'Please, constable,' Harry said meekly, 'my mother is

very shaken. Can I just get her to the ambulance over there?' He pointed to the road nearby, which was now lined with emergency vehicles of all varieties, blue lights flashing.

'Oh, right. Yes, of course. Let me help you.'

'Oh, you are very kind,' Ophelia said, making sure her voice was suitably thin and reedy.

Fitz broke away and walked behind them, watching as Ophelia took her small, unsteady steps towards the ambulance at the front of the line. He could see that there was a paramedic behind the wheel, filling in some paperwork. As they got to the back of the ambulance, Harry climbed in through the open doors and held his hands out. The policeman stood behind Ophelia and helped her up.

Once she was inside and out of sight, the tiny woman allowed the policeman to follow up the steps behind her before she broke out of character. Ophelia spun swiftly around to her right and brought her elbow up under the policeman's jaw; his legs gave way as he went out like a light. Harry caught the copper as he tumbled and gently laid him out on the gurney. Ophelia gave the young man a thoughtful tap on the cheek.

'Nothing personal. Best we get you to hospital.' She looked to Harry. 'Your mother? Cheeky sod.'

They climbed out of the ambulance and Harry shut the doors. He banged twice on the back and the driver, thinking this was a signal that he was loaded with a patient and ready to go, put the big machine in gear and roared away in a scream of sirens. Ophelia led them away as she marched along the pavement, the walk of the struggling old lady had given way to one of single-minded resolve.

Three cars down was an old green van, a royal crest in gold on the side, above the words '*Royal Parks*'. Ophelia pulled back the side door and ushered Fitz inside while Harry climbed in the front next to the driver, who had thick white hair rebelliously jutting out at all angles from his small head. There were padded leather benches on both sides of the van. Fitz sat on the far side and Ophelia positioned herself opposite him.

'Fitz, this is Barnaby Pine. Barnaby, meet Fitz.'

'Afternoon, Fitz,' the man said in a Yorkshire accent and gave a little salute with his left hand.

'Straight back to the shop, I think, Barney,' Ophelia said, looking out of the front window at the traffic.

'Very good, ma'am.'

'Did our guest arrive?'

'Indeed. She's having a coffee while she waits.'

'Wonderful, I think we're going to need all the help we can get.'

She looked at Fitz, who had just noticed that his hands were shaking.

'We need to find Boyd,' he managed to say, almost too quietly for anyone to hear, but Ophelia clearly picked up on it.

She leant over and tapped his hand. 'Fitz, listen to me, we're going to get him back.'

'Good.' That was all Fitz needed to hear. 'I know what he can be like. But it's because no one's ever really had his back, it's not his fault. I can't let him down.'

The Toy Shop

Barnaby pointed the van towards a sign for Regent's Park. He drove under a beautiful, ornate black gateway adorned with gold, before slowly crawling along a tree-lined road. The green van was right at home here, with its *'Royal Parks'* crest emblazoned on the side and the bonnet. Dog walkers and joggers happily moved aside to allow them through and Barnaby replied with a raised hand and a nod.

When he reached a sign pointing left for the English Garden, Barnaby swung the van right down a narrow path. He pulled to a stop near a small café hut and tucked the van under a tree. It wasn't especially busy in this isolated section of the park; most of the tourists and walkers would visit one of the many picturesque gardens rather than choose this remote café for a pit stop.

As they climbed out of the van, Fitz noticed someone sitting at a table – a young woman looking at a phone. She had black and pink hair pulled up into a topknot and wore a baggy animal-print jumper. As Fitz got closer, he could see she was watching a news report showing scenes from the incident at the London Eye: a reporter was standing in front of crowds, with police milling around behind the taped-off tourist attraction.

'Miss Azima,' Barnaby got her attention as he approached the table, 'please allow me to introduce Ophelia, Harry and Fitzgerald.'

'Fitz,' he said, feeling his cheeks flush. 'Just call me Fitz.'

'Whatever you say, lad,' Barnaby continued. 'And this young lady is Azima, an associate of Miss Rake.'

'Ah, okay. Gotcha.' Fitz nodded. 'I'm sorry I couldn't... well, anyway, I'm just sorry.'

'Follow me, please,' Ophelia said. Fitz and Azima didn't move. Ophelia glanced at each one of the group; they looked exhausted and bewildered.

'Wait!' Azima waved her hand. 'Skye told me to go with this guy, so I did. But I have no idea who you are and why I'm here.'

Ophelia glanced around the park, ensuring that they were alone. 'I should have thought that was obvious?'

'Well, it isn't, and from what I've just seen, Skye's been kidnapped. You let that happen, so I'm thinking maybe I just go back to HQ and try my luck with people

I know.'

'I'm very sorry, Azima, *FrakeNews* has gone. You got everyone out before they tore the place apart, but I wouldn't advise you go back there.'

'What do you mean? Who tore the place apart?' Azima's voice cracked.

'Come with me now and I will tell you. I promise.'

'Right, sure. Skye was perfectly safe with you lot, wasn't she?'

Ophelia stood back and looked around the faces in front of her. 'Look, we have all lost a great deal today. Friends have been taken, yes, but I am asking you to look beyond that, just for now. It's a fact that our entire future is being threatened, as is our past. I look at you and, much like what you see when you look at me, this probably isn't the team we would choose for this battle, but we are where we are. So, Azima, I can't offer you any guarantees around your safety. I can't even promise you we will get your friend back, but I can give you my word that you can trust me to do everything in my power to make this right. And at this point, is there anyone offering you a better deal than that?'

Ophelia began to march away from the café. 'Right,

speeches over. Arses in gear. Let's be having you.'

Fitz and Azima looked at each other, grabbed their things and followed her – wherever it was she was leading.

There was a public toilet just beyond the café, with a sign hanging from the door saying, *'Closed to the Public'*. The powder-red brickwork was cracked and the green painted wood around the building's frame was peeling away. The small print on the sign told anyone who needed a comfort break that they could find the nearest convenience five minutes' walk away in Queen Mary's Gardens. Ophelia slid an old-fashioned iron key into the lock on the big, green door. Fitz noticed as she put the key back into her pocket that it was tied onto a green ribbon and the circle at the top of the key had the outline of a roaring lion's head inside it.

'Do you hold all your meetings in a toilet?' Fitz asked, screwing his nose up. 'I know you said you were low on budget, but man.'

'Everyone in, no more questions for now, please.' Ophelia ushered them through the door, then closed it and drew a bolt across the top. 'With me,' she said as she marched down to the last stall.

The building clearly hadn't been open to the public in a very long time. It didn't smell like a toilet. In fact, Fitz was reminded of the smell in his grandad's garage: brick dust and damp wood. There were piles of old leaves gathering in the corners of the tiled floor and sitting on the row of sinks was an old newspaper, turning brown and curled at the edges. Fitz carefully folded back the front cover and saw a colour picture of two ice skaters holding medals; the date in the corner said 15th February 1984.

Ophelia entered the last cubicle as Harry stood against the back wall with Barnaby, giving Azima and Fitz room to peer around the door. Ophelia reached up and carefully took hold of the old flush chain. She turned and faced her two guests, a knowing smile on her face as she placed her thumb over the bottom of the ornate wooden handle. She pulled the flush and held it down. Fitz saw a light move across her thumb, like a photocopier scanning a page.

'No way,' he said, the beginnings of a smile creeping across his face.

'Oh yes, Mr Tork,' Ophelia's smile grew wider. 'Yes way, indeed.'

She let go of the flush and pushed on the big, white cistern that was attached to the wall. It moved back into a recess and, as it did, the floor began to open and the toilet itself dropped down out of sight. A dim light flickered on from below and Fitz could see a set of concrete steps, several spiders and at least one rat.

Ophelia set off down the steps, the light clack of her shoes echoing back up towards the group. Fitz couldn't help but be a little bit excited.

'Well, I'm in!' He set off after Ophelia.

Azima looked at the steps, her eyebrows raised in trepidation. 'Yeah, but into an actual toilet?' She hesitated.

'Don't worry - the plumbing was removed almost 70 years ago,' Harry said reassuringly.

'Wonderful. You're still asking me to follow an old lady into a toilet – which is still a little bit weird.'

'Not averse to a little adventure, are you?' Barnaby asked, with a little edge in his voice.

'I'm a scientist, not an explorer. We tend to like to assess things like going underground with a group of strangers, before we fully commit.'

'Okay,' Harry jumped in. 'Well, you're certainly not

378

a prisoner. No one is forcing you to do anything you don't want to, okay?'

'Not at all,' Barnaby confirmed.

'So I can go down there, hear what you guys have to say and if I don't like it...'

'I will happily show you back up here myself,' Barnaby said reassuringly.

'Good,' Azima replied and set off down the steps, with Harry following close behind.

'As soon as you've signed the Official Secrets Act,' Barnaby whispered to himself as he closed the toilet door.

Ophelia led them down a circular passage that reminded Fitz of some of the narrow tunnels in the London Underground. He thought about how much Boyd would hate being in here; the air was thick and the tunnel seemed to be getting narrower and narrower as they continued deeper underground. As the walls moved closer towards him, Fitz noticed that they were yellowy-brown and slick with dirty condensation. There was a constant drip-dripping that echoed loudly, and the lights – old-fashioned looking bulbs behind wire mesh – flickered on and off constantly.

Finally, they reached the end of the tunnel and Ophelia stood in front of a small, round door that reminded Fitz of the doors in old submarine war movies: thick metal with a wheel in the middle. Ophelia grabbed the wheel and Fitz was about to ask if she needed help with turning it when she bent down. Ophelia lined her eye up with the centre of the wheel, wrenched it counterclockwise and spoke loudly over the noise the mechanism was making.

'X-One – Ten dash Ten dash Seven-Two.'

Fitz then saw a green light shine out of the centre cap of the wheel and meet Ophelia's open eye. The light formed a flat shape that brushed over her eyeball, scanning back and forth before disappearing. The door then clunked and released.

'Right, in we go.' Ophelia pulled the door back and stepped over the threshold. She held the door for the rest of them as they all entered one by one, stopping just inside the door as the lights finally flickered on.

'Welcome to what we affectionately call the Toy Shop,' Ophelia said proudly.

They had entered a cold, underground room about the size of a football pitch. Its walls and ceiling were lined with brownish-white tiles. In front of them were four steps leading down to old wooden desks. They were on a slope, leading to a set of screens on a raised stage at the front, giving the room the appearance of a theatre.

Just like the tunnel, the room smelt musty and damp and Fitz could see that there were several old metal buckets dotted around on the floor and on desks, positioned to catch the drips from a leaky roof. The lights had large, copper shades that hung low on long, gold chains. Fitz looked up at the ceiling and noticed a huge crest painted on it in gold and black. It had the silhouette of a roaring lion's head, the same one as he had seen on Ophelia's key. Under it were the words: '*In Ministerium Scienta*.'

Harry noticed Fitz looking up at it. '*In the Service of Science*,' he said. 'That's the Section X crest.'

Fitz nodded. 'Where's everyone else?' Fitz asked.

'No one else, just us,' Ophelia replied.

She walked purposefully down a walkway through the middle of the desks, picked up a remote control and stopped in front of the bank of televisions that covered the far wall. She pressed the remote control and the screens flickered into life. Fitz swallowed hard as he saw a face emerge in giant form on the screens. The sight of Hornet in actual size was enough to make his skin crawl but a giant version of her face in HD made him shiver.

'Take a seat, please, everyone. We're going to have a short history lesson.'

Hurricane Warning

Fitz stood leaning against a desk whilst Azima sat in a chair, hugging her legs. They faced the bank of screens whilst Ophelia, small and austere, marched up and down in front of them as she spoke. She clicked the remote control and another face appeared on one of the screens.

'That's Lord Ravensbrook, isn't it?' Fitz asked, looking at the image of the dusty adventurer holding a dinosaur bone aloft in triumph.

'It is,' Ophelia nodded.

'He came to speak at our school. Turned up in a super-charged Bentley. Pretty cool bloke.'

'That's exactly the image he likes to convey. What I'm about to tell you all can never leave this room. It is, at the risk of sounding just a little melodramatic, top secret. Am I making myself clear?'

Azima looked at Fitz and they silently nodded their agreement before Fitz answered for them.

'Our friends are missing, so, like, yeah, whatever it takes.'

'Thank you. Ravensbrook's reputation is built around being a philanthropist, a teacher; a man who uses his vast riches for the good of mankind. He makes no secret of the fact that he dedicates a substantial amount of those riches towards his first love: experimental sciences. Around 20 years ago, Ravensbrook funded a little research team and plonked them in the middle of the ocean, near the Bahamas, on a place called Hurricane Island. This team was a carefully selected group of specialists and Ravensbrook managed to keep the security on the island extremely tight. Section X tried to get close, but this man stood in our way.'

Ophelia clicked the remote and an image of chubby, bald man popped up onto the screens. 'This is Arnold Bishop.' She looked to Fitz and raised her eyebrows.

'Oh, right,' he said nervously. 'Yeah, not a clue who that is, never heard of him.'

'That's rather strange, Fitz, seeing as you broke into his flat earlier today.'

'Oh, *that* Arnold Bishop. Gotcha.' Fitz made a face

and Azima smiled in appreciation.

'We believe that Ravensbrook, along with at least one prominent politician and with the skills of Mr Bishop, sought to rebuild an ancient scientific society called the Trinity Guild. The Guild was originally founded by Sir Isaac Newton in 1663.'

'The gravity guy?' Fitz inquired.

'Yes, Fitz, the "gravity guy". Newton left the Trinity Guild after two or three years as he disagreed with their extreme beliefs. They were obsessed with the idea of utilising elements from other planets to make humankind stronger, faster, more powerful. The Guild developed the reputation of a cult, a gaggle of lunatics, and Newton wanted no part in it. The key members of Ravensbrook's reformed Trinity Guild were two scientists, a husband-and-wife team, both with different specialties. But we were pretty certain that the initial project was the same as it had always been: to develop a way to make human beings stronger, faster and deadlier.'

'Super Soldiers?' Fitz inquired.

'Yes, that's the kind of thing. It was a crazy idea of the husband, a scientist called Dr Karl Adler, and, unfortunately, whilst his wife, Erica, was keen to use her discoveries to help humankind, Karl was exceptionally greedy and probably quite insane. Erica was pregnant, so she naturally took a backseat, but she continued her work in secret. Meanwhile, Karl Adler and Trinity were getting nowhere and Ravensbrook was just about ready to pull out of the project. Then, from what we gather, Karl discovered that Erica had made a tremendous breakthrough in her research and he went absolutely mad – they fought and there was a huge fire on the island. The Trinity Guild were only interested in power and wealth, and they bet almost everything on Karl Adler and Operation Hurricane only to watch it fall apart. Ravensbrook made sure everything was cleared up and by the time we had permission from the locals to search through the rubble, there was nothing left, and the Adler family had disappeared. It was after this that Section X was all but closed down. The government and the security service didn't trust us to make sure that this kind of thing never happened again.'

'But this Karl and Lord Ravensbrook and their Trinity Guild – they failed? They left Hurricane Island empty-handed?' Fitz asked.

'We can't be sure. We know that the Guild broke apart and Hurricane was buried; no one ever spoke of it. With Ravensbrook and the politicians having their dirty little fingers all over the project, can you imagine what the public would think if they found out? Human experiments? Ancient societies? It wasn't safe for anyone to talk to us. But the best we can gather is, whatever they managed to create down there, when the Guild broke apart that night, no one had all the pieces of the jigsaw. But they did create something; Bishop eventually revealed that much to Harry. Something happened out there in the middle of the sea that convinced Ravensbrook not to give up entirely. There are rumours, of course.'

'Time travel,' Azima said, confidently.

'That's one of them yes, but…' Ophelia wagged a finger.

'You know as well as I do that is what's causing the power surges.'

'It's too early to confirm that.'

Azima was locked eyes with Ophelia. 'Whatever they were doing in the Bahamas all those years ago, they screwed it up, but out of their mistake they found a way to create some kind of wormhole and travel through time.'

'That's a dangerous assumption. You have to understand, Azima, you're just a blogger and...'

'I'm a scientist, actually. And my professional opinion is that these surges should be shaking the planet to pieces, but they're not. So why? Because they are controlled somehow. Maybe they are using something from another planet, y'know, like Isaac Newton and his squad were looking into. But whatever their method is, it's deliberate and it's bigger than anything we've ever seen.'

'I appreciate you know your field. I know mine, and however you cut it, you work for a YouTube conspiracy theorist.'

Azima dropped her legs to the floor and stood up. She reached out a hand and nudged Fitz. 'Are you coming?'

Fitz looked back to Ophelia, who was stood rigid, her arms folded. Fitz surprised himself with how quickly he stood up to the spymaster's authority. 'Yeah, let's go.' They picked up their bags.

'I wouldn't advise this,' Ophelia said sternly.

Azima stepped forward. 'You said we were free to leave and so I'm leaving. I might be just a vlogger but you work in a place that's falling down around you. You're not exactly hi-tech and the government gave up on you a long time ago – look around you. You're telling your stories to a bunch of kids because no one else will believe in you anymore. You're the one who brought us here. We're all you've got. So, if you want us to stay, start showing some respect.'

Harry looked at Ophelia and tilted his head. 'She's got a point, ma'am.'

Ophelia clenched her jaw, nodded and gestured for them to retake their seats.

'While you're respecting the kids,' Fitz said, 'I have a question: what the hell does all this have to do with Boyd?'

Ophelia started pacing again. 'By the time Ravensbrook had invested in Hurricane, he had already tried and failed in his own similar experiments. He would take in homeless children, people that wouldn't be missed by anyone...'

'Oh my god!' Fitz exclaimed.

'Yes. Not such a cool bloke after all.'

'Hang on, is he going to experiment on Boyd?' Fitz's voice nudged up an octave.

'Not just yet.'

'What does that mean? What does he need him for?'

'From what Bishop told Harry, Ravensbrook had already experimented with several boys and girls by the time Operation Hurricane went up in flames but the closure of that project left him with a distinct advantage over the rest of his former friends in the Trinity Guild. He had a man there the night of the fire, you see. His clean-up man, who, in the confusion, gathered up as much of the materials and research as he could and brought them back here, to England.'

'So if Ravensbrook has the research, he can build it all for himself. So surely he's the one causing the power surges?' Fitz asked.

'He doesn't have everything, and unfortunately, this is the reason why he was using Boyd as bait.'

'Okay, I am really lost now – he was using Boyd as bait? Bait for what? What am I missing here?'

'The man who brought back the materials for Ravensbrook was called Martin Spengler. He was a former British Soldier in the SAS and one of

Ravensbrook's most trusted soldiers.'

'Martin? Boyd's dad is missing and he's called Martin?' Fitz felt a sudden flush through his body, like he was going to be sick.

'Yes, that's right. The man you know as Boyd's dad is Martin Spengler. But he didn't just bring back a box of papers and some research materials. He brought back a lot more than that.' Ophelia took a deep breath and stopped in front of Fitz. 'Martin brought Erica's diary and in it, she revealed that she had hidden her research. In fact, to keep it safe, she had hidden it within herself. So, Erica Adler has been running for her life for 15 years, never truly safe from anyone who knew about Operation Hurricane. But Ravensbrook never hunted her because he didn't need to. Martin left the Bahamas with her baby son, Evan, who then became the fourth boy to live in Ravensbrook's facility. You see, he'd already had a Boy A, Boy B and Boy C...'

'Oh my god!' Fitz leapt to his feet. 'Evan became Boy D.'

'Yes. After a few years of keeping him locked away, they decided to put him out in the open to see who would come looking for him. Karl, Erica, the Trinity

Guild; they would all have reasons to try to find little Evan. So Ravensbrook gave him a normal life, a life with Martin as his father in a nice house in Bloomfield, never too far from the Lockmead estate. Hornet became his aunt and they simply changed Boy D to Boyd. But according to Bishop, Boyd is so much more than just bait. Ravensbrook has no idea who Boyd really is or what he's capable of and we cannot risk him finding out. Whatever they did on Hurricane Island, whatever they created down there 15 years ago, Boyd is the key to everything.'

The Trinity Guild

As Octavius Ogilvy watched two gorillas drag a kid from a helicopter, he nervously tapped his leg with his fingers. He always did this when he was anxious; same fingers, same beat. Jasper Van Cleef looked at him, and then at his hand, letting the politician know that the noise was just about the most irritating thing he could imagine. Ogilvy didn't stop the tapping; his stomach was doing somersaults at being dragged back into this horrendous business, so it was either tapping his fingers or running around the room screaming.

Just a few hours ago he'd been sitting in his office, safe in the knowledge that he was one of the most powerful men in the land. Now he was reminded that the real power did not reside in politics and was certainly not held by people front of cameras. It was tucked in the dark corners of this world, and held by people like Lord Ravensbrook; people who thought nothing of having two thugs trawl a half-conscious kid across the grass of Lockmead House under the nose of the Home Secretary.

'I apologise you had to see that, gentlemen.' The door opened and Lord Ravensbrook swept in.

Ogilvy turned away from the window. He clearly wasn't sorry; the whole event had been stage-managed so the people in the room could see it. Ravensbrook was a man who knew just how important he was and by letting them see the kid, he insisted that everyone else knew it too.

As a member of the government, Ogilvy felt like he had to say something, to do something. Not because he wanted to help anyone else but because he was scared to death of getting caught in the middle of this mess if it all went wrong. He would lose his job, or maybe even his money – god forbid, he could end up in jail – but for now he said nothing. He decided it was best to wait and see what this bunch of lunatics had up their sleeves and then he could decide if he was going to be a part of it again. It's exactly what he had done 20 years ago when the Trinity Guild had first asked for his help; he had always been smart like that.

'Mr Van Cleef,' Ravensbrook said as he sat in his

office chair, 'I believe we have you to thank for bringing us all back together?'

'It was hardly an act of nobility.' Van Cleef smiled as he casually sat in one of the chairs on the other side of the desk. 'Each of us has got as far as we can alone; together, we are more powerful than we are apart, more powerful than any government.' He shot a sideways glance at Ogilvy.

'So, what makes you think Miranda is going to suddenly show herself now, after all these years?' Lord Ravensbrook asked.

'I don't.' Van Cleef let out a burst of laughter and shook his head, as if this was a preposterous suggestion. 'That is not what I think at all.'

Ravensbrook sat forward, agitated. 'So why have we altered the plan? Why have we brought the boy back in?' Clearly he was unhappy being made a fool of at any time, but especially in his own office.

'Because we don't need her. Surely you can see what's happening? The boy is the key, we now have everything we need.'

Ravensbrook flopped back into his chair and removed his glasses. He held them up, removed a handkerchief from his pocket and began to polish them.

'The boy? And we had him right here, under our noses all along. Very well, I'll get my people to start work immediately.'

'No.'

Ravensbrook was not used to hearing that word, and now he had heard it twice in the same exchange. He stopped dead, holding his glasses up again, before sliding them back into place, his eyes fixed on Van Cleef. Now it was Van Cleef's turn to show his strength. He removed a card from his pocket and held it up.

'You will call this man. He is the best in his field, and we need the best. He will be expecting your call. Until he is here, we wait.'

Ravensbrook paused. He held Van Cleef's gaze and didn't blink. His Lordship allowed a long, uncomfortable silence to spread around the room like a bad smell. Then he nodded to Knowles, who emerged from the corner of the room and took the card from Van Cleef.

'Give that to Jagger, tell him to make all the necessary arrangements.' He waved Knowles away with a hand.

Ravensbrook stood and went to a small drinks table. He collected three tumbler glasses in one hand and a chunky crystal decanter filled with dark, brown liquid. His Lordship walked around the other side of the desk, roughly dropped the glasses onto the antique wood and poured three generous measures of whisky. 'Taking our time actually suits me.' He handed a glass to Van Cleef and one to Ogilvy before raising his own in a toast. 'Now, to a matter where I refuse to demonstrate any more patience: my man, Martin Spengler. I want him back, Mr Van Cleef.'

'The father?' Van Cleef nodded. 'Of course, he is unharmed. You can have him with my apologies.'

'In that case, gentlemen,' Ravensbrook said with a smile. 'I propose a toast; to the Trinity Guild.'

Van Cleef and his Lordship brought their glasses together. Ogilvy hesitated long enough that the other men both fired uncertain glances in his direction. The Home Secretary swiftly brought his glass up to meet theirs and it struck with a loud 'CLINK'; some of the sticky liquid spilled over his hand and he smiled nervously. It looked like he was going to be part of this after all.

Can You Hack It?

Fitz was still trying to take in all the revelations about Boyd's past. The story was so extraordinary, it couldn't be true. But then it also made perfect sense; it explained why Boyd was the way he was. Ever since Fitz had known him, Boyd had been unlike anyone else he knew: quick to temper, cold and withdrawn from everyone and everything in life. Ophelia had told them how Martin had set up a home with Boyd as his son when he was just five-years-old. Fitz couldn't even imagine what Boyd had been through up to then and whatever happened must still be lurking inside of him, locked away in his head.

'So where was he up until then?' Fitz asked.

'Where he is now – they've taken him home, in a sense.'

'You know where he is? So we should just call the police or tell someone in the government? My dad might be able to help.'

'It's not that simple. Ravensbrook is extremely well-connected and the location where they are holding Boyd and Skye isn't somewhere you can just walk into, no matter who you are.'

'But we are going to find a way? I mean, we are going in there?'

'Oh, we're definitely going in there,' Harry said. 'But not without your help.' He took the remote control and clicked it. An image of what looked like an aeroplane hangar appeared on the screen; a long building with a curved metal roof, set in the middle of a wooded area.

'This is a top-secret facility on the outskirts of His Lordship's land in Bloomfield. It doesn't have a name, as such, but its nickname is the Barn.'

'If it's so top-secret,' Azima pointed out. 'How do you know about it?'

Harry smiled. 'Because there's a tiny hole in Ravensbrook's operation and he has no idea it's even there.' Harry raised his hand and pressed the remote. An image of a tall, broad man with curly blond hair and a dissatisfied sneer appeared on the screen. 'This fella is such an over-confident fool, he doesn't even know he's passing information to us. I'd like you to meet former

MI5 data analyst, Elliot Jagger. He is now the head of cyber-security for the Lockmead estates. Since he left the secret service, Jagger believes he has been successfully wandering in and out the back door to their network and pinching anything he wants.'

'But he hasn't?' Fitz asked.

'Well, technically, yes, he has, but only because we've not bothered to tell MI5 about it. Unfortunately, Ravensbrook's entire network at the Lockmead estate is all but impenetrable, but Barnaby did have some success when we began tracing Mr Jagger, here.'

'Hang on – Grandpa is your IT guy?'

'What of it, lad?' Barnaby appeared, seemingly from nowhere.

Fitz jumped. 'Whoa, there! Crikey, fella! Where did you crawl out from? No, that's impressive. Great work. Truly,' He composed himself. 'So, Barnaby, what changed when Jagger arrived on the scene?'

'He created and installed a highly sophisticated security system across the Lockmead site, and it became impossible for us to send any electronic device in there and expect to get a signal from it.'

'So how does that help us?' Azima said, quizzically.

'It doesn't, but he is also an arrogant twerp – as is so often the case with kids nowadays.' He smiled at Fitz. 'Elliot Jagger has a bee in his bonnet with MI5, so he likes to play games with their systems. Oh, it's all fairly harmless stuff and we keep a close eye on him to make sure he's not doing anything too disruptive. He enjoys sending dodgy emails between colleagues and changing room bookings so 25 people turn up to the wrong meeting – basically, the electronic version of putting dog poo through someone's letterbox. But the point is, over time, he's got careless and he likes to play his little pranks from the comfort of his own home. One day when he was online at the house he shares with his mum, I combed his system. The fool had all the plans for the security system, right there on his laptop, behind a flimsy firewall.'

'So, I take it we're going to give Mr Dog Poo a bit of a wake-up call?' Fitz smiled.

'Bingo, and here's how.' Harry brought up another image onto the screen. 'Jagger had a call on his way home tonight, from this man: Erlich Schmidt.'

Azima perked upon hearing the name. 'He's a bio-physicist., an expert on nanotechnology.'

'Ten points to Azima. Some say he's the world's best at nano-engineering.'

'And remind me, how small is a nano?' Fitz asked.

'Well,' Azima said, buzzing with enthusiasm, 'a sheet of paper is about 100,000 nanometres thick.'

'Wow. So, he's good.'

'He is,' Harry continued. 'And he's also completely without morals, available to the highest bidder and he's now on his way to the Lockmead estate. He called and left Elliot a voicemail about a change to his travel arrangements. They want him there to start work on Friday but Schmidt wants to fly in earlier so he can have a look around London.'

'And this gives the Toy Department the chance to intercept him,' Ophelia said.

'What's this guy going to be doing at Lockmead?' Fitz asked.

'We presume that they are going to try to find out what Boyd is made of, literally. If they are experimenting on Boyd, well, as I said, we can't let that happen. But they can't start until Friday because of this.' Ophelia pointed to the screen.

Harry pressed the remote and a YouTube clip

exploded into life. There were stock cars smashing into each other, motocross bikes jumping over flaming buses and quad bikes speeding around a dirt track.

'Lockmead's annual SpeedFest starts tomorrow,' Ophelia continued. 'The whole estate will be full of press, the rich and famous, and everyone who is anyone in the motor industry, plus around 200,000 members of the general public. His Lordship will be followed by a camera for the next two days; he hosts a party every night and he can't just disappear to deal with his secret experiments on a teenager. He's waited 15 years and he's going to have to wait for two more days, so, we have a window: 48 hours to get Harry into the Barn under Schmidt's ID and break Boyd and Skye out. And Fitz, that's where you come in.'

'Sure. What do you need?'

'Jagger will have set up a profile for our friend Schmidt to access the Barn and we need to hack it,' Ophelia looked to Barnaby. 'Barnaby…'

'And this is where I start to enjoy myself.' Fitz pulled away from the desk and folded his arms. 'What are we dealing with?'

'To warm us up, the Barn uses voice recognition,'

Barnaby said.

'Okay, that's not too drastic. The key to voice recognition is to have a recording and playback device with a high bit-rate.'

'And the next stage of security is biometric.'

Fitz's eyes widened. 'What kind of biometric security are we talking about?' he asked.

'Vein Authentication.' Ophelia looked at Fitz, her head tilted downward, smiling at the idea of the challenge.

'Crikey. Yeah, that's really not going to be easy.'

Harry clicked the remote and the screens were suddenly filled with diagrams and technical drawings of the Vein Authentication reader they had stolen from Elliot Jagger's laptop. Fitz watched closely as a video showed a mock-up of a hand being lowered onto a soft gel pad before a metal cover closed around it. Then a light shone through the graphic of the hand and the veins were highlighted in blue as the machine scanned the precise location and size of the individual's veins.

Fitz moved closer to the screens, a smile unfolding across his face as his eyes opened wide. 'Now that is a thing of beauty.' He stroked the screen in admiration.

'Remind me how long have I got to figure this out?'

Ophelia looked to Harry; Fitz's eyes followed hers.

'Schmidt lands tomorrow morning at eleven,' Harry said. 'So, no pressure.'

Fire And Ice

Boyd woke up with a start, gasping for air. He had felt like he was falling; he had been reaching out to try to grab something to stop himself, but he just kept tumbling through the air, faster and faster. Then he felt an impact, like he had hit the floor, and he heard a desperate shout.

He realised it had been a dream and the shout had come from him.

He sat up and his head throbbed. He was on a single bed, in a large room that was covered floor-to-ceiling in silver metal panels that curved up from the floor on one side of the room into the middle, like an underground railway station. There was a door to the right of the bed. Boyd reached around to the back of his neck and rubbed at what felt like a mosquito bite. Then he remembered being injected with something when he climbed into the helicopter. He clenched his fists as he recalled Skye's last words to him: 'Keep your head.' Easier said than done.

Boyd closed his eyes and swallowed down his anger. He knew Skye was right; he would need to find out exactly where he was and who he was dealing with if he was going to get them out of here alive. In the meantime, he meant to play them at their own game. That would mean facing whatever they threw at him and letting them think he was the same old Boyd, immature and naive. Because whatever their plan, it was obvious to him that they needed him desperately and he was going to have to convince them that if it helped Skye and Martin, maybe he would be on their side.

So he closed his eyes and drew in another long breath. Boyd felt the familiar fire of rage that usually ran through his veins turn into cold ice as he walked calmly to the door.

Never Doubt My Powers

Erlich Schmidt's flight from Berlin was delayed. Fitz sat with Azima in the arrivals lounge and struggled to stay awake. No matter how much coffee he poured down his neck, with the chronic boredom of inactivity, Fitz's brain just wanted to shut down.

He had called his father last night and told him as much about his activities as he could. Considering Fitz was missing from home and had been involved in a major incident in the middle of London, his dad had reacted very strangely. Roger Tork had tried to make out he was being cool about it, but something was not right, and Fitz had no clue what it was. Fitz had expected shouting and demands to return home, but his dad had just asked Fitz to keep him updated with everything. Fitz hadn't had the time to dwell on it last night; he had to start researching the Vein Authentication system they had to hack to get into the Barn.

Harry had replayed the call Schmidt had made to

Elliot Jagger:

'*Thank you for changing my flight to tomorrow. I will be ready to work Friday as requested. I've sent you the data you asked for.*'

'"*I have sent you the data you asked for…*" I would bet you anything you like that the data he has sent them is a scan of his hand.'

Fitz had nodded slowly as he suddenly realised what Barnaby meant. 'So if he's scanned his own hand and sent them the data, there must be a way for us to scan it too!'

Fitz then spent every minute of the long night working out how they could scan a copy of Schmidt's hand, right down to the size and position of the veins. Finally, at around five am he believed he had cracked it. They all gathered around.

'If we had just wanted Schmidt's fingerprints, then we could simply pinch an object he's touched, but this was always going to be much more complicated than that. So I've adapted a Single Lens Reflex camera, or SLR, by removing the infrared filter, which allowed me to get a perfect image of the veins inside my hand.' Fitz held up an image. Now all he had to do was work out

409

how to create a perfect replica of a human hand in around 24 hours. Absolute doddle. No problem at all.

The arrivals board had finally changed ten minutes ago to show that Schmidt's plane had landed, and the passengers would now be collecting their luggage. Finally, a tall, slim man with a large bald patch at the back of his brown hair emerged through arrivals – Erlich Schmidt. Fitz and Azima could easily follow him from a safe distance, they just had to keep that bald spot in sight.

Barnaby was waiting on the other side of the arrivals barrier, posing as a limo driver. As Schmidt emerged, Barnaby pretended to wave at someone behind him and made his move. As he made his way towards his make-believe client, Barnaby 'accidentally' tripped over a suitcase, right at the feet of Erlich Schmidt. Despite appearances, Barnaby was as lithe and flexible as any man a quarter of his age. His fall may have looked bone-crunchingly painful but he was perfectly in control, fulfilling his clandestine task with precision timing.

'Oh, my goodness,' Barnaby said loudly. 'I am so sorry, sir, I really am.'

Schmidt was pulling his own small roller suitcase with his right hand and he reached down to help Barnaby to his feet using his left. Barnaby only had a hold of the scientist's wrist for around five seconds. He put both hands around there and pulled himself up onto his feet.

'Are you okay?' Schmidt asked.

'I am, thank you for your kindness.' Barnaby gave a smile and stepped aside.

Schmidt walked to the exit, went outside and hailed a taxi. Azima and Fitz exited and jumped in the Royal Parks van, where Harry was behind the wheel. They didn't force their way out into traffic, and Harry didn't put his foot down to keep up with Schmidt's aggressive taxi driver – he didn't need to. Barnaby had perfectly placed a tiny tracker onto the inside of Schmidt's watch strap that would give them twelve hours of signal.

Harry pulled the van into traffic, looked at the screen of his phone and followed the pulsating dot as it headed towards London.

'Well, that was a pretty good start, eh team?' Azima nodded to Fitz.

'Not bad,' he replied. 'Now all we have to do is find

the ideal time to have him stand still for at least 45 seconds so you can scan his hand.'

'I spent a year on the streets of London living on my wits.'

'Meaning what, exactly?'

'Never doubt my powers, Fitzgerald, it won't end well for you,' she said with a grin.

Fitz sighed. He *really* needed another coffee.

Welcome Home

Boyd had knocked on the door twice before going back to his bed and lying on his back. After what felt like around ten minutes, someone on the other side punched a code into the keypad. Hornet walked in. Boyd didn't move; his face remained impassive.

'Hello, Boyd.' She smiled. 'Sorry about the rough ride in.'

'The Tube gets so stuffy at that time of day; it made a lovely change.'

Hornet's smile grew but behind it was a sense of trepidation. She was wary of him; that was an interesting development. 'There's someone I'd like you to meet.'

'A party? For me? How wonderful.' He jumped off the bed as Hornet watched him carefully. 'Everything okay?' Boyd asked her.

'Yes, why wouldn't it be?'

'No reason. You just seem a bit, oh I don't know, on

413

edge?'

He saw a flash of something in her eyes – anger perhaps. She was rattled, and his gloating was only making her more unsettled. She stepped aside and gestured for him to exit first.

'Just get moving.'

'Not very hospitable. I'll mention this on TripAdvisor.'

Boyd walked out of the door and was surprised to be greeted by a group of five men, all dressed in black, all built like rugby players and each of them on their toes, ready for things to get nasty. Two of them had batons: thick black sticks like cattle prods, used to deliver a voltage of electricity into anyone who got caught on the wrong end of it. Boyd took some satisfaction in the fact that they were worried, but he was equally puzzled as to why they were so cautious with him; they were each twice his size.

Just like his room, the hallway had silver panels on the wall and ceiling. A door opposite was opened and Boyd was shown into a room that was set out like a lounge. The walls were white and in the middle of the room were two sofas facing each other. Hornet followed

414

him in, along with the two guards with the cattle prods; the others stayed outside.

Boyd sat in the middle of the sofa that faced the door and crossed his legs. He put both arms up and rested them along the back of the cushions, laid his head back and closed his eyes. He had an eerie feeling about this place, this room, something he couldn't shake off; it was like he had seen it somewhere before. The door opened again but Boyd stayed exactly where he was for a moment and didn't react.

'Well, I am glad to see we're keeping you so comfortable,' the man said.

Boyd lifted his head and opened his eyes, as if he had just been about to drop off into a nice, relaxing sleep. 'Well, now you mention it, I do have one or two minor complaints. Do you have a suggestion box?' he said, keeping his voice neutral.

The man tilted his head and cracked a strained smile. 'Do you know who I am?'

Even though he was dressed in the kind of overalls a racing driver wears, Boyd, like any resident of Bloomfield, had recognised the man immediately.

'You're Lord Ravensbrook.' Boyd sat up slightly and

nodded his head. 'Now this is interesting.'

'And why is that?'

'Because I knew that whoever walked through that door was the complete lunatic who's been chasing me since last week. I wouldn't have put any money on it being you.'

'Good!' Ravensbrook let a loud laugh erupt from his throat. 'I'm rather glad I wasn't on your radar – it means I'm doing something right.' He sat on the sofa opposite Boyd. 'I apologise for all the theatrics, I really do. I'm not one for all that. But sometimes these things are only resolved if you take a certain type of action and that's where she comes in.' Ravensbrook gestured towards Hornet, who was still standing by the door.

'Who is she?' Boyd asked, doing his best to keep his voice from cracking.

'Surely you know your aunt when you see her?'

'I know a liar when I see one.'

'You're right. Good point well made. You have my word, that's the last lie I will tell you. Let me try again: she is Hornet, a lethal and cruel assassin who has worked for me for more than a decade. She was put in place as your aunt to keep watch over you. Now, ask me

416

another; anything you want.'

'Why did you need to keep watch over me?'

'That's a good one! You see, we knew that one day, people would come for you. But we had no idea – it's almost comical really. If we'd known then what we know now, well, it would have saved so much time. The fact is, you are exceptional, Boyd. And there are those that would seek to exploit you, perhaps even destroy you. I will not let that happen. You must understand, you are safe here with us, no matter who tells you any different. The truth you long for is that this world is made up of two kinds of people: those who jump into the fire and those who live in fear of getting burnt. The greatest accomplishments in human history only came about because someone was brave enough to run into the flames, while the rest of the world simply stood at a safe distance and sneered. A time is coming, very soon, where everything will change and you will have to decide which type of person you are, and which side of history you want to be on. Together, we can have everything, you and I. Remember that.'

All the times Boyd had seen Lord Ravensbrook on television or even when he visited his school, the affable adventurer had seemed so ordinary, funny and inspiring. It's why everyone seemed to love him. But looking into his eyes, Boyd saw beyond that now: it was all an act and the real man behind the mask was in front of him, talking about taking over the world. He was barking mad and he did a great job of hiding it, but maybe now was not the right time to bring it up.

'So, what is it that makes me exceptional?'

Ravensbrook checked his watch and waved a hand, he was done. Boyd could see him transform back in front of his eyes. In an instant, the maniacal millionaire became the good-natured adventurer again. He slapped his hands on his thighs. 'We will get to that, my boy, we have plenty of time ahead of us. For now, I want you to settle in here.' Lord Ravensbrook stood and moved back towards the door.

Boyd leant forward onto his knees. 'And where exactly is here?'

Ravensbrook turned around, a smile of surprise etched across his lips. 'You really don't remember, do you? This is where it all began, Boyd. Welcome home.'

Elementary, My Dear Fitz

Schmidt had left the airport, dumped his bags at a hotel and gone straight to the London Underground. Fitz and Azima followed on foot as the tall, German scientist bounded out of his hotel and headed for the Bakerloo Line. Azima had the tracking app on her phone, so they could calmly follow at a distance. But both were aware that they needed to find an opportunity to get this done without rousing Schmidt's suspicion, and time was running out.

They were standing on the platform at Maida Vale, a little too close to Schmidt for Azima's liking. She waited for him to look down the tunnel for the approaching train and she carefully observed everything about him: his clothes, shoes and the book he was carrying. Then she moved them down to the end of the platform and when the train arrived, they boarded the last carriage. They passed through the first few stations in silence, then Fitz turned to Azima and spoke over the clatter of

419

the train.

'So, where are you from?' Fitz asked, making conversation to take his mind off things.

'Syria,' Azima replied, proudly.

'Wow.'

'Yeah, pretty much.'

'How did you… y'know…'

'How did I get out? How did I get to here?'

'Yeah, all of the above.'

'I lost everything: my home, my family. You can't even imagine it. I can't sometimes; it feels unreal,' Azima said, staring into space as the train moved off.

'No, you're right, I can't even begin. I'm not sure I'd be able to carry on.'

'You would, Fitz. You carry on because you have to. It's like this, what we're doing now – you get up off your butt and do it because no one is going to do it for you. I used to feel bad for myself all the time, but it made me sad, it made me different from how my mother would want me to be, so I stopped. Now I think of my family and I am happy. I am lucky. I found Skye and she changed my life. She is my family now. I owe her everything.'

'We'll find them,' Fitz said, but he could see that Azima wasn't really listening, she was looking at the map of the Bakerloo line on the wall of the train.

Azima stood up and dragged him towards the doors. 'Come on, we're getting out here.'

'How do you know that?'

'I just do. Follow me and we can get ahead of him.'

The trained squealed to a halt and Azima was out of the train and up the stairs so fast, Fitz struggled to keep pace. He stepped out into the sunlight at Baker Street Station and she was waiting for him.

'Round here, quick.' She turned right and headed along Baker Street. 'Cross here,' Azima said, dragging Fitz across the road, between a bus and a taxi.

'Whoa! Are you trying to get me killed?' Fitz turned and saw the familiar bald head atop a tall, thin frame as Schmidt weaved along the pavement. 'He's over there, on the other side of the road.'

'Not for long. Get the camera out, get ready with it – I know where he's going. Stop looking at me like I don't know what I'm doing, Fitz.'

'I'm sorry! And it's quite the opposite. I find it quite worrying that you seem to know exactly what you're doing.'

Fitz flipped his backpack around and pulled out the modified SLR camera. The adjustments he had made meant that he just had to get Schmidt to press the shutter-release button once and hold the camera for 45 seconds and they would have a perfect scan of his vein configuration. If he pressed it twice, it would stop the scan. Fitz had also installed a 128-kilobytes-per-second voice recorder in the camera, so they just needed to capture him saying his name and they'd have everything they needed.

Fitz fumbled with the camera as he followed Azima down a packed Baker Street. 'Can you still see him?' he said, flustered.

'Yes. Relax and try to be a little more covert.'

'Has he crossed the street yet?'

'No, but he will. Don't panic.'

'How do you know? What if we lose him?'

Azima slowed and gently tugged at Fitz's arm. He turned to her. 'The book he was reading,' she whispered. Then she amplified her voice along with her accent, 'Here it is! 221B!' She pointed at a black door, next to a shop with an old-fashioned sign that read: '*The Sherlock*

Holmes Museum.'

A horn blared out to their right as Schmidt crossed the road in front of a car. Azima stood in front of the shop and pretended to point at things in the window. In the reflection, Fitz could see Schmidt finding a spot on the edge of the kerb as he struggled to capture an acceptable selfie that didn't have irritable Londoners in the background. Then, as he turned, Fitz saw it: on top of Schmidt's bag was a well-worn paperback book, '*A Study in Scarlet – A Sherlock Holmes Mystery*'.

Azima approached the scientist. 'Excuse me,' she said, her English suddenly broken as if every word was a struggle. 'I can take a photo of you in front of the door if you take one for me and my boyfriend?'

Schmidt took a moment before shaking his head. He clearly wasn't the type to just trust a stranger with his phone. 'No, thank you,' he replied, straight-lipped.

Azima wasn't giving up that easily. She physically shoved the wiry German into place in front of the shop. Then she took his phone and stepped back. She held out her hand to two people who were about to walk in front of her and barked, 'Wait one second, please!' They stopped, their faces a picture of frustration but they didn't say a word. Azima fired off a round of pictures and then waved them through. 'Here.' She handed Schmidt his phone.

He looked at her in disbelief. When he checked the pictures on his phone, he smiled. 'Thank you,' he said, nodding. He smiled and showed her a set of bright white teeth.

'You are very welcome,' she said back. Azima then took the SLR camera from Fitz, handed it to Schmidt and pointed at the shutter release. 'Just press once, okay?'

She and Fitz took up position on the steps. Azima nodded to Schmidt and he pressed the button. Azima left the steps before he could offer to take another picture; she didn't want him to press the button again and abort the scan. She took her time getting across the crowded pavement to him as she counted down from 45. She then remembered her rucksack on the step and went back for it, all the while, the SLR camera would be busy scanning Schmidt's hand. She reached him as the timer in her head arrived at 40 seconds. 'I am Dalila Salah.' Azima purposefully held out her left hand.

Schmidt looked down at it and extended his own. 'I am Erlich Schmidt. Pleased to meet you.'

Fitz joined them. 'Erling Smith?' he asked.

'Erlich,' Schmidt said, a little frustrated. 'Erlich Schmidt.'

'Ah! Gotcha. I had an uncle called Erlich, great guy. Anyway, it's been lovely, cheers.' Fitz nodded and took the camera. 'Bye!' he said as he popped his rucksack back on and marched off towards London Zoo.

Azima waved and smiled as she left a slightly bewildered Schmidt on the pavement. When she caught up with Fitz, he was playing with the camera. 'Did we get it?' she asked him as they dodged the half-term crowds. 'Fitz, did we get it?'

He smiled. 'We got it.'

'Good. Let's get back to the Toy Shop. You've got work to do.'

This Is Our Target

'So, ladies and gentlemen, this is our target.' Harry was waving a pencil towards a 3D projection of the Barn. The flickering image was rising out of a virtual-reality table at the Toy Shop, one of Barnaby's proudest creations. The rest of the team were crowded around, listening intently.

'3D projection table?' Fitz scoffed. 'I thought you lot were broke? You're like Dexter Ferguson at school, pleading poverty when we're at the shop, then turns up the next day in new Nike Air Max 90s. Buy your own *Pot Noodle* then, mate! Right?' Fitz laughed to himself, then noticed that everyone was staring at him. 'Didn't mean to interrupt. Back to you, Harry.'

'Right, thanks for that, Fitz.' Harry raised his eyebrows. 'Getting into the Barn will literally be just the tip of the iceberg. We have plans for the section above ground but from what Bishop told me, there is an underground section that they affectionately refer to as "the Belly". This is where they work on anything particularly nasty that they want to keep from prying eyes, so we can presume that this is where they are holding Boyd and Skye.'

Harry pointed to a room at the rear of the 3D projection. 'As we understand it, this room is empty apart from a single guard, who sits in a chair and watches the door like a hawk. To get into the Belly, we've got to get across that room and into that lift without being seen by the guard. Then, if by some miracle we find a way down into the Belly, we have no idea what the layout is, or what I'm walking into down there.'

'But if you're going in as Schmidt, they'll let you walk straight through, surely?' Azima looked at Harry puzzled.

'Schmidt isn't due until Friday – we're going to hit the place tomorrow, when Ravensbrook is busy. We might be able to get past the front desk and into the Barn posing as Schmidt, but the Belly is highly restricted access; no one goes down there without His Lordship knowing about it. The minute I walk through that door and head towards the lift, that guard will be on their radio to Hornet and our plan is stuffed.'

'So, we need to quietly take that guard out of circulation, without them raising the alarm.' Fitz rubbed his face as his brain whirred.

'How's our fake hand coming along?' Ophelia asked.

'It's good. I'm going with wax, so it'll need some time to dry. I've got an idea for that guard too. Harry, have you got a spare pair of glasses I can borrow?'

Harry raised his eyebrows suspiciously. 'Perhaps. Will I get them back?'

'Of course, they'll be better than ever,' Fitz said, as if he was insulted.

Harry took a pair of metal framed spectacles out of his pocket and handed them to Fitz.

'Perfect. Barney's going to customise them for you,' Fitz winked.

'Why does that not fill me with confidence?' Harry rolled his eyes. 'So I'll be going in, whilst you four run operations from the outside. As Barnaby explained, there's no chance we can get a signal into or out of that place, which means the minute I step over the threshold, my communications will go dark. Now, we need to talk about a plan for when we come out. It would be lovely to think we can quietly slip out the front door, but it's a pretty fair bet that we'll have to make some noise and come out of there running for our lives.'

A silence fell over the team. They all knew that there was a chance that Boyd and Skye wouldn't be coming out of there in the same state as when they'd gone in.

'This is going to work, isn't it?' Fitz asked no one in particular.

'It has to,' Azima said, her voice slightly shaky.

Ophelia looked around the group. 'Listen you lot,' she said as she stepped to the head of the table. 'I've spent a good deal of my life battling against the powerful and corrupt, and the game is always rigged; we never seem to get a fair fight. I look around this table and I couldn't think of a better bunch to take these creatures on. Remember this: they won't be ready for us, they won't have ever seen anything like us and we've got Boyd and Skye on our side too. So let's leave the brooding for another time, yes? We need to bring our people home.'

They all nodded. Azima and Fitz did their best to hold in their emotions.

'Oh, and don't worry,' Ophelia added with a smile. 'I've had an idea for how to get us all away from that wretched place in one piece. You leave that with me.'

What You Do Best

Hornet was not a patient woman but, in some cases, she had to make an exception. One only got in to see Lord Ravensbrook when he was ready and not a moment before. So she stood in the hallway of Lockmead House and distracted herself by studying the huge paintings set in their heavy, gold frames, the dark, wooden antique furniture, and the enormous vases and ornaments that sat on top of them. Hornet had never been one for material possessions. She preferred power and had never needed money to get it. In her experience, fear had always been the best way to influence any situation. But Lord Ravensbrook had been good to her and he had provided a purpose for her chilling talents, so she respected him more than anyone she had ever met. Still, she *really* didn't like waiting.

Knowles appeared and ushered her into a sitting room where His Lordship was sitting by a fire enjoying a glass of brandy. There were no lamps on, and the only light was the glow thrown out from the fireplace. Ravensbrook sat in a high-backed leather chair, swilling the brown liquid around in a glass so large, it resembled a fishbowl. He motioned for Hornet to sit in an identical chair opposite his own.

'Van Cleef's scientist chap has arrived?' Ravensbrook asked.

'Yes, safe and sound. We'll collect him Friday morning.'

'Fine. Let him be a tourist for a day or two. What about Martin?'

'He's in the East Wing. He was unharmed, just as Van Cleef said.'

'Good, I want you to put him in with Boyd tomorrow morning.'

'Is that wise?'

Ravensbrook looked at Hornet; he didn't like being questioned by his own people. 'I think so.'

'If I can speak with Boyd, I think I can bring him over to us if you'll let me try.'

Ravensbrook drained his glass and rested it on the arm of his chair. 'I don't believe you can; I think he's got the beating of you. Somehow, by putting him into the world with only a soldier and an assassin for company, I believe we've created a stone-cold operator with a filthy temper. The lad is 15 years old and yet his ability to think through scenarios and equate outcomes is far beyond what your reports told me. I think it's time you consider the fact that you completely underestimated him.'

'But he isn't heartless. I can play the part and tug at his emotions.'

'I don't think so. He's a complex young man – all teenagers are – and you failed to factor that in.'

'Please, I insist…' Hornet's voice raised a notch.

'You insist?' Ravensbrook suddenly looked up at her, irritation in his voice. 'Please don't embarrass yourself, old friend. I've made my decision and it's final. We need to get beneath that emotional armour he has created for himself. So you will show him to the room and leave him with Martin – that's the way to give his young heart a little squeeze.' He looked into the fire and smiled, the flames dancing in the black of his eyes.

He turned to Hornet, who was seething with anger. 'Anyway, I need you to speak with the girl tomorrow and find out what she knows,' he said, trying to soften the blow. He waved his hand to dismiss her.

Hornet stood and for a moment, looked like she was going to say something, but she couldn't find the right words.

'You're angry, that's good,' Ravensbrook said to her. 'You always do your best work when you're angry. Twist that rage into something sharp, then use it on Skye. Do what you do best.'

Boy D

Boyd had lost all track of time. How long had he been back in this room? He had been replaying the events of the last week over in his mind and realised how everything was building towards a reckoning. And now, those same two words were going around and around in his head: 'Welcome home.'

The minute he had set foot in the lounge across the hallway, he felt like he had been there before. Then when Ravensbrook had uttered those words, it just confirmed what Boyd had known to be true: this place, whatever it was, was where he had spent the first few years of his life; not in a children's home, as his dad had always told him. But then, according to Ophelia, Martin wasn't really his father, so who the hell was he and what was he to Boyd?

This was how his mind had worked for the last few hours as he pulled at threads and tried to see the truth behind the lies. Boyd had lain on the bed, paced the floor and done everything he could to let all of this wash over him now before they came for him again, because he couldn't allow any of it to get in his way. Ravensbrook wanted Boyd confused; he wanted his mind clouded so that he didn't know up from down, left from right. Ophelia had told him to be ready for it and he had to do his best to fight it off. So, as the door opened again, he pushed all the questions to the back of his mind and held onto one thing: if he wanted to find Skye and get the hell out of there, he had to stay smart.

Hornet gestured for Boyd to follow her. She led him a short way down the corridor, to a frosted-glass door that, unlike the rest of the facility, had no keypad next to it. Instead, mounted on the stark, silver wall next to the door handle was a sign that made him do a double-take and stop in his tracks. He swallowed hard; his eyes set on the black letters carved into the brushed metal while all around it blurred into insignificance.

The sign said, "*Boy D*".

'Everything alright, Boyd?' Hornet smiled knowingly as she stood in front of the open door.

Boyd broke his gaze away and looked into her electric green eyes. 'Fine.'

He walked past her and into the room. Like the room

they had been keeping him in, the roof sloped down on one side, but this was bigger, much bigger. The walls were covered in posters, and he could see four screens set into the walls, all showing cartoons. There was a large bookshelf, sofas, chairs and several bean bags. One corner was set up like a bedroom, and an *Iron Man* bedspread was just about visible beneath a pile of soft toys. Boyd felt a sting in his eyes as the tears began to form. He knew his hands were shaking but he couldn't do anything about it. He wouldn't allow himself to look at Hornet; he wouldn't give her the satisfaction.

Every glance at another part of the room was like being placed inside a living photograph, a faded memory. This was his room; this was where his life had begun and he felt as if he had walked out of it just moments ago. There was a small partition that cut off the last part of the room, with an archway shaped into the metal wall to whatever was beyond. A man in a polo shirt and jeans stepped through it.

'Hello Boyd,' Martin said with a small nod and a nervous twitch of a smile.

Boyd could see Hornet watching him intently and he could almost feel her desire for him to lose control. He allowed the sudden burst of heat he felt to evaporate like the steam from a kettle. Boyd settled his pale blue eyes on Martin for a long moment, then he looked away and walked to a small table with a jug of water and some glasses. He poured himself a water.

'Either of you guys want one?' he said casually, keeping his back to them.

'No, thank you,' Martin replied.

'I'm fine,' Hornet said, frustrated.

Boyd turned and took a sip of the water. He held his hand up and shook his head. 'Sorry! Where are my manners? Allow me to propose a toast.' He raised the glass. 'To family.'

Hornet was carefully examining his every move. This had clearly been a ploy to lure some of the old Boyd to the surface by bringing him here, to this room and putting Martin in front of him, but Boyd couldn't let her see if it had worked.

'Well, you two have a good amount of catching up to do.' She turned and walked back to the door. 'I'll leave you to it.'

'Thanks, Aurora,' Boyd said with a mischievous grin.

Hornet stared at Boyd, narrowing her eyes and tilting her head. As she walked out of the door, it hissed shut and a click told Boyd that it was locked.

Boyd moved around to a sofa opposite Martin and sat down. He had no idea where to even begin with the man standing in front of him; the man he had called 'dad' for 10 years. They had never had a perfect relationship, it was true, but they had been the closest companions to one another. They had been on holidays, shared jokes; Martin had taught him how to rock climb, how to scuba dive, how to ride a bike, but Boyd still felt as if he had been cheated.

Martin lowered himself into the seat opposite him, slowly, as if asking permission. Boyd realised that despite having always been so distant, Martin had always made him feel safe and secure. He had taught him to take care of himself, not be afraid or care what anyone else thought of him, and to have confidence in himself; that was surely everything you could want from a parent. But what stood out the most was the shared a bond over the loss of Boyd's mother, and now he had to ask himself how much of that was even true.

Not ready to face Martin yet, Boyd looked at the

books on the shelf in the corner. He felt like he remembered some of them; he was sure he could recall running his hands over the spines and picking a book before jumping into bed. Was that real, or was it his mind playing a cruel trick on him? It was then he knew that the pain he had felt when he first stepped into the room was the agony of loss: not for his mother, not for his father, but for the innocent child that had lived in this room 10 years ago, for Boy D.

'You don't have to put on a show now. There aren't any cameras in here.'

'Right,' Boyd nodded.

'It's true. Ravensbrook could never risk any record of what they do down here. Boyd, listen to me, I don't imagine we have a lot of time. I'm not going to lie to you, you can ask me anything.'

'Strange, that's what His Lordship said. Caretaker.'

Martin bowed his head in shame. 'Okay, I'll prove that they're not watching us or listening in.'

'I'm all ears.'

'You're in a facility called the Barn, on the Lockmead estate. We're underground in what they call "the Belly". 15 years ago, I took you from your mother and brought you here because she created something that could shake the world to its core and Ravensbrook wanted it; it consumed him. You and I lived here for a few years but as you got older, it made sense for you to be out in the real world. You liked me. I used to visit you in here every day; you trusted me.'

'I was five. Five-year-olds trust anyone with ice cream.'

'But you were different.'

'I was bait. It was my mother you wanted.'

'That was true, at first, yes. I know I wasn't exactly a great father.'

'Maybe the fact that you're not actually my father had something to do with that?'

'It wasn't all down to me; you weren't like other kids. You didn't come to me when you had nightmares or sleep in my bed when you got sick; you never asked for help with homework. You just got on with everything, always on your own. You never needed anyone.'

'Maybe I did, I just didn't *have* anyone – there's a difference, Martin.'

Martin stood up and dragged his hands through his

441

hair. Boyd had never seen him like this; he had always been so cool and in control.

'I wanted to be there for you, but I always had all of this hanging over me; I had a responsibility. I couldn't get too close because they could take you away at any time. My job was to put you out there but keep you safe.'

Boyd clapped his hands. 'Well, congratulations on that. You'll be up for 'Employee of the Month' for this.'

'You think this is what I wanted?' Martin shouted, his face red. 'I had no idea this was going to happen!'

Boyd stood and, without warning, all the emotion he had been keeping under the surface exploded. 'What the hell did you think was going to happen? You lied to me my whole life! You were never on my side!'

Martin walked forward and grabbed Boyd's hands. 'You're right, you're so right. So let me make it better, let me change that.'

Boyd wrenched his hands away. 'How? Look around you. I'm stuck here. They have me, they have everything they want.'

'No, they don't. Listen to me. I'm not all bad. I never was.'

'You stole someone's baby to use against them. That makes you a pretty crappy human being in my book.'

'But I didn't. You have to listen, Boyd.'

'I am listening. You said, "*I took you from your mother.*" It couldn't be much clearer. You're a monster, just like the rest of them.'

Boyd turned away and fought back the tears once more. He desperately wanted to ask about his mother, this woman he had never met. Was she alive? Had she been looking for him? For all he knew, she was locked up next door. But he wasn't going to ask Martin – he wanted the truth, he didn't need any more lies.

'I was sent to Hurricane Island by Ravensbrook as private security, to keep an eye on your mother. As soon as they realised that she was the talented one, they wanted to make sure she wasn't doing anything she shouldn't be. And yes, you're right, when Operation Hurricane imploded, I took you from your mother. Erica Adler handed you to me. That was part of her plan all along.'

Boyd couldn't believe what he was hearing.

'She trusted me, and she knew that the best way to keep you safe was to put you with the people who wished her harm, and then disappear from your life forever. I wasn't keeping you safe for them, Boyd, I was doing it for her.'

Getting into Position

The Barn was tucked away in the woods, on the outskirts of the Lockmead estate. Because it was SpeedFest week, the roads all around the Bloomfield Downs were jammed with spectators and racers making their way to the event. Every year His Lordship turned 900 acres of fields into a thrilling celebration of all things speed.

Ophelia and the Section X team had ensured they were in place long before the traffic started to build up. They had found a field surrounded by a thick hedge and tucked the van just inside the gate before the sun came up. Just to be safe, they had covered it with a thick layer of brambles and then Azima had checked to ensure it couldn't be seen from the road. Now it was all about playing the waiting game.

Ophelia's escape plan meant that they couldn't hit the Barn until later in the afternoon, so whilst Fitz and Azima waited in the van with Ophelia, Harry was driving to his starting point near the Barn in a modified black car with oversized wheels. Barnaby had installed a full surveillance kit in the back of the van, with recording equipment and headsets for everyone so the team could speak to Harry and track him right up until the point he got past security at the Barn.

'Harry, are you receiving? Over.' Fitz spoke nervously into the microphone attached to his headset.

'Yes, Fitz, I'm receiving you. Just as I was two minutes ago when you asked me.' Harry had a small, skin-coloured bud in his ear that acted as a microphone and a speaker. He had a few other toys with him too, some of them classic tools of the spy trade that Barnaby had provided, along with some essential new inventions that Fitz had dreamt up. Harry knew that Fitz was nervous; they hadn't had time to fully test everything and the whole mission rested on things going off without a hitch.

He guided the car along a tree-lined road that led up to the long driveway for the Barn, then pulled over and parked up in a break in the trees. He thought of Boyd, Skye and Arnold Bishop. From the information Bishop had given him, Harry knew he was walking into the nest of a particularly cruel and heartless snake. In all his years trading secrets and quietly halting the progress of his enemies, Harry had never known anyone as ruthless as Ravensbrook and the Trinity Guild. He had meant what he said to Skye when they first met in the theatre: Bishop didn't trust him, they didn't even like each other very much. But they were both old spies and that meant you lived by a code, doing anything and everything in the name of Queen and country.

When Harry had asked Bishop why he was betraying the Guild, Bishop had been clear: he could no longer stand by whilst evil flourished. He had been young when Operation Hurricane had started but as far as Bishop was concerned, when it all fell apart, it was a good thing. Once the Guild started to rise again, Bishop had decided to do everything he could to disrupt them. Now Harry was as certain as he could be that it had cost Bishop his life, and he wasn't going to let Boyd and Skye pay the same price.

Skye had been secured to the bed with a strap across her forehead, another across her elbows and one more at her ankles. It was her own fault for breaking a guard's nose. Then, when they had tried to sedate her, she had thrown the doctor against the wall and tried to escape. The latest development had been the threat of a gag if Skye didn't stop singing. So, when the door opened, she presumed they were about to put a premature stop to her run-through of every track from Stormzy's 'Heavy Is The Head', and she was only up to 'Do Better'. What a shame!

When Skye flicked her eyes to the door, she couldn't hide her surprise. Instead of a cautious guard, cattle prod in hand, she saw Hornet, unarmed and smiling like a reptile.

'Don't let me stop you, please.'

'I didn't have you down as a Stormzy kind of girl?'

'No, I'm not, really, but I do so enjoy a dose of fake bravado. So please, you crack on.'

'I tell you what, sweetheart. Why don't you take these restraints off and we'll see how real my bravado is?'

'You know the biggest problem with you kids these days?'

'Why don't you enlighten me?'

'You think that power is all about what you can do on your own. I blame social media – it rams all that self-help rubbish down your throats. What you fail to realise is that the people you're idolising on there have a team behind them, telling them what to do every minute of every day, and you lot lap it up.'

'Is that it? You done? Surely there's so much more you can tell me about my wasteful generation?'

'You're being stupid, you know that?'

'From you, I'll take that as a compliment.'

'I wouldn't. You can break a nose, smash up your room – go ahead. You're a single person fighting against a machine – you'll never be believed, and you'll never win.'

Skye let out a nervous laugh. 'So, what? I should join you? Are you joking with me?'

'Not at all. You're a smart young woman. I actually have a lot of respect for you.'

'A moment ago, you were calling me stupid.'

Hornet crept slowly around the bed and let a long silence hang in the air. Eventually, she stopped next to Skye's head and started to stroke her face. 'I said you were "being stupid"; there's a big difference. Your little project is over; we've taken your base of operations.'

'I can do what I do from anywhere, and anyway, I'm

not one person. They'll come for me and when they do, you're going to be the one with the broken nose.'

'Section X? You think the Toy Department is coming for you? Oh, my dear, you really have no clue, do you? You can shout from the rooftops about power surges, time travel and Operation Hurricane and no one will listen. You're just a conspiracy theorist. But we're not your enemy, Skye, we're not the government or the establishment. We are an underground force that the powers-that-be have tried to stamp out for centuries, trying to make a difference against the people at the top. Does that sound at all familiar? We're just like you, and we're on the cusp of something that you can't even begin to fathom.'

Hornet grabbed both of Skye's cheeks and stared into her eyes. 'And I'm asking you to be a part of it because I was just like you once. So let me help you and we can find the truth together.' She let go of Skye's face and marched to the door. 'I didn't want to be the one to tell you this, I really didn't, but it rips me apart to see you fool yourself like this.'

'What are you talking about?' Skye said, her voice heavy with emotion.

'They won't come for you. They'll come for him, yes, but they'll leave you to your fate. They don't care about you, Skye, you'll see that. But I won't ever leave you, I promise.' Hornet opened the door and walked out.

Pick A Side

The door opened behind Boyd. Martin, who was sat directly facing it, stood up immediately.

'I don't know what more I can say. This is pointless,' he said. 'Call the guards. Let's get him back to his room.'

Boyd furrowed his brow, confused at the change in Martin's demeanour. Then he looked over his shoulder, saw Hornet and everything became clear.

'What a shame,' she said. 'I think we're going to have your friend, Skye, on our side before long. It's a pity you can't see sense. Guards!'

Boyd jumped to his feet and leapt the sofa. He was across the room and heading towards Hornet before Martin could stop him. Hornet didn't even blink and the thin smile remained in place despite Boyd lunging towards her.

Just as he was about to reach her, two guards stepped through the door, batons raised. As Boyd's momentum carried him forward, they stepped in front of Hornet and slammed their fingers on the buttons that triggered the electrical charge. The weapons hit Boyd directly in the chest and each one kicked 15 volts of electricity into him. It was like running at full speed into a charging bull. Boyd's feet flew out from under him and he landed heavily on his back, cracking his head on the floor.

'Get him up,' Hornet said as she turned and left the room.

The two guards went to move him.

'Leave him,' Martin ordered, his voice laced with menace. The two guards stopped in their tracks. 'You get the doors, I'll carry him.'

As Martin lowered Boyd down onto his bed, the guards stood in the doorway. Boyd's eyes flickered as he started to come around, then he scrunched them up as the signals of pain shot all around his body.

'Steady,' Martin said with care. 'I'd stay off your feet for a little while. You've taken a pretty hard bang to the head.'

Boyd felt Martin put something in his hand. It was cold and metallic, sharp in places; it felt like a bracelet. Martin held Boyd's hand where it was and folded it over the object; he was telling Boyd not to look at whatever it was until they were gone. Then he turned and walked to the door. He stopped and put his hand on the wall, tapping his fingers. 'Take your time, I'll be here, and we can talk when you're ready.'

The door closed. Boyd waited for a moment. He hadn't heard the now-familiar click; the door hadn't locked. He lifted his head slowly and brought himself up into a sitting position. Martin had been right: Boyd had come down hard on the floor of the lounge and his head was throbbing. He allowed his eyes to settle, the world slowly crept back into focus and he looked towards the door. Boyd realised that Martin hadn't been tapping his fingers on the wall as he spoke, he must have been tapping an override code into the door lock to disable it. Boyd opened his hand and looked down at the object Martin had given him – an old digital watch from the 1980s.

Before Hornet had come back to the lounge, Martin had told Boyd about Operation Hurricane and how on the night that it all burnt down, he had followed Erica Adler's instructions to the letter. She had wanted him to make sure the Trinity Guild had her diary, which detailed her progress and explained how she had tested her research on herself. But the diary was fake, she had written it to ensure Boyd's safety. So long as Ravensbrook and the Trinity Guild believed that she was the key to Hurricane, then they would never harm Boyd because they needed him to lure her out of hiding.

Boyd let everything sink in for a moment. He had desperately wanted to ask if Martin knew where his mother was, but somewhere inside him, he was petrified that she wasn't alive and he wasn't ready to hear that yet; not now he had a tiny shred of hope.

'I don't understand how you suddenly stopped doing the only thing you'd ever known to help a woman who would put you in so much danger. It doesn't make sense.'

Martin had nodded in agreement.

'I spent over a year as your mother's security detail. She was like no one I had ever met: kind, thoughtful and she seemed to know exactly what I was thinking or feeling before I knew it myself. She became my best friend.'

Boyd had watched as Martin's mind wandered and he'd waited for him to snap back to the story. Then he'd realised he had never seen Martin's eyes shine like they

455

were then: he was lost in a real memory, truly happy.

'She was the first person in my life to tell me I had a choice – I didn't just have to follow orders. Erica said that whichever path I chose, it would change my life, and nothing would ever be the same again. It's the same for you now, Boyd. Nothing is stopping you from working with these people and becoming rich and powerful beyond your dreams. But in the end, you would have to be able to justify your actions, to be able to look at yourself in the mirror. Ravensbrook, Hornet and the Trinity Guild will never give up; they won't stop hunting your mother or chasing the truth behind Hurricane and they will cut down anyone in their way. If you go against them, it will make the last week seem like a walk in the park; it will mean the end of just being a kid, of everything you know. No teachers to tell you what to do and no parents to tell you where to be; you'd be making decisions that result in whether people live or die and you'd have to live with the consequences. Are you ready for that?'

It was at this point that Hornet had returned and interrupted them, so Boyd never had a chance to answer, although he wasn't sure that Martin expected him to. Boyd hadn't felt a shred of genuine anger towards Hornet when he charged her; he was just putting on a show. It was best that she continued to underestimate him, then he'd have two things in his favour. The other one being that he was fairly certain now that he could rely on Martin's help.

He fastened the watch around his wrist and slid his feet onto the ground. It was time to find out just how exceptional he really was.

A Great Day For Rock 'N' Roll

Harry had watched the black Range Rover arrive a while ago. Now he sat in his car, desperately hoping that whoever was behind the tinted glass wasn't planning on staying at the Barn too long; Section X had banked on the place being mostly empty. Finally, at almost 4pm, just as it was getting to the point where they would have to delay the operation, he saw the sleek 4x4 drive away from the Barn and head up towards the Lockmead estate. Harry turned the wheel and guided the car out of the trees.

It wasn't long before he was pulling into the car park. He reversed into a space so that the next time he got behind the wheel, the car would be facing front and ready to go. He climbed out and crunched across the gravel pathway towards the entrance to the Barn. His walk had a little more sway to it than usual. This was because underneath his smart grey suit was a fake stomach that moved along with his steps, just like a real paunch.

Harry looked up at the building. Fitz had commented that it looked like half a toilet roll tube painted silver, and he wasn't far wrong. But then, if you were going to build a facility dedicated to atrocious experimentation on children with the sole aim to create a power that could take over the world, it was probably best to make sure it doesn't attract any undue attention.

He noticed a sound as if a swarm of bees were about to burst into view, then remembered it was the buzz of the bikes and cars at SpeedFest. He smiled to himself, knowing that Lord Ravensbrook would be busy parading his carefully sculpted public persona whilst the Toy Department were stealing his prize asset from right under his nose.

Just like every operation he had ever been on, Harry felt a fizz of excitement mixed with a bite of anxiety. He had lost count of the number of missions he had been on, but it wasn't lost on him that this one was quite extraordinary; he had never been part of anything with stakes this high. Just before he got to the end of the pathway, Harry quietly said the code words he had been given on his first mission and since then he had used them before stepping over the threshold to begin every mission as his good luck mantra: 'This is Four, it looks like a great day for rock 'n' roll.'

'Receiving X-Four. Rock 'n' Roll, affirmative,' Ophelia replied in his ear.

Harry reached into his pocket and put on the glasses Fitz had given back to him. He opened the door and walked into the cool, air-conditioned foyer of the Barn.

The Barn

'We weren't expecting you until tomorrow,' the guard said slowly.

Harry had entered the foyer and made straight for the security office on the right-hand side. There were two guards, both with biceps and chests that were bursting through their black uniforms. The one talking to Harry had a neatly trimmed little beard, the other seemed completely unaware Harry was even in the building as he stared at a monitor, wearing large black headphones and blasting a gang of marauding zombies. Next to the office, directly to Harry's left was what looked like a set of revolving doors inside a black pod, but Harry was well aware that this was much more than just a set of doors. The two guards were behind a panel of clear plastic set into the silver wall.

'When you were expecting my arrival is of zero consequence to me,' Harry replied in German-accented English. His tone was impatient and clipped. 'I am here now so you will kindly let me in, or I will leave and return to my home. Then I will tell Lord Ravensbrook and his associates that you sent me away.' Harry leant on the glass. 'This will make you very popular, I should imagine.'

He leant back and took out his phone to make a call.

'Oh no, sir. Excuse me.' The guard stood up and began to gesture. 'They should have told you; you should leave that outside. We don't allow any phones into the building.'

Harry lowered the phone, shaking his head. 'Are you making jokes with me now? First I can't get in to start my work and now I can't have my phone?'

'I apologise, sir. They just aren't allowed. We can keep it here for you.'

Harry threw the phone into a small silver drawer under the glass window. The guard pulled the drawer from his side and took out the phone.

'I'll keep it right here, on my desk. I promise.' The guard placed the phone down. His colleague looked at it and then at Harry, then went back to killing a zombie with a brick.

'So, make your choice. Will you allow me to enter? Or are you perhaps looking for a career change?'

The guard raised his hands. Thin beads of sweat were beginning to form on his forehead and top lip. 'No, of course, you can come in!' The guard glanced down at the monitor next to him. 'It seems we do have your biometric data on file, so in this case, I am willing to make an exception.'

Harry kept his stern demeanour and tried not to look quite as happy as he felt. 'This "exception" is the smart decision.' He picked up his thin briefcase. 'Congratulations, you won't be getting fired today.' He nodded to the guard.

'Please enter the pod, pop your bag onto the conveyor belt, say your name, then place your hand into the cradle. Once again, I apologise for any confusion. Is there anything else I can do?'

'You have done enough, I think.'

Harry turned left, took two steps and entered the black pod. The semi-circular door hissed to a close around him. That was stage one complete, and from here on, he was relying on Fitz's new toys to get him the rest of the way.

He placed his bag onto the conveyor belt to his right and watched as it disappeared into the scanner. It didn't hold anything that might raise suspicion, so there was absolutely no reason why it wouldn't be waiting for him on the other side. Harry removed his glasses and was glad to notice that his hands were steady as a rock. On the left arm of the frame was a small button hidden in the logo of the manufacturer where Fitz had installed a playback device. In the right arm was a tiny, high-definition speaker. Harry held the frames up so they were level with the microphone in front of him and pressed the button with his fingernail.

'*Erlich Schmidt.*' The voice recording that Fitz and Azima had captured on Baker Street played out so crisp and clear, it was almost as if the German scientist was in the pod with Harry.

After a second, the circle around the microphone went green.

Next, Harry undid the button on his suit jacket, opened his shirt and pushed his hand inside. His new belly was actually a padded, flesh-coloured bag that was strapped around his middle. This meant that the team didn't have to worry about smuggling in certain toys via the briefcase. Harry could slip past security wearing all his essentials around his waist, and to the outside world, he simply looked like a man who wasn't afraid to skip a meal.

Very slowly and carefully, Harry pulled a perfect wax model of Erlich Schmidt's right hand out from under his shirt. He lined it up and placed it on the scanner, then held his breath. If this didn't work, Harry would not be leaving the Barn on his own two legs. Section X wouldn't know anything had gone wrong until he didn't make the rendezvous in an hour and by then, goodness knows what the Guild could have done to him.

The scanner closed around the hand. Harry held onto the solid wrist section that Fitz had built out of plastic and held his breath. The light around the scanner went red and the machine fired out a loud barking noise – strike one. The cover retracted and Harry lifted the hand up. There was no damage, nothing stuck to the wax, so why hadn't it worked? He replaced it on the scanner and waited. The cover sprung up and over the hand and Harry felt his heart in his mouth. 'Come on, play nice,' he said to himself, his right leg starting to twitch.

He quickly assessed his options for getting out of

this should the wax hand not work a second time. There was only one option as far as he could see it, he would have to rely on bluff and bluster. Just as he was about to start banging on the pod and complaining that the stupid English facility had malfunctioned, the light around the scanner went green and he heard a satisfying 'BING!' The curved door in front of him slid back and Harry gratefully stepped through, into the windowless corridors of the Barn. To his right, sitting on the conveyor belt was his bag. He collected it, stuffed the hand back into the pouch around his waist and moved quickly. Checking his watch, he noted it was 4:24pm. He had lost valuable time and the truth of it was, the toughest tests were all ahead of him.

The corridor ran through the centre of the building, between small, windowless offices on both sides. When Harry reached the end, he was faced with a kitchen and a store cupboard, and the only way to turn was left. He followed the corridor and ended up around the back of the kitchen and store cupboard. Now he was at the far end of the Barn and there, in the middle of the back wall, was a door with a small window, just as Bishop had described and exactly as it was on the plans. Harry stopped. He didn't need to look through it, he knew what was beyond this: the security room for the Belly.

He ducked down, shuffled under the window, then he turned right and tucked himself down around the corner in the dead-end of the corridor, safely out of sight. Harry lifted his shoulders and reached again into the pouch around his waist. He took out a small plastic case, popped it open and looked inside at the tiny radio-controlled car that Fitz had given him. It looked just like a toy car, except it had much bigger wheels. Harry then pulled aside the sole of his shoe and took out a silver cylinder around the size of a pen lid. He gently pressed the cylinder down into the slot on the car's roof until it clicked into place. He slid the sole of his shoe back on as he looked out around the corner and took a moment to listen for any movement; there was nothing, not a sound. The place was almost empty, just as they had suspected it would be.

He made his way to the door with the small window, took out his Parker pen and pulled the top off. Inside was a small mirror on an extending stick. He held it up to the window, steadied the mirror and looked carefully at the reflection. The room wasn't very long, but it was the entire width of the building with a set of lift doors at the opposite end. It was completely empty, except for two things: at the far end next to the lift was a chair and sat on it was a guard, who was fast asleep.

'Okay Fitz,' Harry thought to himself. 'Time to see what you're made of.'

He reached for the door handle and slowly turned it.

Burn Baby Burn

Martin left Boyd and went straight to the large laboratory stretching all along the back of the Belly. He had only been in here once before, and although he had never seen what they had done to the children they took from the streets, he had heard the rumours. He had also heard the excuses – that these kids had no family to miss them, and the only future they would have had would be pick-pocketing at train stations, working for drug-dealers and sleeping rough. He didn't believe that was any reason to snatch the life away from a child, but he hated himself for not doing anything about it. He had simply chosen not to listen, to ignore the fact that he worked for tyrants; and just because he hadn't witnessed the pain and grief they had caused, it didn't make him innocent and it no longer eased his conscience.

Martin had helped take care of Boyd from the moment he was born. He looked after him while Erica worked and when he had brought him back to

Lockmead, Boyd was still just a baby. The people at the Belly had noticed that as he grew, the boy felt safe with Martin around. When the suggestion was made that Martin take Boyd and set up home with him, that had been fine with Martin. What better way to keep his promise to Erica than to actually raise Boyd himself?

Martin had tried everything to break down the barriers that stood between him and Boyd, but nothing had worked. The fact that most of the walls between them were of his own making didn't help. Martin had told Boyd the truth: he'd always had to live with the knowledge in the back of his mind that his job was to protect Boyd, but he knew that one day he would probably lose him to someone else. Because of this, because he had protected himself and kept his distance, Boyd had been cast in the same mould. He had grown into a cold, difficult young man who found it almost impossible to trust anyone. But now Martin had a chance to change the future for them both and he wasn't going to fail Erica again.

Inside the labs, they used secure plastic chambers to work on minerals and rock samples that they couldn't expose to oxygen; he had never asked why and he didn't much care. What he did know was that these chambers were like big plastic bags, and to get rid of the normal air you would find in any room, they first introduce nitrogen and then a small amount of hydrogen. Martin wasn't a scientist, but he knew there was a reason why they did this in a specific order. If he didn't remove the oxygen from the six plastic chambers first, if he skipped the nitrogen and just pumped them full of hydrogen, he was pretty certain the result would be explosive.

He found the control room at the back of the lab, wiggled the mouse and woke up the computer. It was time to make some noise.

Climbing The Walls

Harry carefully removed the small radio-controlled car from its case and set it down on the floor, just inside the room. He gently shut the door and then quickly held up the mirror again; the guard hadn't moved, she was still sound asleep. Harry took off the modified glasses once more and held them face down in his hands. He pushed down once on both of the silicone nose pads and a small blue light came on behind each pad; this indicated that the controls for the car were now activated. He knew he had a short window of battery power in the small car to do what needed to be done. Harry pushed the right-hand pad all the way to the right and then gently applied pressure forward on the left-hand pad. On the other side of the door, the little car turned right and moved forward, creeping slowly towards the wall.

'Here goes nothing.'

When it met the wall, instead of stopping, the car's oversized wheels continued to roll, gripping the surface of the wall and pulling it up and away from the floor. Fitz had created tyres covered with 1000s of long microfibre hairs, so the car would work much like the legs of a spider, helped by a coating of adhesive gel. The only problem was, Fitz didn't know how long the car could climb for and it worked best when it remained in motion, so Harry had to work fast and try not to let the car stop in one place for too long.

Now he had his hands full with the controls, he could no longer use the mirror, so he risked a quick glance through the window. The guard was a short woman, her hair pulled back into a bun. She was still slumped forward, fast asleep. Harry allowed himself a smile as he looked up and scanned the wall for the car. It had travelled much farther than he had anticipated and was already almost in the middle of the ceiling, and heading towards a flat, plastic light fitting. Harry released the controls but the momentum carried the car into the light, emitting a small 'crack!'

The last thing Harry saw before he ducked away from the window was the guard's head snap back. He immediately put one arm of the glasses in his mouth, retrieved the small mirror from the floor and raised it slowly up to the window. At first, he checked the location of the car and saw it was still in place on the ceiling, just inside the door and tucked behind the light fitting, so the guard couldn't see it from the chair; but how long it could hang on there, motionless, was anybody's guess.

Harry moved the mirror the smallest of fractions and saw as the guard moved her head side to side. She got to her feet and started towards the door, her eyes darting left and right, up and down, like a small animal searching the skies for a predator. Harry had a simple choice to make: stay put or quickly move back to his staging area around the corner. He decided to stay put; he couldn't risk making any more noise.

He quickly pulled the mirror away as the guard edged closer to the door. Once he had he dropped it below the window, Harry arched the small mirror upwards to get another view of the car. He froze in panic as he saw the wheels had begun to come away from the ceiling. If it fell, he would have to deal with the guard the old-fashioned way and hope she didn't have time to radio for help. That was a huge risk at this stage of the operation; he simply had to work out how to get the car moving again.

The guard's shadow edged along on the wall opposite the window as she moved closer. Harry pulled the mirror away, flattened himself against the wall and held his breath. He could feel the sweat starting to pour down into his eyes. Boyd was just beyond those doors and Harry was so close. This couldn't all end here, now, not like this.

Unexpected Guest

The tall man pulled the small car into the car park and slotted it in, two spaces away from a strange-looking black car with big wheels. He didn't know why English people couldn't just drive normal cars instead of customising their vehicles and creating these ridiculous machines.

He climbed out of his hire car, smoothed his shirt with his hand and collected his bag from the back seat. As he turned to walk up the gravel path, he wondered what that buzzing sound was, then remembered the signs for a motor show nearby. That must be why the traffic had started to build up on his drive in. Maybe that's why his contact had told him not to arrive until tomorrow. Oh well, never mind. He was here now. London had bored him, and English hotels had no idea how to make good food, so last night he decided he needed to work.

It was 4:38pm when Erlich Schmidt walked

purposefully up the pathway to the Barn. A whole day ahead of schedule.

A Little Surprise

Boyd stood just inside the door to his room and waited. If anyone was outside, they weren't moving or talking. He gently pulled the door open, just a fraction, and peered out into the hallway. No one came running. Then he heard a man's laugh; it was coming from across the corridor, inside the lounge where he'd met with Ravensbrook.

He opened the door enough to poke his head out and look right, down towards the double doors that he presumed were the way out. Not a soul, the place was quiet. Except for Chuckles and his mate in the lounge, and Boyd was about to give them a little surprise.

A Coiled Spring

Harry hugged the wall and stayed as low as he could.
He hoped that the guard's field of vision through the
small window would be narrow enough that he would
be able to stay out of sight. He could tell by the shadow
on the wall opposite the door that she was looking
through the glass. He watched as an outline of the
guard's head moved left and then right, scanning the
corridor for the source of the unknown noise. Despite
being flat against the wall, Harry was on his toes, tucked
up like a coiled spring. If she opened the door now, he
would be ready.

Intruder Alert

'What do you mean, I am already here? How is this possible? Can you not see me standing in front of you?' It was now the turn of the real Erlich Schmidt to make life uncomfortable for the bearded guard at the front desk.

'Well, obviously it wasn't you, sir,' Beardy tried to explain. 'But it was Dr Schmidt. He went through the biometric checks – I don't know what to tell you.'

'You tell me nothing. You get your head of security on the phone, right now.'

Beardy picked up the phone, hit a single button and waited for five seconds. Today was going from bad to worse. 'Yes, I know you said not to call this evening. I am sorry to bother you, ma'am – it's just that Dr Schmidt has arrived a day early.' He paused. 'Yes, I would admit him, only I already have. You see, I already signed in Dr Schmidt over half an hour ago.'

A sudden burst of inaudible sound erupted from the

phone and Beardy stood up straight. He leant back and delivered a back-hand slap to the shoulder of his colleague, who had just had a chunk taken out of his neck by a zombie. He pulled off his headphones as Beardy was just finishing the call.

'Yes, immediately. See you down there.' Beardy faced Schmidt. 'Herr Doctor, if you could please go to your car and head to Lockmead House. Just out the drive, the way you came and turn right. His Lordship will be with you later this evening.'

Schmidt slammed his hand down on the small metal counter. 'This is preposterous!'

Headphones turned towards Beardy, a quizzical look on his face. 'What's the drama?'

Beardy reached under the counter, pulled out a baton and held it up in front of him. 'Doctor, do as I say now, please.' He pressed the button on the baton, and they all watched as a blue and white line crackled and fizzed between the two electrical points on the end of the weapon.

Schmidt's eyes widened. He nodded, turned and silently left the building.

Headphones stood up. 'Oi, I said what the hell is

going on?'

Beardy threw him a second cattle prod. 'We've got a code nine. Hornet's incoming with back up but we need to get down there now and contain him.'

Headphones smiled. Finally, something to bash other than digital zombies.

Code Nine

The guard turned on her heels and looked back into the room, confused. Just as she was deciding that the noise that had woken had been inside rather than outside her head, she heard something else. It sounded like someone slowly peeling the back from a sticker. What the heck was that? Was she going completely mad? She stopped and stood still just inside the door of the security room and almost jumped out of her skin as her radio crackled to life.

'All posts. We have an intruder, repeat, an intruder… Code nine!'

Before she could respond, something above her drew her attention. The guard looked up just as an object began to fall directly towards her face.

It's A Gas

Harry heard the squelch of the guard's radio, followed by the message: *'All posts, we have an intruder, repeat, an intruder…'*

He pulled himself up and risked another look through the window. The guard hadn't moved forward, she was standing right in front of the door. It was at this point that she looked up and Harry followed her gaze.

The car was hanging around 20 centimetres from the ceiling, the spider hairs had stretched out to their fullest before they quickly gave way. The guard let out a gasp and caught the tiny toy as it fell towards her.

Harry immediately pulled the glasses from his mouth, grabbed the two nose pads and twisted them, the left pad clockwise and the right pad counterclockwise; then he stood up and looked through the window.

The confused guard extended her neck down to get a closer look at what she held in her hands, then, sensing she was being watched, she looked ahead and saw Harry through the window. There was a sharp puff and a cloud of vapour erupted around her face. The guard's legs folded neatly under her.

Before Beardy at the front desk had finished yelling a description of Harry through the radio, the Belly guard was out cold on the floor and Harry had stepped over her on his way to the lift.

That Makes Two Of Us

Boyd heard the crackle of a radio and the conversation inside the lounge abruptly changed tone. Something was wrong. He stepped back towards his room, opened the door and lay down in the doorway with his legs in the corridor and his upper body inside his room. He stayed perfectly still and waited.

The lounge door burst open and he heard the two guards emerge. This was quickly followed by the sound of their boots squeaking to a halt on the hard floor; they had seen him.

'Hey, kid. Get up.'

Boyd recognised the voice; it was the one with wet, bug eyes.

'I said stop mucking around and get up. What's wrong with you?'

'I don't think he can hear you,' the other one replied.

Boyd knew it was the man with the ponytail and the bad breath. Both men had taken turns in delivering

Boyd's meals for the last couple of days.

'So, what do we do?' Bug Eyes said. He lifted his radio. 'Hey, this is H13 down in the Belly. Your intruder alert just came in and…' He stopped as Boyd suddenly groaned and crawled back into his room.

'Hey, kid. Stop!' Bug Eyes said and they both walked towards the door to Boyd's room.

'You can't tell him to stop, you already told him to get up,' Ponytail protested.

'Stay out of this. Greg put me in charge.'

Bug Eyes caught the door to Boyd's room before it closed, stepped forward and confidently pushed it open. As he did, he was surprised to be met with the sight of Boyd powering towards him, wheeling his bed into the doorway. It hit Bug Eyes with full force in the stomach and the man fell forward onto the pillows as Boyd continued to push from the other end, letting out a guttural roar as he did so.

Ponytail managed to jump clear as Boyd pushed Bug Eyes back through the door, pumped his legs and ran as hard as he could towards the wall opposite. They came to an abrupt stop as Bug Eyes smashed into the metal wall at bone-crunching speed. The bed tipped up, the guard let out a scream and fell to the floor.

Boyd immediately turned to Ponytail, his face a picture of calm, his eyes fixed on the man like a predator stalking its prey. Ponytail brought up his baton, twirling it around in his hand in a perfect, practised motion.

'I bet you do that in front of the mirror, don't you? Does it impress the ladies?' Boyd smirked.

'I don't care how precious you are to Ravensbrook,' Ponytail spat through gritted teeth. 'I don't care how much money you're worth, I'm going to make you beg.'

'You know how you could do that? Breathe on me. Anyone ever told you that you're in serious need of a mint?'

Ponytail snorted and pumped his arm up and down, threatening to strike. 'Laugh it up. You may mean something to them but you're nothing to me. I don't even know who you are, kid.'

'Yeah? Well, that makes two of us, mate,' Boyd replied as he undid his hoodie.

Ponytail watched as Boyd finished unfastening the zip and then held his hands out wide.

'Come on then, big boy. What are you waiting for?' he taunted the guard. 'I'm just a kid, remember? Or maybe you haven't got the bottle to take on a teenager?'

Ponytail's snorts became more and more animated as he screwed his face up tight and then brought the baton up in a high arc. Boyd took an evasive step back and flipped his hoodie over his head. He kept his arms inside it and pulled them out to the ends of the sleeves. As Ponytail brought the baton down fast towards Boyd's skull, Boyd dropped to his knees, raised his hands, pulled the hoodie tight and formed a twisted, fabric shield over his head. The baton landed on Boyd's stretched-out hoodie and stopped, sending shock waves through his shoulders but also leaving Ponytail arms wide and open for an attack.

Then, Boyd took his chance.

Harry's Game

At the entrance to the Belly, outside the lift doors, two muscular guards watched as the light behind the downward-facing arrow above the lift doors came on, which meant that the lift was on its way. They raised their batons and eyed each other encouragingly. Behind them two silver escalators sat under the curved steel roof; one led down to the double doors into the Belly and the other led back up. It looked like the entrance to a London Underground station.

The lift arrived with a '*PING!*' The two men flexed their chests and arms, twitched their batons in a loose grip and stood forward on their toes, prepared to strike. The doors slid back and they both lifted their weapons above their head, took in a deep breath and clenched their jaws. Then they stopped, their arms dropped, their shoulders slackened and their faces scrunched up. The lift was empty.

'Skip?' The shorter man stood to the right of the lift

and looked to his boss for guidance.

Skip blinked quickly; his eyes darted around the lift.

'Skip, what do we do?' The shorter, younger man sounded desperate.

The man in charge tried to think of an explanation for Shorty. 'Hang on.'

Skip carefully edged forward, as if he was walking across a minefield. He put his head inside the lift and gave it a thorough inspection, left and right. Then his shoulders dropped as he relaxed, he stepped back out of the lift and unhooked his radio from his belt. Both men turned away from the door.

'No sign of him at the escalator and he's not in the lift. Repeat, he is NOT in the lift.'

Behind the two men, Harry released his grip on the ceiling of the lift, letting his feet go before his hands. He dropped hard and fast to the floor and landed in a crouch with a loud 'thud'.

The guards swung around. Shorty still had his baton in his hands, and he reacted quickest, lunging forward. Harry took a direct hit, the baton striking him in the body and Shorty pressed the button to deliver the electric charge. To his surprise, Harry didn't even flinch as he grabbed Shorty's hand at his wrist and pressed his thumb hard into the back of the guard's hand. Harry then twisted the wrist around and pushed it back towards Shorty. Shorty had no choice but to bend over; his arm folded up. Harry delivered a sharp kick to the guard's exposed stomach and knocked the wind out of him. Skip started to move towards them, so Harry used the momentum in Shorty's arm to thrust the crackling baton into Skip's neck. The electrical charge made him shudder violently with the shock.

Shorty shuffled his feet in an effort to regain his balance. He pulled his arm back, moving the baton from his stricken comrade's neck, and then swung his elbow in a sharp arc towards Harry's jaw. But Harry saw it coming, pivoted on his right foot and twisted with the impact, using Shorty's momentum to swing him into the empty lift. Harry flung the man and released his arm just as Shorty was losing his balance, sending him colliding with force into the back wall of the lift. Shorty's face was a picture of confusion; Harry knew his opponent was trying to work out why the electrical charge he had pumped into Harry's stomach didn't seem to have had any effect on him at all.

Just as the guard gathered himself to begin another attack, Harry reached inside his shirt and pulled out the large, flesh-coloured bag he had worn around his middle. It was sticky to the touch and snapped out of his clothes just as Shorty stepped into range. Harry whipped the pink padding upwards and it slapped into Shorty's face, where it stuck over his eyes and mouth like a jellyfish. He lurched forward, clawing at thin air.

Harry stepped aside as Shorty blindly staggered out of the lift, then swept his legs and watched as he fell forwards, cracking his head on the metal section between the two escalators. Harry looked at both guards and assessed his work; neither would cause him any worry in the next 10 minutes.

Breathing hard, he started quickly down the escalator towards the Belly. More would be coming; he had to find Boyd and Skye and they had to get out of here.

Ponytail and Bug Eyes

Boyd was crouched down, his hoodie stretched out over his head between his hands. Ponytail had his right hand clamped around the baton, which had come to an abrupt stop on the hoodie. Bug Eyes, the other guard, was still face down on the bed that Boyd had used to hammer him into the steel wall; but he was slowly starting to shake off his injuries.

Boyd moved his left hand up and looped the hoodie around Ponytail's wrist, then stood, taking the guard's right arm with him. Boyd quickly powered a front kick into Ponytail's groin that surprised the larger man and bent him forward. Boyd then swung Ponytail by his captured right arm, through the open doorway into his room, clattering him against the door frame on the way.

He heard movement behind him and turned to see the bed rolling away; Bug Eyes was back on his feet and ready for round two. The groggy guard lunged fast, his baton crackling, catching Boyd flat-footed and unable to avoid the impact. For the second time in his stay at the Barn, electricity was fired into Boyd's body. But this time, with just a single baton in the attack, he didn't hit the floor. As the weapon hissed and jolted against him, Boyd gritted his teeth and grabbed hold of it with his right hand. He looked directly into the guard's bulging, vengeful eyes. Boyd slowly cracked a smile and Bug Eyes just had time to furrow his brow in confusion before he abruptly lost contact with Boyd, and the baton clattered to the floor.

Boyd fell back against the wall and looked to his right.

Martin had charged in from the side and hit the guard, tackling him to the ground. He raised himself up onto Bug Eyes' chest and delivered a sharp right hook to the jaw. Martin then stood, leaving the man in an unconscious heap on the floor.

'Are you okay?' he asked, reaching out a hand, which Boyd accepted.

Boyd opened his mouth to respond but before he could utter a word, the double doors at the end of the corridor hissed open. Boyd and Martin didn't have time to run or hide, so they turned and readied themselves for whatever was on the other side.

Only One Way Out

Harry knew that there was no clever way to fool the enemy this time, so he simply pressed the button to open the doors and got ready to take on whoever was waiting for him. As the doors hissed back into their recesses, he crouched low and reasserted his grip on the baton. Once the gap in the doors grew, he saw Boyd and the man he knew as Martin Spengler, Boyd's guardian provided by the Trinity Guild, both coiled and ready to attack.

Harry moved forward quickly. 'Run, Boyd!' he blurted out as he charged at Spengler.

'Wait!' Boyd stepped into Harry's path, his hands held up.

Harry came to an abrupt halt, his face coloured with confusion.

'He's on our side.'

'No, Boyd. You don't know who he is. He's…'

'I do, Harry.' Boyd nodded, reached up and pushed

Harry's baton hand down. 'I don't have time to explain, so you're going to have to trust me. He's with us.'

Harry tilted his head and looked into the eyes of the young man standing in front of him. He had known him for the past year as a moody, spoilt teenager, far too wrapped up in himself to care about others, who had a warped kind of pride in having no meaningful ties to anyone. Now, for the first time, behind the cold steel in his gaze, Harry saw a kid who was putting himself in harm's way to protect someone he cared about.

'Okay, I trust you,' Harry confirmed. 'Now we need to find Skye, because this party's about to get a few more guests.'

Martin stepped around Boyd. 'We can't stay here; we need to go, now.'

'No,' Boyd insisted. 'We're not leaving here without Skye. They must have her in one of the other rooms.' He only managed a step before Martin grabbed his arm.

'Boyd, listen to me. I've set the lab to blow. We've barely got time to get out before this place becomes a fireball.'

'No, I can't just leave her here, I have to find her!' Boyd pulled at him.

Harry grabbed Boyd and turned him around. 'Listen to me! I'll go, you two get out of here.'

'No, that won't work.' Martin shook his head. 'Hornet's on her way, she's bringing reinforcements. There's only one way Boyd is getting out of here.' Martin took a deep breath. 'Now it's my turn to do something for you. It's my turn to be the bait.'

Hornet Takes Charge

Hornet hadn't heard a word back from the guards in the Belly, so she had told everyone to hold at the lift and wait for her arrival. *Why do I have to work with such incompetents?* she brooded silently as the lift descended, packed with four of her best men, plus the two guards from the front desk. She could not let Boyd escape – she had not spent 10 years babysitting him, play-acting as that dreadful woman, to let him simply walk out of the door.

The lift opened onto the escalators, she stepped out and immediately saw two guards stretched out across the floor. The bearded guard from the front desk moved to check on one of his injured colleagues.

'Leave the fool where he is,' Hornet hissed with disgust. 'Secure the boy, that's all that matters. Now move!'

They all moved quickly and quietly down the escalators and approached the double doors. Whoever

499

had been through here had left them wide open. Hornet peered around towards the room Boyd had been occupying and saw that the door was closed. The light on the keypad was red, meaning the door was locked. Hornet split the team, waving three guards off to the right-hand side of the lounge and taking the other three with her towards Boyd's room.

The near silence was shattered with a sudden hammering on the inside of Boyd's door. Hornet held her hand up at shoulder height and clenched her fist, a military sign for her team to stop immediately; and they did. The banging ceased and every set of eyes remained fixed on the door. Hornet raised two fingers and then pointed twice to the other side of the door. Two of the guards stealthily moved into place as Hornet and the one remaining guard moved to the wall on the near side of the door and waited. Then came a buzzing sound and a small bang, like a firecracker going off. Not a single person on this side of the door jumped, they remained perfectly still and focused.

Hornet knew exactly what had just happened: whoever was in there had just used one of the electrical charges from a baton to fry the door lock, and they were about to step out, right into her path.

The door opened and a face emerged into the hallway.

'Don't move!' a guard shouted.

'It's okay, it's me – it's Spengler!' Martin slowly came out of the door, a baton in his raised hands. His shirt was torn, his face and the back of his head were bloody.

'Where is Boyd?' Hornet spat the question at him, like it was a sour taste in her mouth. How could he have let a boy take him down?

'He's gone to the other side, to look for the girl.'

'Go! Get the others and find him,' Hornet barked and the guards ran off. 'He's got help,' Hornet said.

'I heard. Section X, I am guessing. I told Boyd about the storage room down below the labs, I thought if they went down there it would distract him, buy us some time until you arrived.'

Hornet looked at him suspiciously. 'Very good thinking, Martin.'

He felt the back of his head and grimaced. He brought his hand away and it was covered in blood.

'Let me take a look at that for you,' Hornet said, moving around behind him.

'No,' Martin twisted to move away from her. 'Thank you, but I'll live.'

Hornet smiled and half turned, before snapping back and driving the heel of her palm into the space below Martin's right ear. He collapsed onto the floor; the blow had made his senses fuzzy.

'That's for me to decide.'

Hornet pulled her radio out. 'All teams: Boyd and Section X operative are in the wind. I need security response on the roads surrounding the Barn and air support in play as soon as possible. Find them!'

Hornet felt a gentle rumble under her feet, like a small earthquake. She instinctively turned her head to the left, towards the laboratory. Then came another rumble that nearly knocked her off her feet. She reached out to the wall to steady herself.

Finally, the security doors to the lab flew across the corridor like bullets from a gun, slamming into the walls, chased by chunks of debris and huge orange flames that instantly turned the silver walls black. That was when Hornet was launched off her feet and slammed back through the doorway into Boyd's room.

Up In Smoke, Away In Flames

Harry had carefully positioned himself so he could see Hornet and the guards step off the escalator and enter the Belly. Without moving his head, he held his breath and peered through his half-open eye as they descended.

As soon as the last guard was clear of the doorway and inside the Belly, he reached out and tapped Boyd, who was lying a few feet away. Both were face-down outside the lift, at the top of the escalator, posing as the guards Harry had injured not five minutes earlier.

Once Martin had told them his plan, they had moved quickly. They dressed in the guard's black sweaters and combat trousers, then dumped the two men in Boyd's room before running up the escalator and getting into place. Boyd had only just managed to get to the floor when the lift doors had opened. He was drenched in sweat; his heart had been pounding so hard in his ears, he could barely hear Hornet as she instructed the bearded guard not to check on him and get down to the Belly.

'Let's go.' Harry lifted himself up into a crouch and kept his eyes on the doors at the bottom of the escalator.

He and Boyd moved back into the lift and pressed the button to take it back up. Boyd bent over, hands on his knees.

'Don't worry, Martin will find Skye,' Harry said, putting a hand on Boyd's back.

'And if he can't? If Hornet doesn't believe him, or they can't get out in time? We should have stayed. We could have fought them off and got everyone out.'

'No, there were too many of them. Martin was right, this is the right thing to do.'

'Then how come it doesn't feel like it?' Boyd stood up, getting agitated.

Before Harry could reply, a '*ping!*' echoed around the lift as it arrived at the ground floor.

'Are you ready?' Martin looked over to Boyd.

He raised his stolen baton and nodded to Harry.

The doors slid open and the room was empty. Harry took a cautious step out from the lift, his eyes pinched in confusion.

'You were expecting someone?' Boyd asked.

'I left a guard here. Doesn't matter, she must've had the sense to get out.'

They ran across the floor of the security room and Harry bent down to collect the small radio-controlled car.

'What's that?' Boyd asked.

'One of Fitz's new toys, and he wants it back.' Harry threw the car in the air and Boyd caught it.

Boyd looked at the gadget, then cracked an affectionate smile before putting the car in his pocket.

Harry looked out through the window and raised a thumb; the coast was clear. 'Follow me, stay close.'

Harry opened the door, turned right and followed the corridor around until there, in front of them, at the far end of the building, was the black biometric pod.

'What are we waiting for?' Boyd said, impatiently and went to move.

'Steady on. Stop for a second.' Harry pointed to the pod. 'That's a biometric pod. It won't let you out until it scans the veins in your hand and determines you're friendly. Which we are clearly not.'

'Wonderful. So how did you get in? Let me guess –

Fitz?'

Harry smiled and nodded. 'Oh, you should have seen it, it was beautiful. But how we get out? Well, that's a little more rudimentary.' He took the glasses from his pocket and pushed the two arms in until they were touching. Then there was a huge rumble, the floor began to shake, and Harry dropped the glasses onto the floor.

Boyd put his hand on the wall to steady himself. 'Was that us? Did we do that?'

'No. I'm guessing that's Martin's little surprise.' Harry picked up the glasses, then grabbed a stunned Boyd by the sleeve. 'We need to go. Now!'

'Harry, we can't leave them!' Boyd pleaded as they started to run.

Then came another rumble, followed by a burst of hot air hitting them in the back as the Belly erupted beneath them and the flames forced their way up to ground level. Harry grabbed Boyd by the shoulders and shouted over the ever-growing noise.

'Listen to me – if we stay, there will be no one left to stop them. We have to move, now!'

As they ran towards the pod, Harry tapped the arms of the glasses frame together once, then two times, then three; then he held them together. This was a colossal risk, but he knew he had no choice.

'What the hell are you doing?' Boyd asked him.

'Just making a phone call.'

At the end of the corridor, inside the office at the entrance to the Barn, the phone Harry had left with the bearded security guard flashed on and vibrated as the call connected. It auto-answered after two rings, then it triggered the C4 explosive inside the phone. The explosion ripped through the front of the building, tearing the metal structure into pieces as if it were a stick of dynamite in a baked-bean can.

Right next to the office, the glass in the pod shattered, the rest of it was fired almost in one piece, down the corridor towards Harry and Boyd. Boyd launched himself into Harry, pushing him sideways against the wall, then taking both of them crashing down to the floor as the pod shot by them like a speeding train.

'Holy crap!' Boyd shouted as he crouched against the wall.

Both men allowed a few seconds to pass before lifting their heads. Harry looked at the bent frames in his hand.

'Fitz certainly knows how to open doors.' He stood up and held out his hand for Boyd.

They reached what was left of the entrance to the building and clambered over shards of scorched metal. As soon as they were out into the fresh air, Harry led Boyd to the black car. He pulled the keys off the front tyre and opened the door.

'Get in.'

He checked the time; the whole operation had only taken a shade over 40 minutes and yet it felt like hours ago he had parked up and walked into the Barn. Now he looked at the facility, a torn shell, coughing smoke out into the evening air.

'This is Four, I hope you can hear me. Exfiltration complete. I've got Six with me – en route to rendezvous. Over.'

'*Receiving Four.*' Azima's voice came through Harry's earpiece. '*It looks like there's a helicopter inbound and you have one hostile vehicle moving in to engage.*'

'Roger, over.' Harry skidded the huge wheels of the car across the gravel and put his foot to the floor.

'Who are you talking to?' Boyd asked, only hearing

Harry's side of the conversation.

'Don't worry about that. Just listen. Under your seat there's a thing that looks like a long tube, with a handle and a trigger – find it.'

Boyd let go of the seat and took his other hand off the door handle. Harry threw the car down the driveway like they were on the dodgems and Boyd bounced around, hitting the door with his shoulder.

'I had only just managed to get your wonderful driving skills out of my mind, and here we are again. You know that no one is behind us, right?'

'And I'd like to keep it that way.'

Harry pulled the car out onto the narrow country road as Boyd scratched around under the seat with his hand. His fingers brushed against something. He lunged and grabbed it, dragging it free and immediately saw that Harry was right. The strange object looked like a cardboard kitchen roll tube, but it had a curved handle on one end, with a button above the handle and a trigger on the underside; a bit like a toy shotgun.

'Hold down that button on the top until the light goes green, and whatever you do, don't pull the trigger yet,' Harry said.

'Yeah, I figured the trigger part out for myself. What is this thing?'

Before Harry could answer, a car appeared in his rear-view mirror and accelerated towards them at speed. 'Oh hell. You're about to find out. Hang on.'

Boyd looked up and saw a queue of traffic just coming into view around the corner. The tiny, narrow lane was jammed with 1000s of cars leaving the SpeedFest event and they were on a collision course, heading right for it. 'Harry,' he said, nervously. 'You see that, right? Tell me you can see that?'

Harry's eyes flicked from the road to his mirrors. He dropped a gear and the engine burst with a throaty roar as the car jolted forwards.

'Harry!' Boyd shouted and pointed towards the stack of stationary cars blocking their path.

Harry ignored him, pushed his head back into the head rest and stretched his arms out as if he were bracing himself.

'I really hope you've got a plan!' Boyd shouted as he scrambled back into his seat, turned his face away and prepared for impact.

Then, at the last second, he felt the car lurch to the right as Harry wrenched the steering wheel all the way around. The big wheels bit into the grass bank at the side of the road and the car took off, over a ditch. It ripped through a hedge and bounced unevenly as it landed in a field. Both Harry and Boyd lifted up, high out of their seats before coming down hard.

'I didn't doubt you for a minute,' Boyd said, shaking his head and smiling.

Harry fired a quick look at Boyd and cracked a small smile. 'Is the light green?' Harry pointed to the contraption in Boyd's hand.

'Yep.'

Boyd looked in his wing mirror and saw that the hostile vehicle had found a way into the field and was quickly gaining on them. When he looked forward again, he saw that Harry was taking them towards two huge stacks of hay bales.

'Get the sunroof open,' Harry said, his voice juddering from the bumps in the terrain. 'Then wait until I say the word. We're going to let them catch up a bit.'

Boyd turned his head and furrowed his brow. 'Let

them catch up? What is wrong with you?'

Harry smiled at him, looking relaxed for the first time in the whole operation. 'Have a little faith, Boyd.' He checked his mirror. 'Any second now.'

Boyd twisted his shoulders and looked out of the back window. The chasing car was close and would be right on their back bumper if Harry didn't do something soon. 'Whatever you're going to do, it had better work.'

Boyd popped himself up out of the sunroof. As they got closer to the hay bales, Harry put his foot down and pulled right, skidding their car between the two high stacks, then turned another sharp right and stopped. The chasing car could travel fast in a straight line but it couldn't make turns over the rough terrain of the field that quickly, so it was forced to take the long way around both the large stacks of hay.

'Aim at the hay bales, two shots, go!'

Boyd pointed the barrel at the far stack of hay and pulled the trigger just as the chasing car disappeared behind it. There was almost no kick from the weapon at all, but the effect out of the other end was absolutely devastating. Boyd heard a 'WHUMP!' and noticed his ears pop as a massive projectile of air flew at the far stack of hay, bursting some bales open and sending others crashing down onto the chasing car.

Boyd quickly adjusted his aim, then fired at the nearest stack of bales and got the same results, sending clouds of yellow straw flying everywhere – but this time the chasing car went with them. The driver was still side-on, bringing the car around the stacks and Boyd watched as it got caught by the blast and flipped over twice.

Boyd lowered himself back into the car, just as Harry stepped on the accelerator. He stared with surprise at the weapon in his hands.

'We call it a pop gun,' Harry said.

'Of course, you do,' Boyd said with a wry smile.

Harry powered the car towards the exit on the opposite side of the field to where they had smashed through the hedge. The gate was open, and just inside it, Boyd could see a trailer attached to a green van. Harry slowed down, lined up the big wheels with the trailer and drove the car up straight up onto the back.

'Let's go,' he said as he jumped from the driver's seat. He pointed to the pop gun. 'Bring that with you.'

Boyd saw Fitz and Azima jump out of the van and

around the back of the car before he had even climbed out; neither of them acknowledged him as they leapt into action.

'I'll get the bonnet, you get the roof!' Harry shouted to Boyd.

Boyd gave him a puzzled look. Then he watched as Azima picked at the paintwork on his side of the car until she had a handful of the black material that covered it. She pulled it away, revealing bright racing-car colours and the names of sponsors. Boyd saw Harry doing the same on the bonnet. He jumped up onto the trailer, reached up to the roof and pulled at the corner of the black paintwork until it started to come away in his hands. He saw Azima scrunch up the black covering and run for the van, so he did the same.

Boyd climbed in the side door behind Harry, just as Fitz and Azima climbed in the front. Ophelia pulled the van out and drove for no more than five seconds before they hit traffic. She pulled to a halt behind a mobile home pulling a stock car on a trailer. Boyd lifted his head up and saw a queue of vehicles in front, all towing cars just like theirs.

There was a familiar sound overhead as a helicopter

emerged over the horizon, seemingly scanning the area, no doubt looking for a black car carrying a man and a teenage boy. They wouldn't find it.

This Is The Life

Harry's flat was tucked away in London, in a place called Notting Hill. It was a terraced house in what Harry said was called a 'mews'; Boyd didn't much care. It seemed like Harry wanted to talk about everything from his first undercover operation, to what type of tea Boyd wanted, or whether he liked Chinese takeaway or pizza; anything to avoid talking about how Section X planned to find Martin and Skye.

Ophelia had driven them to an old, disused farm building on the outskirts of Bloomfield, where they split up and headed off in different directions. Ophelia told Boyd to go with Harry in his old MG sports car and they would catch up tomorrow. When Boyd had asked what they were going to do next, she had simply told him that they had to regroup and find out if anyone had survived the blast at the Barn, but it would take time. Getting Boyd out alive had been their priority.

He had felt a surge of frustration at this. He couldn't

be any more important than Skye; he wouldn't have got this far without her help. He didn't lose his temper, he didn't argue, or storm off alone; tonight, he would do whatever Ophelia asked him to. Tomorrow, he would listen to what she had to say, then quietly assess his options.

For now, he sat on Harry's cracked leather sofa, in a lounge that had a lot of paintings but not many photographs. Harry came in and put two over-sized teacups on a small wooden coffee table.

'How are you feeling? Anything broken?' Harry asked, settling back into a matching leather club chair with a small groan that acknowledged everything he had put his body through in the last few hours.

'Nope. I'm fine,' Boyd responded without emotion.

'Right, of course you are.'

'What do you want me to say, Harry? I'm just peachy. The guy who raised me and the one person who put everything she believed in on the line for me were taken by a psychotic multi-millionaire and some nut-job cult he's involved with, and they have probably been blown to pieces in a raid that wouldn't have happened if it weren't for me. In fact, none of it would have happened if I had just gone with them in the first place and not dragged Skye into this.'

'Skye was already involved. She was on the government's radar and making all the wrong noises to get her noticed by all the wrong people. Trust me, it was just a matter of time before she got snared in their trap.'

'That doesn't help, Harry. She isn't here now because I dragged her into my drama.'

'So, tell me then, what else could you have done back there?'

'I could have stayed. I could have gone to find her.'

'We've been through this – you would have been blown to pieces.' Harry sat forward. 'Do you think I don't know what you're feeling? I've been right where you are, son, and I know that leaving there without them goes against everything you feel as a human being. But you didn't have any choice. It was between everyone staying and no one getting out or making the smart play. For the first time in your life, you used your head, and now the consequences hurt like hell, but it doesn't mean it was the wrong move. I've been doing this stuff a long time and those questions you've just asked, they never go away. If you're a decent human being, then you'll always question your actions. So, it's good that you feel that pain, it's part of this life we chose.'

'When did I get to make a choice, tell me that? It's not part of my life. I'm not like you or Ophelia bloody Bletchley. I'm going to hear what she has to say tomorrow and it had better be a plan to go back in there because I can't leave Martin and Skye with those people.'

'If I know you at all, then you will do what you have to do, son, and I respect that.' Harry leant back against the soft leather of his chair and closed his eyes.

A few moments of silence went by and Boyd realised that that he owed Harry something. 'But thanks.'

'For what?'

'For risking your neck for me. I won't forget it.'

Harry allowed himself a smile. 'No problem. Like I said, kid – it's part of the life.'

The Worst Kind Of Betrayal

Fitz woke up in his own bed for the first time in a few days and wondered for a moment where he was. He had slept like a baby. His dreams had been all about the unrelenting drama of the last few days and nights. He could barely believe that he had turned his ideas into real, working gadgets that had helped saved his friend's life. He had got home last night still buzzing with excitement. But this morning, he couldn't muster the same feelings. Despite his relief that Boyd was safe, he was worried about Skye; what could he do to help her? When Ophelia dropped him off at the end of his road last night, it had all felt a little final and he wasn't sure that they would need him anymore. For the first time in his life, Fitz had felt like he had a purpose, like he was needed, but now it had just come to a sudden end and he didn't know what to do about it.

His dad had been strange with him again when he got home. Roger had been on the phone, pacing up and down in the back garden in the early hours of the morning, so there was obviously some big emergency at work. His mum seemed to believe that Fitz had gone away on a hike in Wales for his Duke of Edinburgh Award; he guessed that was a cover story of his dad's creation, so he had just gone along with it. At least his mum was proud of him again, which always made for an easier life.

Fitz slowly trudged downstairs, taking his stack of bowls and plates with him into the kitchen. His mum was just heading out to her office in the back garden.

'Look at this, cleaning up after himself now!' She tousled his hair. 'Whoever you went away with, they've obviously had a good influence on you.'

Fitz smiled.

'Time to go and see what kind of a mess your father made in my office last night. He was working out there until all hours. The front room looks lovely by the way, thank you, Fitz.' And she disappeared out the back door.

The front room! The painting! He had completely forgotten about that. Fitz put the crockery down and ran back down the hallway to the front room. He pushed open the door and found beautifully painted walls, with no sign of his radio-controlled car. His dad must have covered for him again. He owed him big time – and his mum was right, it looked good. In fact, it was a better job than Fitz could have managed had he stayed at home and used a paint brush.

Just as he was about to go and make himself some breakfast, Fitz noticed a car pull up outside – a black Range Rover. It stopped at the end of their path and someone got out. Fitz stood on tiptoes but still couldn't see who it was over the bushes in the front garden. The gate opened and his dad started down the path; Fitz headed straight for the front door. Had he stayed in the front room, Fitz would have seen that his father wasn't alone, as another figure exited the car and followed Roger down the path.

Fitz's dad opened the door and stepped into the hallway as he was greeted by his son.

'Man, do I owe you some serious payback!' he said in hushed tones. 'Massive, huge! Maybe I need to paint the whole house or something, with a brush this time!'

Roger moved into the house, away from the open door. 'No, don't be silly, it's fine.' He attempted a laugh, but it fell flat. His face was ashen, like he hadn't slept in days.

'Dad, are you alright?' Fitz was suddenly concerned. He moved past his dad to close the front door, turned to face him, with his back to the outside. 'And whose car is that?'

Hornet stepped around the porch and into the open doorway, behind Fitz. He saw her in the hallway mirror over his dad's shoulder. Her face was covered on one side by deep, angry scars, criss-crossed with red-raw burn marks.

Before Fitz could move or utter a word, Hornet clasped a large hand over his mouth and his eyes exploded with fear. She raised her right hand and brought down the point of the 'T' on her ring, breaking the skin on Fitz's neck. Before he could grab at the door frame, the powerful woman had dragged him away from the house, his arms and legs thrashing in desperation. But his eyes didn't move from his father. Roger stood inside the doorway, his face down, unable to look at his son.

Fitz was unconscious by the time Hornet reached the gate. She closed it carefully, carried the boy to the Range Rover and laid him down on the backseat. She then smoothed her leather suit, climbed into the passenger seat and gave Bull the signal to pull away.

Without looking outside, Roger Tork closed the front door.

Call Me Six

Harry had taken Boyd to the Toy Shop and Ophelia had filled him in on everything they knew about the Trinity Guild and Lord Ravensbrook. Boyd then explained Martin's version of events and Ophelia, ever the spy, was sceptical that he had done what he did for Erica Adler.

'There's one way we can find out,' Boyd said. 'We can go back in there and get them – him and Skye.'

They were sitting in a room away from the main operations centre. Harry had led Boyd through a door and up a rusted metal staircase to a glass office where Ophelia was sitting behind a desk; Boyd and Harry were now sitting opposite her.

Ophelia looked at Harry. 'Could you give me a moment with Six, please?'

Harry stood up and left the room.

'Six?' Boyd tilted his head. 'That's the second time you've called me that.'

'Yes, we were hoping you'd join Section X, and we know that Six is the number you wear when you run and play football.'

'Well, you have done your homework. It's actually the day I was supposedly born on, but for some reason I'm now having trouble believing anything I thought was true.'

Ophelia had a file in front of her, she closed it. 'No, from what we can gather, your birth date is genuine.'

'Oh, well, that's a relief,' Boyd said sarcastically. 'Alright if I go now? Get back to my life?' He stood and half turned away. 'Whatever's left of it.'

'Tell me, Boyd, do you plan to stop whining anytime soon? To stop being such a child?'

'I am a child! That's kind of my point!'

Ophelia considered him for a moment. 'You're right. Your life, the one you knew, is over. What you do now is up to you, but the job's not done. Getting you out was just the first step. Finding Martin and Skye – Harry and Barnaby can do that. It's what they're good at. You're needed for something else.'

Ophelia stood up and walked around the desk. She sat on the edge of it, in front of Boyd. 'Did you actually listen to what I said about the Trinity Guild? They won't stop, Boyd, not until they have everything they want, and we can't let that happen.'

'They made me who I was then, and they made me who I am now. I'm going after my friend and I'm going to use that against them.'

'And if Skye is dead and you're walking into a trap?'

'Then I'll take them all down.'

'Revenge? That's your grand plan? You go in there alone and they'll just rebuild whatever you knock down. Whoever you take out, they'll just find someone stronger, quicker, faster. You'll have achieved nothing.'

'So what? Join Section X?'

Ophelia picked up a black control, clicked it and pointed him towards a TV screen in the corner of the room. 'If you won't do it for me, do it for her.'

Boyd turned to the TV. A woman appeared on screen. She was in her early forties, with blonde hair and soft features. Boyd immediately recognised Miranda Capshaw. The image was a warm sepia and there was a whirring sound like Boyd had seen with old-fashioned movies on projectors. The picture broke up a couple of times before she started talking.

'Evan, I don't have a lot of time.' She swallowed hard and looked down, steadying her nerves. 'I wish I could see your face, I wish I could tell you everything you need to hear. I can't imagine how all over the place you must feel. Just know, you are special, my boy. You have something inside you that makes you different.' She nodded and smiled. 'You know what I'm talking about, don't you.? You've felt it from time to time. I know because I have it too.' Miranda laughed nervously.

Boyd realised that the voice he heard in his dreams, the woman who called his name when he slept, was Miranda Capshaw. His pale blue eyes fixed on her face and he felt like she was right there in the room.

'All you need to know for now is that it will help you be strong for what's ahead. So I need you to do two things – find this,' Miranda held up a Casio digital watch.

Boyd instinctively reached down and touched the watch on his wrist – the watch Martin had given him – and he hadn't taken off.

'Now, this bit is going to take a leap of faith, it's going to sound crazy, but I promise you, it's not just the truth, it's your destiny. Inside these watches, I placed something very unique, called a Sutter Clock. This allows you to focus the energy of a wormhole to an exact date and time in the past and, because you're special, you can jump to it. I have a friend, a woman called Rose, and I need you to meet her. You see, there's something I need to do, but I can't do it on my own.'

She sat forward and stared intently.

'There are dark forces gathering – they are going to follow me here and I need your help. Find Rose in Paris, in 1986. I've sent some written instructions in the package I left for Harry Lazenby, but the truth is I don't even know if you'll get this message.' A tear escaped and slowly slid down her cheek.

'Oh, my boy. I wish… I wish I could have seen you grow up. I am so sorry this has all landed on you. I hope you'll see one day that I had to disappear to keep you safe, though I'm not sure that worked out very well. You can hate me, you can blame me, but for now, Section X needs you. Someone always has to save the world, and I'm afraid that this time, it has to be you.' A sudden noise broke the silence and Miranda snapped her head around. 'I have to go, I've run out of time – maybe you can bring me some more, please, Evan. I love you.'

The screen turned from sepia to white and the room was filled with a whirring sound as the film ran out. Ophelia clicked the remote and switched off the TV. Boyd took a moment, still facing away from Ophelia. She saw him reach up and wipe his face with his sleeve.

'Miranda Capshaw is my mother.' His voice cracked. He coughed and then turned to face her. 'My mum is Erica Adler, that's why they were chasing her and this...' he held up the watch on his wrist... 'this is how she disappeared.'

'That's right.'

'When did she leave this for Harry?'

'She left it with a courier more than 30 years ago, with instructions to deliver it to Harry – yesterday. All this time you've felt out of place and this is why – this is who you really are. Now, I know it's a lot to take in and it's a lot to ask, but you heard her – we need you. Personally, I'm not sure you're ready for it and I'm damn well sure you're not up to it. You're no more than a child and you let your heart rule your head most of the time. But Harry tells me you're a fast learner. He also says you're colder than a penguin's arse and as hard as an anvil, and I happen to trust Harry Lazenby implicitly.

In this case, I have little choice.'

Ophelia stood and placed her hands on her hips. Her frame may have been slight, but her demeanour was still imposing; it was like being stared down by the Queen. 'Your life up to now has been a mess of secrets and lies and we're offering you a chance to find some answers. You help Erica, and leave me to search for Martin and Skye. Trust me to do that for you.'

She paused, sizing him up, trying to decipher his intentions but realising that the young man in front of her had become adept at hiding his emotions over the last few days. 'So, what's it to be, Evan – are you ready to save the world, or is it not your problem?'

He stood and placed his hands in the pocket of his hoodie. A determined look blazed in his pale blue eyes. 'I'm ready. And you can call me Boyd, or Six.'

Make Them Pay

'You're very lucky to be here, very lucky indeed,' Ravensbrook said with a nod and a gentle smile.

His guest said nothing, her eyes remained blank, giving nothing away.

'Hornet saved your life. If she hadn't put herself in between you and our aggressors, they would have succeeded in their plan and wiped out every last one of us, every trace of anyone or anything that could reveal the truth.'

'And what is that, exactly – the truth, I mean?' the guest finally responded. Next to her, Hornet leant over, her scarred face a mask of pain.

'They saved Boyd and blew the place up. He even left his father here to die in the flames, a man I had called my brother for 10 years.'

The actual truth was that Skye had never been in the Barn and she would never know it had even existed. She had been unconscious when they had dragged her across the lawn from the helicopter and placed her in the basement of Lockmead House. Skye and Boyd had been kept apart, but she wasn't to know that. As far as Skye knew, she had been locked in a room, there had been a battle and people had died. Boyd had been rescued, but no one had come for her.

Skye looked at Hornet, then at Ravensbrook. Her blank expression gave way to a rage that burnt like a thousand fires behind in her eyes. 'I warned him what would happen if he betrayed me.'

God Speed, Six

'Right, are we all set?' Ophelia addressed the room.

After everything that had happened in the last few days, for the first time, Boyd thought he saw a flash of uncertainty cross Ophelia's face. The good news was that Azima looked totally confident; in fact, she was struggling to contain her excitement.

'I've studied the Sutter Watch and, thankfully, Erica included detailed operating instructions, and a set of plans.' She tapped a pile of yellowed papers on the desk. 'Mechanics aren't my strong point, we may need to get Fitz in here at some point. In a nutshell, that thing on your wrist manipulates the tiny pieces of technology in your bloodstream, called nanos, and creates something called a wormhole.'

'Sounds pretty straightforward,' Boyd said sarcastically. He stood in the middle of the floor in the Toy Shop, holding his backpack, the team assembled around him.

'And we're sure this is safe?' Harry asked, unable to mask his concern for the kid.

'Oh no,' Azima replied, matter-of-factly, 'we can't be sure of that at all. Sutter created this in the 1940s, can you imagine that? It's insane how advanced this is – and as for the nano-tech, well…' she turned to Boyd… 'let's just say your mother is a genius! It's beyond anything I've seen, and if you do make it back there, it might well turn you inside out.'

They all stood open-mouthed, looking anywhere except at Boyd's wide-eyed expression.

'But you'll have travelled through time, which would be, well, pretty amazing.' Azima tried to smile.

'Absolutely.' Boyd nodded. 'Let's hope my eyes are still on the outside of my body so I can enjoy it. Shall we crack on before I think about this too much and decide it's the craziest thing I've ever done?'

He put the pack on his back, shuffled his legs into a walking stance and raised the Sutter Watch to chest height. He brought his right hand up to it and suddenly realised that he had adopted the same position he took when he started a race: on his toes, fingers poised over the timer on his stopwatch.

'We've talked through how it works: we've set the date, time and location on the watch. You just have to press all three buttons together, then each one in sequence, one, two and three,' Azima said.

'Then what?' Ophelia asked.

'Then we hope for the best.' Azima exhaled through a strained smile.

Boyd didn't waste any more time; he pressed all three buttons together and the face of the watch glowed blue. The date, time and location shone up at him and suddenly, he felt completely calm and relaxed.

It struck him that his mother had done this exact same thing, she had stood somewhere and followed the same sequence of actions he was going through now. He hadn't known a single thing about her before today, but this was a fact he knew for sure, and that made him feel like he knew a little bit more about himself.

'I'm coming for you,' he whispered under this breath.

'Sorry, what?' Azima asked him.

'I said, it looks like a great day for rock 'n' roll.' He fired Harry a wink.

Boyd pressed the three buttons in sequence: one, two and three. The blue glow on the face of the watch grew brighter and everyone quickly reached up to shield their eyes; everyone except Boyd. The blue light began to spread out from the watch and up his arm.

Whatever it was, he could feel the effects; it was as if someone had injected ice into his veins and it was slowly creeping around every inch of his body. After just a few seconds it crawled into his head and his vision started to fade. Azima, Harry and Ophelia all seemed to be drifting into a blur. Then it happened; a sudden, crippling pain inside his head, like the worst ice-cream brain-freeze you could imagine, and Boyd closed his eyes and screamed.

When Harry took his arm away from his face, Boyd was gone. Azima and Ophelia withdrew their hands from their eyes, and they all looked to the same spot.

'Did it work?' Harry looked to Azima, a pleading in his eyes.

'Let's hope so.'

'Godspeed, Six,' Ophelia said quietly and bowed her head.

The pain had eased somewhat but Boyd's vision was still blurred. He could still see the glowing outlines of Harry, Azima and Ophelia.

'Crap, that hurts. Okay, it didn't work but let me get over this pounding in my head and we can try again.' He shuffled his legs and blinked hard.

'Guys, why can't you hear me?' Boyd rubbed his eyes. He could see some movement, but the outline of the team was starting to fade from view; what was going on here? Was he losing his sight? Was he blind?

'*Qui es-tu?*' A voice erupted, sudden and sharp.

Boyd stumbled in shock, lost his balance and fell against a wall. What the heck was he doing next to a wall? He was in the middle of the floor at the Toy Shop, wasn't he?

'*Qui veux-tu?*' The voice came again, more impatient this time. Then something poked him in the chest.

Boyd rubbed his eyes again and then opened them. The light around him was dazzling. The Toy Shop had gone; there was no Harry, no Azima and no Ophelia. As his eyesight started to return, he could make out snow, a lot of snow; and an angry man forcing him backwards with a gun.

They wouldn't have to try again because it had worked perfectly well on the first try. Boyd was in France; it was 1986 and he had travelled back in time.

Evan Boyd

WILL RETURN...

New Novella Coming Soon!

Section X: The Thief & The Phantom

Go back to where it all began, with a thrilling new adventure!

London: 1942

Charlie is just a schoolboy thief, going about his business when he makes an enemy of the most feared gangster in London. Things get more complicated when Charlie is forced to work for the crew for a night. But why is Charlie being followed by a mysterious man in a long, black coat? And why does the man believe Charlie can lead him to a powerful machine capable of changing the course of World War II?

Charlie is about to find out that he's linked to the most secretive department in British Intelligence, Section X – and this is the night his life changes forever...

Be part of the adventure!

www.benjaminshawbooks.com

Acknowledgments

So many people have contributed to this book in so many different ways. My brother, Ken - who one night watching football turned to me and said, 'You should write a book about a boy who can travel through time.' My wonderfully supportive wife, Maria - who turned to me after I'd left my job and said, 'You should write that book about a boy who can travel through time.' My Mum and Step-dad who always call to make sure I'm writing and my best mate Humphrey, who has to put up with me trying out dialogue on him all day. To The Captain, for the feedback and inspiration.

To the brilliant Clem Moulaert; sorry about all the commas.

Finally, the ridiculously supportive and wonderful Liz Hawkins; who despite only seeing me every couple of years, has never not been there for me whenever I've needed a friend, an ear, an editor or, now a web designer. You're truly one of the best, thank you.

About the Author

Benjamin Shaw was born in Hampshire, in the UK. After studying English at university, he worked in computers, despite not knowing much about them. He then went back to college, became a film journalist and was lucky enough to travel the world, interviewing people like James Bond.

After a decade in publishing, he decided to become an author and is currently writing the hotly anticipated Evan Boyd Adventures; the young adult fiction series about a reluctant teen hero.

Combining Mission: Impossible, with a dash of Indiana Jones and a healthy dollop of Back To The Future, the Evan Boyd books are bursting with action, stunts, gadgets and a little bit about the pain of growing up.

Benjamin lives on the south coast of the UK, with his lovely wife and his rather awesome dog, Humphrey.

Printed in Great Britain
by Amazon

65434546R00312